THE PLAYBOY OF PUERTO BANÚS

BY

CAROL MARINELLI

MILLS & BOON

First published in Great Britain 2013
by Mills & Boon, an imprint of Harlequin (UK) Limited.
Harlequin (UK) Limited, Eton House, 18-24 Paradise Road,
Richmond, Surrey TW9 1SR

© Carol Marinelli 2013

ISBN: 978 0 263 90705 6

Harlequin (UK) policy is to use papers that are natural, renewable and recyclable products and made from wood grown in sustainable forests. The logging and manufacturing process conform to the legal environmental regulations of the country of origin.

Printed and bound in Spain
by Blackprint CPI, Barcelona

'It's not every day you get offered a million dollars.' Estelle could at least be honest about that. **'Nor move to Marbella…'**

'You will love it,' Raúl said. 'The night life is fantastic…'

He didn't know her at all, Estelle realised. 'I just hope everyone believes us,' she said.

'Why wouldn't they? Even when we divorce we'll maintain the lie. You understand the confidentiality clause?' Raúl checked. 'No one is ever to know that this is a marriage of convenience only.'

'No one will ever hear it from me,' she assured him. The prospect of being found out was abhorrent to Estelle. 'Just a whirlwind romance and a marriage that didn't work out.'

'Good,' he said. 'And, Estelle, even if we do get on—even if you do like—'

'Don't worry, Raúl,' she interrupted. 'I'm not going to be falling in love with you.' She gave him a tight smile. 'I'll be out of your life as per the contract.'

Carol Marinelli recently filled in a form where she was asked for her job title and was thrilled, after all these years, to be able to put down her answer as 'writer'. Then it asked what Carol did for relaxation and, after chewing her pen for a moment, Carol put down the truth—'writing'. The third question asked, 'What are your hobbies?' Well, not wanting to look obsessed or, worse still, boring, she crossed the fingers on her free hand and answered 'swimming and tennis'. But, given that the chlorine in the pool does terrible things to her highlights, and the closest she's got to a tennis racket in the last couple of years is watching the Australian Open, I'm sure you can guess the real answer!

Recent titles by the same author:

PLAYING THE DUTIFUL WIFE
BEHOLDEN TO THE THRONE*
BANISHED TO THE HAREM*
AN INDECENT PROPOSITION

linked titles

**Carol also writes for
Mills & Boon® Medical Romance™!**

**Did you know these are also available as eBooks?
Visit www.millsandboon.co.uk**

THE PLAYBOY OF
PUERTO BANÚS

For Anne and Tony
Thank you for all your love and support.
It means so much.
C xxxx

CHAPTER ONE

'ESTELLE, I PROMISE, you wouldn't have to do anything except hold Gordon's hand and dance....'

'And?' Estelle pushed, pulling down the corner on the page she was reading and closing her book, hardly able to believe she was having this conversation, let alone considering going along with Ginny's plan.

'Maybe a small kiss on the cheek or lips...' As Estelle shook her head Ginny pushed on. 'You just have to look as if you're madly in love.'

'With a sixty-four-year-old?'

'Yes.' Ginny sighed, but before Estelle could argue further broke in, 'Everyone will think you're a gold-digger, that you're only with Gordon for his money. Which you will be...' Ginny stopped talking then, interrupted by a terrible coughing fit.

They were housemates rather than best friends, two students trying to get through university. At twenty-five, Estelle was a few years older than Ginny, and had long wondered how Ginny managed to run a car and dress so well, but now she had found out. Ginny worked for a very exclusive escort agency and had a long-term client— Gordon Edwards, a politician with a secret. Which was why, Ginny had assured her, nothing would happen or be expected from Estelle if she took Ginny's place as his date at a very grand wedding being held this evening.

'I'd have to share a room with him.'

Estelle had never shared a room with a man in her life. She wasn't especially shy or retiring but she certainly had none of Ginny's confidence or social ease. Ginny thought the weekends were designed for parties, clubs and pubs, whereas Estelle's idea of a perfect weekend was looking around old churches or ruins and then curling up on the sofa with a book.

Not playing escort!

'Gordon always takes the sofa when we share a room.'

'No.' Estelle pushed up her glasses and returned to her book. She tried to carry on reading about the mausoleum of the first Qin Emperor but it was terribly hard to do so when she was so worried about her brother and he *still* hadn't rung to let her know if he had got the job.

There was no mistaking the fact that the money would help.

It was late Saturday morning in London, and the wedding was being held that evening in a castle in Scotland. If Estelle was going to go then she would have to start getting ready now, for they would fly to Edinburgh and then take a helicopter to the castle and time was fast running out.

'Please,' Ginny said. 'The agency are freaking because they can't get anyone suitable at such short notice. He's coming to pick me up in an hour.'

'What will people think?' Estelle asked. 'If people are used to seeing him with you...'

'Gordon will take care of that. He'll say that we had an argument, that I was pushing for an engagement ring or something. We were going to be finishing soon anyway, now that I'm nearly through university. Honestly, Estelle, Gordon really is the loveliest man. There's so much pressure on him to appear straight—he simply cannot go to this wedding without a date. Just think of the money!'

Estelle couldn't stop thinking about the money.

Attending this wedding would mean that she could pay her brother's mortgage for an entire month, as well as a couple of his bills.

Okay, it wouldn't entirely solve their dilemma, but it would buy Andrew and his young family a little bit more time and, given all they had been through this past year, and all that was still to come, they could certainly use the reprieve.

Andrew had done so much for her—had put his own life on hold to make sure that Estelle's life carried on as normally as possible when their parents had died when Estelle was seventeen.

It was time for Estelle to step up, just as Andrew had.

'Okay.' Estelle took a deep breath and her decision was made. 'Ring and say that I'll come.'

'I've already told him that you've agreed,' Ginny admitted. 'Estelle, don't look at me like that. I know how badly you need the money and I simply couldn't bear to tell Gordon that I didn't have someone else lined up.'

Ginny looked more closely at Estelle. Her long black hair was pulled back in a ponytail, her very pale skin was without a blemish, and there was no last night's makeup smudged under Estelle's green eyes because Estelle rarely wore any. Ginny was trying not to show it but she was actually more than a little nervous as to what a madeup Estelle would look like and whether or not she could carry it off.

'You need to get ready. I'll help with your hair and things.'

'You're not coming near me with that cough,' Estelle said. 'I can manage.' She looked at Ginny's doubtful expression. 'We can all look like tarts if we have to.' She smiled and Ginny laughed. 'Though I don't actually have anything I can wear...would anyone notice if I wore something of yours?'

'I bought a new dress for the wedding.' Ginny headed to the wardrobe in her bedroom and Estelle followed.

Estelle's jaw dropped when she held the flimsy gold fabric up.

'Does that go under the dress?'

'It looks stunning on.'

'On *you*, perhaps...' Estelle said, because Ginny was a lot slimmer and had a tiny pert bust, whereas, though small, Estelle was curvy. 'I'm going to look like...'

'Which is the whole point.' Ginny grinned. 'Honestly, Estelle, if you just relax you'll have fun.'

'I doubt it,' Estelle said, wrapping her long dark hair in heated rollers at Ginny's dressing table, and setting to work on her face under her housemate's very watchful eye. Gordon was supposed to be a womanizer, and somehow Estelle had to get the balance right between looking as if she adored him while being far, far too young for him too.

'You need more foundation.'

'More?' Estelle already felt as if she had an inch on.

'And lashings of mascara.'

Ginny watched as Estelle took out the heated rollers and her long dark hair tumbled into ringlets. 'Okay, loads of hairspray...' Ginny said. 'Oh, and by the way, Gordon calls me Virginia, just in case anyone mentions me.'

Ginny blinked a few times when Estelle turned around. The smoky grey eyeshadow and layers of mascara brought out the emerald in her green eyes, and the make-up accentuated Estelle's full lips. Seeing the long black curls framing her friend's petite face, Ginny started to believe that Estelle could carry this off.

'You look amazing! Let's see you in the dress.'

'Won't I change there?'

'Gordon's schedule is too busy. Once you land I would imagine you'll be straight into the wedding.'

The dress was beautiful—sheer and gold, it clung everywhere. It was far too revealing but it was delicious too. Ginny gaped when Estelle wobbled on very high shoes.

'I think Gordon might dump me.'

'This,' Estelle said firmly, 'is a one-off.'

'That's what I said when I first started at the agency,' Ginny admitted. 'But if it goes well...'

'Don't even *think* it!' Estelle said as a car tooted in the street.

'You'll be fine,' Ginny said as Estelle nearly jumped out of her skin. 'You look stunning. I know you can do this.'

Estelle clung onto that as she stepped out of her cheap student accommodation home. Teetering on the unfamiliar high heels, she walked out of the drive and towards a sleek silver car, more than a little terrified to meet the politician.

'I have amazing taste!'

Gordon greeted her with a smile as his driver held open the door and Estelle climbed in. He was chubby, dressed in full Scottish regalia, and he made her smile even before she'd properly sat down.

'And you've got far better legs than me! I feel ridiculous in a kilt.'

Instantly he made her relax.

As the car headed for the airport he brought Estelle up to speed. 'We met two weeks ago...'

'Where?' Estelle asked.

'At Dario's...'

'Dario who?'

Gordon laughed. 'You really don't know anything, do you? It's a bar in Soho—sugar daddy heaven.'

'Oh, God...' she groaned.

'Do you work?' Gordon asked.

'Part-time at the library.'

'Maybe don't mention that. Just say you do a little bit of modelling,' Gordon suggested. 'Keep it all very vague, or say that right now keeping Gordon happy is a full-time job.' Estelle blushed and Gordon noticed. 'I know. Awful, isn't it? I seem to have created this terrible persona.'

'I'm worried that I shan't be able to pull it off.'

'You'll be fine,' Gordon said, and he went through everything with her again.

They practised their story over and over on the short flight to Edinburgh. He even asked after her brother and niece, and she was surprised that he knew about their plight.

'Virginia and I have become good friends this past year,' Gordon said. 'She was ever so upset for you when your brother had his accident and when the baby was born so unwell...' He gave her hand a squeeze. 'How is she now?'

'Waiting for surgery.'

'Just remember that you're helping them,' Gordon said as they transferred to the helicopter that would take them to the castle where the very exclusive wedding was being held.

As they walked across the immaculate lawn Gordon took her hand and she was grateful to hold onto it. He really was nice—if they had met under any other circumstances she would be looking forward to this evening.

'I can't wait to get inside the castle,' Estelle admitted. She'd already told Gordon she was studying ancient architecture.

'There won't be much time for exploring,' Gordon said. 'We'll be shown to our room and there will just be time to freshen up and touch up your hair and make-up before we head down for the wedding.'

'Okay.'

'And just remember,' Gordon said, 'this time tomorrow it will all be over and you'll never have to see any of them again.'

CHAPTER TWO

THE SOUND OF seagulls and the distant throb of music didn't wake Raúl from his slumber; instead they were the sounds that soothed him when he was startled in his sleep. He lay there, heart pounding for a moment, telling himself it was just a dream, while knowing that it was a memory that had jolted him awake.

The gentle motion of his berthed yacht almost tempted him back to sleep, but then he remembered that he was supposed to be meeting with his father.

Raúl forced his eyes open and stared at the tousled blonde hair on his pillow.

'Buenos días,' she purred.

'Buenos días.' Raúl responded, but instead of moving towards her he turned onto his back.

'What time do we leave for the wedding?'

Raúl closed his eyes at her presumption. He had never actually asked Kelly to join him as his guest, but that was the trouble with dating your PA—she knew your diary. The wedding was to be held this evening in the Scottish Highlands. It was nothing for Raúl to fly from Spain to Scotland for a wedding, but Kelly clearly thought that a few weeks out of his office and in his bed meant she was automatically invited.

'I'll speak to you about that later,' Raúl said, glancing at the clock. 'Right now I have to meet with my father.'

'Raúl…' Kelly turned to him in a move that was suggestive.

'Later,' he said, and climbed out of bed. 'I am supposed to be meeting with him in ten minutes.'

'That wouldn't have stopped you before.'

He took the stairs and walked up onto the deck, picking his way through the debris and the evidence of another wild Raúl Sanchez Fuente party. A maid was already starting the mammoth clean up and she gave a cheery wave to Raúl.

'Gracias,' she said as he gave her a substantial cash bonus without apologising for the mess. She did not mind his excesses—Raúl paid and treated her well, unlike the owners of some of the yachts, who expected her to work without complaint for very little.

Raúl put on his shades and walked along the Puerto Banús marina, where his yacht was moored. Here, Raúl belonged. Here, despite his decadent ways, he fitted in—because he was not the wildest. Raúl could hear a party continuing on, the music throbbing, the sound of laughter and merriment carrying across the sparkling water, and it reminded Raúl why he loved this place. Rarely was it ever silent. The marina was full of luxurious yachts and had the heady scent of filthy money. Ludicrously expensive cars were casually parked, all the fruits of serious wealth were on display here, and Raúl—dishevelled, unshaven and terribly beautiful—blended in well.

A couple of tourists stumbling home from a club nudged each other as Raúl walked past, trying to place him. For he was as good-looking as any film star and clearly he was *someone*. People-watching was a regular activity in Puerto

Banús, for amongst the tourists and locals were the rich, the famous and the notorious too.

Raúl scored two out of three—though he *was* famous in the business world.

Enrique, his driver, was waiting for him, and Raúl climbed in and gave a brief greeting, and then sat silently as he was driven the short distance to the Marbella branch of De La Fuente Holdings. He had no doubt as to what his father wanted to discuss, but his mind was going over what Kelly had just said.

'That wouldn't have stopped you before.'

Before what? Raúl asked himself.

Before he lost interest?

Before the chase had ended?

Before she assumed that a Saturday night would be shared?

Raúl was an island.

An island with frequent visitors and world-renowned parties, an island of endless sun and unlimited luxury, but one who preferred guests not to outstay their welcome, only allowed the superficial. Yes, Raúl was an island, and he intended to keep it that way. He certainly didn't want permanent boarders and he chose not to let anyone get too close.

He would never be responsible again for another's heart.

'I shan't be long,' Raúl told Enrique as the car door was lifted and he climbed out.

Raúl was not looking forward to this conversation, but his father had insisted they meet this morning and Raúl just wanted it over and done with.

'Buenos días.' He greeted Angela, his father's PA. 'What are you doing here on a Saturday?' he asked, because Angela usually flew home to her family for the weekend.

'I am trying to track down a certain Spaniard who said he would be here at eight a.m.,' Angela scolded mildly. She was the one woman who could get away with telling Raúl how it was. In her late fifties, she had been employed by the company for as long as Raúl could remember. 'I've been trying to call you—don't you ever have your phone on?'

'The battery is flat.'

'Well, before you speak with your father I need to go through your diary.'

'Later.'

'No, Raúl. I'm flying home later this morning. This needs to be done now. We also need to sort out a new PA for you—preferably one you *don't* fancy!' Angela was less than impressed with Raúl's brief eye-roll. 'Raúl, you need to remember that I'm going on long service leave in a few weeks' time. If I'm going to train somebody up for you, then I need to get on to it now.'

'Choose someone, then,' Raúl said. 'And you're right; perhaps it would be better if it was someone that I did not fancy.'

'Finally!' Angela sighed.

Yes, after having it pointed out to him on numerous occasions, Raúl was finally accepting that mixing business with pleasure had consequences, and sleeping with his PA was perhaps not such a good idea.

What was it with women? Raúl wondered. Why, once they'd made it to his bed, did they decide that they could no longer both work *and* sleep with him? Raúl could set his watch by it. After a few weeks they would decide, just as Kelly now had, that frequent dates and sex weren't enough. They wanted exclusivity, wanted inclusion, wanted commitment—which Raúl simply refused to give. Kelly would be found another position—or paid off handsomely, if that was what she preferred.

'All your flights and transfers are arranged for this afternoon,' Angela said. 'I can't believe that you'll be wearing a kilt.'

'I look good in a kilt.' Raúl smiled. 'Donald has asked that all the male guests wear them. I'm an honorary Scotsman, you know!' He was. He had studied in Scotland for four years, perhaps the best four years of his life, and the friendships he had made there had long continued.

Bar one.

His face hardened as he thought of his ex, who would be there tonight. Perhaps he *should* take Kelly after all, or arrive alone and get off with one of his old flames just to annoy the hell out of Araminta.

'Right, let's get this done...'

He went to walk towards his father's office but Angela called him back. 'It might be an idea to have a coffee before you see him.'

'No need,' Raúl said. 'I will get this over with and then go to Sol's for breakfast.' He loved Saturday mornings at Sol's—a beautiful waterfront café that moved you out quickly if you weren't one of the most beautiful. For people like Raúl they didn't even bother with a bill. They wanted his patronage, wanted the energy he brought to the place. Yes, Raúl decided, he would head there next—except Angela was calling him back again.

'Go and freshen up and I will bring you in coffee and a clean shirt.'

Yes, Angela was the only woman who could get away with speaking to him like that.

Raúl went into his own huge office—which was more like a luxurious hotel suite. As well as the office there was a sumptuous bedroom, and both rooms were put to good use. Heading towards the bathroom, he glanced at the bed and was briefly tempted to lie down. He had had two, possibly three hours' sleep last night. But he forced himself on to the bathroom, grimacing when he saw himself in the mirror. He could see now why Angela had been so insistent that he freshened up before facing his father.

Raúl's black eyes were bloodshot. He had forgotten to shave yesterday, so now two days' worth of black growth lined his strong jaw. His usually immaculate jet-black hair was tousled and fell over his forehead, and the lipstick on his collar, Raúl was sure, *wasn't* the colour that Kelly had been wearing last night.

Yes, he looked every inch the debauched playboy that his father accused him of being.

Raúl took off his jacket and shirt and splashed water on his face, and then set about changing, calling out his thanks to Angela when he heard her tell him that she had put a coffee on his desk.

'Gracias!' he called, and walked out mid-shave. Angela was possibly the only woman who did not blush at the sight of him without a shirt—she had seen him in nappies, after all. 'And thanks for pointing me in this direction before I meet with my father.'

'No problem.' She smiled. 'There is a fresh shirt hanging on the chair in your office also.'

'Do you know what it is that he wants to see me about?' Raúl was fishing. He knew exactly what his father would want to discuss. 'Am I to be given another lecture about taming my ways and settling down?'

'I'm not sure.' Only now did Angela's cheeks turn pink. 'Raúl, please listen to what your father has to say, though. This is no time for arguments. Your father is sick...'

'Just because he is ill, it does not necessarily make him right.'

'No,' Angela said carefully. 'But he does care for you, Raúl, even if he does not easily show it. Please listen to him... He is worried about you facing things on your own...' Angela saw Raúl's frown and stopped.

'I think you *do* know what this is about.'

'Raúl, I just ask that you listen—I can't bear to hear you two fighting.'

'Stop worrying,' Raúl said kindly. He liked Angela; she was the closest thing to a mum he had. 'I have no intention of fighting. I just think that at thirty years of age I don't have to be told my bedtime, and certainly not who I'm going to bed *with*...'

Raúl got back to shaving. He had no intention of being dictated to, but his hand did pause. Would it be such a big deal to let his father think that maybe he was actually serious about someone? Would it hurt just to hint that maybe he was close to settling down? His father was dying, after all.

'Wish me luck.' Raúl's voice was wry as, clean-shaven and bit clearer in the head, he walked past Angela to face his father. He glanced over, saw the tension and strain on her features. 'It will be fine,' he reassured her. 'Look...' He knew Angela would never keep news from his father. 'I *am* seeing someone, but I don't want him getting carried away.'

'Who?' Angela's eyes were wide.

'Just an old flame. We ran into each other again. She lives in England but I'm seeing her at the wedding tonight...'

'Araminta!'

'Stop there...' Raúl smiled. That was all that was needed. He knew the seed had been sewn.

Raúl knocked on his father's door and stepped in.

There should have been flames, he thought afterwards.

Or the smell of sulphur. Actually, there should have been the smell of car fuel and the sound of thunder followed by silence. There should at least have been some warning, as he was walked through the door, that he was returning to hell.

CHAPTER THREE

ESTELLE FELT AS if everyone knew what a fraud she was.

She closed her heavily made-up eyes and dragged in a deep breath. They were standing in the castle grounds, waiting to be led to their seating, and some pre-wedding drinks and nibbles were being served.

Why they hell had she agreed to this?

You know why, Estelle told herself, her resolve hardening.

'Are you okay, darling?' Gordon asked. 'The wedding should start soon.'

He'd been nothing but kind, just as Ginny had promised he would be.

'I'm fine,' Estelle said, and held a little more tightly onto his arm, just as Gordon had told her to do.

'This is Estelle.'

Gordon introduced her to a couple and Estelle watched the slight rise of the woman's eyebrow.

'Estelle, this is Veronica and James.'

'Estelle.' Veronica gave a curt nod and soon moved James away.

'You're doing wonderfully,' Gordon said, squeezing her hand and drawing her away from the mingling wedding guests so that they could speak without being overheard. 'Maybe you just need to smile a bit more,' he suggested gently, 'and, I know it calls for brilliant acting, could you try and look just a little more besotted with me? I've got my terrible reputation with women to think of.'

'Of course,' Estelle said through chattering teeth.

'The gay man and the virgin,' Gordon whispered in her ear. 'If only they knew!'

Estelle's eyes widened in horror and Gordon quickly apologised. 'I was just trying to make you smile,' he said.

'I can't believe that she *told* you!'

Estelle was horrified that Ginny would share something as personal and as sensitive as that. Then again, she could believe it—Ginny found it endlessly amusing that Estelle had never slept with anyone. It wasn't by deliberate choice; it wasn't something she'd actively decided. More that she'd been so shell shocked by her parents' death that homework and books had been her escape. By the time she'd emerged from her grief Estelle had felt two steps behind her peers. Clubs and parties had seemed frivolous. It was ancient ruins and buildings that fascinated her, and when she did meet someone there was always a panic that her virgin status must mean she was looking for a husband. More and more it had become an issue.

Now it would seem it was a joke!

She'd be having strong words with Ginny.

'Virginia didn't say it in a malicious way.' Gordon seemed devastated to have upset her. 'We were just talking one night. I really should never have brought it up.'

'It's okay,' Estelle conceded. 'I guess I am a bit of a rarity.'

'We all have our secrets,' Gordon said. 'And for tonight we both have to cover them up.' He smiled at her strained expression. 'Estelle, I know how hard it was for you to agree to this, but I promise you have nothing to feel nervous about. I'm soon to be a happily married man.'

'I know,' Estelle said. Gordon had told her on the plane about his long-term boyfriend, Frank, and the plans they had made. 'I just can't stand the disapproving looks and that everyone thinks of me as a gold-digger,' she admitted. 'Even though that's the whole point of the night.'

'Stop caring what everyone thinks,' Gordon said.

It was the same as she said to Andrew, who was acutely embarrassed to be in a wheelchair. 'You're right.'

Gordon lifted her chin and she smiled into his eyes. 'That's better.' Gordon smiled back. 'We'll get through this together.'

So Estelle held onto his arm and did her best to look suitably besotted, ignoring the occasional disapproving stare from the other guests, and she was just starting to relax and get into things when *he* arrived.

Till that moment Estelle had thought it would be the bride who would make an entrance, and it wasn't the sight of a helicopter landing that had heads turning—helicopters had been landing regularly since Estelle had got there— no, it was the man who stepped out who held everyone's attention.

'Oh, my, the evening just got interesting,' Gordon said as the most stunning man ducked under the blades and then walked towards the gathering.

He was tall, his thick black hair brushed back and gleaming, and his mouth was sulky and unsmiling. His Mediterranean colouring should surely mean that he'd look out of place wearing a kilt, but instead he looked as if he'd been born to wear one. Lean-hipped and long-limbed, but muscular too, he could absolutely carry it off.

He could carry me off right now, Estelle thought wildly—and wild thoughts were rare for Estelle.

She watched as he accepted whisky from a waiter and then stood still. He seemed removed and remote from everyone else. Even the women who flocked to him were quickly dismissed, as if at any minute he might simply walk off.

Then he met her eyes.

Estelle tried to flick hers away, except she found that she couldn't.

His eyes drifted down over the gold dress, but not in the disapproving way that Veronica's had. Although they weren't approving either. They were merely assessing.

She felt herself burn as his eyes moved then to her sixty-four-year-old date, and she wanted to correct him—wanted to tell him that the rotund, red-faced man who was struggling with the heat in his heavy kilt and jacket was not her lover. Though of course she could not.

She wanted to, though.

'Eyes only for me, darling,' Gordon reminded her, perhaps picking up on the crackle of energy crossing the lawn. His glance followed Estelle's gaze. 'Though frankly no one would blame you a bit for looking. He's completely divine.'

'Who?' Estelle tried to pretend that she hadn't noticed the delicious stranger—Gordon was paying her good money to be here, after all—but she wasn't fooling anyone.

'Raúl Sanchez Fuente,' Gordon said in a low voice. 'Our paths cross now and then at various functions. He owns everything but morals. The bastard even looks good in a kilt. He has my heart—not that he wants it…'

Estelle couldn't help but laugh.

Raúl's eyes lazily worked over the guests. He was questioning now his decision to come alone. He needed distraction tonight, but when he had thought of the old flames that he might run into he had been thinking of the perky breasts and the narrow waists of yesteryear, as if the clock might have stopped on his university days. Instead the hands of time had moved on.

There was Shona. Her once long red hair was now cut too severely and she stood next to a chinless wonder. She caught his eye and then blushed unbecomingly and shot him a furious look, as if their once torrid times could be erased and forgotten by her wedding ring.

He knew, though, that she was remembering.

'Raúl...'

He frowned when he saw Araminta walking towards him. She was wearing that slightly needy smile that Raúl recognised only too well and it made his early warning system react—because temporary distraction was his requirement tonight, not desperation.

'How are you?'

'Not bad,' she said, and then proceeded to tell him about her hellish divorce, how she was now single, how she'd thought about him often since the break-up, how she'd been looking forward to seeing him tonight, how she regretted the way things had worked out for them...

'I told you that you would at the time.' Raúl did not do sentiment. 'You'll have to excuse me. I have to make a call.'

'We'll catch up later, though?'

He could hear the hope in her voice and it irked him.

Was he good enough for her father now? Rich enough? Established enough?

'There's nothing to catch up on.'

Just like that he dismissed her, his black eyes not even watching her as she gave a small sob and walked off.

What on earth was he doing here? Raúl wondered. He should be getting ready to party on his yacht, or to hit the clubs—should be losing himself instead of getting reacquainted with his past. More to the point, there was hardly a limitless choice of women in this castle in the Scottish

Highlands. And after what Raúl had found out this morning his own company wasn't one he wanted to keep.

His hand tightened on the whisky glass he held. The full impact of what his father had told him was only now starting to hit him.

So black were his thoughts, so sideswiped was he by the revelations, Raúl actually considered leaving—just summoning his pilot and walking out. But then a tumble of dark hair and incredibly pale skin caught his eye and held it. She looked nervous and awkward—which was unusual for Gordon's tarts. They were normally brash and confident. But not this one.

He held her gaze when she caught his and now there was only one woman he wanted to walk towards him—except she was holding tightly to Gordon's arm.

She offered far more than distraction—she offered oblivion. Because for the first time since his conversation with his father he forgot about it.

Perhaps he would stay. At least for the service…

A deep Scottish voice filled the air and the guests were informed that the wedding would soon commence and they were to make their way to their seats.

'Come on.' Gordon took Estelle's hand. 'I love a good wedding.'

'And me.' Estelle smiled.

They walked through the mild night. The grounds were lit by torches and there were chairs set out. With the castle as a backdrop the scene looked completely stunning, and Estelle let go of her guilt, determined to enjoy herself. She'd been on a plane and, for the first time in her life, a helicopter, she was staying the night in a beautiful castle in the Scottish Highlands, and Gordon was an absolute delight. Despite having dreaded it, she was enjoying herself, Estelle realised as they took their seats and she made more small talk with Gordon.

'Donald says that Victoria's so nervous,' he told her. 'She's such a perfectionist, apparently, and she's been stressing over the details for months.'

'Well, it all seems to have paid off,' Estelle said. 'I can't wait to see what she's wearing.'

Just as she'd finally started to relax as the music changed and they all stood for the bride, just as she'd decided simply to enjoy herself, she turned to get a first glimpse of the bride—only to realise that Raúl was sitting behind her.

Directly behind her.

It should make no difference, Estelle told herself. It was a simple coincidence. But even coincidence was too big a word—after all, he had to sit *somewhere*. Estelle was just acutely aware that he was there.

She tried to concentrate on the bride as she made her way to Donald. Victoria really did look stunning. She was wearing a very simple white dress and carried a small posy of heather. The smile on Donald's face as his bride walked towards him had Estelle smiling too—but not for long. She could feel Raúl's eyes burning into her shoulder, and a little while later her scalp felt as if it were on fire. She was sure his eyes lingered there.

She did her best to focus on the service. It was incredibly romantic. So much so that when they got to the 'in sickness and in health' part it actually brought tears to her eyes as she remembered her brother Andrew's wedding, just over a year ago.

Who could have known then the hard blows fate had in store for him and his pregnant bride, Amanda?

Ever the gentleman, Gordon pressed a tissue into her hand.

'Thank you.' Estelle gave a watery smile and Gordon gave her hand a squeeze.

* * *

Please! Raúl thought. *Spare me the crocodile tears.* It had been the same with Gordon's previous girlfriend—what was her name? Raúl smiled to himself, as he had the day they were introduced.

Virginia.

This one, though, even if she wasn't to Raúl's usual taste, was stunning. Raven-haired women were far from a rarity where Raúl came from, and for that reason he certainly preferred a blonde—for variety, two blondes!

He wanted raven tonight.

Turn around, Raúl thought, for he wanted to meet those eyes again.

Turn around, he willed her, watching her shoulders stiffen, watching the slight tilt of her neck as if she was aware of but resisting his silent demand.

How she was resisting.

Estelle sat rigid and then stood in the same way after the service was over, when the bride and groom were letting doves fly. They fluttered high into the sky and the crowd murmured and pointed and turned to watch them in flight.

Reluctantly she also turned, and she must look up, Estelle thought helplessly as two black liquid pools invited her to dive in. She should, like everyone else, move her gaze upwards and watch the doves fly off into the distance.

Instead she faced him.

What the hell are you doing with him? Raúl wanted to ask. *What the hell are you doing with a man perhaps three times your age?*

Of course he knew the answer.

Money.

And Raúl knew then what to do—knew the answer to the dilemma that had been force-fed to him at breakfast-time.

His mouth moved into a smile and he watched as her head jerked away—watched as she stared, too late, up into the sky. And he saw her pale throat as her neck arched and he wanted his mouth there.

A piper led them back to the castle. He walked in front of her and Gordon. Estelle's heels kept sinking into the grass, but it was nothing compared to the feeling of drowning in quicksand when she had been caught in Raúl's gaze.

His kilt was greys and lilacs, his jacket a dark purple velvet, his posture and his stride exact and sensual. She wanted to run up to him, to tap him on the shoulder and tell him to please leave her alone. Yet he had done nothing. He wasn't even looking over his shoulder. He was just chatting with a fellow guest as they made their way back to the castle.

Very deliberately Raúl ignored her. He turned his back and chatted with Donald, asked a favour from a friend, and then flirted a little with a couple of old flames—but at all times he knew that her eyes more than occasionally searched out his.

Raúl knew exactly what he was doing and he knew exactly why.

Mixing business with pleasure had caused a few problems for Raúl in the past.

Tonight it was suddenly the solution.

CHAPTER FOUR

'Excuse me, sir.'

A waiter halted Estelle and Gordon as they made their way into the Grand Hall and to their table.

'There's been a change to the seating plan. Donald and Victoria didn't realise that you were seated so far back. It's all been rectified now. Please accept our apologies for the mistake.'

'*Oooh,* we're getting an upgrade,' Gordon said as they were led nearer to the front.

Estelle flushed when she saw that the rather teary woman she had seen earlier speaking with Raúl was being quietly shuffled back to the bowels of the hall. Estelle knew even before they arrived at the new table which one it would be.

Raúl did not look up as they made their way over. Not until they were being shown into their seats.

She smiled a greeting to Veronica and James, but could not even attempt one for Raúl—both seats either side of him were empty.

He had done this.

Estelle tried to tell herself she was imagining things, or overreacting, but somehow she knew she was right. Knew that those long, lingering stares had led to this.

The chair next to him was being held out. She wanted

to turn to Gordon, to ask if they could swap seats but she knew that would look ridiculous.

It was a simple change of seating, Estelle told herself. She acknowledged to herself that she lied.

'Gordon.' Raúl shook his hand.

'Raúl.'

Gordon smiled as he took the seat next to Estelle, so she was sandwiched between them, and she leant back a little as they chatted.

'I haven't seen you since...' Gordon laughed. 'Since last wedding season. This is Estelle.'

'Estelle.' He raised one eyebrow as she took her seat beside him. 'In Spain you would be Estela.'

'We're in England.' She was aware of her brittle response, but her defences were up—though she did try to soften it with a brief smile.

'Of course.' Raúl shrugged. 'Though I must speak with my pilot. He was most insistent, when we landed, that this was *Scotland.*'

She tried so hard not to, but Estelle twitched her lips into a slight smile.

'This is Shona and Henry...' Raúl introduced them as a waiter poured some wine.

Estelle took a sip and then asked for water—for a draughty castle, it felt terribly warm.

There was brief conversation and more introductions taking place, and all would have been fine if Raúl were not there. But Estelle was aware, despite his nonchalant appearance, that he was carefully listening to her responses.

She laughed just a little too loudly at one of Gordon's jokes.

As she'd been told to do.

Gordon was busy speaking with James, and for something to do Estelle looked through the menu, squinting because Ginny had suggested that she leave her glasses at home.

Raúl misconstrued it as a frown.

'Vichyssoise,' came his low, deep voice. 'It is a soup. It's delicious.'

'I don't need hand-holding for the menu.' Estelle stopped herself, aware she was coming across as terribly rude, but her nerves were prickling in defensiveness. 'And you failed to mention it's served cold.'

'No.' He smiled. 'I was just about to tell you that.'

Soup was a terribly hard ask with Raúl sitting next to her, but she worked her way through it, even though her conversation with Gordon kept getting interrupted by his phone.

'I can't even get a night off.' He sighed.

'Important?' Estelle checked.

'It could be soon. I'll have to keep it on silent.'

The main course was served and it was the most gorgeous beef Estelle had ever tasted. Yet it stuck in her throat—especially when Veronica asked her a question.

'Do you work, Estelle?'

She took a drink of water before answering. 'I do a bit of modeling.' Estelle gave a small smile, remembering how Gordon had told her to respond to such a question. She just hadn't expected to be inhaling testosterone when she answered. 'Though, of course, taking care of Gordon is a full-time job...'

Estelle saw the pausing of Raúl's fork and then heard Gordon's stab of laughter. She was locked in a lie and there was no way out. It was an act, Estelle told herself. Just one night and she would never have to see these people again—and what did she care if Raúl thought her cheap?

'Could you pass me the pepper?' came the silk of his voice.

Was it the fact that it had been asked with a Spanish accent that made the question sound sexy, or was it that she was going mad?

She passed it, holding the heavy silver pot and releasing it to him, feeling the brief warmth of his fingertips as he took it. He immediately noticed her error. 'That's the salt,' Raúl said, and she had to go through it again.

It was bizarre. He had said hardly two words to her, had made no suggestions. There were no knees pressing into hers under the table and his hands had not lingered when she'd passed him the pepper, yet the air between them was thick with tension.

He declined dessert and spread cheese onto Scottish oatcakes. 'I'd forgotten how good these taste.'

She turned and watched as he took a bite and then ran his tongue over his lip, capturing a small sliver of quince paste.

'Now I remember.'

There was no implication. He was only making small talk.

It was Estelle's mind that searched every word.

She spread cheese on an oatcake herself and added quince.

'Fantastic?' Raúl asked.

'Yes.'

She knew he meant sex.

'Now the speeches.' Gordon sighed.

They were long. Terribly long. Especially when you had no idea who the couple were. Especially when you were supposed to be paying attention to the man on your right but your mind was on the one to your left.

First it was Victoria's father, who rambled on just a touch too long. Then it was the groom Donald's turn, and he was thankfully a bit quicker—and funnier too. He moved through the formalities and, on behalf of himself and his new wife, especially thanked all who had travelled from afar.

'I was hoping Raúl wouldn't make it, of course,' Donald said, looking over to Raúl, as did the whole room. 'I'm just thankful Victoria didn't see him in a kilt until *after* my ring was on her finger. Trust a Spaniard to wear a kilt so well.'

The whole room laughed. Raúl's shoulders moved in a light, good-natured laugh too. He wasn't remotely embarrassed—no doubt more than used to the attention and to having his beauty confirmed.

Then it was the best man's turn.

'In Spain there are no speeches at a wedding,' Raúl said, leaning across her a little to speak to Gordon.

She could smell his expensive cologne, and his arm was leaning slightly on her. Estelle watched her fingers around the stem of her glass tighten.

'We just have the wedding, a party, and then bed,' Raúl said.

It was the first hint of suggestion, but even so she could merely be reading into things too much. Except as he leant over her to hear Gordon's response Estelle wanted to put her hand up, wanted to ask for the lights to come on, for this assault on her senses to stop, to tell the room the inappropriateness of the man sitting beside her. Only not a single thing had he done—not a word or hand had he put wrong.

So why was her left breast aching, so close to where his arm was? Why were her two front teeth biting down on her lip at the sight of his cheek, inches away?

'Really?' Gordon checked. 'I might just have to move to Spain! In actual fact I was—'

Gordon was interrupted by the buzz of his phone and

Raúl moved back in his seat. Estelle sat watching the newly wed couple dancing.

'Darling, I am so sorry,' Gordon said as he read a message on his phone. 'I am going to have to find somewhere I can make some calls and use a computer.'

'Good luck getting internet access,' drawled Raúl. 'I have to go outside just to make a call.'

'I might be some time.'

'Trouble?' Estelle asked

'Always.' Gordon rolled his eyes. 'Though this is unexpected. But I'll deal with it as quickly as I can. I hate to leave you on your own.'

'She won't be on her own,' Raúl said. 'I can keep an eye.'

She rather wished that he wouldn't.

'Thanks so much,' Gordon said. 'In that dress she deserves to dance.' He turned to Estelle. 'I really am sorry to leave you…' For appearances' sake, he kissed her on the cheek.

What a waste of her mouth, Raúl thought.

Once Gordon had gone she turned to James and Veronica, on her right, desperately trying to feed into their conversation. But they were certainly not interested in Gordon's new date. Over and over they politely dismissed her, and then followed the other couples at their table and got up to dance—leaving her alone with Raúl.

'From the back you could be Spanish…'

She turned to the sound of his voice.

'But from the front…'

His eyes ran over her creamy complexion and she felt heat sear her face as his eyes bored into hers. And though they did not wander—he was far too suave for that—somehow he undressed her. Somehow she sat there on her seat beside him at the wedding as if they were a

couple. And when he looked at her, she felt, for a bizarre
second, as if she was completely naked.

He was as potent as that.

CHAPTER FIVE

'IRISH?' HE CHECKED, and Estelle hesitated for a moment before nodding.

She did not want to give any information to this man— did not even want to partake in conversation.

'Yet your accent is English?'

'My parents moved to England before I was born.' She gave a tight swallow and hoped her stilted response would halt the conversation. It did not.

'Where in England are they?'

'They're not,' Estelle answered, terribly reluctant to reveal *anything* of herself.

Raúl did not push. Instead he moved the conversation on.

'So, where did you and Gordon meet?'

'We met at Dario's.' Estelle answered the question as Gordon had told her to, trying to tell herself he was just being polite, but every sense in her body seemed set to high alert. 'It's a bar—'

'In Soho,' Raúl broke in. 'I have heard a lot about Dario's.'

Beneath her make-up her cheeks were scalding.

'Not that I have been,' Raúl said. 'As a male, I would perhaps be too young to get in there.' His lips rose in a slight smile and he watched the colour flood darker in her neck and to her ears. 'Maybe I should give it a try...'

He looked more closely at Estelle. She had eyes that were a very dark green and rounded cheeks—she really was astonishingly attractive. There was something rather sweet about her despite the clothes, despite the make-up, and there was an awkwardness that was as rare as it was refreshing. Raúl was not used to awkwardness in the women he dated.

'So, we both find ourselves alone at a wedding…'

'I'm not alone,' Estelle said. 'Gordon will be back soon.' She did not want to ask, but she found herself doing just that as she glanced to the empty chair beside him. 'How come…?' Her voice faded out. There was no polite way to address it.

'We broke up this morning.'

'I'm sorry.'

'Please don't be.' He thought for a moment before continuing. 'Really to say we broke up is perhaps an exaggeration. To break something would mean you had to have something, and we were only going out for a few weeks.'

'Even so…' Still she attempted to be polite. 'Breakups are hard.'

'I've never found them to be,' Raúl said. 'It's the bit before that I struggle with.'

'When it starts to go wrong?'

'No,' Raúl said. 'When it starts to go right.'

His eyes were looking right into hers, his voice was deep and low, and his words interesting—because despite herself she *did* want to know more about this fascinating man. So much so that she found herself leaning in a little to hear.

'When she starts asking what we are doing next weekend. When you hear her saying "Raúl said…" or "Raúl thinks…"' He paused for a second. 'I don't like to be told what I'm thinking.'

'I'm sure you don't.'

'Do you know what I'm thinking now?'

'I wouldn't presume to.' She could hardly breathe, because she was surely thinking the same.

'Would you like to dance?'

'No, thank you,' Estelle said, because it was far safer to stay seated than to self-combust in his arms. He was sinfully good-looking and, more worryingly, she had a sinking feeling as she realised he was pulling her in deeper with each measured word. 'I'll just wait here for Gordon.'

'Of course,' Raúl said. 'Have you met the bride or groom?'

'No.' Estelle felt as if she were being interviewed. 'You're friends with the groom?'

'I went to university with him.'

'In Spain?'

'No, here in Scotland.'

'Oh!' She wasn't sure why, but that surprised her.

'I was here for four years,' Raúl said. 'Then I moved back to Marbella. I still like to come here. Scotland is a very beautiful country.'

'It is,' Estelle said. 'Well, from the little I've seen.'

'It's your first time?'

She nodded.

'Have you ever been to Spain?'

'Last year,' Estelle said. 'Though only for a few days. Then there was a family emergency and I had to go home.'

'Raúl?'

He barely looked up as a woman came over. It was the same woman who had been moved from the table earlier.

'I thought we could dance.'

'I'm busy.'

'Raúl…'

'Araminta.' Now he turned and looked at her. 'If I wanted to dance with you then I would have asked.'

Estelle blinked, because despite the velvet of his voice his words were brutal.

'That was a bit harsh,' Estelle said as Araminta stumbled off.

'Far better to be harsh than to give mixed messages.'

'Perhaps.'

'So…' Raúl chose his words carefully. 'If taking care of Gordon is a full-time job, what do you do in your time off?'

'My time off?'

'When you're not *working*.'

She didn't frown this time. There was no mistake as to what he meant. Her green eyes flashed as she turned to him. 'I don't appreciate the implication.'

He was surprised by her challenge, liked that she met him head-on—it was rare that anyone did.

'Excuse me,' he said. 'Sometimes my English is not so good…'

When it suited him.

Estelle took a deep breath, her hand still toying with the stem of her glass as she wondered how to play this, deciding she would do her best to be polite.

'What work do you do?' She looked at him. She had absolutely no idea about this man. 'Are you in politics too?'

'Please!'

He watched the slight reluctant smile on her lips.

'I am a director for De La Fuente Holdings, which means I buy, improve or build, and then maybe I sell.' Still he watched her. 'Take this castle; if I owned it I would not have it exclusively as a wedding venue but also as a hotel. It is under-utilised. Mind you, it would need a lot of refurbishment. I have not shared a bathroom since my university days.'

She was far from impressed and tried not to show it. Raúl, of course, could not know that she was studying ancient architecture and that buildings were a passion of hers. The castle renovations she had seen were modest, the rooms cold and the bathrooms sparse—as it should be. The thought of this place being modernised and filled to capacity, no matter how tastefully, left her cold.

Unfortunately *he* didn't.

Not once in her twenty-five years had Estelle even come close to the reaction she was having to Raúl.

If they were anywhere else she would get up and leave.

Or, she conceded, if they were anywhere else she would lean forward and accept his mouth.

'So it's your father's business?' Estelle asked, trying to find a fault in him—trying to tell herself that it was his father's money that had eased his luxurious path to perfection.

'No, it was my mother's family business. My father bought into it when he married.' He saw her tiny frown.

'Sorry, you said De La Fuente, and I thought Fuente was *your* surname…'

For an occasional model who picked up men at Dario's she was rather perceptive, Raúl thought. 'In Spain it is different. You take your father's surname first and then your mother's…'

'I didn't know that.' She tried to fathom it. 'How does it work?'

'My father is Antonio Sanchez. My mother was Gabriella De La Fuente.'

'Was?'

'She passed away in a car accident…'

Normally he could just say it. Every other time he revealed it he just glossed over it, moved swiftly on—tonight, with all he had learnt this morning, suddenly he could not.

Every man except Raúl had struggled in the summer heat with full Scottish regalia. Supremely fit, and used to the sun, Raúl had not even broken a sweat. But now, when the castle was cool, when a draught swirled around the floor, he broke into one—except his face drained of colour.

He tried to right himself, reached for water; he had trained his mind not to linger. Of course he had not quite mastered his mind at night, but even then he had trained himself to wake up before he shouted out.

'Was it recent?' Estelle saw him struggle briefly, knew surely better than anyone how he must feel—for she had lost her parents the same way. She watched as he drained a glass of water and then blinked when he turned and the suave Raúl returned.

'Years ago,' he dismissed. 'When I was a child.' He got back to their discussion, refusing to linger on a deeply buried past. 'My actual name is Raúl Sanchez De La Fuente, but it gets a bit long during introductions.'

He smiled, and so too did Estelle.

'I can imagine.'

'But I don't want to lose my mother's name, and of course my father expects me to keep his.'

'It's nice that the woman's name passes on.'

'It doesn't, though,' Raúl said. 'Well, it does for one generation—it is still weighted to the man.' He saw her frown.

'So, if you had a baby…?'

'That's never going to happen.'

'But if you did?'

'God forbid.' He let out a small sigh. 'I will try to explain.'

He was very patient.

He took the salt and pepper she had so nervously passed to him and, heads together, they sat at the table while he made her a small family tree.

'What is your surname?'

'Connolly.'

'Okay, we have a baby and call her Jane...'

How he made her burn. Not at the baby part, but at the thought of the part to get to that.

'Her name would be Jane Sanchez Connolly.'

'I see.'

'And when Jane marries...' he lifted a hand and grabbed a fork as he plucked a name from the ether '...Harry Potter, her daughter...' he added a spoon '...who shall also be called Jane, would be Jane Sanchez Potter. Connolly would be gone!' He looked at her as she worked it out. 'It is simple. At least the name part is simple. It is the fifty years of marriage that might prove hard.' He glanced over to today's happy couple. 'I can't imagine being tied down to another, and I certainly don't believe in love.'

He always made that clear up-front.

'How can you sit at a wedding and say that?' Estelle challenged. 'Did you not see the smile on Donald's face when he saw his bride?'

'Of course I did,' Raúl said. 'I recognised it well—it was the same smile he gave at the last wedding of his I attended.'

She laughed. There was no choice but to. 'Are you serious?'

'Completely,' Raúl said.

Yet he was smiling, and when he did that she felt as if she should scrabble in her bag for sunglasses, because the force of his smile blinded her to all faults—and she was quite positive a man like Raúl had many.

'You're wrong, Raúl.' She refused to play his cynical game. 'My brother got married last year and he and his wife are deeply in love.'

'A year.' He gave a light shrug. 'It is still the honey-moon phase.'

'They've been through more in this year than most have been through in a lifetime.' And she'd never meant to but she found herself opening up to him. 'Andrew, my brother, was in an accident on their honeymoon—a jet ski...'

'Serious?'

Estelle nodded. 'He's now in a wheelchair.'

'That must take a lot of getting used to.' He thought for a moment. 'Is that the family emergency you had to fly home from your own holiday for?'

Estelle nodded. She didn't tell him it had been a trip around churches. No doubt he assumed she'd been hauled out of a club to hear the news. 'I raced home, and, really, since then things have been tough on them. Amanda was already pregnant when they got married...'

She didn't know why she was telling him. Perhaps it was safer to talk than to dance. Maybe it was easier to talk about her brother and the truth than make up stories about Dario's and seedy clubs in Soho. Or perhaps it was the black liquid eyes that invited conversation, the way he moved his chair a little closer so that he could hear.

'Their daughter was born four months ago. The pros-pect of being a dad was the main thing that kept Andrew motivated during his rehabilitation. Just when we thought things were turning around...'

Raúl watched her green eyes fill with tears, saw her rapid blink as she tried to stem them.

'She has a heart condition. They're waiting till she's a little bit bigger so they can operate.'

He watched pale hands go to her bag and Estelle took out a photo. He looked at her brother, Andrew, and his wife, and a small frail baby with a slight blue tinge to her skin, and he realised that they hadn't been crocodile tears he had witnessed during the wedding ceremony. He looked back to Estelle.

'What's her name?'

'Cecelia.'

Raúl looked at her as she gazed at the photo and he knew then the reason she was here with Gordon. 'Your brother?' Raúl asked, just to confirm things in his mind. 'Does he work?'

'No.' Estelle shook her head. 'He was self-employed. He...' She put away the photo, dragged in a breath, could not stand to think of all the problems her brother faced.

Exactly at that moment Raúl lightened things.

'My legs are cold.'

Estelle laughed, and as she did she blinked as a photographer's camera flashed in her face.

'Nice natural shot,' the photographer said.

'We're not...' Oh, what did it matter?

'I need to move.' He stood. 'And Gordon asked that I take care of you.' Raúl held out his hand to her. This dance was more important than she could ever know. This dance must ensure that tonight she was thinking only of *him*— that by the time he approached her with his suggestion it would not seem so unthinkable. But first he had to set the tone. First he had to make her aware that he knew the sort of business she was in. 'Would you like to dance?'

Estelle didn't really have a choice. Walking towards the dance floor, she had the futile hope that the band would break into something more frivolous than sensuous, but all hope was gone as his arms wrapped loosely around her.

'You are nervous?'

'No.'

'I would have thought you would enjoy dancing, given that you two met at Dario's.'

'I do love to dance.' Estelle forced a bright smile, remembered who she was supposed to be. 'It's just a bit early for me.'

'And me,' Raul said as he took her in his arms. 'About now I would only just be getting ready to go out.'

She couldn't read this man. Not in the least. He held her, he was skilled and graceful, but the eyes that looked down at her were not smiling.

'Relax.'

She tried to—except he'd said it into her ear, causing the sensitive skin there to tingle.

'Can I ask something?'

'Of course,' Estelle said, though she would rather he didn't. She just wanted this duty dance to end.

'What are you doing with Gordon?'

'Excuse me?' She could not believe he would ask that—could not think of anyone else who would be so direct. It was as if all pretence had gone—all tiny implications, all conversation left behind—and the truth was being revealed in his arms.

'There is a huge age difference...'

'That's none of your business.' She felt as if she was being attacked in broad daylight and everyone else was just carrying on, oblivious.

'You are twenty, yes?'

'Twenty-five.'

'He was ten years older than I am now when you were born.'

'They're just numbers.'

'We both work in numbers.'

Estelle went to walk off mid-dance, but his grip merely tightened. 'Of course...' He held her so she could feel the lean outline of his body, inhale the terribly masculine scent of him. 'You want him only for his money.'

'You're incredibly rude.'

'I'm incredibly honest,' Raúl corrected. 'I am not criticizing—there is nothing wrong with that.'

'*Vete al infierno!*' Estelle said, grateful for a Spanish schoolfriend and lunchtimes being taught by her how to curse. She watched his mouth curve as she told him in his own language to go to hell. 'Excuse me,' Estelle said. 'Sometimes my Spanish is not so good. What I mean to say is...'

He pressed a finger to her lips before she could tell him, in her own language and rather more crudely, exactly where he could go.

The contact with her mouth, the sensual pressure, the intimacy of the gesture, had the desired effect and silenced her.

'One more dance,' Raúl said. 'Then I return you to Gordon.' He removed his finger. 'I'm sorry if you thought I was being rude—believe me, that was not my intention. Accept my apology, please.'

Estelle's eyes narrowed in suspicious assessment. She was aware of the pulse in her lips from his mere touch. Logic told her to remove herself from this situation, yet the stir of first arousal won.

The music slowed and, ignoring brief resistance, he pulled her in tighter. If she thought he was judging her, she was right—only it was not harshly. Raúl admired a woman who could separate emotion from sex.

Raúl needed exactly such a woman if he were to see this through.

He did not think her cheap: on the contrary, he intended to pay her very well.

She should have gone then—back to the table, to be ignored by the other guests. Should have left this man at a safer point. But her naïve body was refusing to walk away; instead it was awakening in his arms.

He held her so that her head was resting on his chest. She could feel the soft velvet of his jacket on her cheek. But she was more aware of his hand resting lightly on the base of her spine.

A couple dancing, each in a world of their own.

Raúl's motives were temporarily suspended. He enjoyed the soft weight that leant against him, the quiet of his mind as he focused only on her. The hand on her shoulder crept beneath her hair, his fingers lightly stroking the back of her neck, and again he wanted his mouth there, wanted to lift the raven curtain and taste her.

His fingers told her so—they stroked in a soft probing and they circled and teased as she swayed in time to the music. Estelle felt the stirring between them, and though her head denied what was happening her body shifted a little to allow for him. Her nipples hurt against his chest. His hand pressed her in just a little tighter as again he broke all boundaries. Again he voiced what perhaps others would not.

'I always thought a sporran was for decorative purposes only...'

She could feel the heat of its fur against her stomach.

'Yet it is the only thing keeping me decent.'

'You're *so* far from decent,' Estelle rasped.

'I know.'

They danced—not much, just swaying in time. Except she was on fire.

He could feel the heat of her skin on his fingers, could feel her breath so shallow that he wanted to lower his head and breathe into her mouth for her. He thought of her dark hair on his pillow, of her pink nipples in his mouth at the same time. He wanted her more than he had wanted any other, though Raúl was not comfortable with that thought.

This was business, Raúl reminded himself as motive returned. Tonight she would think of *his* lean, aroused body. When she was bedded by Gordon it would be *his* lithe body she ached for. He must now make sure of that. It was a business decision, and he made business decisions well.

His hand slid from beneath her hair down to the side of her ribs, to the bare skin there.

She ached. She ached for his hand to move, to cup her breast. And again he confirmed what was happening.

'Soon I return you to Gordon,' Raúl said, 'but first you come to *me*.'

It was foreplay. So much so she felt that as if his fingers were inside her. So much so that she could feel, despite the sporran, the thick outline beneath his kilt. It was the most dangerous dance of her life. She wanted to turn. She wanted to run. Except her body wanted the feel of his arms. Her burning cheeks rested against purple velvet and she could hear the steady thud of his heart as hers tripped and galloped. No one around them had a clue about the fire in his arms.

He smelt exquisite, and his cheek near hers had her head wanting to turn, to seek the relief of his mouth. She did not know the range of *la petit mort* or that he was giving her a mere taste. Estelle was far too innocent to know that she was building up to doing exactly as instructed and coming to him.

Raúl knew exactly when he felt the tension in his arms slowly abate, felt her slip a little down his chest as for a brief moment she relaxed against him.

'Thank you for the dance.' Breathless, stunned, she went to step back.

But still he held her as he lifted her chin and offered his verdict. 'You know, I would like to see you *really* cuss in Spanish.'

He let her go then, and Estelle headed to the safety of the ladies' room and ran her wrists under the tap to cool them.

Careful, she told herself. *Be careful here, Estelle.*

There was a blaze of attraction more intense than any she had known. What Estelle *did* know, though, was that a man like Raúl would crush her in the palm of his hand.

She looked up into the mirror and took out her lipstick, she could not fathom what had just taken place—nor that she had allowed it.

That she had partaken in it.

And willingly at that.

'There you are.'

Gordon smiled as she headed back to the table and she could not feel more guilty: she'd even failed as an escort.

'I'm so sorry to have left you—some foreign minister wanted to speak urgently with me, but we couldn't get him on the line and when we did...' Gordon gave a weary smile. 'He had no idea what he wanted to speak to me about. I've been going around in circles.' Gordon drained his drink. 'Let's dance.'

It felt very different dancing with Gordon. They laughed and chatted as she tried not to think about the dance with Raúl.

Yes, she danced with Gordon—but it was the black eyes still on her that held her mind. Raúl sat at the table drinking whisky.

'I think you've made quite an impression. Raúl can't keep his eyes off you.'

She started in his arms. 'It's okay, Estelle.' Gordon smiled. 'I'm flattered—or rather my persona is. To have Raúl as competition is a compliment indeed.'

He kissed her cheek and she rested her head on his shoulder, and then her eyes fell to Raúl's black eyes that still watched and there was heat in her body, and she tried to look away but she could not. She watched his mouth move in a slow smile till Gordon danced her so that Raúl was out of her line of vision. Then, a moment later, her eyes scanned the room for him and prayed that the dangerous part of her night was now over.

Raúl was gone.

CHAPTER SIX

'Sorry!'

Gordon apologised profusely for scaring her, after Estelle had walked into the guest room much later that night to find a monster!

He whipped the mask off. 'It's for my breathing. I have sleep apnoea.'

Estelle had changed in a tiny bathroom along the draughty hall and was now wearing some very old, very tatty pale pink pyjamas that she only put on when she was sick or reading for an entire weekend. It was all she'd had at short notice, but Estelle was quite sure Gordon wasn't expecting cleavage and sexy nightdresses.

She offered to take the sofa bed—he was paying her, after all—but true to his word he insisted that she have the bed.

'Thank you so much for tonight, Estelle.'

'It's been fine,' Estelle said as she rubbed cold cream into her face and took her make-up off. 'It must be so hard on you, though,' she mused, trying to get off the last of her mascara. 'Having to hide your real life.'

'It certainly hasn't been easy, but six months from now I'll be able to be myself.'

'Can't you now?'

'If it was just about me then I probably would have by

now,' Gordon explained. 'Frank is so private, though—it would be awful for him to have our relationship discussed on the news, which it would be. Still, six months from now we'll be sunning it in Spain.'

'Is that where you're going to live?'

'And marry,' Gordon said. 'Gay marriage is legal there.'

Estelle was really tired now; she slipped into bed and they chatted a little while more.

'You know that Virginia has nearly finished her studies…?'

'I know.' Estelle sighed—not only because she would miss her housemate, but also because she would need to find someone else to share if she continued with *her* course. But then she realised what Gordon was referring to.

'She's starting work next month. I don't want to offend you by suggesting anything, but if you did want to accompany me to things for a few months…'

He didn't push, and for that Estelle was grateful.

'Have a think about it,' Gordon said, and wished her goodnight.

Estelle was soon drifting off, thinking not about Gordon's offer but about Raúl and his pursuit.

And it *had* been a pursuit.

From the moment their eyes had locked he had barely left her thoughts or her side, whether standing behind her at the wedding or sitting beside her at dinner. She still could not comprehend what had taken place on the dance floor; she had been searching for the bells and whistles and sirens of an orgasm, but how delicious and gentle that had been—how much more was there to know?

She didn't dare think too much about it now. Exhausted from a long and tiring day, Estelle was just about to drift off to sleep when Gordon turned on his ventilation machine.

Ginny hadn't told her about this part.

She lay there, head under pillow, at two a.m., still listening to the CPAP machine whirring and hissing. In the end she gave in.

She padded through the castle, her bare feet making not a sound on the stone floor. She headed to the small bathroom and took a drink from the tap, willing the night to be over.

Then she looked at her surroundings and regretted willing it over.

She stepped out onto a huge stone balcony, stared out to the loch. It was incredibly light for this time of the morning. She breathed in the warm summer night air and now her thoughts *did* turn to Gordon and his offer.

Estelle had already been coming to a reluctant decision to defer her studies and work full-time. It was all so big and scary—a future that was unknown.

She turned as the door opened, her eyes widening as Raúl stepped out.

He was wearing only his kilt.

Estelle would have preferred him with clothes on. Not because there was anything to disappoint—far from it— but the sight of olive skin, the light fan of hair on his chest and the way the kilt hung gave her eyes just one place to linger. There was nothing safe about meeting his gaze.

It was only then that she realised he had not followed her out here—that instead he was speaking on the phone.

He must have come out to get better reception. She gave him a brief smile and went to brush past, to get away from him without incident, but his hand caught her wrist and she stood there as he spoke into the phone.

'You don't need to know what room I am in…' He rolled his eyes. 'Araminta, I suggest that you go to bed.' He let out an irritated hiss. 'Alone!'

He ended the call and only then dropped Estelle's wrist.
She stood as he examined her face.

'You know, without all the make-up you slather on...'
His eyes searched her unmade-up skin. Her hair was tied
in a low ponytail and she was dressed in a way he would
not expect Gordon to find pleasing.

Raúl did.

She looked young—so much younger without all the
make-up—and her baggy pyjamas left it all to Raúl's imagination. Which he was using now.

And then came his verdict.

'You look stunning,' Raúl said. 'I'm surprised Gordon
has let you out of his sight.'

'I just needed some air.'

'I am hiding,' Raúl admitted.

'From Araminta?'

'Someone must have given her my phone number. I am
going to have to change it.'

'She'll give in soon.' Estelle smiled, feeling a little sorry
for the other woman. If Araminta had had a fling with
him a few years ago and had known he would be here tonight—well, Estelle could see why her hopes might have
been raised.

His phone rang again and he rolled his eyes and chose
not to answer. 'So, what are you doing out here at this
time of morning?'

'Just thinking.'

'About what?'

'Things.' She gave a wry smile, didn't add that far too
many of her thoughts had been about him.

'And me,' Raúl admitted. 'It has been an interesting
day.'

He looked out to the still, silent loch and felt a world
away from where he had woken this morning. He didn't

even know how he was feeling. He looked over to Estelle, who was gazing out into the night too, a woman who was comfortable with silence.

It was Raúl who was not—Raúl who made sure his days and nights were always filled to capacity so that exhaustion could claim him each night.

Here, for the first time in the longest time, he found himself alone with his thoughts—and that was not pleasant. But he refused to pick up to Araminta, knowing the chaos that might create.

It was Raúl who broke the silence. He wanted to hear her voice.

'When do you go back?'

'Late morning.' Estelle stared out ahead. 'You?'

'I will leave early.'

He walked to lean over the balcony, gazed into the night, and Estelle saw the huge scar that ran from his shoulder to his waist. He glanced around and saw the slight shock on her face. Usually he refused to offer an explanation for the scar—he did not need sympathy. Tonight he chose to explain it.

'It's from the car accident...'

'That killed your mother?'

He gave a curt nod and turned back to look into the night, breathing in the cool air. He was glad that she was here. For no other reason, Raúl realised, than he was glad. It was two a.m. in the second longest night of his life, and for the first one he had been alone.

'Can I ask again?' He had to know. 'What are you doing with Gordon?'

'He's nice.'

'So are many people. It doesn't mean we go around...' He did not complete his sentence yet he'd made his rather crude point. 'Are you here tonight for your brother?'

Estelle could not answer. She had agreed to be here for Gordon, yet she knew they both knew the truth.

'Do you have siblings?' Estelle asked.

There was a long stretch of silence. His father had asked that he not reveal anything just yet, but it would all be out in the open soon. Estelle came and stood beside him as she awaited his answer. Perhaps she would go straight to the press in the morning. Raúl actually did not care right now. He could not think about tomorrow. It was taking all his control to get through the night.

'Had you asked me that yesterday the answer would have been no.' He turned his head, saw her frown at his answer and was grateful that she did not push for more detail. Instead she stayed silent as Raúl admitted a little of the truth. 'This morning my father told me that I have a brother—Luka.' It felt strange to say his name. 'Luka Sanchez Garcia.'

From their little lesson earlier, Estelle knew they did not share the same mother. 'Have you met him?'

'Unwittingly.'

'How old is he?'

She asked the same question that he had asked his father, though the relevance of the answer she could not know.

'Twenty-five,' Raúl said. 'I walked into my father's office this morning, expecting my usual lecture—he insists it is time for me to settle down.' He gave a small mirthless laugh. 'I had no idea what was coming. My father is dying and he wants his affairs put in order. My affairs too. And so he told me he has another son...'

'It must have been the most terrible shock.'

'Skeletons in the closet are not unique,' Raúl said. 'But this was not some long-ago affair that has suddenly come to light. My father has kept another life. He sees his mis-

tress in the north of Spain. I thought he went there so regularly for work. We have a hotel in San Sebastian. It is his
main interest. Now I know why.'

Estelle tried to imagine what it was like, finding out
something like this, and Raúl stood trying to comprehend
that he had actually told another—how readily he had
opened up to her. Then he reminded himself why. For his
solution to come to fruition of *course* Estelle had to be told.

Some of it, at least.

He would never reveal all.

'His PA—Angela—she has always been…'

He gave a tight shrug. Angela had not been so much
like a mother, but she had been a constant—a woman he
trusted. Raúl closed his eyes, remembered walking out of
his father's office and the words he had hurled to the one
woman he had believed did not have an agenda.

'We have always got on. It turns out the son she speaks
of often is in fact my half-brother.' He gave a wry smile.
'A lot of my childhood was spent with my aunt or uncle.
I assumed my father was working at the hotel in San Sebastian. It turns out he was with his mistress and his son.'
Black was the hiss that came from his mouth. 'It's all sorry
and excuses now. I always prided myself on knowing what
goes on, on being astute. It turns out I knew nothing.'

He had said enough. More than enough for one night.

'So, in answer to your question—yes. I have a brother.'

He shrugged naked shoulders and her fingers balled
into her palms in an effort not to rest her hand on them.

'Unlike you, I care nothing for mine.'

'You might if you knew him.'

'That's not going to happen.'

She felt a small shiver, put it down to the night air. But
his voice was so black with loathing it could have been
that. 'I'm going to go in.'

'Please don't.'

Estelle had to get back—back to the safety of Gordon—yet she did not want to walk away from him.

She had to.

'Goodnight, Raúl...'

'Stay.'

She shook her head, grateful for the ringing of his phone—for the diversion it offered. But as she went to open the door she heard a woman's frantic voice coming down the corridor.

'Pick up Raúl. Where the hell are you?'

He had lightning reflexes. Quickly Raúl turned his phone off and pulled Estelle into the shadows.

'I need a favour.'

Before she knew what was happening she was in his arms, his tongue prising her lips open, his hand at her pyjama top. Estelle struggled against him before realising what was happening. She could hear Araminta calling out to Raúl, and if she saw the balcony any moment now she would come out.

But Araminta didn't. She stumbled past the balcony, the couple on it unseen.

He could stop now, Estelle thought. Except her pyjama top was completely open, her breasts splayed against his naked chest.

We *should* stop now, she thought as his tongue chased hers.

He made a low moan into her mouth; it was the sexiest thing she had ever heard or felt. He slid one hand over her bottom and his tongue was hot and moist.

Suddenly sending a message to Araminta was the last thing on Raúl's mind.

Estelle wanted his kiss to end, and yet she yearned for it to go on—like a forbidden path she was running down, wanting to get to the end, to glimpse again the woman he made her. It was a kiss that should not be happening, but it was one she did not want to end.

'Don't go back to him…' Raúl's mouth barely left hers as he voiced his command.

He had intended to speak with her at a later point, perhaps get her phone number, but having tasted her, having kissed her, he could not stand the thought of her in Gordon's bed. He would reveal his plan right now.

He peeled his mouth off hers, his breath coming hard on her lips. 'Come now with me.'

It was then that she fully realised her predicament. Raúl assumed this was the norm for her, that she readily gave her body.

As he moved in to kiss her again she slapped him. It was the only way she knew how to end this.

'You pay more, do you?' She was disgusted with his thought processes.

'I did not mean it like that.' Raúl felt the sting on his cheek and knew that it was merited—knew how his suggestion must have come across. But business had been the last thing on his mind. He had simply not wanted her going back to another man. 'I meant—'

'I know exactly what you meant.'

'Bastard!'

They both turned at the sight of a tear-streaked Araminta. 'You said you were tired, that you were in bed.'

'Can I suggest that you go back to your bed?' Raúl snapped to Araminta, clearly not welcoming the intrusion.

Estelle saw again just how brutal this man could be when he chose.

'How much clearer can I make it that I have absolutely no interest in you?'

He turned and came to help a mortified Estelle with her buttons, but her hand slapped him off.

'Don't touch me!'

She flew from the balcony and back to her room, stepped quietly in and slipped into bed, listened to the whirring of Gordon's machine, trying to forget the feel of Raúl's hands, his mouth.

Trying to deny that she lay there for the first time truly wanting.

CHAPTER SEVEN

'ESTELLE...'

Gordon was lovely when she told him what had happened. Well, not all of it. She didn't tell him about her conversation with Raúl, just that he had been trying to avoid a woman and had kissed her...

It was a terribly awkward conversation, but Gordon was writing her a cheque, so as not to embarrass her in front of his driver, and Estelle simply couldn't accept it and had to tell him why.

'Frank and I have three free passes.'

Estelle blinked as Gordon smiled and held out the cheque.

'We have three people each who, should something happen, wouldn't be construed as cheating with.' He gave her a smile. 'It's just a game, of course, and it's mainly movie stars, but Raúl could very easily make it to my list. No one can resist him when he sets his sights on them—especially someone as darling and innocent as you.'

'I feel awful.'

'Don't.' Gordon closed her hand around the cheque. 'My being in competition with Raúl Sanchez Fuente could only do wonders for my reputation, if word were ever to get out. It might even be the reason for our breaking up and me realising just how much I care for Virginia.'

'I'm sorry.'

'Don't be,' Gordon said, and gave her a kiss on the cheek. 'Just be careful.'

'I'll never see him again,' Estelle said. 'He doesn't know anything about me.'

'Mere details to a man like Raúl—and he takes care of them easily.'

Estelle felt the hairs on her arms stand up as she remembered that she had given him her name.

'Just do your hair and put on a ton of make-up and we'll head down for breakfast,' Gordon told her. 'If anyone says anything about last night just laugh and shrug it off.'

It was a relief to hide her blushes behind thick make-up. Estelle put on a skirt that was too short and some high wedges, and tied her hair in a high ponytail and then teased it with a comb and sprayed it.

'I feel like a clown,' she said to Gordon as she checked her reflection in the mirror.

'Well, you make *me* smile.'

Raúl had gone, and all Estelle had to endure were some daggers being thrown in her direction by Araminta as they ate a full Scottish breakfast. She was relieved not to see him, yet there was a curious disappointment at his absence which Estelle chose not to examine.

Finally they were on their way, but it was late afternoon before Gordon dropped her at her home.

'Think about what I said,' Gordon reminded Estelle as she climbed out.

'I think I've had my excitement for the year,' Estelle admitted as she farewelled him.

She let herself step into familiar surrounds and released a breath before calling out to Ginny that she was home.

'How are you feeling?' Estelle asked as she walked into the lounge.

'Awful!'

Ginny certainly looked it.

'I'm going to go home for a couple of days. My dad's coming to pick me up—I need Mum, soup and sympathy.'

'Sounds good.'

'How was it?

'It was fine,' Estelle said, really not in the mood to tell Ginny all that had happened.

Ginny would no doubt find out from Gordon, given how much the two of them discussed. Estelle was still irritated that Ginny told Gordon about her virginity but, seeing how sick Ginny was, Estelle chose to save that for later.

'Gordon was lovely.'

'I told you there was nothing to worry about.'

'I'm exhausted,' Estelle admitted. 'You didn't tell me about Gordon's sleep apnoea. I got the fright of my life when I walked in and he was strapped to a machine.'

Ginny laughed. 'I honestly forgot. Your brother's been calling you. A few times, actually.'

The phone rang then, and Estelle's heart lurched in hope when she saw that it was her brother. 'Maybe he's got that job.'

He hadn't.

'I found out on Friday,' Andrew said. 'I just couldn't face telling you.'

'Something will come up.'

'I'm not qualified for anything.'

Estelle could hear the hopelessness in his voice.

'I don't know what to do, Estelle. I've asked Amanda's parents if they can help—'

His voice broke then. Estelle knew the hell that would have paid with his pride.

'They can't.'

She could feel his mounting despair.

'Something will come up,' Estelle said, but she was finding it harder and harder to sound convincing. 'You've just got to keep applying for work.'

'I know.' He blew out a long breath in an effort to compose himself. 'Anyway, enough about me,' Andrew said, 'Ginny said you were in Scotland. How come?'

'I was at a wedding.'

'Whose?'

'I'll tell you all about it tomorrow.'

'Tomorrow?'

'I want to speak to you about something.' As a car tooted outside, Ginny stood. 'Andrew, I've got to go,' Estelle said. 'I'll call in tomorrow.'

Estelle didn't know how to tell Andrew she had some money for him, but anyway she knew that one month's mortgage payment would only be a Band-Aid solution. She was relieved that Ginny would be out for a few days because she really wanted some time to go over what she was considering.

The library was offering her more hours. Perhaps she could defer her studies and move in with Andrew and Amanda for a year, pay them rent, help out with little Cecelia, maybe even take Gordon up on his offer… Yes, she was glad Ginny would be away, because she needed to think properly.

'Your dad's here,' Estelle said.

'Thanks so much for last night, Estelle,' Ginny said, grabbing her bag and heading out of the door, waving to her father, who had climbed back into the car when he saw her.

Ginny was too dosed up on flu medication even to notice the expensive car a little further down the road.

Raúl noticed *her*, though—and a frown appeared on his face as he saw Virginia, Gordon's regular date, disappearing into a car driven by another older male. After Raúl's father's revelations he was past being surprised by anything, but there was a curious feeling of disappointment as he thought of Estelle and Virginia together with Gordon.

No.

He did not like the images that conjured, so he settled for the slightly more palatable version—that Estelle hadn't picked him up at Dario's; instead Estelle and Virginia must both work for the same escort agency.

He needed someone tough, Raúl told himself. He needed a woman who could separate sex from emotion, who could see what he was about to propose as a financial opportunity rather than a romantic proposition.

Except his knuckles were white as he clutched the steering wheel. Since last night there had been an incessant gnawing in his stomach when he thought of Estelle with Gordon. Now that gnawing had upgraded to a burn in the lining of his gut.

Estelle would be far better with him.

Was he arrogant to think so? Raúl pondered briefly as he walked up her garden path.

Perhaps, he conceded, but he was also assured enough to know that he was right.

'What did you forget...?' Estelle's voice trailed off when she saw that it wasn't Ginny.

Raúl preferred the way she'd looked last night on the balcony, but her appearance now—the short skirt, the heavy make-up, the lacquered hair—actually made things easier.

'What do you want?'

'I wanted to apologise for what I said last night. I think it was misconstrued.'

'I think you made things perfectly clear.' She drew in

a breath and then gave a small nod. 'Apology accepted. Now, if you'll excuse me?'

Her hand was ready to close the door on him. There was just a moment and Raúl knew he had to use it wisely. There was no time for mixed messages. He knew he had better reveal the truth up-front.

'You were right—I didn't want you to go back to Gordon, but not just because…' The door was closing on him so Raúl told her exactly what he was here for. 'I wanted to ask you to marry me.'

Estelle laughed.

After the tension of the last twenty-four hours, then her brother's tears on the phone, and now Raúl, standing absolutely immaculate in black jeans and a shirt at her door with his ridiculous proposal, all she could do was throw her head back and laugh.

'I'm serious.'

'Of course you are,' Estelle answered. 'Just as you were serious last night when you told me just how much you don't want to marry—ever.'

'I don't want to marry for love,' Raúl said, 'but I do need a bride. One with a level head. One who knows what she wants and goes for it.'

There was that implication again, Estelle realised. She was about to close the door, but then she looked down to the cheque Raul was holding—one with her name on it—and she saw the ridiculous amount he was offering. He surely wasn't serious. She looked up at him and realised that possibly he was—that he could pay for her services. As Gordon had.

Estelle gave a nervous swallow, reminding herself that whatever happened, whatever Raúl thought, she must not betray Gordon's confidence.

'Look—whatever you think, Gordon and I…'

'Should that be, Gordon, *Virginia* and I?' He watched her flaming cheeks pale. 'I just saw her leave. Are you both dating him?'

'I don't have to explain anything to you.'

'You're right,' Raúl conceded.

'How did you know where I lived?'

'I checked your bag when you were dancing with Gordon.'

Estelle blinked. He was honest, brutally honest—and, yes, she couldn't help herself. She was curious.

'Are you going to ask me in or do I stand and speak here?'

'I don't think so.' Common sense told her to close the door on him, but as she stared into black eyes curiosity was starting to win. Things like this—conversations like this—simply didn't happen to Estelle. But, more than that, she wanted to find out more about this man who had been on her mind from the second their eyes had locked.

'I ask for ten minutes,' Raúl said. 'If you want me to leave then, I shall, and I will never bother you again.'

He spoke in such a matter-of-fact voice. This was business to him, Estelle realised, and he assumed it was the same for her. She chose to keep it that way.

'Ten minutes,' Estelle said, and opened the door.

He looked around the small house. It was typical student accommodation, yet she was not your typical student.

'You are studying?'

'Yes.'

'Can I ask what?'

Estelle hesitated, not keen on revealing anything to him, but surely it could do no harm. 'Ancient architecture.'

'Really?' Raul frowned. Her response was not the one he'd been expecting.

She offered him a seat and Raúl took it. Estelle chose a

chair on the opposite side of the room to him. He wasted no time getting to the point.

'I have told you that my father is sick?' Raúl said, and Estelle nodded. 'And that for a long time he has wanted to see me settled? Now, with his death nearing, more and more he wishes to see his wish fulfilled—he has convinced himself that a wife will tame my ways.'

Estelle said nothing. She just looked at this man she doubted would ever be tamed; she had tasted his passion, had heard about his appalling reputation. A ring on his finger certainly wouldn't have stopped what had taken place last night.

'You might remember I told you my father revealed he has another son?'

Again Estelle nodded.

'He has said that if I do not comply, if I do not settle down, then he will leave his share of the business to my...' He could not bring himself to call Luka his brother. 'I refuse to allow that to happen.'

She could see the determination in his eyes.

'Which is why I have come this evening to speak with you.'

'Why aren't you having this conversation with Araminta? I'm sure she'd be delighted to marry you.'

'I did briefly consider it,' Raúl admitted, 'but there are several reasons. The main one being she would not be able to reconcile the fact that this is a business transaction. She would agree, I think, but it would be with hope that love would grow, that perhaps a baby might change my mind. It will not,' Raúl said. His voice was definite. 'Which is why I come to speak with you. A woman who understands a certain business.'

'I really think you have the wrong idea about me.'

'I am not here to judge you. On the contrary, I admire a woman who can separate love from sex.'

He did not understand the wry smile on her face. If only he knew. It faded as he continued.

'We are attracted to each other.' Raúl said it as a fact. 'Surely for you that can only be a bonus?'

Estelle blew out a breath; he was practically calling her a hooker and yet she was in a poor position to deny it.

'We both like to party,' Raúl said. 'And we like to live life in the fast lane—even if we know how to take things seriously at times.'

He was wrong about the fast lane, and Estelle knew if she admitted the truth he'd be gone. But, yes, she *was* undeniably attracted to him. Her skin was tingling just from his presence. Her mind was still begging for a moment of peace just to process the dance and the kiss they had shared last night.

He interrupted her wandering thoughts.

'Estelle. I have spoken with my father's doctor; it is a matter of weeks rather than months. You would only be away for a short while.'

'Away?'

'I live in Marbella.'

Now she definitely shook her head. 'Raúl, I have a life here. My niece is sick. I am studying...'

'You can return to your studies a wealthy woman—and naturally you will have regular trips home.'

He looked at her, with her gaudy make-up and teased hair. He chose to remember her fresh-faced on the balcony, recalled the comfort she had given even before they had kissed. He should not care, but he did not like the life she was leading. Suddenly it was imperative for reasons other than appeasing his father that she take this chance.

'I do not judge you, Estelle, but you could come back

and start over. You can live the life you want to without ever having to worry about the rent.'

Estelle stood and walked to the window, not wanting him to see the tears that sprang in her eyes because for a moment there he had sounded as if he actually cared.

'You certainly won't have to host dinner parties or cook for me. I work hard all day. You can shop. We'll eat out every night. And there are many clubs to choose from, parties to attend. You would never be bored.'

He had no idea about her at all.

'After my father's death, after a suitable pause, we will admit our whirlwind marriage cannot deal with the grief— that with regret we are to part. No one will ever know you married for money. That would be written into the contract.'

'Contract?'

'Of course,' Raúl said. 'One that will protect both of us, that will lay down all the rules. I have asked my lawyer to fly in for a meeting at midday tomorrow. Naturally it will be a lengthy meeting. We will have to go over terms.'

'I won't be there.'

He didn't look in the least deterred.

'Raúl, my brother would never believe me.'

'I will come with you and speak to him.'

'Oh, and he'll believe *you*? He'll believe we met yesterday and fell madly in love? He'll have me certified insane before he lets me fly off with a stranger—'

'We met last year.' Raúl interrupted her tirade. It was clear he had thought it all through. 'When you were in Spain. It was then that we fell madly in love, but of course with your brother's accident it was not the time to say so, or to make plans to move, so we put it down to a holiday romance. We met again a few weeks ago and this time around I had no intention of letting you go.'

'I don't want to lie to him.'

'You are always truthful?' Raúl checked. 'Does he know about Gordon, then? Does he know—?'

'Okay,' she interrupted. Because of course there were things her brother didn't know. She was actually considering it—so much so that she turned to him with a question. 'Would *your* family believe it?'

'Before I found out about my father's other life I chose to let him think I was serious about someone I used to date. It was not you I had in mind, but they do not know that.'

It could work.

The frown that was on her brow was smoothed, the impossibility of it all was fading, and Raúl knew it was time to leave.

'Sleep on it,' Raúl said. 'Naturally there is more that I have to tell you, but I am not prepared to discuss certain things until after the marriage.'

'What sort of things?'

'Nothing that impacts on you now—just things that a loving wife would know all about. It is something I would not reveal to anyone I did not trust or love.'

'Or pay for?'

'Yes.' He placed the cheque on the coffee table and handed her two business cards.

'That is the hotel my lawyer will be staying at. I have booked an office there. The other card contains my contact details—for now.'

'For now?'

'I am changing my phone number tomorrow,' Raúl said. 'One other thing...' He ran a finger along her cheek, looked at the full mouth he had so enjoyed kissing last night. 'There will be no one else for the duration of our contract...'

'It's not going to happen.'

'Well, in case you change your mind—' he handed her an envelope '—you might need this.'

She opened it, stared at the photo that had been taken last night. His arm was on the chair behind her, she was laughing, and there was Raúl—smiling, absolutely beautiful, his eyes on her, staring at her as if he was entranced.

He must have known the photographer was on his way, Estelle realised. He had been considering this even last night.

Raúl *had* rearranged the seating—she was certain of it now.

She realised then the lengths he would go to to get his way.

'Did you arrange for Gordon to be called away?'

'Of course.'

'You don't even try to deny it?'

He heard her anger.

'You'd prefer that I lie?' Raúl checked.

She looked to the mantelpiece, to the photo of her brother and Amanda holding a tiny, frail Cecelia. She was so tired of struggling. But she could not believe that she was considering his offer. She had considered Gordon's, though, Estelle told herself. Tomorrow she had been going to tell her brother she was deferring her studies and moving in with them.

She had already made the decision to up-end her life.

This would certainly up-end it—but in a rather more spectacular way.

She went into the kitchen with the excuse of making coffee, but really it was to gather her thoughts.

Bought by Raúl.

Estelle closed her eyes. It was against everything she believed in, yet it wasn't just the money that tempted her. It was something more base than that.

A man as beautiful as Raúl, for her first lover. The thought of sharing his bed, his life—even for a little while—was as tempting as the cheque he had written. Estelle blew out a breath, her skin on fire, aroused just at the thought of lying beside him. Yet she knew that if Raúl knew she was a virgin the deal would be off.

'Not for me.'

He was standing at the kitchen door, watching as she spooned instant coffee into two mugs.

'I'll leave you to think about it. If you do not arrive at the appointment then I will accept your decision and stop the cheque. As I said, tomorrow my phone number will be changing. It will be too late to change your mind.'

It really was, Estelle knew, a once-in-a-lifetime offer.

CHAPTER EIGHT

'I WILL FLY your family out for the wedding...'

They were sitting in Raúl's lawyer's office, going over details that made Estelle burn, but it was all being dealt with in a cool, precise manner.

'I will speak with your parents and brother.'

'My parents are both deceased.' Estelle said it in a matter-of-fact way. She was not after sympathy from Raúl and this was not a tender conversation. 'And my brother and his wife won't be able to attend—Cecelia is too sick to travel.'

'You should have *someone* there for you.'

'Won't your family believe us otherwise?' There was a slight sneer to her voice, which she fought to check. She had chosen to be here, after all. It was just the mention of her parents, of Cecelia, that had her throat tightening— the realisation that everything in this marriage bar love would be real and she would be going through it all alone.

'It has nothing to do with that,' Raúl said. 'It is your wedding day. You might find it overwhelming to be alone.'

'Oh, please,' Estelle responded, determined not to let him see her fear. 'I'll be fine.'

'Very well.' Raúl nodded. 'It will be a small wedding, but traditional. The press will go wild—they have been waiting a long time for me to marry—but we will not let them know we are married till after.'

They had been talking for hours; every detail from wardrobe allowance to hair and make-up had been discussed.

Estelle had insisted she could choose her own clothes.

'I have a reputation to think of,' had been Raúl's tart response.

Estelle was entitled to one week every month to come back to the UK and visit her family for the duration of the contract.

'I am sure we will both need the space,' had been Raúl's explanation. 'I am not used to having someone permanently around.'

There was now an extremely uncomfortable conversation—for Estelle, in any case—about the regularity of sex, and also about birth control and health checks. Raúl didn't appear in the least bit fazed.

'In the event of a pregnancy—' the lawyer started.

Raúl was quick to interrupt. Only now did he seem concerned by the subject matter being discussed. 'There is to be no pregnancy.' There was a low menace to his voice. 'I don't think my bride-to-be would be foolish enough to try and trap me in *that* way.'

'It still needs to be addressed.' The lawyer was very calm.

'I have no intention of getting pregnant.' Estelle gave a small nervous laugh, truly horrified at the prospect. She had seen the stress Cecelia had placed on Andrew and Amanda, and they were head over heels in love.

'You might change your mind,' Raúl said, for he trusted no one. 'You might decide that you like the lifestyle and don't want to give it up.' He looked to his lawyer. 'We need to make contingency plans.'

'Absolutely,' the lawyer said.

It could not be made clearer that this was all business.

Estelle sat as with clinical detachment he ensured that he would provide for any child they might have on the condition that the child resided in Spain.

If she moved back to England, Estelle would have to fight against his might just to make the rent.

'I think that covers it,' the lawyer said.

'Not quite.' Estelle cleared her throat. 'I'd like us to agree that we won't sleep with each other till after the wedding.'

'There's no need for quaint.'

'I've agreed to all your terms.' She looked coolly at him. It was the only way for this to work. If he knew she was a virgin this meeting would close now. 'You can surely agree to one of mine? I'd like some time off before I start *working*.' She watched his jaw tighten slightly as she made it clear that this *was* work.

'Very well.' Raúl did not like to be told that sleeping with him would be a chore. 'You may well change your mind.'

'I shan't.'

'You will be flown in a couple of days before the wedding. I will be on my yacht, partying as grooms do before their marriage. You shall have the apartment to yourself.' He had no intention of holding hands and playing coy for a week. He waited for her nod and then turned to his lawyer. 'Draft it.'

They waited in a sumptuous lounge as the lawyer got to work, but Estelle couldn't relax.

'You are tense.'

'It's not every day you get offered a million dollars.' She could at least be honest about that. 'Nor move to Marbella…'

'You will love it,' Raúl said. 'The night-life is fantastic...'

He just didn't know her at all, Estelle realised yet again.

'How did your parents die?' Raúl asked, watching as her shoulders stiffened. 'My family are bound to ask.'

'In a car accident,' Estelle said, turning to him. 'The same as your mother.'

He opened his mouth to speak and then changed his mind.

'I just hope everyone believes us,' Estelle said.

'Why wouldn't they? Even when we divorce we'll maintain the lie. You understand the confidentiality clause?' Raúl checked. 'No one is ever to know that this is a marriage of convenience only.'

'No one will ever hear it from me,' she assured him. The prospect of being found out was abhorrent to Estelle. 'Just a whirlwind romance and a marriage that didn't work out.'

'Good,' Raúl said. 'And, Estelle—even if we do get on...even if you do like—'

'Don't worry, Raúl,' she interrupted. 'I'm not going to be falling in love with you.' She gave him a tight smile. 'I'll be out of your life, as per the contract.'

CHAPTER NINE

RAÚL HAD BEEN RIGHT.

Estelle stood on the balcony of his luxurious apartment, looking out at the marina, on the morning of her wedding day, and was, as Raúl had predicted, utterly and completely overwhelmed.

She had arrived in Marbella two days ago and had barely stopped for air since. Stepping into this vast apartment, she had fully glimpsed his wealth. Every room bar the movie screening room was angled to take in the stunning view of the Mediterranean, and every whim was catered for from Jacuzzi to sauna. There was a whole new wardrobe waiting for her too. The only thing lacking was that the kitchen cupboards and fridge were empty.

'Call Sol's if you don't want to go out,' Raúl had said. 'They will bring whatever you want straight over.'

The only vaguely familiar thing had been the photo of them both, taken at Donald's wedding, beautifully framed and on a wall. But even that had been dealt with by Raúl. It had been manipulated so that her make-up was softer, her cleavage less revealing.

It had been a sharp reminder that he thought her a tart.

Raúl knew the woman he wanted to marry, and it wasn't the woman he had met, so there had been trips to a beauty salon for hair treatments and make-up lessons.

'I don't *need* make-up lessons,' Estelle had said.

'Oh, baby, you do,' had been his response. 'Subtle is best.'

Constantly she had to remind herself to be the woman he thought he had met. A woman who acted as if delighted by her new designer wardrobe, who didn't mind at all when he told her to wear factor fifty-plus because he liked her pale skin.

But it wasn't that which concerned Estelle this morning as she looked out at the glittering sea and the luxurious yachts, wondering which one was Raúl's.

Tonight she would be on his yacht.

This night they would be sharing a bed.

Estelle wasn't sure if she was more terrified of losing her virginity, or of him finding out that she had never slept with anyone before.

Maybe he wouldn't notice, she thought helplessly. But she knew she didn't have a hope of delivering to his bed the sexually experienced woman that Raúl was expecting. Last night, before heading off with his sponsors for his final night as a single man, Raúl had kissed her slowly and deeply. The message his tongue had delivered had been an explicit one.

'Why do you make me wait?'

Tonight he would find out why.

'You have a phone call.' Rosa, his housekeeper, brought the phone up to the balcony. It was Amanda on the line.

'How are you doing?' Amanda asked.

'I'm petrified.' It was nice to be honest.

'All brides are,' Amanda said. 'But Raúl will take good care of you.'

He had utterly and completely charmed Amanda, but had not quite won over Andrew.

'I am not letting her go again.' He had looked Andrew

straight in the eye as he said it. 'If I move Estelle to Spain I want to make a proper commitment. That is why she will come to be my wife.'

So easily he had lied.

Estelle knew she must remember that fact.

'How did the dress turn out?' Amanda asked.

'It's beautiful,' Estelle said. 'Even better than I imagined it would be.'

It was the only thing Estelle had been allowed to organise. It had all be done online and by phone, and the final adjustments made when she had arrived.

'How is Cecelia?' Estelle asked, desperate for news of her niece.

'She's still asleep.'

It was nine a.m. in Spain, which meant it was eight a.m. in the UK. Cecelia had always been an early riser. More and more she slept these days, though Amanda always did her best to be upbeat.

'I'm going to dress her up for the wedding and take a photo and send it. Even if we can't be there today, know that we're thinking of you.'

'I know.'

'And I'm not your sister, but I do think of you as one.'

'Thank you,' Estelle said, her eyes welling up. 'I think of you as a sister too.'

They weren't idle words; many hours had been spent in hospital waiting rooms this past year.

'Is that the door?' Amanda asked.

'Yes. Don't worry, someone else will get it.'

'Do you have a butler?'

'No!' Estelle laughed, swallowing down her tears. 'Just Raúl's housekeeper. Though it's going to start to get busy soon, with the hairdresser...' She turned around as she heard her name being called, and Estelle's jaw dropped as she saw her brother coming through the door.

'Andrew!'

'Is that where he's got to?' Amanda laughed, and then she was serious. 'I'm so sorry that I couldn't be with you today—I'd have given anything. But with Cecelia…'

'Thank you,' Estelle said, and promptly burst into tears, all her pent-up nerves released.

'I think she's pleased to see me,' Andrew said, taking the phone and chatting to Amanda briefly before hanging up.

'I can't believe you're here,' Estelle admitted.

'Raúl said he thought you might need someone today, and of course I wanted to give you away. If anything happens with Cecelia he's assured me I'll be able to get straight back.'

She couldn't believe that Raúl would do this for her. Until now she hadn't fully realised how terrifying today was, how real it felt.

Raúl had.

'When did you get in?'

'Last night,' Andrew said. 'We went to Sol's.'

'You were out with Raúl?'

'He certainly knows how to party.' Andrew smiled. 'I'd forgotten how.'

Even if she was doing all this for her brother and his wife, of the many benefits of marrying Raúl, this was one Estelle had not even considered—that her brother, who was still having trouble accepting the diagnosis that he would never walk again, who had, apart from job interviews and hospital appointments, become almost reclusive, would fly not just to Spain but so far out of his comfort zone.

It was a huge and important step, and it was thanks to Raúl that he was here.

'I've got something for you.'

Estelle bit her lip, hoping they hadn't spent money they didn't have on a gift for a wedding that wasn't real.

'Remember these?' Andrew said as she opened the box. 'These' were small diamond studs that had belonged to her mother. 'Dad bought them for her for their wedding day.'

She had never felt more of a fraud.

'Enough tears,' Andrew said. 'Let's get this wedding underway.'

Raúl was rarely nervous, but as he stood at the altar and waited for Estelle, to his own surprise, he was.

His father had almost bought their story, and Raul's future with the company was secure, but instead of a gloating satisfaction that his plans were falling into place today he thought only of the reasons he had had to go to these lengths.

His head turned briefly and he caught a glimpse of Angela in the middle of the church. She was seated with his father, as ever-present PA. His mother's family were still unaware of the real role she played in his father's life—and the role she had played in his mother's death.

He stared ahead, anger churning in his gut that Angela had the gall to be here. He wouldn't put it past her to bring her bastard son.

Then he heard the murmur of the congregation and Raúl turned around. The churning faded. Just one thought was now in his mind.

She looked beautiful.

He had wondered how Estelle might look—had worried that, left to her own devices, a powder-puff ball would be wobbling towards him on glittery platform shoes, smiling from ruby-red lips.

He had not—could not have—imagined this.

Her dress was cream and made of intricate Spanish lace. It was fitted, and showing her curves, but in the most elegant of ways. The neckline was a simple halter neck. She carried orange blossom, as was the tradition for Spanish brides, and her lipstick was a pale coral.

'*Te ves bella.*' He told her that she looked beautiful as she joined him, and he meant every word. Not one thing would he change, from her black hair, piled high up on her head, to the simple diamond earrings and elegant cream shoes. She was visibly shaking, and he made a small joke to relax her. 'Your sewing is terrible.'

She glanced at his shirt and they shared a smile. With so little history, still they found a piece now, at the altar—as per tradition, the bride-to-be must embroider her groom's shirt.

'I'm not marrying a billionaire to sit sewing!' she had said teasingly, and Raúl had laughed, explaining that most women did not embroider all of the front of the shirt these days. Only a small area would be left for her, and Estelle could put on it whatever she wanted.

He had half expected a € but had frowned this morning when he had put on his shirt to find a small pineapple. Raúl still couldn't work out what it meant, but it was nice to see her relax and smile as the service started.

They knelt together, and as the service moved along he explained things in his low, deep voice, heard only by her.

'*El lazo,*' he said as a loop of satin decorated with orange blossom was placed over his shoulders and then another loop from the same piece was placed over hers. The priest spoke then for a moment, in broken English, and Estelle's cheeks burnt red as he told them that the rope that bound them showed that they shared the responsibility for this marriage. It would remain for the rest of the ceremony.

But not for life.

She felt like a fraud. She *was* a fraud, Estelle thought, panic starting to build. But Raúl took her hand and she looked into his black eyes. He seemed to sense that she was suddenly struggling.

'He asks now that you hand him the Arras,' Raúl said and she handed over the small purse he had given her on arrival. It contained thirteen coins, he had explained, and it showed his financial commitment to her.

It was the only honest part of the service, Estelle thought as the priest blessed them and handed it back to her.

Except it felt real.

'It's okay,' he said to her. 'We are here in this together.'

It felt far safer than being in it alone.

The service ended and an attendant removed the satin rope and presented it to Estelle; then they walked out to cheers and petals and rice being thrown at them. Raúl's hand was hot on her waist, and he gripped her tighter when she nearly shot out of her dress at the sound of an explosion.

'It's firecrackers,' Raúl said. 'Sorry I forgot to warn you.'

And there would be firecrackers later too, Estelle thought, when they got to bed and she told him the truth! But it was far too late now to warn him.

It really was a wonderful wedding.

As Raúl had told her on the night they had met, there were no speeches; instead it was an endless feast, with dancing and celebration and congratulations from all.

She met Paola and Carlos, Raúl's aunt and uncle, and they spoke of Raúl's mother, Gabriella.

'She would be so proud to be here today,' Paola said. 'Wouldn't she, Antonio?'

Estelle saw how friendly they were with Raúl's father,

and also with Angela, who was naturally seated with them. No longer were they names, but faces, and a shiver went down her arms as she imagined their reaction when the truth came out.

'My son has excellent taste.' Antonio kissed her on the cheek.

Estelle had met him very briefly the day before, and Raúl had handled most of the questions—though both had seen the doubt in his eyes as to whether this union was real.

It was slowly fading.

'It is good to see my son looking so happy.'

He *did* look happy.

Raúl smiled at her as they danced their first dance as husband and wife, with the room watching on.

'Remember our first dance?' Raúl smiled.

'Well, we shan't be repeating *that* tonight.'

'Not till later.' Raúl gazed down, saw her burning cheeks, and mistook it for arousal.

He could never have guessed her fear.

'I ache to be inside you.'

Other couples had joined them. The music was low and sensual and it seemed to beat low in her stomach. His hand dusted her bare arm and she shivered at the thought of what was to come, wondered if those eyes, soft now with lust and affection, would darken in anger.

'Raúl…' Surely here was not the place to tell him, but it felt better with people around them rather than being alone. 'I'm nervous about tonight.'

'Why would you be nervous?' he asked. 'I will take good care of you.'

He would, Raúl decided. He was rarely excited at the thought of monogamy but he actually wanted to take care of her, could not stand to think of what she might have put her body through. There was a surge of protectiveness that shot through him then, and his arms tightened around her. He could feel her tension and nervousness and again he wanted to make her smile.

'Can I ask why,' he whispered into her ear as they danced, 'you embroidered a pineapple on my shirt?'

'It's a thistle!'

A smile spread on her lips and he felt her relax a little in his arms.

'For Scotland.'

Raúl found himself smiling too. 'All day I have been trying to work out the significance of a pineapple.'

She started to laugh and Raúl found himself laughing a little too.

He lowered his head and kissed her lightly.

It was expected, of course. What groom would *not* kiss his bride?

Many times since he had put his proposition to her Estelle had had doubts—the morality of it, the feasibility of it, the logistics—but as he kissed her, as she felt his warm lips and the soft caress of his hand near the base of her spine, true doubt as to her ability to go through with the deal surfaced. For once it had nothing to do with her hymen. She was suddenly more worried about her heart.

It was the music. It was the moment. It was having her brother here. It was Raúl's kiss. All these things, she told herself, were the reasons she felt as she did—as if this were real…as if this were love.

Estelle excused herself a little while later and went to the bathroom, just so she might collect herself, but brides could not easily hide on their wedding day.

'Estelle?' She turned at the sound of a woman's voice. 'I am Angela—Raúl's father's PA.'

'Raúl has spoken about you,' Estelle responded carefully.

'I'm sure what he had to say was not very flattering.' There were tears in the older woman's eyes. 'Estelle, I don't know what to believe…'

'Excuse me?'

'About this sudden marriage.' Angela was being as up-front with Estelle as she was with Raúl. 'I do know, though, that Raúl seems the happiest I have seen him. If you *do* love your husband…'

'If?'

'I apologise,' Angela said. 'Given that you surely love your husband, I ask this not for me, and not even for Antonio's sake. Whatever Raúl thinks of me, I care for him. I want him to come and visit us. I want us to be a family, even for a little while.'

'You could have had that years ago.' Estelle answered as she hoped Raúl would expect his loyal wife to.

'I want him to make peace with his father while there is still time. I don't want him to have any guilt when his father passes. I know how much guilt he has over his mother.'

Estelle blinked, unsure how to respond because there was so much she didn't know about Raúl. What did he have to feel guilty about? Raúl had been a child, after all. He had agreed to tell her more on their honeymoon—had said that he would be the one to deal with any questions tonight.

'I have always loved Raúl. I have always thought of him as a son.'

'So why did you leave it so late to tell him?' Perhaps it was the emotion of the day, but the tears that flashed in Estelle's eyes were real. 'If you cared so much for him—'

Estelle halted. It wasn't her place to ask, and Raúl certainly wouldn't thank her for delving. She was here to ensure his father left his share of the business to him, that was all. She would do well to remember that.

'I *do* care,' Angela responded. 'Whatever Raúl thinks of me, from a distance I have loved him as a son.'

'From a distance?' Estelle repeated, making the bitter point.

Turning on her heel, she walked out and straight into Raúl's arms.

'She wanted to speak about you,' Estelle told him. 'I don't know how well I handled it.'

'We'll discuss it later,' Raúl said, for he had seen Angela follow her in. 'Now we have to hand out the favours.'

It really was an amazing party, and for reasons of her own Estelle didn't particularly want it to end.

As per tradition, the bride and groom had to see off all their guests and be the last to leave. Antonio tired first, and she felt the grip of Raúl's hand tighten on hers as his father left with his loyal PA.

'It's been great,' Andrew said as he prepared to head back to the hotel he was staying in. 'Once Cecelia is well, and I'm working, I'm going to bring Amanda and Cecelia here for a holiday, to visit you.'

'You do that,' Estelle said, and bent down and gave her brother a cuddle, then stood as Raúl shook his hand.

'Look after my sister.'

'You do not have to worry about that.'

'Have a great honeymoon.'

A driver sorted out the wheelchair and they waved Andrew off and then headed back inside.

Apart from the staff it was just Raúl and Estelle now, and still the music went on as they danced their last dance of the night.

'It really helped having Andrew here.' Her hands were round the back of his neck, he held her hips, and she would give anything not to disappoint him tonight—anything to be the experienced lover he assumed she was.

'I thought it might.'

'It didn't just help me,' Estelle admitted, and started to tell him about how Andrew's confidence had been lacking.

But he dropped a kiss on her shoulder. 'Enough about others.'

Estelle swallowed. She could feel his fingers exploring the halter neck, his other hand running down the row of tiny buttons that ran to the base of her spine, and she knew he was planning his movements, undressing her slowly in his mind as they danced.

'Raúl…' His mouth was working over her bare shoulder, kissing it deeply; she could feel the soft suction, feel the heat of his tongue and his ardour building. 'I've never slept with anyone before.'

He moaned into her shoulder and pulled her tighter into him, so she could feel every inch of the turn-on he thought she was giving him.

'I mean it.' Her voice was shaking. 'You'll be my first.'

'Come on, then.' His mouth was now at her ear. 'Let's go and play virgins.'

CHAPTER TEN

THEY WERE DRIVEN the short distance to the marina, but for Estelle it just passed in a blur.

It was almost morning, yet despite the hour the celebrations continued.

Alberto, the skipper, welcomed them, and briefly introduced the staff—but Estelle barely took in the names, let alone her surroundings. All she could think of was what was soon to come as the crew toasted them and then Raúl dismissed them.

'Tomorrow I will show you around properly,' Raúl said, taking her champagne glass. 'But for now…'

There was no escaping. He pulled her towards him, his tongue back on her neck, at the crease between her neck and shoulder. He *had* been mentally undressing her before, for now his hands moved straight to the halter neck and expertly unravelled the carefully tied bow.

He had been expecting a basque, had anticipated another contraption to disable, but the dress had an inbuilt bra and he gave a low growl of approval as one of the breasts that had filled his private visions in recent days fell heavy and ripe into his palm.

'Raúl, someone might come…'

'That would be *you*,' he said, but she did not relax. 'No one will disturb us.'

Raúl lowered his head and licked around the pale areola, flicked a nipple that had been crushed all day by fabric back into rapid life, surprised that she was concerned that someone might come in. The staff on his yacht had seen many a decadent party—a husband and wife on their wedding night paled in comparison with what usually took place. He took the breast he craved in his mouth again, felt her hand try to push him back. He was at first surprised by her reticence—but then he remembered their game.

'Of course.' He smiled. 'You are nervous.'

He lifted her up and carried her down to the master stateroom, kissing her the entire way. He lowered her to the ground, turning her around so he could work on the tiny buttons from behind. It did not halt his mouth; his tongue kissed every inch of newly exposed flesh till her spine felt as if it were on fire.

He peeled off her dress, then her shoes and stockings. As his tongue licked and nibbled her sex through her silk panties the sensations his mouth delivered drove her wild. He only removed her panties when the moisture his mouth had made matched the dampening silk.

'Raúl…' Her hands were on his head—contrary hands that tried to halt him, while her moans of mounting desire urged him on.

'I want you so bad.' He peeled off her panties and, kneeling, parted her lips, his tongue darting to the swelling bud over and over as her hands knotted in his hair.

'Raúl…' she whimpered, lost between bliss and fear. 'I'm serious. I really haven't slept with anyone before.'

He simply didn't believe her. As she came under his mouth she had a hopeless thought that maybe he wouldn't guess, maybe he wouldn't know. Because despite her naïveté her body responded with ease. She throbbed against his mouth, more aroused than sated as he softly kissed the lingering orgasm.

He relished her taste, was assured she was moist. He was desperate now to take her.

He rose to his full height then, and shrugged his jacket off.

Breathless, aroused, moving on instinct, her hands shaking with want, she undid the buttons of his shirt. He was so dark and sultry, and he wore it well. His lips parted as her hands roamed his chest and she licked at his nipples as she undid his belt.

Raúl wanted her fingers at his zipper, and he wished she would hurry, but she lingered instead, feeling his thick heat through the fabric, her fingers lightly exploring. His already aching erection hardened further beneath her fingers. 'Estelle…' He could barely get the word out, but thankfully she read the urgency and slid the zipper down, and he let out a breath as she freed him.

He was delicious to her hands. She ran her fingers along his length, felt the soft skin that belied the strength beneath. She was petrified at the thought of him inside her, but wanting him just the same. She could see a trickle of silver and caught it with her finger, then swirled it around the head, entranced by its beauty.

Raúl closed his eyes in a mixture of frustration and bliss, for he wanted her hand to grip him tight, yet conversely he liked the tentative tease and exploration, liked the feel of her other hand gently weighing him.

Deeply they kissed, his tongue urging her to move faster, his erection twitching at the pleasure of her teasing, till he could take it no more.

'Te quiero.'

He told her he wanted her in Spanish as he pushed her

onto the bed. *'Tengo que usted tiene.'* He told her he had to have her as he parted her legs.

'Be gentle.' She was writhing and hot beneath him, her words contrary to the wanton woman in his arms. Her sex was slippery and warm and engorged as his hand stroked her there. She was as close to coming as Raúl, and his answer to her final plea was delivered as he nudged her entrance.

'It's way too late for gentle, baby.'

How he regretted those words as he seared and tore into her.

Raúl heard her sob, heard her bite back a scream.

Estelle knew then she had been a fool to think he might somehow not notice. He tore through her barrier but the pain did not end there. His fierce erection drove through tight muscles full of resistance. Too late to halt, too late to be tender, he froze—just not quickly enough. He leant on his elbows above her as she tried to work out how to breathe with Raúl inside her.

He attempted slow withdrawal. She begged that he did not. She lay there, trying to accommodate him, waiting for the heat and pain to subside, her muscles clamped around him.

'I take it out slowly,' Raúl said. He felt sick—appalled by his own brutality—and guilty too at the pleasure of her, hot and tight around him. He was so close to coming and trying to hold on. 'I'll just—'

'Don't.'

Her eyes were screwed tight as he moved a fraction backwards, but when he halted, when he stilled, her body relaxed a little. Estelle tried to release herself. She moved to slide away from him. Yet the pain was subsiding to a throbbing heat so she moved again, warming to the sensation of him inside her.

It was a different type of command she gave next.
'Don't stop.'

'Estelle?' He did not want to stop, and yet he did not
want to hurt her; he moved slowly a little within her, his
breath shallow, panting as if he had already come.

Her hands moved to his buttocks and she felt them
tauten beneath her fingers. It was Estelle who pressed and
dictated the tempo and, rarely for Raúl, he let her. Rarely
for Raúl, he was humbled. He did not think of the questions he must ask her, just focused on the tight grip and the
heat of her on his unsheathed skin, and all he could do was
kiss her. Every inch of him held back, resisting the beck-
oning of oiled muscles that gripped as he slid past them,
that urged him now to move faster, to take her deeper.

Estelle's breath was quickening. He felt the somewhat
impatient rise of her groin, the press of her hands in his
buttocks, and he could hold back no more.

Still he had not taken her fully, but now he thrust in.
Estelle's neck arched as he probed and located fresh virgin
flesh with each deepening thrust, and when he had filled
her, when every part of her was consumed, he moved out
and did it again, angling his hips, hitting her deep inside
till she was moaning.

He was moving fast now, and she wrapped her legs
around him, could not believe how her body had just taken
over. For she lifted to him, was building to him, working
with him, both heading to the same mutual goal.

No longer naïve, her body shattered in an orgasm like
nothing she had ever given herself—for there she could
stop, there she could halt. And it was nothing like the teasing he had given her either, for here in Raúl's bed he urged
her on further, broke all limits, ensured that she screamed.

She pulsed around the head of him. He was stroking
her deep inside—one spot that had her sobbing, one tender

spot that he hit over and over—till she sobbed, and then he released himself into her. Her thighs were in spasm as a fresh wave of orgasm crashed through her body—and, yes, just as he had warned her, she cussed him in Spanish till he kissed her, till she was lying beneath him no longer a virgin.

She looked up at him, expecting a barrage of questions, a demand for an explanation, but instead he moved onto his side and put his arm around her, pulling her into him.

'I should have known' was his reprimand.

'I tried to tell you.'

'Estelle…' he warned.

She gave a small nod, conceding that tonight might have been rather too late.

'We will speak about it in the morning.'

For now, they held each other, lay in each other's arms, tired and sated and both in a place they had never thought they might be.

Estelle a bought bride; Raúl a man who had married and made love to a virgin.

CHAPTER ELEVEN

ESTELLE WOKE AND had no idea where she was for a moment.

Her body was bruised and sore. She could hear a shower.

She rolled over in bed and saw the evidence of their union, and moved the top sheet to cover it.

'Hiding the evidence?'

Estelle turned and was shocked at the sight of him. There was a towel round his hips, but his chest was covered in the bruises she now remembered her mouth making. He turned and took a drink from the breakfast table that had presumably been delivered and she saw the scratches on his back, remembered the wanton place he had taken her to.

'I need to have a shower.'

'We need to talk.' But then he conceded, 'Have some lunch and a shower. Then we will talk.'

'Lunch?'

'Late lunch,' Raúl said. 'It is nearly two.'

Estelle quickly gulped down some grapefruit juice and then headed to the bathroom. When she had found out they would be honeymooning on a yacht she had expected basic bathroom facilities; instead it was like a five-star hotel. The bathroom was marble, the taps and lighting incredible, yet she barely noticed. Her only thought was getting to her make-up bag.

The doctor had told her how important it was to take her pill on time every day. She was still getting used to it. Her breasts felt sore and tender, as if she were getting her period, and she still felt a little bit queasy from the new medication.

Estelle swallowed down the pill, making a mental note to change the alarm on her phone to two p.m.—or should she take it at seven tomorrow?

Her mind felt dizzy. She had seen that Raúl was less than impressed with her this morning and no doubt he would want a thorough explanation. She still hadn't worked out what to say.

Estelle showered and put on the factor fifty he insisted on, then sorted out her hair and make-up, relieved when she headed back into the bedroom and Raúl wasn't there. She selected a bikini from the many he had bought her, and also a pale lilac sarong. Her head was splitting from too much champagne and too much Raúl. She sat on the bed and put on espadrilles. Then, dressed—or rather barely dressed, as Raúl would want her to be—she stood. But her eyes did not go to the mirror—instead they went to the bed.

Mortified at the thought of a maid seeing the stained sheets, Estelle started to strip the bed.

'What are you doing?'

'I'm just making up the bed.'

'If I had a thing for maids then it would have been stipulated in the contract,' Raúl said. 'And if I had a thing for virgins,' he added, 'that would have been stipulated too.'

Estelle said nothing.

'Just leave it.' His voice was dark. 'The crew will take care of that. I will show you around.'

'I'll just wander…' She went to walk past.

'You can't hide from me here,' he warned, taking her wrist. 'But we will discuss it later. I don't want the staff getting even a hint that this is anything but a normal honeymoon.'

'Don't you trust your staff?' It was meant as a small dig—because surely a man in his position could easily pay for his privacy?

'I don't trust anyone,' Raúl said, watching the fire mount on her cheeks as his words sank in. 'And with good reason.'

She followed him up onto the deck. The sun blinded her for a moment.

'Where are your sunglasses?'

'I forgot to bring them.' She turned to head back down, but Raúl halted her, calling out to one of the crew. 'I can get them myself.'

'Why would you?'

Sometimes she forgot just how rich and spoilt he was. This was not one of those times. Despite the fact there were some of the crew around, he pulled her into his arms and very slowly kissed her.

'Raúl....' She was embarrassed by his passion. She looked into his black eyes and knew he was making a point.

'We are here for two days, darling. The plan is for us to fully enjoy them.'

His words were soft, the message not.

'I'll show you around now.'

A maid handed her her sunglasses and then Raúl showed her their abode for the next few days. The lounge that she had barely noticed last night was huge, littered with low sofas; another maid was plumping the cushions. There was a huge screen and, though nervous around him, Estelle did her best to be enthusiastic. 'This will be lovely for watching a movie.'

Raúl swallowed and caught the maid's eyes, and as Estelle went over to look at his DVD collection he quickly led her away.

'Here is the gym.' He opened a door and they stepped in. 'Not that you'll need it. I will ensure that you get plenty of exercise.'

Only there, with the door safely closed, did he let his true frustration slip out. He closed the door and gave her a glimpse of what was to come.

'If you think we are going to be sitting around watching movies and holding hands—'

'I know what I'm here for.'

'Make sure that you do.'

Raúl had woken at lunchtime from his first decent sleep in days, from his first night without nightmares. For a moment he had glimpsed peace—but then she had stirred in his arms and he had looked down to a curtain of raven hair and felt the weight of her breast on his chest. The sheet had tumbled from them; he'd seen her soft pale stomach and the evidence of their coupling on her inner thigh.

He had gone to move the sheet to cover them, but the movement had disturbed her a little and he had lain still, willing her back to sleep, fighting the urge to roll over and kiss her awake, make love to her again. He had felt the heat from her palm on his stomach and had physically ached for that hand to move down. His erection had been uncomfortable.

He'd fought the bliss of the memories of last night as his hand had moved down—and then halted when he'd realised his own thought-processes.

Sex Raúl could manage—and often.

Making love—no.

Last night had been but one concession, and he reminded himself she had lied.

He had removed her hand from him then and spent a

full ten minutes examining her face—from the freckles dusting her nose to the full lips that had deceived him.

He stood in the well-equipped gym and looked at them now. Absolutely he would make things clear.

'We have several weeks of this,' Raúl said. 'I wanted a woman who could handle my life, who knew how to have fun.' He did not mince words. 'Who was good in bed.'

He watched her cheeks burn.

'I'm sure I'll soon learn. I'll keep up my end of the deal—I don't need hand-holding.'

'There will be no holding hands.' He took her hand and placed it exactly where it had been agreed it would visit regularly. 'You knew what you were signing up for...'

He had to hold her back; he had to be at his poisonous worst. He could not simply dump her, as he usually did when a woman fell too hard. They had weeks of this and he could not risk her heart.

Instead he would put her to work.

'Let's have a spa.'

She saw the challenge in his eyes, knew that he was testing her, and smiled sweetly. 'Let's!'

She followed him up onto the deck, trying to ignore the fact that he had fully stripped off as she took off her espadrilles and dropped her sarong.

'Take off your top.'

'In a moment...'

He could sense rather than see that she was upset, and it made him furious. He was actually wishing his father dead, just so this might end.

'Take off your top,' he said again. Because if she thought she was here to discuss the passing scenery, or for them to get to know each other better, then she was about to find out she was wrong.

Estelle might have taken him for a fool.

He wasn't one.

Her face was one burning blush as her shaking hands undid the clasp, and she sank beneath the water as she removed it and placed the bikini top on the edge.

'Good morning!' The skipper made his way over. Naked breasts were commonplace on the Costa Del Sol—and especially on Raúl Sanchez Fuante's boat. He had no trouble at all looking Estelle in the eye as he greeted her. She, though, Raúl noted, was close to tears as she attempted to smile back.

'We are heading towards Acantilados de Maro-Cerro Gordo,' Alberto said, and then turned to Raúl. 'Would you like us to stop there tonight? The chef is looking forward to preparing your dinner and he wondered if you would like us to set up for you to eat on the bay?'

'We'll eat on the boat,' Raúl said. 'We might take a couple of jet skis out a little later and take a walk.'

'Of course,' Alberto said, then turned to Estelle.

'Do you have any preferences for dinner? Any food choices you would like the chef to know about?'

'Anything.'

Raul heard her try to squeeze the word out through breathless lips.

'It's a beautiful bay we are stopping at.' Albert happily chatted on. 'It's not far at all from the more built-up areas, but soon we will start to come into the most stunning virgin terrain.'

He wished them a pleasant afternoon and headed off.

'I've already explored the virgin terrain...' Raúl drawled, once he was out of earshot.

Estelle said nothing.

'Here.' Annoyed with himself for giving in, but hating her discomfort, he threw her the bikini top. 'Put it on if you want.'

She really was shaken, Raúl thought with a stab of guilt as he watched her trembling hands trying to put the damp garment on. Going topless was nothing here—nothing at all—but then he remembered last night: her shaking, her asking him to be gentle. Pleas he had ignored.

He strode through the water and turned her around, helping her with the clasp of her bikini top. Then, and he didn't know why, he pulled her into his arms and held her till she had stopped shaking—held her till the blush had seeped from her skin.

And then he made her burn again as he dropped a kiss on her shoulder and admitted a truth to her about that virgin terrain.

'...and it was stunning.'

CHAPTER TWELVE

NORMALLY RAÚL'S YACHT sailed into the busiest port, often with a party underway.

This early evening, though, they sailed slowly into Acantilados de Maro-Cerro Gordo. The sky was an amazing pink, the cliffs sparkling as they dropped anchor near a secluded bay.

'The beaches are stunning here,' Alberto said, 'and the tourists know it. But this one has no road access.' He turned to Raúl. 'The jet skis are ready for you both.'

Only as they were about to be launched did Raúl remember. He turned and saw her pale face, saw that she was biting on her lip as she went to climb on the machine, and his apology was genuine.

'Estelle, I'm sorry. I forgot about your brother's accident.'

'It's fine,' she said through chattering teeth. 'He was showing off...mucking around...' She was trying to pretend that the machine she was about to climb on *didn't* petrify her. 'I know we'll be sensible.'

Raúl had had no intention of being sensible. He loved the exhilaration of being on a jet ski and had wanted to share it with her—had wanted to race and to chase.

Instead he was taking her hand. 'It's not fine. You don't have to pretend.'

Oh, but she did. At every turn she had to pretend, if she was to be the temporary woman he wanted.

'Come on this one with me,' Raúl said. 'Alberto, take her hand and help her on.'

They rode towards the bay in a rather more subdued fashion than Raúl was used to.

The maid who was setting up the dinner table caught Alberto's eye when he came to check on her progress and they shared a brief smile.

His bride and the effect she was having on Raúl was certainly not one they had been expecting.

'I think I might go and reorganise his DVD collection,' the maid suggested and Alberto nodded.

'I think that might be wise.'

Estelle held tightly onto Raul's waist as the jet ski chopped through the waves, and because her head kept knocking into his back in the end she gave in and rested it there, not sure if her rapid heart-rate was because she was scared by the vehicle, by the questions she would no doubt soon be facing, or just by the exhilaration.

Making love with Raúl had been amazing. She was sore and tender but now, feeling his skin beneath her cheek, feeling the ocean water sting her and the wind whip her hair, she could not regret a moment. Even her lie. Feeling his passion as he had seared into her was a memory she would be frequently revisiting. For now, though, Estelle knew she had to play it tough—had to convince him better than she had so far that she was up to the job he had paid her for.

He skidded into the shallows and she unpeeled herself from him and stepped down.

'It's amazing…' She looked up at the cliffs, shielding her eyes. 'Look how high it is.'

He did, but only briefly. Estelle was too busy admiring the stunning view to notice his pallor.

'What did Angela say to you at the wedding?' Raúl asked.

She had been expecting a barrage of questions about her lack of experience, and was momentarily sideswiped at his choice of topic for conversation, but then she reminded herself his interest in her was limited.

'She wasn't sure whether or not we were a true couple,' Estelle said.

'You corrected her?'

'Of course,' Estelle said. 'She seems to think that *if* I love my husband, then I should encourage you to make peace with your father while there is still time.' She glanced over to him as they walked. 'She wants us to go there and visit.'

'It is too late to play happy families.'

'Angela said that she doesn't want you to suffer any guilt, as you did over your mother's death…'

'Misplaced guilt,' Raúl said, but didn't elaborate any more.

He stopped and they sat on the beach, looking out to the yacht. She could see the lights were on, the staff on deck were preparing their meal. It was hard to believe such luxury even existed, let alone that for now it was hers to experience. It was the luxury of *him* she wanted, though; there was more about Raúl that she needed to know.

'I didn't know how to answer her,' Estelle admitted. 'You said there was more you would tell me. I have no real idea about your family, nor about you.'

'So I will tell you what you need to know.' He pondered for a moment on how best to explain it. 'My grandfather—my mother's father—ran a small hotel. It did well and he built another, and then he purchased some land in the north,' Raúl explained.

'In San Sebastian?' Estelle asked.

He nodded. 'On his death the business was left to his three children—De La Fuente Holdings. My father and mother married, and my father started to work in the family business. But he was always an outsider—or felt that he was, even though he oversaw the building of the San Sebastian hotel. When I was born my mother became unwell. In hindsight I would say she was depressed. It was then he started to sleep with Angela. Apparently Angela felt too much guilt and left work, moved back to her family, but they started seeing each other again...'

'How do you know all this?'

'My father told me the morning I met you.'

It was only then that Estelle fully realised this was almost as new to him as it was to her.

'Angela got pregnant, the guilt ate away at him, and he told my mother the truth. He wanted to know if she could forgive him. She cried and wailed and screamed. She told him to get out and he went to Angela—the baby was almost due. He assumed my mother would tell her family, that she would turn to them. Except she did not. When she had the car accident and died my father returned and soon realised no one knew he had another son. Instead they welcomed him back into the company.' He was silent for a moment. 'Soon they will find out the truth.'

'Angela said that you blamed yourself for your mother's death?'

'That is all you need to know.' He looked over to her. 'Your turn.'

'I don't know what to tell you.'

'Why you lied?'

'I didn't lie.'

'The same way my father didn't lie when he didn't tell me had another son? The same way Angela didn't lie when she failed to tell mention her son, Luka, was my brother?' He did not want to think about that. 'Okay, if you didn't outright lie, you *did* deceive.'

He watched her swallow, watched as her face jerked away to look out to the ocean.

'I wanted an experienced woman.'

'Sorry I don't know enough tricks—'

'I wasn't talking about *sex*!' Raúl hurled. 'I wanted a woman who could handle things. Who could keep to a deal. Who wasn't going to fall in love…'

'Again you assume!' Estelle flared. 'Why would I fall in love with some cold bastard who thinks only in money—who has no desire for true affection? A man who tells me what to wear and whether or not I can tan.'

Her eyes flashed as she let out some of the anger she had suppressed over the past few days while every decision apart from her wedding dress had been made by him.

'Raúl, I would not have a man choose my clothes or dictate to the hairdresser the style of my hair, or the beautician the colour of my nails. You're getting what you paid for—what you wanted—what you demanded. Consider my virginity a bonus!'

She dug her heels deep into the sand and almost believed her own words. Tried to ignore that last night, as she'd been falling asleep in his arms, foolish thoughts had invaded. Raúl's doubts about her ability to see this through perhaps had merit, for he would be terribly easy to love…

She turned around and faced him.

'I'm here for the money, Raúl.' And not for a single second more would she allow herself to forget it. 'I'm here with you for the same reason I was with Gordon.'

He could not stand the thought of her in bed with him—

could not bear to think about it. But when he did, Raúl frowned.

'If you were with Gordon for money, how come you were trying to change the sheets before the maid got in.'

'I was never with Gordon in that way. I just stood in for Ginny.'

'You shared his bed,' Raúl said. 'And we all know his reputation…'

'Unlike you, Gordon didn't feel comfortable going to a wedding alone,' Estelle said carefully.

'So he paid you to look like his tart?' Raúl checked. 'What about Dario's…?' His voice trailed off and he frowned as he realised the lengths Gordon had gone to, then frowned a little more as realisation hit. 'Is Gordon…?' He didn't finish the question—knew it was none of his business. 'You needed the money to help out your brother?'

She conceded with a nod.

'Estelle, it is not for me to question your reasons—'

'Then don't.'

Her warning did not stop him.

'Andrew would not want it.'

'Which is why he will never find out.'

'I know that if I had a sister I would not want her—'

'Don't compare yourself to my brother. You don't even have a sister, and the brother you *do* have you don't want to know.'

'What's that got to do with it?'

'We're two very different people, Raúl. If I discovered that I had a brother or sister somewhere I'd be doing everything I could to find out about them, to meet them—not plotting to bring them down.'

'I'm not plotting anything. I just don't want him taking what is rightfully mine. Neither do I want to end up working alongside him.'

She looked at the seductive eyes that invited you only to bed, at the mouth that kissed so easily but insisted you did not get close.

'You miss out on so much, Raúl.'

'I miss out on nothing,' Raúl said. 'I have everything I want.'

'You have everything money can buy,' Estelle said, remembering the reason she was here. 'Including me.'

When he kissed her it tasted of nothing. It tasted empty. It was a pale comparison to the kiss he had been the recipient of last night. And when he took her top off he knew she was faking it, knew she was thinking of the boat and of people watching, knew she was trying not to cry.

'Not here,' Raúl said for her.

'Please, Raúl…'

Her mouth sought his. She was still playing the part, too inexperienced to understand that he knew her body lied.

He wanted it back, the intimacy of last night, which meant taking care of her.

For now.

Surely for a couple of days he could take care of her. They could just enjoy each other and break her in properly. The last thing he wanted was her tense and teary, feeling exposed.

He had glimpsed her toughness, admired the lengths she would go to for her family, and he believed her now— she did not want his love

'Later.' Raúl pulled his head back from her mouth. 'I'm starving.'

He helped her with her bikini, used his chest as a shield as he did up the clasp, just in case any passing fish were having a peek, or telescopes were trained on them. But rather than making him feel irritated, her coyness now made him smile.

Especially when he thought of her unleashed.

'Come on,' Raúl said, despite the ache in his groin. 'Let's head back.'

CHAPTER THIRTEEN

'WE WILL GO and shower and get dressed for dinner,' Raúl said as they boarded and Alberto took the jet ski. 'Do you want me to ask Rita to come down and do your hair?'

'Rita?'

'She is a masseuse and a beautician. If you want her to come and help just ask Alberto,' Raúl said, heading off to the stateroom.

Estelle called him back. She could smell the food and was honestly starving. 'Why do we have to get dressed for dinner?' Estelle did not notice the twitch of his lips, though Alberto did. 'It's only us.'

'On a yacht such as this one, when the chef…' Raúl began. But he was torn, because etiquette often had no place on board and it seemed petty to put her right. 'Very well.' He turned to Alberto, who was already on to it.

'I'll let the chef know.'

They rinsed off under the shower on deck and then took their seats.

Raúl was rather more used to a well-made-up blonde in a revealing dress sitting opposite him, but there was something incredibly appealing about sitting for dinner half-naked and scooping up the delicacies the waiters were bringing.

'I could get far too used to this,' Estelle started, and

then stopped herself, remembering his words at the lawyer's. 'I meant…'

'I know what you meant.'

She was relieved to see he was smiling.

'The food really is amazing,' Raúl agreed. 'They chef is marvellous. Chefs on yachts generally are—that is why we keep coming back for more.'

They chatted as they ate, far more naturally than they had before, and it wasn't just for the benefit of the staff.

It was simply a blissful night.

They danced.

On the deck of his yacht they danced when the music came on.

'I understand now why we should have changed for dinner,' Estelle admitted. 'Do you think I've offended anyone?'

'I don't think you could if you tried.'

The sky was darkening and Raúl looked out to the cliffs, and rather than remembering hell he buried his face in her hair. It took only the smell of the ocean in her hair for him to escape.

'And for the record,' Raúl said, 'although you accuse me being a controlling bastard, I was worried about you burning. I have never seen paler skin.'

'I think I *am* a bit sunburnt.'

'I know.'

They moved down to the lounge room. Estelle was starting to relax—so much so that she didn't spring from his arms when some dessert wine was brought through to them.

'Let's go to bed…' His hand was in her bikini top, trying to free her breast.

'Not yet,' she breathed into his mouth. 'I'll never sleep.'

'I have no intention of letting you sleep.'

'Let's watch a movie,' Estelle said, unwrapping herself from him and heading over to his collection.

'Estelle—no!'

'Oh, sorry.' She'd forgotten what he'd told her in the gym, about no hand-holding and movies, and she turned and attempted a smile. 'Sure—let's go to bed.'

'I didn't mean that,' Raúl said through gritted teeth, wondering how he'd ended up with the one hooker to whom he'd have to apologise for his DVDs. 'I just don't think there will be anything there to your taste.'

He braced himself for the rapid demise of a pleasant night as Estelle flicked through his collection.

'I love this one.'

'Really?' Raúl was very pleasantly surprised.

'Actually…' She skimmed through a couple more. 'This one's my favourite.' She held up the cover to him and didn't understand his smile.

'Of course it is,' Raúl said, pulling her down beside him, smiling into her hair. One day he would tell her how funny that was—one day when it wouldn't offend, when she knew him better. He would laugh about it with her.

But there would not *be* that day, he reminded himself.

This was just for now.

He had not lain on a sofa and watched a movie—not one with a plot, anyway—since he couldn't remember when.

Estelle shivered. The doors were open and the air was cooling. He pulled down a rug from the back of the sofa and covered them, felt her bottom curving into him.

'Sore?' He kissed her pink shoulders as he made light work of her bikini top.

'A bit.'

Estelle concentrated on the movie as Raúl concentrated on Estelle. He kissed her neck and shoulders for ages, then played with her breasts, massaging them with his palms, taking her nipples between thumb and fingers. Then slowly, when he knew there would be no qualms from Estelle, moved one hand down and untied her bikini bottoms.

His question, when repeated, was a far more personal one as his fingers crept in.

'Sore?'

'A bit,' she said again, but he was so gentle, and it felt so sublime.

She could feel the motion of the boat, and him huge and hard behind her; she could feel the urging of his mouth to turn to him and growing insistence from behind.

'Turn around, Estelle.' His breathing was ragged.

'In a minute.' She wasn't even watching the film. Her eyes were closed. She was just loving the feel of him playing with her and longing for it to go on. 'It's coming to the best bit.'

He pulled her up a little further, so that her naked bum was against his stomach, and he angled her perfectly. She felt the long, slow slide of him where he had stabbed into her last night. She was still bruised and swollen and hot down below, and yet she closed around him in relief.

'*This* is the best bit,' Raúl's low voice corrected her.

He pressed slowly into her, his fingers playing with her clitoris, slid slowly and deeply, with none of the haste of last night, and it was Estelle who was fighting to hold back.

'I'm going to come.'

'Not yet,' he told her, teasing her harder with his fingers, thrusting himself deeper inside.

'I am.' She was trembling and trying to hold on.

'Not yet.'

He stroked her somewhere so deep, the feeling so intense that she let out a small squeal.

'There?' he asked.

Estelle didn't know what he meant, but then he stroked her there again and she sobbed. 'There!' She was begging as over and over he massaged her deep, hitting her somewhere she hadn't even known existed. 'There…'

She was starting to cry, but with intense pleasure, and then she could no longer hold it. There was no point even trying.

There was a flood of release as she pulsed around him, and Raúl moaned as she tightened over and over around his thick length. He felt the rush of her orgasm flowing into him and he shot back in instant response, spilling deep into her, loving her abandon, loving the Estelle his body revealed.

Loving too the tinge of embarrassment that crept in as she struggled to get her breath back.

'What was that?'

'Us,' he said, still inside her. And it was not the cliffs he feared now, but the perfume of the ocean in her hair as he inhaled it—a fear that was almost overwhelming as he realised how much he had enjoyed this night.

Not just the sex, not just the talking, not just dinner.

But *now*.

'We should head back.'

They had been snorkelling. It had all started off innocently, but had turned into a slightly more grown-up activity. Raúl did not know if it was her laughter, or the feel of her legs wrapped around him, or just that he was simply enjoying her too much, but he kissed her cheek and unwrapped her legs from his waist.

'Is it dinner-time?'

'I meant we should head back for Marbella…'

It had been two nights and two amazing days, and more of a honeymoon than Raúl had ever intended for it to be.

They *were* dressing for dinner tonight, because they wouldn't be dawdling on their return. Which meant this would be their last night on the yacht.

She missed it already.

Even as Rita did her hair and make-up she missed the yacht, because it had been the most magical time. As if they had suspended the rules of the contract, their time had been spent talking, laughing, eating, making love— but Raúl had made it clear that things would be different when they returned to Marbella.

She felt as if they were approaching that already as Rita pushed the last pin into Estelle's hair. Raúl's expression was tense as he picked up his ringing phone.

'I will tell the chef you will be up soon,' Rita said, and Estelle thanked her and started to put on her dress.

She didn't understand what was being said on the phone, but given the terse words, she guessed it wasn't pleasant.

'They are getting married.' Raúl hung up and was silent.

By the time he told her what the call had been about he was doing up his tie, but kept getting the knot wrong.

'Oh.' She didn't know what else to say, just went on struggling with her zip.

'Come here.' He found the side zipper. 'It's stuck.'

She stood still as he tried to undo it.

'My father says he wants to do the right thing by Angela—wants to give her the dignity of being his wife and his widow. He wants her to have a say in decisions by the medical staff.'

'What did you say?'

'That it was the first decent thing I had heard on the subject.'

'Are you going to attend?'

He didn't answer her question; instead he hurried her

along. 'Come on. They will be serving up soon. It is not fair to keep the chef waiting.'

Since when was Raúl thoughtful about his staff? Estelle thought, but said nothing.

It was an amazing dinner. The chef had made his own paella, and even Raúl agreed, it was the best he had tasted.

Yet he barely touched it.

He looked at Estelle; she looked exquisite. Her hair was up, as it had been on their wedding day, her black dress looked stunning, and he told himself he could do it—that it wasn't a problem after all.

'What would you think if we did not turn around for Marbella?'

Estelle swallowed the food she was relishing and took a drink of water, nervous for the same reasons as Raúl.

'We could head to the islands, extend our trip…'

'So that you miss your father's wedding?'

'He has chosen to marry when I am on my honeymoon. He doesn't know we were to be on our way back.'

'You'll have to face him at some point.'

'You don't tell me what I have to do!' he snapped, and then righted himself, trying to explain things a little better. 'He wants a wedding—one happy memory with his wife. I doubt that will be manageable with me there. Especially if Luka attends.' He took a breath. 'So how about a few more days?' He made it sound so simple. 'I have not had a proper holiday in years…'

'I thought your life was one big holiday?'

'No,' Raúl said. 'My life is one big party. We will return to that in a few days.' He issued it as a warning, telling her without saying as much that what happened at sea stayed at sea.

He was waiting for her decision. But then Raúl remembered the decision was entirely his. He was paying for her company—not her say in their location.

'I will let the staff know.'

'Now?'

'They have to plot the route, inform...'

He didn't finish, just headed off to let the crew know, and Estelle sat there, suddenly nervous.

She wanted to be back on safe water—because living with Raúl like this, seeing this side of him, she was struggling to remember the rules.

Their 'couple of days' turned into two weeks.

They sailed around Menorca and took their time exploring its many bays. Estelle's skin turned from pale to pink, from freckles to brown. He watched her get bolder, loved seeing her stretch out on a lounger wearing only bikini bottoms, not even a little embarrassed now. Her sexuality was blossoming to his touch, before his eyes.

Finally they sailed back into Marbella. Normally the sight of it was the one he loved best in the world, yet there was a moment when he wanted to tell the skipper to keep sailing, to bypass Marbella and head to Gibraltar, take the yacht to Morocco, just to prolong their time. Except he was growing far too fond of her.

She put a hand on his shoulder, joined him to watch the splendid sight, but she felt his shoulder tense beneath her touch.

Raúl turned. She was wearing espadrilles and bikini bottoms, his own wedding shirt knotted beneath her now rosy bust, her cheeks flushed and her lips still swollen from their recent lovemaking.

'You'd better get dressed.'

Usually Raúl was telling her she was *over*dressed.

'The press may be there. The cream dress,' he told her. 'And have Rita do your make-up.'

As easily at that he demoted her, reminded her of her place.

Back on dry land he took her hand. But it was just for the cameras that he put his shoulders around his new wife.

It was in case of a long lens that he picked up her and carried her into his apartment, back to the reality of his life.

CHAPTER FOURTEEN

It was a life she could never have imagined.

Raúl worked harder than anyone she knew.

His punishing day started at six, but rather than coming in drained at the end of it he would have a quick swim in the pool, or they'd make love—or rather they'd have sex. Because the Raúl from the yacht was gone now. A quick shower after that and then they'd get changed for dinner. Meals were always eaten out, and then they would hit the pulsing nightlife, dancing and partying into the early hours.

Estelle couldn't believe this was the toned-down version of Raúl.

'I can cook,' Estelle said, and smiled one night as they sat at Sol's and waited for their dishes to be served. 'It might be a novelty...'

'Why would you cook when a few steps away you can have whatever you choose?'

It was how he lived: life was a smorgasbord of pleasure. But six weeks married to Raúl, even with a week off to visit her family, was proving exhausting for Estelle—and she wasn't the one working. Or rather, she corrected herself as the waiter brought her a drink, she *was* working, twenty-four-seven, because no way would she be dining out every night, no way would she be wandering along streets that still pumped with music well after midnight on a Tuesday.

It had been Cecelia's cardiology appointment today, and Estelle was worried sick and doing her best not to show it. But she kept glancing at her phone, willing it to ring, wondering when she'd hear.

'How's your new PA?' Estelle asked as she bit into the most gorgeous braised beef, which had been cooked over an open fire.

'Okay.' Raúl shrugged. 'Angela trained her well...'

He looked down at her plate, stabbed a piece of beef with a fork and helped himself. Estelle was getting used to the way they shared their meals; it was the norm here.

'It *is* much more difficult without Angela,' Raúl admitted. 'Only now she is gone are we seeing how much she did around the place.'

'When will she be back?'

'She won't,' Raúl said. 'She is taking long service leave to nurse my father. Once he dies and it gets out about her she won't be welcome there.'

'Oh, well, you'll only have to see her at the funeral, then.'

Raúl glanced up. He could never be sure if she was being flip or serious. 'When are you going to see your father?' she asked him.

She was being serious, Raúl quickly found out.

'He chose to live in the north—he chose to end his days with his other family. Why should I....?' He closed his tense lips. 'I do not want to discuss it.'

'Angela called again today.'

'I told you not answer to her.'

'I was waiting for my brother to ring,' Estelle said. 'It was Cecelia's cardiology appointment today. I didn't think to look when I picked up.' Estelle could not finish her dinner and pushed the plate away.

'You're not hungry?'

'Just full.'

'I was thinking...' Raúl said. 'There is a show premiering in Barcelona at the weekend. I think it might be something we would enjoy.'

'Raúl...' She just could not sit and say nothing—could not lie beside him at night and sleep with him without caring even a bit, without having an opinion. Surely he could understand that? 'I was riddled with guilt when my parents died.'

'Why?'

'For every row, for every argument—for all the things we beat ourselves up about when someone dies. Guilt happens whatever you do. Why not make it about something you couldn't have changed, instead of something you can?' On instinct she went to take his hand, but he pulled it back.

'You're starting to sound like a wife.'

She looked at him.

'Believe me, I don't feel like one.'

Estelle pounced on her phone when it rang.

'I need to take this.'

'Of course.'

It was Amanda, doing her best, as always, to sound upbeat. 'They're going to keep Cecelia in for a few nights. She's a bit dehydrated...'

'Any idea when she's going to have surgery?'

'She's too small,' Amanda said. 'They've put a tube in, and we're going to be feeding her through that. She might come home on oxygen...'

Raúl watched Estelle's eyes filling with tears but she turned her shoulders and hunched into the phone in an effort to hide them. He heard her attempt to be positive even while she was twisting her hair around and around her finger.

'She's a fighter,' Estelle said, but as she did so she closed her eyes.

'How is your niece?' Raúl asked as she rang off.

'Much the same.' She didn't want to discuss it for fear she might break down—Raúl would be horrified! Seeing that he'd finished eating, Estelle gave him a bright smile. 'Where do you want to go next?'

'Where do *you* want to go?' Raúl offered.

Home, her body begged as they walked along the crowded street. But that wasn't what she was here for. She'd been transferring money over to Andrew since he'd gone back to England. The first time she'd told Andrew it was money she'd been saving to get a car. The second time she'd said it was a loan. Now she'd just given him a decent sum that would see them through the next few months, telling Andrew that she and Raúl simply wanted to help.

It was time to earn her keep.

They passed a club that was incredibly loud and very difficult to get into. It was a particular favourite of Raúl's. 'How about here?'

Estelle woke to silence. It was ten past ten and Raúl would long since have gone to work.

She sat up in bed and then, feeling dizzy, lay back down.

How the hell he lived like this on a permanent basis, Estelle had no idea. All she knew was she was not going out tonight.

He could, she decided, dressing and heading out not for the trendy boutiques but for the markets. She just wanted a night at home—or rather a night in Raúl's home—and something simple for dinner. There must be some subclause in the contract that allowed for the occasional night off?

Marbella was rarely humid, the mountains usually shielded it, but it struggled today. The air was thick and oppressive and the markets were very busy. Estelle had bought the ripest, plumpest vine tomatoes, and was deciding between lamb and steak when she passed a fish stall and gave a small retch. She tried to carry on, to continue walking, tried to focus on a flower stall ahead instead of the appalling thought she had just had.

She couldn't be pregnant.

Estelle took her pill at the same time every day.

Or she had tried to.

All too often Raúl would come home at lunchtime, or they'd be in a helicopter flying anywhere rather than to his father's—the one place he needed to be.

She couldn't be pregnant.

'Watch where you're going!' someone scolded in Spanish as she bumped into them.

'Lo sierto,' Estelle said, changing direction and heading for the *Pfarmacia*, doing the maths in her head and praying she was wrong.

Less that half an hour later she found out she was right.

Raúl didn't get home from work till seven, and when he did it was to the scent of bread baking and the sight of Estelle in his underutilised kitchen, actually cooking.

'Are we taking the wife thing a bit far?' Raúl checked tentatively. 'You don't have to cook.'

'I want to,' Estelle said. She was chopping up a salad. 'I just want to have a night in, Raúl.'

'Why?'

'Because.' She frowned at him. 'Do you ever stop?'

'No,' he admitted, then came over and give her a kiss. 'Are you okay?'

'I'm fine. Why?'

'You didn't wake up when I left this morning. You seem tense.'

'I'm worried about my niece,' Estelle said, removing herself from him and adding two steaks to the grill.

She was curiously numb. Since she'd done the test Estelle had been operating on autopilot and baking bread, which she sometimes did when she didn't want to think.

She just couldn't play the part tonight.

They carried their food out to the balcony and ate steak and tomato salad, with the herb bread she had made, watching a dark storm rolling in.

Estelle wanted to go home, wanted this over. Though she knew there was no getting out of their deal. But she needed a timeframe more than ever now. She wanted to be far away from him before the pregnancy started showing.

She could never tell him.

Not face to face, anyway.

Estelle could not bear to watch his face twist, to hear the accusations he would hurl, for him to find another reason not to trust.

'I spoke with my father today.'

She tore her eyes from the storm to Raúl. 'How is he?'

'Not good,' Raúl said. 'He asks that I go and see him soon.'

'Surely you can manage to be civil for a couple of days?' She was through worrying about saying the wrong thing. 'Yes, your father had an affair, but clearly it meant something. They're together all this time later...'

'An affair that led to my mother's death.' He stabbed at his steak. 'Their lies left the guilt with *me*.' He pushed his plate away.

The eyes that lifted to hers swirled with grief and confusion and now, when all she wanted was to be away from him, when she must guard her heart properly, when she needed it least, Raúl confided in her.

'I had an argument with my mother the night she died. She had missed my performance at the Christmas play—as she missed many things. When I came home she was crying and she said sorry. My response? *Te odio*. I told her I hated her. That night she lifted me from my sleep and put me in a car. The mountains are a different place in a storm,' Raúl explained. 'I had no idea what was happening; I thought I had upset her by shouting. I told her I was sorry. I told her to slow down...'

Estelle could not imagine the terror.

'The car skidded and came off the mountain, went down the cliffside. My father returned from his so-called work trip to be told his wife was dead and his son was in hospital. He chose not to tell anyone the reason he'd been gone.'

'Did they never suspect he and Angela?'

'Not for a moment. He just seemed to be devoting more and more time to the hotel in San Sebastian. Angela was from the north and she resumed working for him again. Over the years, clearly when Luka was older, she started to come to Marbella more often with my father. We had a flat for her, which she stayed in during the working week.'

'He had two sons to support,' Estelle said. 'Maybe it was the only way he could see how.'

'Please!' Raúl scoffed. 'He was with Angela every chance he could get, leaving me with my aunt and uncle. Had he wanted one family he could have had it. Perhaps it would have been a struggle, but his family would have been together. He chose this life, and those choices caused my mother's death.'

'Instead of you?'

'I blamed myself for years for her death. I thought the terrible things I said...'

'You were a child.'

'Yes,' he said. 'I see that now. The night she died was two days after Luka's birth. I realise now that she was on her way to confront them.'

'In a storm, with a five-year-old in the back of her car,' Estelle pointed out.

'I thought she was trying to kill me.'

'She was ill, Raúl.'

He nodded. 'It would have been nice to know that she was,' Raúl said. 'It would have been nice to know that it was not my words that had her fleeing into the night.'

'It sounds as though she was sick for a long time, and I would imagine it was a very tough time for your father...' Estelle did not want involvement. She wanted to remove herself as much as she could before she told him. Yet she could not sit back and watch his pain. 'He just wants to know you're happy, that you're settled. He just wants peace.'

'We all want peace.' He was a moment away from telling her the rest, but instead he stood and headed through the balcony door. 'I'm going out.'

Estelle sat still.

'Don't wait up.'

'I won't.'

She didn't want him going out in this mood, and she followed him into the lounge while knowing he wouldn't welcome her advice. 'Raúl, I don't think—'

'I don't pay you to think.'

'You're upset.'

'Now she tells me what I'm *feeling*!'

'Now *she* reminds you that she read that contract before she signed it. If you think you're going to go out clubbing and carrying on in your usual way I'll be on the next plane home…' she watched his shoulders stiffen '…with every last cent you agreed to pay me.'

He headed for the door.

'Hope the music's loud enough for you, Raúl!' she called out to him.

'It could never be loud enough.'

There was a crack from the storm and the balcony doors flew wide open. He turned then, and she glimpsed hell in his eyes. There was more than he was telling her, she knew that, and yet she did not need to know at this moment.

He was striding towards her and she understood for a moment his need for constant distraction, for *she* was craving distraction now. She was pregnant by the man she loved, who was incapable of loving her. How badly she didn't want to think about it. How nice it would be for a moment to forget.

His mouth was, perhaps for the last time, welcome. The crush of his lips was so fierce he might have drawn blood. Yet it was still not enough. He wrestled her to the floor and it was still too slow.

Here beneath him there were no problems—just the weight of him on her.

He was pulling at his zipper and pressing up her skirt. She was kissing him as if his lips could save them both. The balcony doors were still wide open. It was raining on the inside, raining on them, yet it did not douse them.

He had taught her so much about her body, but she learned something new now—how fast her arousal could be.

He was coming even before he was inside her; she could feel the hot splash on her sex. Estelle was sobbing as he thrust inside her, holding onto him for dear life. Each thrust of his hips met with her own desperation. It was fast and it was brutal, and yet it was the closest they had ever been.

He was at her ear and breathing hard when he lifted his face. She opened her eyes to a different man.

'Come with me to see them?'

He was asking, not telling.

'Yes.'

'Tomorrow?'

'Yes.'

It felt terribly close to love.

CHAPTER FIFTEEN

THEY FLEW EARLY the next morning, over the lush hills of Spain to the north, and even as his jet made light work of the miles there was a mounting tension. Had they run out of time?

Far from anger from Raúl, there was relief when Angela came out of the door to greet them, a wary smile on her face.

'Come in,' she said. 'Welcome.'

She gave Estelle a kiss on the cheek, and gave one too to Raúl. 'We can do this,' she said to him, even as he pulled back. 'For your father. For one day…'

Raúl nodded and they headed through to the lounge.

If Estelle was shocked at the change in his father, it must be hell for Raúl.

'Hey,' he greeted his son. 'You took your time.'

'I'm here now,' Raúl said. 'Congratulations on your wedding.' He handed Antonio a bottle of champagne as he kissed him on the cheek. 'I thought we could have a toast to you both later.'

'I finally make an honest woman of her,' Antonio said.

Estelle watched as Raúl bit back a smart response. There really was no time for barbs.

'Your brother is flying in from Bilbao tonight. Will you stay for dinner?' Antonio's eyes held a challenge.

'I'm not sure that we can stay…'

'A meeting between the two of you is inevitable,' Antonio said. 'Unless you boycott my funeral. I am to be buried here,' he added.

She watched Raúl's jaw tighten as he told his son that this was the home he loved. Yet he had denied his first son the chance of having a real home.

'I will make a drink,' Angela said to Estelle. 'Perhaps you could help me?'

Estelle went into the kitchen with her. It was large and homely, and even though she was hoping to keep things calm for Raúl, Estelle was angry on his behalf.

'We will leave them to it,' Angela said as Estelle sat at the table. 'You look tired.'

'Raúl doesn't live a very quiet life.'

'I know.' Angela smiled and handed her a cup of hot chocolate and a plate of croissants.

Estelle took a sip of her chocolate, but it was far too sickly and she put the cup back down.

'I can make you honey tea,' Angela offered. 'That is what I had when…' Her voice trailed off as she saw the panic in Estelle's eyes and realised she must not want anyone to know yet. To Angela it was obvious—she hadn't seen Estelle since her wedding day, and despite the suntan her face was pale, and there were subtle changes that only a woman might notice. 'Perhaps your stomach is upset from flying.'

'I'm fine,' Estelle said, deliberately taking another sip.

'I am worried that when Antonio dies I will see no more of Raúl…'

Estelle bit her lip. Frankly she wouldn't blame him. Because being here, seeing first-hand evidence of years of lies and deceit, she understood a little better the darkness of his pain.

'He is like a son to me.'

Estelle simply couldn't stay quiet. 'From a distance?' She repeated Angela's own words from the wedding day and then looked around. There were pictures of Luka, who looked like a younger Raúl.

'Raúl is here too.' Angela pointed to a photo.

'He wasn't, though.' Estelle could not stand the pretence. 'You had a home here—whereas Raúl was being shuffled between his aunt and uncle, occasionally seeing his dad.'

'It was more complicated than that.'

'Not really.' Estelle simply could not see it. 'You say you think of him as a son, and yet…'

'We did everything the doctor said,' Angela wrung her hands. 'I need to tell you this—because if Raúl refuses to speak with me ever again, then this much I would like you to know. The first two years of Luka's life Antonio hardly saw him. He did everything to help Raúl get well, and that included keeping Luka a secret. The doctor said Raúl needed his home, needed familiarity. How could we rip him away from his family and his house? How could we move him to a new town when the doctor insisted on keeping things as close to normal as possible?'

Estelle gave a small shrug. 'It would have been hard on him, but surely no harder than losing his mother. He thought it was because of something he had said to her.'

'How could we have known that?'

'You could have spoken to him. You could have asked him about what happened. Instead you were up here, with his dad.'

There was a long stretch of silence, finally broken by Angela. 'Raúl hasn't told you, has he?'

'He's told me everything.'

'Did Raúl tell you that he was silent for a year?' She

watched as Estelle's already pale face drained of colour. 'We did not know what happened that day, for Raúl could not tell us. The trauma of being trapped with his dead mother…'

'How long were they trapped for?'

'For the night,' Angela said. 'They went over a cliff. It would seem Gabriella died on impact. When the *médicos* got there he was still begging her to wake up. He kept telling her he was sorry. Once they released him he said nothing for more than a year. How could we take him from his home, from his bed? How could we tell him there was a brother?'

'Excuse me—'

Estelle retched and cried into the toilet, and then tried to hold it together. Raúl did not need her drama today. So she rinsed her mouth and combed her hair, then headed back just as Raúl was coming out from the lounge.

'Are you okay?'

'Of course.'

'My father is going to have a rest. As you heard, my brother is coming for dinner tonight. I have agreed that we will stay.'

Estelle nodded.

'Somehow we will get through dinner without killing each other, and then,' Raúl said, 'as my reward for behaving…' He smiled and pulled her in, whispered something crude in her ear.

Far from being offended, Estelle smiled and then whispered into *his* ear. 'I can do it now if you want.'

She felt him smile on her cheek, a little shocked by her response.

'It can wait.' He kissed her cheek. 'Thank you for today. Without you I would not be here.'

'How is he?'

'Frail…sick…'

'He loves you.'

'I know,' Raúl said. 'And because I love him also, we will get through tonight.'

She wasn't so sure they'd get through it when she met Luka. He was clearly going through the motions just for the sake of his parents. Angela was setting up dinner in the garden and Antonio was sitting in the lounge. It was Estelle who got there first, and opened the door as Raúl walked down the hall.

The camera did not lie: he was a younger version of Raúl—and an angrier one too.

Luka barely offered a greeting, just walked into his family home where it seemed there were now two bulls in the same paddock. He refused Raúl's hand when he held it out to him and cussed and then spoke in rapid Spanish.

'What did he say?' Estelle asked as Luka strode through.

'Something about the prodigal son's homecoming and to save the acting for in front of his father.'

'Come on,' Estelle said. There would be time for dwelling on it later.

He caught her wrist. 'You're earning your keep tonight.'

He saw the grit of her teeth and the flash of her eyes.

'Do you do it deliberately, Raúl?' she asked 'Does it help to remind me of my place on a night like tonight?'

'I am sorry. What I meant was that things are particularly strained. When I asked you I never anticipated bringing you here. Certainly I never thought I would set foot in this house.'

They could not discuss it properly here, so for now she gave him the benefit of the doubt. They went out to the garden, where Luka was talking with his father, and they all sat at the table for what should have been a most difficult dinner. Instead, for the most part, it was nice. It was little uncomfortable at first, but soon conversation was flowing as Estelle helped Angela to bring out the food.

'I never thought I would see this day,' Antonio said. 'My family all at the same table...'

Antonio would never see it again.

He was so frail and weak it was clear this would be the last time. It was for that reason, perhaps, that Luka and Raúl attempted to be amicable.

'You work in Bilbao?' Raúl asked.

'I do,' Luka said. 'Investment banking.'

'I had heard of you even before this,' Raúl said. 'You are making a name for yourself.'

'And you.' Luka smiled but it did not meet his eyes. 'I hear about your many acquisitions...'

Thank God for morphine, Estelle thought, because Antonio just smiled and did not pick up on the tension.

The food was amazing—a mixture of dishes from the north and south of Spain. There was *pringá*, an Andalusian dish that was a slow-cooked mixture of meats and had been Raúl's favourite as a child. And there was *marmitako* too, a dish from the Basque Country, which was full of potatoes and pimientos and, Antonio said, had kept him going for so long.

'So you study?' Antonio said to Estelle.

'Ancient architecture.' Estelle nodded. 'Although, I haven't been doing much lately.'

'Yes, what happened to your online studies?' Raúl teased.

'Sol's happened.' Estelle smiled.

Raúl laughed. 'Being married to me is a full-time job...'

Raúl used the words she had used about Gordon. It was a gentle tease, a joke that caused a ripple of laughter—

except their eyes met for a brief moment and it hurt her that he was speaking the truth.

It *was* a job, Estelle reminded herself. A job that would soon be over. But then she thought of the life that grew inside her, the baby that must have the two most mismatched parents in the world.

Not that Raúl knew it.

He thought she loved the clubs and the parties, whereas sitting and eating with his family, as difficult as it was, was where she would rather be. This night, for Estelle, was one of the best.

'You would love San Sebastian.' Antonio carried on speaking to her. 'The architecture is amazing. Raúl, you should take Estelle and explore with her. Take her to the Basilica of Santa Maria—there is so much she would love to see…'

'Estelle would prefer to go out dancing at night. Anyway,' Raúl quipped, 'I haven't been inside a church for years.'

'You will be inside one soon,' his father warned. 'And you should share in your wife's interests.'

Estelle watched thankfully as Raúl took a drink rather than delivering a smart response to his father's marital advice.

And, as much as she'd love to explore the amazing city, she and Raúl were simply too different. And the most bizarre thing was Raúl didn't even know that they were.

She tried to imagine a future: Raúl coming home from a night out to a crying baby, or to nannies, or having access weekends. And she tried to picture the life she would have to live in Spain if she wanted his support.

Estelle remembered the menace in his voice when he had warned that he didn't want children and decided then that she would never tell him while this contract was between them. When she was back home in England and there was distance, when she could tell him without breaking down, or hang up on him if she was about to, *then* she would confess.

And there would be no apology either. Estelle surged in sudden defensiveness for her child—she wasn't going to start its life by apologising for its existence. However Raúl dealt with the news was up to him.

'So…' Still Antonio was focused on Estelle. 'You met last year?'

'We did.' Estelle smiled.

'When he said he was seeing an ex, I thought it was that…' Antonio snapped his fingers. 'The one with the strange name. The one he really liked.'

'Antonio.' Angela chided, but he was too doped up on morphine for inhibition.

'Araminta!' Antonio said suddenly.

'Ah, yes, Araminta.' Estelle smiled sweetly to her husband. 'Was that the one making a play for you at Donald's wedding?'

'That's the one.' Raúl actually looked uncomfortable.

'You were serious for a long time,' Antonio commented.

Estelle glanced up, saw a black smile on Luka's face.

'Weren't you engaged to her?' he asked. 'I remember my mother saying that she thought there might soon be a wedding.'

'Luka,' Angela warned. 'Raúl's wife is here.'

'It's fine,' Estelle attempted—except her cheeks were on fire. She was as jealous as if she had just found out about a bit of her husband's past she'd neither known of nor particularly liked. 'If I'd needed to know about all of Raúl's past before I married him we'd barely have got to his twenties by now.'

She should have left it there, but there was a white-hot

feeling tearing up her throat when she thought of how he'd so cruelly dismissed Araminta—and that was someone he'd once cared about.

It was for that reason her words were tart when she shot Raúl a look. 'Though you failed to mention you'd ever been engaged.'

'We were never engaged.'

'Please!'

Antonio's crack of laughter caught them all by surprise and he raised a glass to Estelle. 'Finally you have met your match.'

It wasn't a long night. Antonio soon tired, and as they headed inside Luka farewelled his father fondly. But the look he gave to Estelle and Raúl told them both he didn't need them to see him to the door in *his* home.

They headed for bed. Estelle was a bit embarrassed by her earlier outburst, especially as everyone else seemed to have managed to behave well tonight.

'I'm sorry about earlier,' she said as she undressed and climbed into bed. 'I shouldn't have said anything about Araminta.'

'You did well,' Raúl said. 'My father actually believes us now.'

He thought she had been acting, Estelle realised. But she hadn't been.

It felt very different sleeping in his father's home from sleeping in Raúl's apartment or on his yacht. Even Raúl's ardour was tempered, and for the first time since she had married him Estelle put on her glasses and pulled out a book. It was the same book she had been reading the day she had met him, about the mausoleum of the First Qin Emperor.

She was still on the same page.

As soon as this was over she was going to focus on

her studies. It had been impossible even to attempt online learning with Raúl around.

'Read me the dirty bits,' Raúl said, and when she didn't comment he took the book from her and looked at the title. 'Well, that will keep it down.'

For his effort he got a half smile.

'You really like all that stuff?'

'I do.'

His hand was on her hip, stroking slowly down. 'They should hear us arguing now,' he teased lightly. 'You demanding details about my past.'

'I don't need to know.'

'My time in Scotland was amazing.' Raúl spoke on regardless. 'I shared a house with Donald and a couple of others. For the first time since my mother died I had one bedroom, one home, a group of friends. We had wild times but it was all good. Then I met Araminta, we started going out, and I guess it was as close to love as I have ever come. But, no, we were never engaged.'

'I really don't need to hear about it.' She turned to him angrily. 'Do you remember the way you spoke to her?' She struggled to keep her voice down. 'The way you treated her?' She looked at his black eyes, imagined running into him a few years from now and being flicked away like an annoying fly. She wasn't hurting for Araminta, Estelle realised. She was hurting for herself—for a time in her future without him.

'So, should I have slept with her as she requested?'

'No!'

'Should I have danced with her when she asked?'

Estelle hated that he was right.

'Anyway, we were never engaged. Her father looked down on me because I didn't come with some inherited title, so I ended things.'

'You dumped her for that?'

'She was lucky I gave a reason,' Raúl said.

Estelle let out a tense breath—he could be so arrogant and cold at times.

'Normally I don't.'

She returned to her book, tried to pick up where she had left off. Just as she would try to pick up her life in a few weeks' time. Except now everything had changed.

'Put down the book,' Raúl said.

'I'm reading.'

'You are the slowest reader I have ever met,' Raúl teased. 'If we ever watch a movie with subtitles we will have to pause every frame.'

She gave up pretending to read, and as she took off her glasses and put down the book he was suddenly serious.

'Not that we will be watching many more movies.'

She lay on her pillow and faced him.

'I could not have done this without you,' Raúl said. 'I nearly didn't come here in time.' He brushed her hair back from his face with her hand.

'You made it, though.'

'It will be over soon.' He looked into her eyes and didn't know if he was dreading his father dying or that soon she would be gone. 'You'll be back to your studies...'

'And you'll be back on your yacht, partying along the coastline.'

'We could maybe go out on the yacht this weekend?' Was he starting to think of her in ways that he had sworn not to? Or was he simply not thinking straight, given that he was here? 'We had a good time.'

'We did have a good time,' Estelle said, but then she shook her head, because she was tired of running away from the world with Raúl. 'But can we just leave it at that?'

She did not want to taint the memory—didn't want to

return to the yacht with hope, only to find out that what they had found there no longer existed.

But for one more night it did.

He held her face and kissed her—a very slow kiss that tasted tender. She felt as if they were back on the boat, could almost hear the lap of the water as he pulled her closer to him and wrapped her in his arms, urged her to join him in one final escape.

Estelle did.

She kissed him as though she were his wife in more than name. She kissed him as though they were really the family they were pretending to be, sharing and loving each other through difficult times.

He had never known a kiss like it; her hands were in his hair, her mouth was one with his, their bodies were meshing, so familiar with each other now. And he wanted her in his bed for ever.

'Estelle....' He was on the edge of saying something he must not, so he made love to her instead.

His hands roamed her body; he kissed her hard as he slid inside her. Side on, they faced each other as he moved and neither closed their eyes.

'Estelle?'

He said it again. It was a question now—a demand to know how she felt. She could feel him building inside her but she was holding back—not on her orgasm. She was holding back on telling him how she felt. They were making love and they both knew it, though neither dared to admit it.

She stared at this man who had her heart. She didn't even need to kiss him to feel his mouth, because deep inside he consumed her. She was pressing her hips into him, her orgasm so low and intense that he moaned as she gripped him. He closed his eyes as he joined her, then forced them open just to watch the blush on her cheeks, the grimace on her face, just to see the face he loved come to him.

She knew he would turn away from her afterwards. Knew they had taken things too far, that there had been true tenderness.

She looked at the scar on his back and waited till dawn for his breathing to quicken, for Raúl to awake abruptly and take her as he did most mornings.

It never happened.

CHAPTER SIXTEEN

HE WOKE AND he waited for reason.

For relief to flood in because he had held back his words last night.

It never came.

He turned and watched her awaken. He should be bored by now. She should annoy him by now.

'What am I thinking?' he asked when she opened her eyes and smiled at him.

'I wouldn't presume to know.'

'I *did* meet you that night,' he said. 'Despite the dress and the make-up, it *was* Estelle.'

He was getting too close for comfort. Raúl had never been anything other than himself. She, on the other hand, changed at every turn—he didn't actually know her at all. Sex was their only true form of communication.

Estelle could hear noises from the kitchen and was relieved to have a reason to leave. 'I'll go and give Angela a hand.' She went to climb out of bed, wondering if she should say anything about what Angela had told her last night. 'I spoke to her yesterday...'

'Later,' Raúl said, and she nodded.

Today was already going to be painful enough.

* * *

'Buenos días,' Raúl greeted Angela.

'Buenos días.' Angela smiled. 'I was just making your father his breakfast. What would you like?'

'Don't worry about us,' Raúl said. 'We'll have some coffee and then Estelle and I might go for a walk.'

'What time are you going back?'

'I'm not sure,' Raúl said. 'Maybe we might stay a bit longer?'

'That would be good,' Angela said. 'Why don't you take your father's tray in and tell him?'

He was in there for ages, and Angela and Estelle shared a look when at one point they heard laughter.

'I am so glad that they have had this time,' Angela said, and then Raúl came out, and he and Estelle headed off for a walk along the sweeping hillsides on his father's property.

'Have you been here before?' Estelle asked. 'To San Sebastian, I mean?'

'A couple of times,' Raúl said. 'Would you like to explore?'

'We're here to spend time with your father,' Estelle said, nervous about letting her façade down, admitting just how much she would like to.

'I guess,' Raúl said. 'But, depending on how long we stay, I am sure the newlyweds would like some private time too.'

'Wouldn't you be bored?'

'If I am I can wait in the gift shop.' Raúl smiled, and so did she, and then he told her some of what he had been talking about with his father. 'He has told my aunt and uncle about Angela and Luka.'

'When?'

'Yesterday. When he knew I was on my way,' Raúl said. 'He didn't want to leave it to me to tell them.'

'How did they take it?'

'He asked if we heard any shouting while we were flying up.' Raúl gave a small mirthless laugh. 'They want him dead, of course. He told them they wouldn't have long to wait.'

They walked for ages, hardly talking, and Raúl was comfortable with silence, because he was trying to think—trying to work out if she even wanted to hear what he was about to ask her.

'You miss England?'

'I do,' Estelle said. 'Well, I miss my family.'

'Will you miss me?' He stopped walking.

She turned to him and didn't know how to respond. 'I won't miss the clubs and the restaurants...'

'Will you miss *us*?'

'I can't give the right answer here.'

'You can.' He took her in his arms. 'You were right. I miss out on so much...'

It was a fragile admission, she could feel that, and she was scared to grasp it in case somehow it dispersed. But she could not deny her feelings any longer. 'You don't have to.'

His mouth was on hers and they were kissing as if for the first time—a teenage kiss as they paused in the hills, a kiss that had nothing to do with business; a kiss that had nothing to do with sex. His fingers were moving into her hair, touching her face as if he were blind, and she was a whisper away from telling him, from confessing the truth. Just so they could tell his father—just so there might be one less regret.

'Raúl...'

He looked into her eyes and she thought she could tell him anything when he looked at her like that. But for the moment she held back. Because a child was something far bigger than this relationship they were almost exploring. She remembered her vow to do this well away from their contract.

'Let's get back.'

They walked down the hill hand in hand, talking about nothing in particular—about France, so close, and the drive they could maybe take tomorrow, or the next day. They were just a couple walking, heading back home to their family—and then she felt his hand tighten on hers.

'It's the *médico*.'

They ran the remaining distance, though he paused for just a moment to collect himself before they pushed open the front door. Because even from there they could hear the sound of Angela sobbing.

'Your father…' Angela stumbled down the hall and Raúl held her as she wept into his arms. 'He has passed away.'

CHAPTER SEVENTEEN

ESTELLE COULDN'T BELIEVE how quickly things happened.

Luka arrived soon after, and spent time with his father. But it was clear he did not appreciate having Raúl and Estelle in his home.

'Stay,' Angela said.

'We'll go to a hotel.'

'Please, Raúl…'

Estelle's heart went out to her, but it was clear that Luka did not want them there and so they spent the night in a small hotel. Raúl was pensive and silent.

The next morning they stood in the small church to say farewell. The two brothers stood side by side, but they were not united in their grief.

'I used to think Luka was the chosen one,' Raúl said as they flew late that afternoon back to Marbella for the will to be read, as per his father's wishes. 'When I found out—when my father said he wanted to die there—I felt his other family were the real ones.' His eyes met hers. 'Luka sees things differently. He was a secret—his father's shame. I got to work alongside him. I was the reason he did not see much of his father when he was small. His hatred runs deep.'

'Does yours?'

'I don't know,' Raúl admitted. 'I don't know how I feel. I just want to get the reading of the will over with.'

It wasn't a pleasant gathering. Paola and Carlos were there, and the look they gave Angela as she walked in was pure filth.

'She doesn't need this—' Estelle started, but Raúl shot her a look.

'It was never going to be nice,' he said.

Estelle bit her lip, and tried to remember her opinion on his family was not what she was here for. But she kept remembering the night they had made love, their walk on the hill the next morning, and tried to hold on to a love that had almost been there—she was sure of it.

She sat silent beside him as the will was read, heard the low murmurs as the lawyer spoke with Angela. From her limited Spanish, Estelle could make out that she was keeping the home in San Sebastian and there were also some investments that had been made in her name.

And then he addressed Luka.

Estelle heard a shocked gasp from Paola and Carlos and then a furious protest started. But Raúl sat still and silent and said nothing.

'What's happening?'

He didn't answer her.

As the room finally settled the lawyer addressed Raúl. He gave a curt nod, then stood.

'Come on.'

He took her by the arm and they walked out.

Angela followed, calling to him. 'Raúl…'

'Don't.' He shrugged her off. 'You got what you wanted.'

Estelle had to run to keep up with his long strides, but finally he told her what was happening.

'His share of the business goes to Luka.' His face was grey when he turned and faced her. 'Even dying still he plays games, still he lies.' He shook his head. 'I get a vine-yard...'

'Raúl,' Angela had caught up with them. 'He saw how happy you two were the night before he died.'

'He did not change his will.'

'No, but it was his dream that his two sons would work side by side together.'

'He should have thought about that twenty-five years ago.'

'Raúl...'

But Raúl was having none of it. He strode away from Angela and all too soon they were back in his apartment and rapid decisions were being made.

'I'll sell my share,' he said. 'I will start again.' He would. Raúl had no qualms about starting again. 'And I will sell that vineyard too...'

'Why?'

'Because I don't want it,' he said. 'I don't want anything from *him*. I don't want to build bridges with my brother.' *His* mother's business was being handed over to her husband's illegitimate son—it would kill her if she wasn't dead already.

Raúl was back in the mountains—could hear her furious shouts and screams, the storm raging; he could hear the screech of tyres and the scrape of metal. He was over the cliff again. But that part he could manage—that part he could deal with. It was next part he dreaded.

It was the silence after that, and he would do anything never to hear it again.

'You don't have to make any decisions tonight. We can talk about it—'

'We?' His lips tore into a savage smile. '*We* will talk about *my* future? Estelle, I think *you* are forgetting your place.'

'No.' She refused to deny it any longer. 'The morning your father died, when were talking, we were *both* choosing to forget my place. If you want a relationship you can't pick and choose the times!'

'A relationship?' He stared at her for the longest time.

'Yes,' Estelle said, and she was the bravest she had ever been. 'A relationship. I think that's what you want.'

'Now she tells me what I want? You *love* me, do you? You *care* about me, do you? Have you any idea how boring that is to hear? I *bought* you so we could avoid this very conversation. You'd do well to remember that.'

Estelle just stood there as he stormed out of the apartment. She didn't waste her breath warning him this time.

She refused to be his keeper.

CHAPTER EIGHTEEN

RAÚL SAT IN Sol's with the music pumping and stared at the heaving dance floor.

A vineyard.

A vineyard which, if he sold it, wouldn't even pay for his yacht for a year—would Estelle stick around then?

Yes.

He had never doubted his ability to start again, but he doubted it now—could not bear the thought of letting her down.

'Te odio.' He could hear his five-year-old voice hurling the words at his mother, telling her he hated her for missing his play.

He'd been a child, a five-year-old having a row, yet for most of his life he had thought those words had driven his mother to despair that day.

Could he do it?

Whisk Estelle away from a family that loved her to live in the hills with a man who surely wasn't capable of love?

Except he did love her.

And she loved him.

He had done everything he could think of to ensure it would not happen, had put so many rules in place, and yet here it was—staring at him, wrapping around him like a blanket on a stifling day.

He did not want her love, did not want the weight of it. Did not want to be responsible for another's heart.

She would stand by him, Raúl knew, but the fallout was going to be huge. The empire was divided. He could smell the slash and burn that would take place and he did not want her exposed to it.

His phone buzzed in his pocket but he refused to look at it, because if he saw her name he would weaken.

Raúl looked across the dance floor, saw an upper-class hooker, ordered her a drink and gestured her over.

He took out some money and as she opened her bag made his request.

'Lápiz de labios,' Raúl said, and pointed to his neck.

He did not have to explain himself to her. She delivered his request—put her mouth to his neck and did as he asked.

'Perfume,' he ordered next, and she took out her cheap scent and sprayed him.

'Gracias.'

It was done now.

Raúl stood and headed for home.

CHAPTER NINETEEN

'AMANDA.' ESTELLE ATTEMPTED to sound normal when she answered the landline. She was staring at the picture of them on Donald's wedding night, trying to fathom the man who simply refused to love.

'I tried your mobile.'

'Sorry...' Estelle had started to talk about the charger she'd left in San Sebastian, started to talk about little things that weren't important at all, when she realised that for once Amanda wasn't being upbeat. 'What's happened?'

'I tried to ring Raúl—I wanted him to break the news to you.'

Estelle felt her heart turn to ice.

'We're at the hospital and the doctors say that they're going to operate tomorrow.'

'Has she put on any weight?'

'She's lost some,' Amanda said. 'But if they don't operate we're going to lose her anyway.'

'I'm coming home.'

'Please...'

'How's Andrew?'

'He's with her now. He's actually been really good. He's sure she's going to make it through.'

'She will.'

'I don't think so,' Amanda admitted, and her sister-in-law who was always so strong, always so positive, finally broke down.

Estelle said everything she could to comfort her, but knew they were only words, that she needed to be there.

'I'm going to hang up now and book a flight,' Estelle told her. 'And I'll try and sort out my phone.'

'Don't worry about the phone,' Amanda said. 'Just get here.'

Estelle grabbed her case and started piling clothes in. Getting to the airport and onto a flight was her aim, but the thought of Cecelia, so small and so weak, undergoing something so major was just too overwhelming and it made Estelle suddenly fold over. She sobbed as she never had before—knew that she had to get the tears out now, so she could be strong for Amanda and Andrew.

Raúl heard her tears as he walked through the apartment and could not stand how much he had hurt her—could not bear that *he* had done this.

'Estelle…' He saw the case and knew that she was leaving.

'Don't worry.' She didn't even look at him. 'The tears aren't for you. Cecelia has been taken back into hospital. They can't wait for the surgery any longer…' She thought of her again, so tiny, and of what would happen to her parents if they lost her. The tears started again. 'I need to get back to them.'

'I'll fix it now.'

He couldn't *not* hold her.

Could not stand the thought of her facing this on her own, not being there beside her.

He held her in his arms and she wept.

And he could not fight it any more for he loved her.

'We'll go now.'

'No.' She was trying to remember that she was angry, but it felt so good to be held.

'Estelle, I've messed up, but I know what I want now. *I know...*'

She smelt it then—the cheap musky scent; she felt it creep into her nostrils. She moved out of his arms and looked at him properly, smelt the whisky on his breath and saw the lipstick on his neck.

'It's not what you think,' Raúl said.

'You're telling me what I think, are you?' Oh, she didn't need him to teach her to cuss in Spanish! 'You win, Raúl!' Her expression revealed her disgust. 'I'm out of here!'

The tears stopped. They weren't for him anyway. She just turned and went on filling her case.

'Estelle—'

'I don't want to hear it, Raúl.' She didn't even raise her voice.

'Okay, not now. We will speak about it on the plane.'

'You're not coming with me, Raúl.'

'Your brother will think it strange if I do not support you.'

'I'm sure my brother has other things on his mind.' She looked at him, dishevelled and unshaven, and scorned him with her eyes. 'Don't make this worse for me, Raúl.'

He went to grab her arm, to stop her.

'Don't touch me!'

He heard her shout, heard the pain—not just for what was going on with her niece, but for the agony of the betrayal she perceived.

'You can't leave like this. You're upset...'

'I'm upset about my niece!' She looked at him. 'I would *never* cry like this over a man who doesn't love me.' She didn't care how much she hurt him now. 'I'm not your mother, Raúl, I'm not going fall apart, or drive over a cliff-edge because the man I'm married to is a cheat. I'm far stronger than that.'

She was.

'All I want now is to get home to my niece.'

He'd lost her. Raúl knew that. Arguing would be worse than futile, for she needed to be with her family urgently.

'I will call my driver and organise a plane.'

'I can sort out transport myself.' Tears for him were starting now, and she didn't want Raúl to see—love was not quite so black and white.

'If you take my plane it will get you there sooner,' Raúl said.

And it would get her away from him before she broke down—before she told him about the baby…before she weakened.

It was the only reason she said yes.

CHAPTER TWENTY

RAÚL STOOD IN the silence.

It was the sound he hated most in the world.

It was his nightmare.

Only this was one *he* had created.

The scent that filled his nostrils was not leaking fuel and death but the scent of cheap perfume and the absence of *her*.

He wanted to chase Estelle—except he was not foolish enough to get in a car, and he could not follow her as his driver was taking her to the airport.

Raúl called a taxi, but even as he climbed in he knew she would not want him with her on the flight. Knew he would be simply delaying her in getting to where she needed to be. They passed De La Fuente Holdings and he looked up, trying to imagine it without his father and Angela, and with Luka working there. Trying to fathom a future that right now he could not see.

Noticing a light on, he asked the driver to stop...

'Raúl!'

Angela tried not to raise her eyes as a very dishevelled Raúl appeared from the elevator.

He was unshaven, his eyes bloodshot. His hair was a mess, and there was lipstick on his collar...

It was the Raúl she knew well.

'What are you doing here at this time, Raúl?'

'I saw the light on,' Raúl said. 'Estelle's niece is sick.'

'I am sorry to hear that. Where is Estelle?'

'Flying back to London.'

'You should be with her, then.' Angela refused to mince her words. He might not want to hear what she had to say to him—he could leave if that were the case.

'She didn't want me to go.'

'So you hit the clubs and picked up a *puta*?'

'No.'

'Don't lie to me, Raúl,' Angela said. 'Your wife would never wear cheap perfume like that.'

'I wouldn't cheat on her. I couldn't.'

Angela paused. Really, the evidence was clear—and yet she knew Raúl better than most and he did not lie. Raúl never attempted to defend the inexcusable.

'So what happened?' Angela asked.

He closed his eyes in shame.

'You know, when you live as a mistress apparently you lose the right to an opinion on others—but of course you have them.' Harsh was the look she gave Raúl. 'Over and over I question your morals.'

'Over and over I do too,' Raúl admitted. 'She got too close.'

'That's what couples do.'

'I did not cheat. I wanted her to think that I had.'

'So now she does.' Angela looked at him. 'So now she's on her own, dealing with her family.'

Angela watched his eyes fill with tears and she tried not to love him as a son, tried not to forgive when she should not. But when he told her what had happened, told her what he had done, the filthy place his head had been, she believed him.

'You push away everyone who loves you. What are you scared of, Raúl?'

'This,' Raúl admitted. 'Hurting another, being responsible for another…'

'We are responsible for ourselves,' Angela said. 'I have made mistakes. Now I pay for them. Now I have till the morning to clear out my office. Now your aunt and uncle turn their backs on me. I would do it all again, though, for the love I had with your father. Some things I would do differently, of course, but I would do it all again.'

'What would you do differently?'

'I would have insisted you were told far sooner about your father and I. I would have told you about your brother,' she said. 'We were going to before you went to university, but your father decided not to at the last moment. I regret that. I should have stood up to him. I should have told you myself. I did not. And I have to live with that. What would *you* have done differently, Raúl?'

'Not have gone to Sol's.' He gave a small smile. 'And many, many other things. But that is the main one now.'

'You need to go to her. You need to tell her what happened—why you did what you did.'

'She doesn't want to hear it,' Raúl said. 'There are more important things on her mind.'

He could not bring himself to tell Angela that their marriage was a fake. If this was fake, then it hurt too much.

And if it was not fake, then it was real.

'If you are not there for her now, with her niece so ill, then it might be too late.'

Raúl nodded. 'She has my plane.'

'I will book you on a commercial flight,' Angela said. 'You need to freshen up.'

He headed to his office, stared in the mirror and picked

up his razor. He called his thanks as she brought him in coffee and a fresh shirt.

'This is the last time I do this for you.'

'Maybe not,' Raúl said. 'Maybe your sons might have a say in that.'

Angela's eyes welled up for a moment as finally he acknowledged the place she had in his heart. But then she met his eyes and told him, 'I meant this is the last time I help you cover up a mistake. Estelle deserves more.'

'She will get it.'

'Your father was so pleased to see how you two were together,' Angela said. 'He was the most peaceful I have ever seen him. He knew he had not allowed time for you and Luka to sort things out, but you are brothers and he believes that will happen. The morning he passed away we were watching you and Estelle walking in the hills. We saw you stop and kiss.'

Raúl closed his eyes as he remembered that day, when for the first time in his life he had been on the edge of admitting love.

'He knew you were happy. I am so glad that I told him about the baby.'

Raúl froze.

'Baby?'

There was no mistaking his bewilderment.

'She has not told you?'

'No!' Raúl could not take it in. 'She told *you*?'

'No,' Angela said. 'I just knew. She did not have any wine; she was sick in the morning...'

Yes, Estelle was tough.

Yes, she could do this without him.

He did not want her to.

'Book the flight.'

CHAPTER TWENTY-ONE

'RAÚL!'

The only possible advantage to being in the midst of a family crisis was that no one noticed the snap to her voice or the tension on Estelle's features when a clean-shaven, lipstick-free Raúl walked in.

'I'm sorry I couldn't get here sooner.' He shook Andrew's hand.

'No, we're grateful to you for getting Estelle here,' Andrew said. 'We're very sorry about your father.'

It was strange, but in a crisis it was Andrew who was the strong one. Amanda barely looked up.

'Is she in surgery?' Raúl sat down next to Estelle and put his arm around her. He felt her shoulders stiffen.

'An hour ago.' Her words were stilted. 'It could be several hours yet.'

The clock ticked on.

Raúl read every poster on the wall and every pamphlet that was laid out. She could hear the turning of the pages and it only served to irritate her. Why on earth had he come? Why couldn't she attempt to get over him with him still far away?

'Why won't they give us an update?' asked Amanda's mother. 'It's ridiculous that they don't let us know what's going on.'

'They will soon,' Andrew said, and Raúl watched as Andrew put his arm around his wife and comforted her, saw how she leant on him, how much she needed him.

Despite everything.

Because of everything, Raúl realised.

'Why don't you wait in the hotel?' Estelle suggested when she could not stand him being in the room a moment longer. 'I've got a room there.'

'I want to wait with you.'

He headed out to the vending machine and she followed him. 'I need some change,' he said. 'I haven't got any pounds.'

'Why would you make this worse for me?'

'I'm not trying to make it worse for you,' Raúl said. 'I know this is neither the time nor the place, but you need to know that nothing happened except my asking a woman to kiss my neck and spray me with her perfume.' He looked her right in the eye. 'I wanted you gone.'

'Well, it worked.'

'I made a mistake,' Raúl said. 'The most foolish of mistakes. I did not want to put you through what was to come.'

'Shouldn't that be *my* choice?' She looked at him.

'Yes,' he said simply. 'As it should be mine.'

Estelle didn't understand his response, was in no mood for cryptic games, and she shook her head in frustration. She wanted him gone and yet she wanted him here—wanted to forgive, to believe.

'I can't do this now,' Estelle said. 'Right now I have to concentrate on my niece.'

As much as Raúl longed to be there for her, that much he understood. 'Do you want me to wait in the hotel or stay with you here?'

'The hotel,' Estelle said—because she could not think straight with him around, could not keep her thoughts where they needed to be with Raúl by her side. She wanted his arms around her, wanted the comfort only he could give, and yet she could not stand what he had done.

'Could I get a coffee as well?' Andrew wheeled himself over.

'Of course,' Raúl said as Estelle handed him some change.

'Estelle, could you take Amanda for a walk?' Andrew asked. 'Just get her away from the waiting room. Her parents are driving her crazy, asking how much longer it will be.'

'Sure.'

Estelle's eyes briefly met Raúl's, warning him to be gone by the time she returned, and Raúl knew the fight he had on his hands. He watched as Estelle suggested a walk to Amanda and he saw a family in motion, supporting each other, a family that was there for each other. A family who helped, who fixed—or tried to.

He looked to Andrew. 'You have the best sister in the world.'

'I know,' Andrew said. 'I'd do anything for her.'

As would Estelle for him, Raúl thought. She'd sold her soul to the devil for her family, but now he understood why.

'I am going to wait in the hotel,' Raúl said. 'I didn't sleep at all last night.'

'I know.' Andrew nodded. 'I'm sure Estelle will keep you up to date.'

'What hotel is she staying at?'

'Over the road,' Andrew told him. 'Good luck—I'm sure it's not at all what you're used to.'

'It will be fine.'

'You just wait.' Andrew gave a pale smile. 'I had to wait fifteen minutes just for them to find a ramp.'

They chatted on for a while—Andrew trying to keep

his mind out of the surgery, Raúl simply because Andrew wanted to talk.

'I had my reservations about the two of you at first,' Andrew admitted. 'You're so opposite.'

And then Raúl found out from his wife's brother just how much Estelle hated clubs and bars, found out exactly the lengths she had gone to for her family.

There was one length she would not go to, though. Raúl was certain of that now.

He walked alongside Andrew's chair, down long corridors, past the operating theatres and Intensive Care, and back again a few times over—until he saw Estelle returning and knew it was better for her that he leave.

He paced the small hotel room, waiting for news—because surely it was taking too long. It was now nine p.m., and he was sick to his stomach for a baby he had never met and a family he wanted to be a part of.

'She made it through surgery.'

Raúl could hear both the relief and the strain in Estelle's voice when the door opened.

'When did she get out of Theatre?'

'About six.' She glanced over to him. 'Was I supposed to ring and inform you?'

He could hear the sarcasm in her voice. 'I just thought it was taking too long. I thought...'

'I'm sorry.' Estelle regretted her sarcastic response—she could see the concern on his face was genuine. 'It was just a long wait till they let Andrew and Amanda in to see her. They've only just been allowed.'

'How is she?'

'Still here.' Estelle peeled off her clothes. 'I've lost my phone charger. I gave Andrew your number in case anything happens overnight.'

It was, though she would never admit it, a relief to have him here, to know that if the phone rang in the night he would be the one to answer it. It was a relief, too, to sink into bed and close her eyes, but there was something that needed to be dealt with before the bliss of sleep.

'I'm not going to tell them we're over yet,' Estelle said. 'It would be too much for them to deal with now. But after we visit in the morning can you make your excuses and leave.'

'I want to be here.'

'I don't want you here, though, and given what's happened you don't own me any more.' She stared into the dark. 'Exclusive, remember?'

'I've told you—nothing happened,' Raúl said. 'Which means I do still own you.'

'No,' Estelle said, 'you don't. Because whatever went on I've decided that I don't want your money. It costs too much.'

'Then pay me back.'

'I will…' she attempted, but of course a considerable amount had already been spent. 'I fully intend to pay you back. It just might take some time.'

'Whatever you choose. But it changes nothing now, Estelle…' He reached for her, wanted to speak with her, but she shrugged him off and turned to her side.

'I'd like the night off.'

'Granted.'

She woke in his arms and wriggled away from them, and then rang her brother. Raúl watched as she went to climb out of bed, saw the extra heaviness to her breasts and the darkening pink of her areolae, and he loved her all the more for not telling him, for guarding their child from the contract that had once bound them. It was the only leverage he had.

'You'll leave after visiting?' Estelle checked.

'Why would I leave my wife at a time like this?' Raúl asked. 'I'm not going anywhere, Estelle.'

'I don't want you here.'

'I don't believe you,' Raúl said. 'I believe you love me as much as I love you.'

'Love you!' Estelle said. 'I'd be mad to love you.' She shook her head. 'You might have almost sent me crazy once, Raúl, but if I possibly did love you then it's gone. My love has conditions too, and you didn't adhere to them. I don't care about technicalities, Raúl. Even if you didn't sleep with someone else, what you did was wrong.'

'Then we go back to the contract.' He caught her wrist. 'Which means I dictate the terms.'

'Your father's dead. Surely it's over?'

'We agreed on a suitable pause. You should read things more closely before you sign them, Estelle.' He watched her shoulders rise and fall. 'But I agree it has proved more complicated than either of us could have anticipated. For that reason, I will agree that the contract expires tomorrow.'

'Tomorrow?' Estelle asked. 'Why not now?'

'I just want one more night. And if I have to exercise the terms of the contract to speak with you—believe me, I shall.'

CHAPTER TWENTY-TWO

'SHE'S PINK!'

Estelle couldn't believe the little pink fingers that wrapped around hers. Even Cecelia's nails were pink—it was suddenly her favourite colour in the world.

'That's the first thing we said.' Andrew was holding Cecelia's other hand. 'She's been fighting so much since the day she was born.' Andrew smiled down at his daughter.

All were too entranced by the miracle that was Cecilia to notice how much Raúl was struggling.

Raúl looked down at the infant, who resembled Estelle, and could hardly believe what he had almost turned his back on.

'I have to go and do some work,' Raúl said. 'Do you want to get lunch later?'

Estelle looked up, about to say no, but he was talking to Andrew.

'Just at the canteen,' he added.

'That would be great.' Andrew smiled. 'Estelle, could you take Amanda for some breakfast? She wants one of us with Cecilia all the time but she needs to get out of the unit and get some fresh air.'

'Sure.' Estelle stood.

'I thought we could go for dinner tonight.'

This time Raúl *was* speaking to Estelle.

'I'm here to be with my niece.'

'Andrew and Amanda are with her. As long as she continues to improve I am sure they expect you to eat.'

'Of course we do,' Andrew said. 'Go out tonight, Estelle. You need a break from the hospital too!'

It was a long day. The doctors were in and out with Cecelia, and talked about taking her breathing tube out if she continued to hold her own. Amanda's parents went home, to return at the weekend, and after they had gone Estelle finally persuaded Amanda to have a sleep in one of the parents' rooms.

It was exhausting.

As she closed the door and went to head back to Cecelia she wondered if she had, after all, grown far too used to Raúl's lifestyle—she would have given anything to be back on his yacht, just drifting along, with nothing to think about other than what the next meal might be and how long it would be till they made love again.

Being Raúl's tart hadn't all been bad, Estelle thought with a wry smile as she returned to Cecelia.

It was being his wife that was hell.

'Amanda's asleep,' Estelle said. 'Well, for a little while.'

'Thanks for being here for us,' Andrew said. 'Both of you. Raúl's great. I admit I wasn't sure at first, but you can see how much he cares for you.'

She felt tears prick her eyes,

'Did you ask him to offer me a job?'

'A job?'

She couldn't lie easily to her brother, but instantly he knew that Estelle's surprised response was real, that she'd had no idea.

'Raúl said that when things are sorted with Cecelia there will be a job waiting for me. He wants me to check out his hotels, work on adjustments for the disabled. There will be a lot of travel, and it will be tough being away at first. But once Cecelia's better he says we can broaden things so it's not just about travelling with disabilities but with a young child as well.'

It was a dream job. She could see it in her brother's eyes. Soon he would be earning, travelling, and more than that his self-respect and confidence would start to return.

'It sounds wonderful.' Estelle gave him a hug, but though she smiled and said the right thing she was furious with Raúl—his company was about to implode, and she and Raúl were soon to divorce quietly.

How dared he enmesh himself further? How dared he involve Andrew in the chaos they had made?

She wanted it to be tomorrow, she wanted Raúl gone so she could sort out how she felt, sort out her life, sort out how to tell him that the temporary contract they had signed would, however tentatively, bind them for life.

There was a note from Raúl waiting for her when she reached the hotel, telling her that he was tied up in a meeting but would see her at the restaurant at eight.

'You signed up for this,' Estelle told herself aloud as she put on her eye make-up. She wondered if it would be just dinner, or perhaps a club after, or…

Estelle closed her eyes so sharply that she almost scratched her eyeball with her mascara wand. He surely wouldn't expect them to sleep together?

He surely wouldn't insist?

Then again, Estelle told herself as she took a taxi to the restaurant, this was Raúl.

Of course he would insist.

Worse, though, she knew she must comply—no matter the toll on heart.

* * *

He turned heads. He just did.

He was waiting for her at the bar, and when they walked into the smartest of restaurants he might as well have being stepping out of a helicopter in a kilt—because everybody was looking at him.

'You look beautiful,' Raúl told her as they sat down.

'Thank you,' she said.

He could feel the anger hissing and spitting inside her, guessed that she must have spoken to Andrew since lunch-time.

'It's a lovely dress,' he commented. 'New?'

'I chose it.'

'It suits you.'

'I know.'

He ordered wine. She declined.

He suggested seafood, which he knew she loved, but he had read in one of the many leaflets he perused in the hospital waiting room that pregnant woman were advised not to eat it.

'I thought you loved seafood?' Raúl commented when she refused it, wondering what her excuse would be.

'I've had enough of it.'

She ordered steak, and he watched her slice it angrily before she voiced one of the many things that were on her mind.

'Did you offer my brother a job?'

'I did.'

'Why would you do that? Why would you do that when you're about to walk away? When you know the company's heading for trouble?'

'We're not heading for trouble,' Raúl said. 'I have been speaking with Luka at length today, and Carlos and Paola too. There is to be a name-change. To Sanchez De La

Fuente… Anyway, if there is trouble ahead it will only be in the office. Your brother will not be dealing with it.'

'What about when we divorce? Will you use him as a pawn then?'

'Never. I tell you this: it is a proper offer, and as long as your brother does well he will have a job.'

'You say that now…'

'I always keep my word.' He looked at her. 'I don't lie,' Raúl said. 'From the start I have only been myself.' He watched the colour spread up her cheeks. 'You get the truth, whether you like or not. I think we both know that much about me.'

Reluctantly she nodded.

'It is only wives that I employ on a whim. I am successful because I choose my employees carefully and I don't give out sympathy jobs. Your brother pointed out a few things that could be changed at the hotel. He would like the menu outside the restaurant to be displayed lower too. He said he would not like to find out about the menu and the prices from a woman he was perhaps dating with.'

Estelle gave a reluctant smile. It was the sort of thing Andrew *would* say.

'He said that a lower table at Reception would be a nice touch, so that anyone in a wheelchair could check in there. That means I do not have to refurbish our reception areas. He has saved me more than his year's wage already.'

'Okay.'

'I don't want my hotels to be good, I want them to be the best—and by the best I mean the best for everyone: businessmen, people with families, the disabled. Your brother, as I told him, will soon be all three.' He looked at her for a long moment, wondering if now she might tell him. 'It is good to see Cecelia improving,' Raúl said. 'It must be a huge relief.'

'It is,' Estelle admitted. 'I think we're only now realising just how scary the last few months have been.'

'Does seeing your niece make you consider ever having a baby?'

She gave a cynical laugh.

'It's just about put me off for life, seeing all that they have had to go through.'

'But they've made it.'

She wasn't going to tell him about the baby, Raúl realised. But, far from angering him, it actually made him smile as he sat opposite the strongest woman he knew.

'Here…' At the end of the meal he smeared cream cheese on a cracker, added a dollop of quince paste and handed it to her.

'No, thanks. I'm full.'

'But remember the night we met…'

'I'd rather not.'

He saw tears prick her eyes and went to take her hand. He could not believe all that they had been through in recent weeks. As she pulled her hand away Raúl wasn't so sure they'd survived it.

'I'm sorry for hurting you. I overreacted—thought I was going to lose everything, thought I might not be able to give you the lifestyle—'

'Like I need your yacht,' Estelle spat. 'Like I need to eat out at posh restaurants seven nights a week, or wear the clothes you chose.'

'So if you don't want all that,' Raúl pointed out, 'what *do* you want?'

'Nothing,' Estelle said. 'I want nothing from you.'

He called for the bill and paid, and as they headed out of the restaurant he took her hand and held it tightly. He turned her to him and kissed her.

It tasted of nothing.

He kissed her harder.

She wanted to spit him out. Not because she loathed his mouth but because she wanted to sink into it for ever—wanted to believe his lies, wanted to think for a moment that she could hold him, that he'd want their baby as much as she did, that he'd want the real her if he knew who she was.

'Where now?' Raúl asked. 'I know...' He held her by the hips. 'You could show me Dario's...'

'I didn't meet Gordon at Dario's,' Estelle said. 'I told you that.'

'We could go anyway,' Raúl said. 'It's our last night together, and it sounds like fun.'

He saw the conflict in her eyes, saw her take a breath to force another lie. He would not put her through it, so he kissed her instead.

'Let's get back to the hotel.'

'Raúl...' She just couldn't go through with it—could not keep up the pretence a moment longer, could not bear to be made love to just to have her heart ripped apart again.

'What?' He took her by the hand again, led her to a taxi.

'Come on, Estelle...' He undressed speedily. 'It's been a hell of a day. I would like to come.'

'You can be *so* romantic.'

'But you keep insisting this is not about romance,' Raúl pointed out.

Her face burnt.

'I don't understand what has suddenly changed. We have been having sex for a couple of months now...' He was undoing her zipper, undressing her. He was down on one knee, removing her shoes. 'Tomorrow we are finished. Tonight we celebrate.'

'I don't want you.'

'So you did the other times?' he checked.

At every exit he blocked her. At every turn he made her see it had never been paid sex for her—not for one single second, not for one shared kiss. She had been lying from the very start. For she had loved him from the start.

'Estelle, after tonight you have the rest of the century off where we are concerned.'

He laid her on the bed and kissed her, felt her cold in his arms. His mouth was on her nipple and he swirled it with his tongue then blew on it, watching it stiffen and ripen. Then he took it deep in his mouth, his fingers intimately stroking her. He filled her mouth with his tongue and she just lay there.

This was what she had signed up for, Estelle reminded herself. She didn't have to enjoy it. Except she was.

It was like a guilty secret—a *filthy* guilty secret. Because she wanted him so—wanted him deep inside her. She turned her cheek away but he turned it back and kissed her. She did not respond—or her mouth did its best not to.

He felt the shift in her…kissed her back to him.

He felt the motion of her tongue on his, felt *her*.

'Tell me to stop and I will,' Raúl said.

She just stared at him.

'Tell me…'

She couldn't

'You can't stop this any more than I can…'

He moved up onto his elbows and she tried not to look at him, looked at his shoulder, which moved back and forth over her.

'Tell me…' he said.

She held on.

'Tell me how you feel…'

In a moment she would. In a moment she'd be sobbing

and begging in his arms. She lifted her hips, and then lifted them again, just so she could hurry him along.

'I'm going to come...' she moaned.

'Liar.'

He pushed deeper within her, hit that spot she would rather tonight he did not, for her face was burning, and her hands were roaming, and her hips were lifting with a life of their own as she let out a low, suppressed moan.

She felt a flood of warmth to her groin, felt the insistence of him inside her, the demand that she match his want.

'You couldn't pay for this...' He was stroking her deep inside and seducing her with his words. 'You could never fake this...'

He slipped into Spanish as she left the planet; he toppled onto her and bucked rapidly inside her as she sobbed out her orgasm. She didn't know where she started or ended, didn't know how to handle the love in her heart and the child in her belly. All belonged to the man holding her in his arms.

'You want me just as much as I want you.'

'So?' She stared back at him. 'What does that prove? That you're good in bed?' She turned away from him and curled up like a ball. 'I think you already knew that.'

'It proves that I am right to trust you. That it is nothing to do with contracts or money. That you *do* love me as much as I love you.'

'You don't know me, though.' She started to cry. 'I've been lying all along.'

'I know you far more than you think,' Raúl said.

'You don't. Your father was right. I like churches and reading...'

'I know that.'

'And I hate clubs.'

'I know that too.'

'I'm nothing like the woman you thought you met.'

'Do you not think I'd long ago worked that out?' Raúl kissed her cheek. 'My virgin hooker.'

He heard her gurgle of laughter, born from exhausted tears.

'I don't get how you're the one with no morals, yet I'm the one who's lied.'

'Because you're complicated,' Raúl said. 'Because you're female.' He kissed her mouth. 'Because you loved me from the start.'

She went to object, but he was telling the truth.

'Do you know when I fell in love with you?' Raúl said. 'When I saw you in those tatty pyjamas and I did not want you in Gordon's bed. It had nothing to do with me paying you. I deserved that slap, but you really did misinterpret my words.'

She was so scared to love him, so scared to tell him about the baby. But if they were to survive, if they were to start to trust, then she had to. It never entered her head that he already knew.

'When were you going to tell me you're pregnant, Estelle?'

She felt his hand move to her stomach, felt his kiss on the back of her neck. All she could be was honest now. 'When I was too pregnant to fly.'

'So the baby would be English?'

'Yes.'

'And you would support it how?'

'The same way that billions of non-billionaires do.'

'Would you have told me?'

'Yes.' She needed the truth from him now and she turned in his arms. 'Are you still here because of the baby?'

'No,' Raúl said. 'I am here because of you.'

She knew he was telling her the truth—not just because he always did, but because of what he said.

'I have had three hellish nights in my life. The first I struggle to speak about, but with you I am starting to. The second was the night after I'd found out about my brother and you were there. I went to bed not thinking about revenge or hate, but about a kiss that went too far and a slap to my cheek. I guess I loved you then, but it felt safer not to admit that.'

'And the third?'

'Finding myself in a nightmare—but not the one I am used to,' Raúl said. 'I was not in a car calling out to my mother. I was not begging her to slow down, and nor was I pleading with her to wake...'

Tears filled her eyes as she imagined it, but she held onto them, knew she would only ever get glimpses of that time and she must piece them together in the quiet of her mind.

'Instead I realised, again, that a woman I loved was gone because of my harsh actions and words. Worse, though. This time it *was* my fault.'

She heard him forgive what his five-year-old self had said as the past was looked at through more mature eyes.

'I went to Angela. She was always the one I went to when I messed up, and I had messed up again. I asked her what to do. I was already on my way to you. It was then that she told me that at least my father had known about the baby... It would seem I was the last to know.'

'I never told her.'

'I'm glad that she guessed. She told my father that morning. I'm glad that he knew, even if I did not.' He looked at her and smiled. 'Opposites attract, Estelle.' He kissed her nose. 'It's law. You can't argue with that.'

'I'm not arguing.'

'Did you hate every dance?' he asked.

She shook her head. 'Of course not.'

'We'll have to get babysitters when we want to go out soon.'

He blew out a breath at the thought of the changes that were to come and she saw that he was smiling.

'Who'd have thought?'

'Not me,' Estelle admitted.

'So, how do you tell your wife you want to marry her all over again?'

'We don't need to get married again,' Estelle said. 'Though a second honeymoon might be nice.'

'Where?'

He was going to make her say it.

'Where?'

'On the yacht.'

Yes, she could get used to that—especially when he made love to her all over again. Especially when he made her laugh about the maid's secret swapping of his DVDs.

No, he had never lied. But he'd never been more honest—and it felt so good.

'Do you think your family will notice a change in us?'

'No.' Estelle smiled. 'They think we met and fell head over heels in love.'

'They were right.' Raúl pulled her to him and then kissed her again. 'We were the only ones who couldn't quite believe it.'

EPILOGUE

IT WAS A beautiful wedding, held on the yacht, which had dropped anchor in Acantilados de Maro-Cerro.

It was Raúl's wedding gift to Gordon for bringing Estelle to him.

The grooms wore white and, contrary to Spanish tradition, there *were* speeches.

'I never thought I'd be standing declaring my love amongst my closest family and friends…' Gordon smiled, and then the dancing started.

Estelle leant against Raúl, feeling the kicks of their baby inside her.

'Is that Gordon's son Ginny is dancing with?' Estelle asked.

'They've been going out for a while.'

'Really?' Estelle smothered a smile. Raúl noticed everything. 'Gordon was once married before—ages ago, apparently.'

'How will they say they met? She can hardly admit she was his father's…' He stopped as Estelle dug him in the ribs. 'Sorry,' Raúl said. 'Sometimes I forget your other life.'

She didn't laugh this time, because the feeling was starting again—like a tight belt pulling around her stomach.

'Do you remember when we stopped here?' Raúl asked.

'When we took out a jet ski and you were scared and trying not to show it.'

'Of course I do.' Estelle attempted to answer normally. 'And I remember when we went snorkeling, and I—'

'Estelle?' He heard her voice break off mid-sentence.

Estelle had been trying to ignore the tightenings, but this one she could not ignore. Raúl's hand moved to her stomach, felt it taut and hard beneath his hands.

'I'll organise a speedboat to take us back to Marbella.'

'It might be ages yet. I don't want to make a fuss.'

'I think it would be a bit more awkward for Gordon if you have the baby here.' He glanced around at the guests and then went to have a word with Alberto, who soon organised transport.

'We are going to head off,' Raúl said when Gordon cornered them. 'Estelle is tired…' But then he couldn't lie—because Estelle was bent over.

'Oh, my!' Gordon was beaming.

'Please,' Estelle begged. 'I don't want everyone to know.'

There was no chance of keeping it quiet as she was helped down to the swimming platform, from where she was guided onto a speedboat. They sped off to the cheers and whistles of the wedding party.

'I wanted to have it in England…'

'I know.' They were supposed to have been flying there the next morning. 'But you wanted to be at the wedding too,' he reminded her.

'I know.'

'You can't have everything,' he teased. 'That's only me.'

She groaned with another pain and buried her face in his neck, wondering how much worse the pains would get, grateful that Raúl was so calm.

He *was* calm—he had everything he wanted right here on this small boat.

He looked up at the cliffs. He had long ago let go of that night, but there was a brief moment of memory just then. It didn't panic him. For a minute he thought of his mother and prayed for her peace.

It was the longest night, and her labour went on well into the next day.

Estelle pushed and dug her nails into his arms, and just when she was sure she could not go on any longer, finally the end was in sight.

'No empujen!'

'Don't push,' Raúl translated.

He had been incredibly composed throughout, but he was starting to worry now, watching the black hair of his infant and realising that soon he would be a father for real.

And then he saw her.

Red, angry, with black hair and fat cheeks.

And as he held her he was more than willing to be completely responsible for this little heart.

The midwife asked if they had a name as she went to write on the wristband and he looked at Estelle. They had chosen a few names, but had opted to wait till the baby was here before they decided. There was one name that had not been suggested till now.

'Gabriella?' Estelle said, and he nodded, unable to speak for a moment. The name that had once meant so much pain was wrapped now in love, and his mother's name would go on.

'Gabriella Sanchez Connolly,' Raúl said.

'She needs a middle name,' Estelle said.

'What about your mother's?' Raúl said, but Estelle already had her mother's name, and thanks to Spanish tradition Connolly was there, too.

Together they held and gazed at their very new daughter, quietly deciding what her full name would be.

'I want to ring Andrew and tell him he's an uncle,' Estelle said, her eyes filling with selfish tears—because though she could not be happier still she wanted to share the news. She wanted her brother to see Gabriella, as she had held Cecelia the day she was born.

'Why would you ring?' Raúl asked. 'They are waiting outside. I will go and bring them in now.'

Raúl stepped out into the waiting room.

His eyes were bloodshot, his hair unkempt, he was unshaven and there was lipstick on his collar—only this time Angela was smiling.

'It's a girl,' Raúl said. 'Both are doing really well,' he said.

Amanda burst into tears and Andrew shook his hand.

'Baby!' Cecelia said, pointing to her little cousin as Estelle showed off the newest arrival to the Connolly clan and thought that Raúl had somehow made an already perfect day even better.

'Come and see,' Raúl said to Angela, who was standing back at the door.

'She's beautiful.' Angela looked down and smiled at the chubby cheeks, seeing the eyes of Luka and Raúl. 'Just perfect—does she have a name?'

'Gabriella,' Raúl said, and looked at the woman who had been like a mother to him, even if it had been from a distance. 'Gabriella Angela Sanchez Connolly.'

Yes, Spanish names could be complicated at times, but they were very simple too.

It was a perfect day, and later came a blissful night, with

Estelle sharing a drink of champagne with her family till Cecelia was drooping in Andrew's arms.

'We're going to get back to the hotel,' Andrew said, looking down at Gabriella. He gave Estelle's hand a squeeze. 'Mum and Dad would have been really proud.'

'I know.'

And then it was just the two of them, lying in bed together, on their first night with Gabriella here.

'There is a text from Luka.' Raúl gave a brief eye-roll as he read the message. 'I have a feeling Angela may have hijacked his phone and typed it.' Raúl's voice was wry. Things were still terribly strained with Luka, but Raúl, very new to being a brother, was trying to work through it.

Not that Luka wanted to.

'You'll get there,' said Estelle.

'Perhaps,' Raúl said.

'Thank you for today.'

Gabriella, who was snuggled up in her cot beside them, made a small noise, and Raúl thought his heart might burst with pride and love as he gazed at his sleeping daughter.

'Thank *you*,' he said. 'I never thought I could feel so much happiness.'

'I meant for bringing my family over. It means so much to me to have them here.'

'I know it does.' He turned his gaze from his daughter to his wife. 'I know, thanks to you, the importance of family—even a difficult one.' He kissed her tired mouth. 'And no matter what happens I am never going to forget it.'

* * * * *

Lilly squared her shoulders and pulled in a deep breath as Riccardo stopped in front of them. He leaned down and brushed a kiss against her cheek.

"Late and wearing pink. One would think you're deliberately trying to antagonize me, Lilly."

Her pulse sped into overdrive. "Maybe I'm celebrating my new-found freedom."

"Ah, but you don't have it yet," he countered, moving his lips to the other cheek. "And you aren't putting me in the kind of mood to grant it to you."

Lilly was aware of the eyes on them as he pulled back and stung her face with a reprimanding look that made her feel like a fifth-grader. "Don't play games with me, Riccardo," she said quietly. "I will turn around and walk out of here so fast you won't know what hit you."

His dark eyes glinted and his mouth tipped up at the corners. "You've already done that, *tesoro*, and now you're back."

Jennifer Hayward has been a fan of romance and adventure since filching her sister's Harlequin® Presents novels to escape her teenage angst.

Jennifer penned her first romance at nineteen. When it was rejected, she bristled at her mother's suggestion that she needed more life experience. She went on to complete a journalism degree, before settling into a career in public relations. Years of working alongside powerful, charismatic CEOs and travelling the world provided perfect fodder for creating the arrogant alpha males she loves to write about.

A suitable amount of life experience under her belt, she sat down and conjured up the sexiest, most delicious Italian wine magnate she could imagine, had him make his biggest mistake and gave him a wife on the run. That story, THE DIVORCE PARTY, won her Harlequin's *So You Think You Can Write* contest and a book contract. Turns out Mother knew best.

A native of Canada's gorgeous east coast, Jennifer now lives in Toronto with her Viking husband and their young Viking-in-training. She considers the meetings of her ten-year-old book club, comprising some of the most amazing women she's ever met, as sacrosanct dates in her calendar. And some day they will have their monthly meeting at her fantasy beach house, waves lapping at their feet, wine glasses in hand.

You can find Jennifer on Facebook and Twitter.

This is Jennifer's stunning debut,
we hope you love it as much as we do!

Did you know these are also available as eBooks?
Visit www.millsandboon.co.uk

THE DIVORCE PARTY

BY
JENNIFER HAYWARD

MILLS & BOON

First published in Great Britain 2013
by Mills & Boon, an imprint of Harlequin (UK) Limited.
Harlequin (UK) Limited, Eton House, 18-24 Paradise Road,
Richmond, Surrey TW9 1SR

ISBN: 978 0 263 90705 6

Harlequin (UK) policy is to use papers that are natural, renewable and recyclable products and made from wood grown in sustainable forests. The logging and manufacturing process conform to the legal environmental regulations of the country of origin.

Printed and bound in Spain
by Blackprint CPI, Barcelona

Dear Reader

This story begins on a cold winter day with a cup of coffee, a newspaper and a real-life party that sparked a tale that just had to be told.

On the front page of my newspaper that morning was the story of a lavish divorce party a Manhattan billionaire was throwing to celebrate the end of his three-year marriage. The embossed invitations, the incredibly civilized approach to the end of a union due to irreconcilable differences fascinated me. What would bring a couple to this point? Why would anyone want to end their marriage in front of family and friends?

I started to wonder—what if the billionaire didn't really want a divorce? What if what he really wanted was his wife back and this was the only way he could get her in the same room with him? What if they were madly in love but the very act of being together destroyed them? Could this marriage ever be saved?

My billionare became sexy Italian wine magnate, Riccardo De Campo, and his feisty, on-the-run wife, Lilly.

I've dreamed of writing romances for as long as I can remember, but the story of Riccardo and Lilly's tempestuous relationship was special. It got me out of bed one night to write the first chapter while I was knee-deep in another book and wouldn't let me go until I'd written 'the end.'

I entered Riccardo and Lilly's story, *The Divorce Party*, in Harlequin's 2012 *So You Think You Can Write* contest, hoping others would love it as much as I did. Never dreaming the De Campos would capture the imagination of so many people and win me the publishing contract I've always wanted. Every minute of that journey was magical.

I've had a hard time letting Riccardo and Lilly go. I hope you do, too.

Enjoy!

Jennifer

I'd love to hear from you! I can be reached at www.jenniferhaywardromance.com.
or on Twitter: @jenhayward_

For my husband, Johan,
who gave me the chance to fly.

And Sharon Kendrick, Connie Flynn and Linda Style
for being the most amazing mentors a writer could have.

CHAPTER ONE

IT WAS GOING to be bad.

Lilly Anderson winced and put a hand to her pounding head. If she held herself in just that position, with the pressure building in her head like the vicious storms that picked up intensity across the plains of the midwest, it might not become a full-on migraine.

Might not.

Except staying in the dim confines of Riccardo's Rolls-Royce, driven by his long-time driver Tony, wasn't an option tonight. She was late for her own divorce party. Excessively late for the one thing that would give her what she wanted above all else. Her freedom from her husband.

"Oh, my God."

Her twin sister Alex made a sound low in her throat. "How can they print this stuff?"

"What?"

"Nothing."

"Alex, read it to me."

"It's Jay Kaiken's column. You don't want me to."

"Read it."

"Okay, but I warned you." She cleared her throat. "In what's expected to be the most scandalous, juiciest, talked-about water cooler event of the season, billionaire wine magnate Riccardo De Campo and former Iowa farmgirl-turned-sports-physiotherapist Lilly De Campo host their divorce party tonight. I once suggested they were the only passionately in love couple left in New York. But apparently even that fairytale doesn't actually exist. Rumors of heartthrob Riccardo's infidelity surfaced and this once solid marriage ended up in the toilet. So it's with mixed feelings that I bid this partnership adieu tonight. I have the invite and will bring you all the salacious details."

She crumpled up the tabloid and threw it on the floor. "He's such an SOB."

Lilly closed her eyes, a fresh wave of nausea rolling over her. No matter how many times she'd envisioned this moment, this freedom from Riccardo, she had never envisioned this. Nor the insanely mixed feelings she had right about now.

"Sorry, Lil. I shouldn't have started on those."

"You're a PR person, Alex. You're addicted."

"Still, I suck. I'm really sorry."

Lilly smoothed her fuchsia silk dress over her knees. It was elegant enough—and in Riccardo's most hated color, which was an added bonus—but it felt as if it was clinging in all the wrong places. A glance in the mirror before they'd left had told her she was paper-white, with dark bags under her hazel eyes. Haunted. In fact the only thing that *was* right was her hair, blowdried to glossy, straight perfection by her savior of a stylist.

It was a problem—this not feeling together. She felt she was already at a disadvantage. Facing Riccardo without her mask, without all her defences in place, was never a good way to start.

"You look a little too good," Alex murmured. "I think you should have put something frumpier on. And maybe messed your hair up a bit."

Lilly took the compliment and felt a bit better. Her sister was, if nothing else, the bluntest person she'd ever met. "Now, why would I do that?"

"Because Riccardo is like a banned substance for you,"

her sister said drily. "And your marriage almost destroyed you. Be ugly, Lilly, it's the easiest way."

Lilly smiled, then winced as her head did another inside-out throb. "He's finally agreed to give me the divorce. You should be doing a happy dance."

"If I thought he was giving in I might be. Has he given you the papers yet?"

"I'm hoping he'll do that tonight."

Alex scowled. "It's not like him to do this. He's up to something."

Her heart dropped about a thousand feet. "Maybe he's decided it's time to replace me."

"One can only hope."

A stab of pain lanced through her. She should be elated Riccardo had finally seen the light. Seen that there was no way they could ever reconcile after everything that had happened. So why had his decree that they finally end this with an official public announcement hit her with the force of an eighteen-wheeler? She certainly hadn't been pining away the past twelve months, hoping his refusal to divorce her meant he still loved her. And there was no way she'd harbored any silly notions that he was going to come climbing through her window and carry her back home, like in some Hollywood movie, with a promise to do everything differently.

That would have been stupid and naive.

She squared her shoulders. He likely did have another prospect in mind. Everything Riccardo did was a means to an end.

"If I ever want to be free to pursue a real relationship with Harry I need Riccardo's signature on that piece of paper."

"Oh, come on, Lil." Her sister's beautiful face twisted in a grimace. "Harry Taylor might be a decorated cardiothoracic surgeon, Doctors Without Borders and all that lovely stuff, but *really?* He's dull as dishwater. You might as well marry him and move back to Mason Hill."

"He's also handsome, smart and sweet," Lilly defended tartly, not needing to tell her sister there wasn't a hope in hell of her moving back to the miserable existence they'd escaped at eighteen. "I'm lucky to have him."

Alex waved a hand at her. "You can't tell me after Riccardo he doesn't seem like some watered-down version—like grape juice instead of Cabernet."

"You just told me Riccardo was bad news for me."

"So is Harry Taylor. He'll bore you to death."

Lilly had to steel herself not to laugh out loud, because that just would have hurt too much. "I'm through with men who make my heart pound and my palms go sweaty. It's self-destructive for me."

"The particular one you picked might have been… What time were we supposed to have been there, by the way?"

Lilly checked her watch. "A half-hour ago."

Alex gave her a wicked smile. "Riccardo's going to love that."

She squirmed in her seat. She was always late. No matter how hard she tried. Because it was just in her nature to try and squeeze too much into the day, and also because her multi-million-dollar athletes kept waltzing in half an hour late. But Riccardo had never seemed to care what the reason was. He wanted what he wanted when he wanted it. And that was all.

Alex's expression shifted. "I talked to David today."

Lilly froze. Alex talking to their brother back in Iowa only meant one thing. "How's Lisbeth?"

Alex frowned. "He said she had a really bad week. The doctor is saying she needs that experimental treatment within the next few months if it's going to do any good."

Dammit. Lilly twisted her hands together in her lap, feeling that familiar blanket of hopelessness settle over her. Her youngest sister Lisbeth had leukemia. She'd been told three months ago she was out of remission, and her doctor was advocating a ground-breaking new treatment as the one thing that might give her a fighting chance. But the treatment cost a fortune.

"I can't ask Riccardo for the money, Alex. I know it's crazy, but I can't give him that kind of power over me."

"I know." Alex put her hand over hers and squeezed. "We'll figure it out. There has to be a way."

Lilly pursed her lips. "I'm going to go back to the bank tomorrow. Maybe they'll let me do it in installments."

There had to be a way. Lisbeth *had* to get that treatment. Tonight, however, she had to focus on survival.

Her hands shook in her lap and her head throbbed like a jackhammer as they turned down a leafy, prestigious street toward the De Campo townhouse. She had taken one look at the beautiful old limestone mansion and fallen in love. Riccardo had taken one look at her face and bought it for her. "You love it," he'd said, not even blinking at the thirty-five-million-dollar price tag. "We'll buy it."

They swung to a halt in front of the home she'd run out of with only a suitcase twelve months ago, when she'd finally had the guts to leave him. It was the first time she'd been back and it occurred to her she was truly crazy making that time tonight. Divorce parties might be in vogue, but did she really want to detonate her and Riccardo's relationship in front of all the people who'd made her life miserable?

She didn't have a choice. She scooted over as Tony came around to open the door. Riccardo had been adamant. *"We need to end this standoff,"* he'd said. *"We need to make the state of our relationship official. Be there, Lilly, or this isn't happening."*

She forced herself to grasp Tony's hand. But her legs didn't seem to recognize the need to function as she stepped out of the car on trembling limbs that wanted to cave beneath her. The long, snakelike line of limousines made her suck in a breath. The memory of Riccardo sweeping her out of this car the night of their first anniversary and carrying her upstairs made it catch in her throat. He had made love to her with an intensity that night that had promised he would love her forever.

The images of the beginning and the end collided together in an almost blinding reminder of how quickly things could turn bad.

How hearts could be shattered.

"We can still turn around," her sister said quietly, coming to stand by her side. "If Riccardo really wants this divorce he'll come to you."

No, he wouldn't. Lilly shook her head. "I need to do this."

Do this and you won't ever have to live in a world you don't belong in again.

She walked woodenly up the front path alongside Alex. A dark-haired young man in a catering uniform opened the door and ushered them inside.

"How weird to have someone invite you into your own home," Alex whispered.

"It's not my home anymore."

But everything about it was. She couldn't help but stare up at the one-of-a-kind Italian cut-glass chandelier that was the centerpiece of the entryway. She and Riccardo had chosen it together on their honeymoon in the little town of Murano, famous for its glass. They had hand-picked a crystal to have their initials carved into, which had been placed on the bottom row. Riccardo had insisted on adding two entwined hearts beside their initials.

"It symbolizes us," he'd said. "We're no longer two separate people—we are one."

She lurched on her high heels, feeling whatever composure she'd had disintegrate. The urge to run far away from here as fast as she could was so overwhelming she could barely keep her feet planted on the floor.

"Lilly…" Alex murmured worriedly, her gaze on her face.

"I'm okay." She forced herself to smile at the young man offering to show them up the staircase to the ballroom. "We know the way."

She climbed the gleaming wooden staircase alongside Alex, her heartbeat accelerating with every step she took. By the time they'd reached the top of the stairs and turned toward the glimmering ballroom it was in her mouth.

You can do this. You've done this hundreds of times before.

Except Riccardo had been by her side then. A rock in a world that had never been hers. And tonight was the beginning of LAR—Life After Riccardo.

She paused at the entrance, taking in the glittering colors and jewels of the beautifully dressed crowd, set off by the muted glow of a dozen priceless antique chandeliers that dated back to the English Regency period. A jazz band played in the corner of the room, but the buzz of a hundred conversations rose above it.

Her back stiffened. She hated jazz. Was Riccardo trying to make a statement? To illustrate to her how he'd moved on?

Alex grabbed her arm and propelled her forward. "You need a drink."

Or ten, Lilly thought grimly as dozens of curious gazes turned on them and a buzz ran through the crowd. She switched herself on to autopilot—the only way she knew how to function in a situation like this—and started walking.

She lifted her chin when she saw Jay Kaiken and kept walking. As they moved toward the bar at the back of the room the strangest thing happened. Like the parting of the Red Sea, the crowd moved aside, dividing down the center of the room. On her left she recognized friends and acquaintances who had chosen to keep in touch with her rather than Riccardo after their separation. On her right she saw Riccardo's business associates, his brother, cousins and political contacts.

"It's like our wedding all over again," she breathed, remembering how she'd walked into that beautiful old Catholic cathedral on the Upper East Side to find her family and friends on one side—the neatly dressed, less-than-glamorous Iowa farm contingent alongside her girlfriends and schoolmates—and Riccardo's much larger, understatedly elegant clan on the other—all ancient bloodlines and aristocratic heritage.

As if their marriage was to be divided from the beginning.

Maybe that should have been her first clue.

She held her head high and kept walking. A tingle went down her spine. Her skin went cold. Riccardo was in the room. Watching her. She could feel it.

Turning her head, she found him—like a homing pigeon seeking its target. He looked furious. Seething. She swallowed hard, a flock of butterflies racing through her stomach. Riccardo spoke four languages—English, Spanish, German and his native Italian. But he did not have to utter a single word from those sensuous, dangerous lips for her to understand the emotion radiating from his eyes.

Hell. She touched her face in a nervous gesture that drew his gaze. Only Riccardo had ever been able to pull off that passionate intensity while still calling himself a twentieth-century man.

"Don't let him intimidate you," Alex murmured. "This is your divorce party, remember? Own it."

Easier in theory than in practice. Particularly so when Riccardo relieved a waiter of two glasses of champagne and strode toward them, with a look of intent on his face that shook her to her core. She absorbed this new Riccardo. He looked as indecently gorgeous as ever in a black tux that set off his dark good looks. But it was the hard edge to him that was different. The strongly carved lines of his face seemed to have deepened, harshened. He'd shaved off the thick, dark waves that had used to fall over his forehead in favor of a short buzz cut that made him look tougher, even more dangerously attractive if that was possible. And the ruthless expession on his face, the glitter in those dark eyes, had never been used on her quite like that before.

Her tongue cleaved to the roof of her mouth, her pulse picking up into a rapid, insistent rhythm that had her nails digging into her palms. Why, after everything they'd gone through, was he still the only man who could simply look at her and make her shake in her shoes?

Alex nudged her. "Dangerous controlled substance, remember?"

Lilly squared her shoulders and pulled in a deep breath as Riccardo stopped in front of them. He leaned down and brushed a kiss against her cheek. "Late and wearing pink. One would think you're deliberately trying to antagonize me, Lilly."

Her pulse sped into overdrive. "Maybe I'm celebrating my new-found freedom."

"Ah, but you don't have it yet," he countered, moving his lips to the other cheek. "And you aren't putting me in the kind of mood to grant it to you."

Lilly was aware of all the eyes on them as he pulled back and stung her face with a reprimanding look that made her feel like a fifth-grader. "Don't play games with me, Riccardo," she said quietly. "I will turn around and walk out of here so fast you won't know what hit you."

His dark eyes glinted. His mouth tipped up at the corners. "You've already done that, *tesoro,* and now you're back."

Something exploded in her head. She was about to tell him exactly what she thought of his ultimatum, but he was bending down and kissing Alex.

"*Buonasera.* I trust you're well?"

"Never better," Alex muttered.

"Do you think I might have a word with my wife alone?"

Wife. He'd said the word with such supreme confidence—a statement of fact that hung on the air between them like a challenge. A tremor went down Lilly's spine.

"Whatever you have to say you can say it in front of my sister."

"Not *this.*" His gaze bored into hers. "Unless you want every gossip columnist in New York reporting on our conversation, I suggest we do it in private."

Considering it was only in the last few months Lilly's name had finally *disappeared* from those columns, she conceded that might be a good idea. "Fine."

Riccardo turned to Alex. "Gabe is getting you a drink at the bar."

Alex rolled her eyes. "Determined to force a confrontation between all the members of the De Campo and Anderson families tonight?"

"You're only antagonistic toward the people who evoke strong emotions in you," Riccardo taunted. "Try not to rip him in two, will you?"

"You think that's a good idea?" Lilly murmured, more to distract herself from the warm pressure of Riccardo's big hand splayed against her back as he directed her from the room than out of concern for her sister, who could hold her own.

"They love baiting each other. It'll be the highlight of their evening."

She struggled to keep up with his long strides as he walked her up the stairs to the third floor, where the bedrooms were, nodding at the security guard stationed there. "Why are we coming up here?" she murmured, flushing at the guard's interested gaze. "Why don't we just talk in your study?"

He kept walking past the guest bedrooms toward the

master suite. "I won't risk being overheard. We'll talk on the patio off our bedroom."

"*Your* bedroom," Lilly corrected. "And I don't think—"

"*Basta,* Lilly." He glared at her. "I'm your husband, not some guy trying to come on to you."

Lilly clamped her mouth shut and followed him through the double doors of the master suite. She would not, whatever she did, look at the huge canopy bed they had shared. The scene of more erotically charged encounters than she cared to remember.

Their marriage bed. The place where she and Riccardo had always been able to communicate.

He pushed open the French doors to the large patio. The rose bushes he'd had planted for her along the edge had already started to bloom, emitting the gorgeous perfume she'd always loved.

Ugh. She shoved her sentimentality down with a determined effort and spun to face him.

"So?" she prompted, hostility edging her words. "What is it you have to say?"

His gaze darkened. "You're not too big for me to put you over my knee, *tesoro.* Push me a little harder and I will."

Lilly's cheeks burned at that very seductive image. To her horror, her mind took her there—took her to a vision of Riccardo holding her over his muscular thighs, her naked behind squirming as he brought his hand down in a stinging reprimand.

Dear God.

A satisfied expression crossed his face. "Unnerving, isn't it, that we only have to speak to each other in a certain way and that happens?"

"*Damn you,* Riccardo." She planted her feet wide and faced him head-on. "For over a year I've been trying to get you to give me a divorce and you've flatly denied it. Then you call me out of the blue with this crazy idea of making it official with a party, and now you're playing cat and mouse with me. What the hell are you playing at?"

He crossed his arms over his chest and leaned back against the railing. "Maybe if you'd agreed to see me I wouldn't have resorted to this."

"Nothing good ever comes of us being together. You know that."

His eyes glimmered as they swept over her. "That's a big fat lie and you know it."

She wrapped her arms around herself. "Sex is not a good basis for a marriage."

"We had more than sex, Lilly." His deep voice softened, taking on those velvet undertones that could make her melt in a nanosecond. "We had way, way more than that."

"It wasn't enough! Do you know how happy I've been this past year?"

He paled beneath his deep tan. "*We* were happy once."

She hugged her arms tighter around herself and fought the ache in her chest that threatened to consume her. "We're better off apart and you know it."

"I will never agree to that."

She lifted her chin. "I want a divorce. And if you won't give it to me I'll have my lawyer fight you until you do."

His mouth flattened. "I will drag it out for years."

"Why?" She pushed her hair out of her face and gave him a desperate look. "We're done. We've hurt each other enough for a lifetime. We need to move on with our lives."

He jammed his hands into his pockets. The fierce, fighting expression in his eyes was one she knew all too well. But he said nothing. Silence sceamed between them until she thought she'd jump out of her skin.

"All right."

She stared at him. "All right what?"

"I will give you the divorce. On one condition."

She knew she should leave now—get the hell out of here as fast as she could. But she couldn't force her feet to move.

"I need you to remain my wife for six more months."

Her jaw dropped open. "Wh-what?"

"My father feels I need to present a more grounded image to the board before they make their decision on a CEO." He lifted his shoulders and twisted his lips in a cynical smile. "They apparently still haven't bought my reformed image."

Lilly came crashing back to earth with the force of a meteorite bent on destruction. Any illusions she'd harbored—and she realized now she *had* harbored a few— about Riccardo not wanting to divorce her because he still loved her vanished at the point of impact. Something hot and bright burned the back of her eyes.

"That's ridiculous," she managed huskily. "You left racing three years ago."

He shrugged. "It is what it is. I can't change their perception."

Lilly almost choked on the irony of it. Everything Riccardo had ever done when they were together had been to dispel the image of himself as a reckless young racecar driver who hadn't been committed to the family business.

She shook her head. "Our *marriage* fell apart because of your obsession with your job. Your single-minded fixation on becoming CEO."

"One of any number of issues our marriage had," he corrected grimly. "Be that as it may, my father wants us back togther. He thinks the media coverage will go a long way toward stabilizing my image with the board, and he's made it a condition in my having his support."

His father wanted her back in his life? She'd always believed Antonio De Campo had thought her far beneath his son, with her poor upbringing, but he had been too polite to say it.

"My father thinks you're a good influence on me." He gave a wry half-smile that softened those newly hardened features of his. "He's quite likely right about that."

"This is crazy." Lilly shook her head and paced to the opposite end of the patio. "We aren't even *capable* of pretending we're a happily married couple."

"You have a short memory, Lilly."

His soft reprimand drew her gaze to his face.

"Six months. That's all I'm asking."

"I want a divorce," she repeated, raising her voice as this insane conversation kept plowing forward. "What makes you think I would ever consider helping you?"

He tilted his head to one side. "What are you afraid of? That we have way more unfinished business than you care to admit?"

She squared her shoulders. "We are over, Riccardo. And this is not a good idea."

"It's a great idea. Six months buys you your freedom."

"What other conditions has your father imposed?" she asked helplessly. "Are you to stop driving fast cars and dating international supermodels?"

He scowled. "Not one of those rumors are true. There's been no one since you."

She stiffened. "We all know there's truth to the tabloids."

"Not one, Lilly."

"*Riccardo,*" she said desperately. "No."

He stalked over, invading her space. "What is it, *tesoro?* Got plans with Harry Taylor?"

How did he know about Harry? They'd been so low-key as to be socially non-existent. "Yes," she snapped. "I'd like to move on, and maybe you should do the same."

He lifted his hand and took her chin in his fingers. "You forget we made a vow, *amore mio.* 'For richer and poorer, in sickness and in health…'"

"That was before you broke it."

A dangerous glimmer entered his eyes. "I never slept with Chelsea Tate. We've had this conversation."

"We are never going to agree on *that*," she bit out, throwing his words back at him. "Nor could we ever fake any real affection for each other. It would be laughable."

"Oh, but I think we could," he murmured, lowering his head to hers. "Even the thought of me spanking you turns you on."

She pulled out of his grip. "Riccardo—"

He slid a hand into her hair and brought her back. "You went there, Lilly. And so did I."

"No, I—"

He smothered her reply with a kiss Lilly felt down to her toes, deep and sensuous. He didn't bother with the pre-liminaries. He simply took—kissing her exactly the way he knew she liked it, using every weapon at his disposal. Lilly curled her fingers into his shirt, intending to push him away, but she didn't quite seem to be able to do it.

He pulled her closer, anchored her against him. "Ric—" she murmured as he changed angles and came back to her.

"Shut up, Lilly," he commanded, sliding his fingers up her bare arms and closing his mouth over hers.

This time his kiss was softer, more persuasive than con-trolling, pleasurable rather than punishing. And something fell apart inside her. It had been too long since he'd kissed her like this, too long since she'd been in his arms, and God help her…of all the things they had *not* been good at, it hadn't been this.

"Dammit." She grabbed a handful of shirt to steady herself. "This is not fair."

He slid a hand down over the curve of her hip and brought her body into full contact with his. The feel of his hard body against her made her shiver, remembering everything.

"Nothing was ever fair between us. It was like a wild rollercoaster ride we couldn't get enough of."

He shifted her between the hard muscles of his thighs and brought his mouth down on hers again with a look of pure intent. His rigid, pulsing arousal pressed against her, making Lilly ache all over.

No, an inner voice warned. But all that came out was a groan.

He dragged her even closer, a satisfied growl escaping his throat. "Open your mouth, Lil."

Caught up in the pure, hot sexual power he had over her, she obeyed. She didn't think about the one hundred and fifty people downstairs, or even what a huge mistake this was. She just wanted this kiss, this magic, the hot intimacy of his tongue tangling with hers.

Oh. She melted into him as her knees threatened to give way. It was like someone offering an alcoholic a double shot after months of abstinence. Pure hedonism. And she wrapped herself in it.

A flash of light exploded around them. She stumbled backward, disoriented, blinking into the bright light that kept coming and coming.

Riccardo cursed and pulled her away from the railing. "*Dio.* How did they get here?"

"A photographer?" Lilly asked dazedly.

He nodded.

She touched her fingers to her mouth, still burning from his kiss. Riccardo had security everywhere. It didn't make sense that a photographer would be able to get up here. "You planned that," she said flatly. "You set that up for your father's benefit."

"I set this party up for my father's benefit," he agreed darkly. "For the board's benefit. Not that photo."

She pressed her palms to her temples. She didn't want to be back here. She couldn't go on walking around like a half-alive person, going through the motions but never really feeling anything. She needed this divorce.

His face tightened. "What? Afraid the good doctor won't understand a six-month hiatus?"

She shook her head. "The answer is no. No, no and no."

He straighened his shirt and raked a hand through his hair. "We'll make the announcement at ten."

She turned her back on him and started for the door.

"I'll give you the house."

She stopped in her tracks.

"You've never wanted anything from me, but I know you love this house. I'll sign it over to you at the end of the six months."

Lilly opened her mouth to tell him where he could put his offer, but the words died in her mouth. The house would pay for Lisbeth's treatment. Fifty times over.

"Tempting, isn't it? Your dream house…without me in it?"

She counted to five before she turned around. As if any amount of money would be enough to convince her that revisitng their ruin of a marriage was worth it.

But she was desperate. And she didn't have the luxury of time.

She lifted her gaze to his. "I will think about it."

"Ten o'clock, Lilly." His smile didn't quite reach his eyes. "Think of yourself as Cinderella, only your deadline isn't midnight—it's ten. And I'm the devil you know."

CHAPTER TWO

LILLY SPENT THE intervening hours coming up with a million different reasons why she would be crazy to agree to Riccardo's proposal. He was once again using her in his single-minded pursuit of the De Campo CEO job. He didn't really want her—he wanted Lilly De Campo the figurehead, his perfect society wife who could smile and say intelligent things to the very intelligent people they met. And, dammit, her life was finally back on track! She had built up her practice, she had started to do the things she loved again, and she had a life.

Whether or not she was just going through the motions was irrelevant. She had been moving on.

Until that kiss tonight.

She touched her fingers to her mouth and tightness seized her chest. How could she kiss Riccardo like that when the same from Harry inspired only lukewarm affection?

"Which do you prefer, Lilly? Snakeskin or alligator?"

She gave the trendy young shoe designer who had cornered her and Alex a blank look. "Sorry?"

"I was asking if you prefer snakeskin or alligator... If I'd known you were doing this tonight I would have begged you to wear *my* shoes."

If *she'd* known she was doing this tonight she would be halfway across the Atlantic!

"Snakeskin, definitely," she murmured.

The other woman nodded and continued her relentless discussion of fashion.

She *would* be crazy to go back to Riccardo. But what choice did she have? The idea that the bank would lend her the money—more than she'd make in ten years of work—was laughable. Even in installments. Her parents were barely getting by on the farm, and although Alex had a great job with one of the city's top PR firms they would never, collectively, be able to scrape up that kind of money.

She had the power to help Lisbeth. Her stomach seemed to go into freefall at the thought of what that might entail. The question was, could she?

Alex gave her an *I need to talk to you* look and politely whisked her away from the designer. "People keep stealing you away," she hissed, dragging Lilly toward the windows. "What *did* he say to you?"

Lilly stared at her sister's flashing blue gaze—the only thing that differentiated them as twins. Her eyes were a mirror image of their sister Lisbeth's. And suddenly her guilt for never having been there for her younger sister made her next move crystal-clear.

She forced herself to smile. Riccardo had made it clear no one was to know about their deal. Not even family. There was too much of a chance for someone to say the wrong thing at the wrong time to the wrong person. The press would blow it wide open.

"We had a really good talk, Alex. I—"

The music stopped. She spun around to find Riccardo standing at the front of the room, his gaze trained on her. She swallowed hard as he nodded for her to join him.

Judgement time.

She steeled herself and raised a trembling hand to push her hair out of her face. "I'll explain afterward," she whispered to her sister. Then she walked to Riccardo's side.

Her presence there said everything.

A satisfied gleam lit her husband's eyes. He raised a hand to quiet the room. The elegantly dressed crowd fell silent as every eye moved to them and hushed anticipation blanketed the air. The first marriage in the history of the De Campo family to disintegrate. A golden couple at that.

She was distracted by a waitress, who presented a bottle for Riccardo's inspection. "The 1972 Chianti."

A 1972 Chianti? The same wine as on their wedding? Her gaze flew to her husband's, which was impaling hers with a burning darkness that seared her soul. He was really doing *this* to her?

What kind of a game was he playing?

The waitress passed each of them a glass of the ruby-red wine. Its deep, rich color was hypnotizing, reminding Lilly of the emotional blood the two of them had spilled. Her hands shook so much around the crystal she was terrified the wine was going to end up down the front of her dress.

Riccardo turned to face their guests, with a controlled, purposeful ease to his movements. "Lilly and I would like to thank you all for coming. You are our closest family, friends and acquaintances and we wanted you to be the first to share in our news."

He paused. The room grew so silent you could have heard a pin drop. Lilly's fingers tightened around the glass, her heart pounding in tandem with her head.

"Sometimes it takes a momentous occasion to bring true feelings to the surface." Riccardo returned his gaze to her face. "For Lilly and I, it took contemplating divorce to realize how much in love we still are."

A gasp rang out. Alex gaped at her from the front row, where she stood with Gabe.

Riccardo cast his gaze over the crowd. "Lilly and I are reconciling."

A shocked buzz filled the room—the sound of a hundred conversations starting at once. Flashbulbs exploded in her face. Hearing the words spoken out loud made her knees go weak. But she kept her gaze trained on her husband's and forced what might have passed for a smile to her lips.

Now her acting role began.

Riccardo tilted his glass toward her. "To new beginnings."

Lilly lifted the glass to her mouth and drank. Her lashes fluttered down over her cheeks as the heady, intoxicating flavor of the Chianti transported her back to the day when her life had seemed poised at the beginning of a rainbow that stretched forever.

The day she had married Riccardo.

And at that moment she knew her mistake for what it was. She had never been, and never would be, in control of her feelings for her husband. Six months wasn't just going to be self-destructive. There was going to be collateral damage.

Riccardo poured himself a two-finger measure of Scotch and sank down in the chair by the window, his gaze on his wife, who lay sleeping in their bed. She had swayed on her feet after the toast, her hands moving to her head in a warning sign that one of those migraines that had always terrified him was about to take her out. He was fairly sure she would have hit the deck had he not slid a subtle arm around her waist and hustled her from the room.

He had left Gabe in charge of winding up the evening and, although Alex had flatly refused to leave her sister, had overridden her and sent her home with his brother. There was still some of Lilly's migraine medication in their medicine cabinet and the key to these attacks, he knew, was to get it into her as soon as possible and put her to bed. Which he'd done—right after she'd been violently ill in their bathroom.

He took a sip of the smoky single malt blend and moved his gaze over her face. It was ghostly white and pinched even in sleep, and for a moment guilt rose up in him. He had dangled the one thing she loved more than anything else in front of her when he knew she wanted nothing to do with him. But then again, he thought, his lips twisting, she hadn't given him any warning when she'd walked out on him. When she'd called it quits on their marriage and left without even having the guts to face him.

A fury long dormant raged to life inside him, pulsing like an untamed beast. Who *did* that? Who took a perfectly good marriage with a few of the usual speed bumps and just quit? Who thought so little of what she had that it was easier to turn into an ice queen and refuse him than to talk it out?

The woman who'd turned into a stranger before his very eyes. The woman who'd taken a lover—a world-renowned cardiothoracic surgeon so highly decorated for his work that he made Riccardo look like the most heartless of corporate raiders. That was who.

His fingers tightened around the glass, drawing his gaze to the fiery amber liquid. No, he wouldn't feel any regret. His wife might have looked at him with those accusing, pain-soaked cat's eyes of hers and begged him to let her go home. But he was through giving her time and space to come to her senses. She was back in his bed, where she belonged, and she was staying there.

Not for six months.

For good.

He lifted the glass to his lips and let the Scotch burn a path down his throat. It had been that conversation he'd overheard that had set him off. Not his father's bullish suggestion that he repair his marriage in order to present the kind of image the De Campo board was looking for in a CEO.

The trash-talking locker room chatter he'd heard on his way out of the gym after a squash game with Gabe had amused him at first. There were things guys said in a locker room that were never repeated outside of them. He had smiled, remembering the crude conversations he and his fellow drivers had had after their races, when all the tension was gone, and then started packing up his stuff. But the conversation had turned to injuries and rehabilitation and he'd heard Lilly's name.

He'd pulled the zipper shut on his bag and had frozen in place as the three men he'd figured must be professional athletes from their height and brawn, went on.

"She's the best there is," one of them had said. "Fixed my bum leg in a month."

"Seriously hot," added one of the others. "I bet you'd like to have more than her hands on you."

He'd been halfway across the room before Gabe had intercepted him and shoved him bodily out the door.

"Not worth it," his brother had muttered. "She's your estranged wife, remember?"

But it had been too much. *Troppo.* It was time Lilly remembered who she was. Who she belonged to.

He skimmed his gaze over her still form. If anything, she had grown more beautiful since that day he'd bumped into her in that SoHo bar. She'd reminded him of a young colt, tripping over those long legs of hers, over *him,* as he'd stopped to put his wallet back in his pocket. She'd apologized, biting her lip in that trademark gesture of hers, and everything about her—her beautiful shoulder-length glossy brown hair, her big hazel eyes and her air of extreme innocence—had knocked him sideways. He wasn't used to women without artifice. And it had made him want to possess her like no other.

He hadn't let her leave the bar until he'd had her reluctantly given number. Then he'd pursued her, called her every day for a week, until she'd agreed to go out with him.

Finding out she was a virgin had been the end for him. He'd put a ring on her finger the week after.

She shifted restlessly onto her back and rubbed her hand against her face. Her vulnerability hit him like a punch to the chest. Lilly was different from any other woman he'd met. She hadn't been attracted to his power or money. In fact it had made her distinctly uncomfortable, given her poor upbringing. But he'd pushed his agenda through anyway, like the big, forceful bull of a man he was. Because that was what a De Campo did. Took what he wanted. Success at all costs.

Lilly fought her way out of the drug-induced fog that held her under, reaching desperately for the glass of water she kept on the nightstand. But her hand grasped only air, and this didn't feel like her bed. It felt bigger, softer, familiar and yet...

It was her old bed.

She bolted upright.

"Here—drink," a husky, fatigue-deepened male voice urged, pressing a glass to her lips.

A strong arm slid around her waist. She blinked and opened her eyes and stared straight into the worried dark-as-night gaze of her husband.

Oh, God. She was in bed with Riccardo.

She pushed the glass away and pulled, panicked, at the sheets.

"Lilly." He placed firm hands on her shoulders and held her down. "Drink for *God's* sake. Those pills are always rough on you."

She shook her head and reached for the side of the bed, but a series of wheezing coughs racked her body. She reached desperately for the glass and drank greedily. Her thirst quenched, she pushed the glass away. "What time is it?"

"One a.m."

A dull, deep throb at the front of her head made her sit back against the pillows. "I want to go home."

"You are home," he said quietly. "Stay in the bed, Lilly. You're in no shape to be going anywhere."

It was then that she realized he was still fully dressed. Hazy memories filled her head. Him holding her hair out of her face while she vomited. Him carrying her to bed. Her cheeks heated with mortification. *She needed to get out of here.*

"My home is my apartment." She swung her legs over the side of the bed, wincing as the movement made her head throb. *Her legs were bare.* And she was drowning in one of Riccardo's white T-shirts. "Did you *undress* me?" she demanded, flicking him an accusing look.

An amused glitter flashed in his eyes. "That's the way it's usually done, *tesoro,* but I stopped at the underwear. I prefer to dispense of that when you're fully conscious."

Her face felt as if it was on fire. She scanned the floor desperately for her things. "Give me my goddamned clothes, Riccardo."

His expression hardened. "Are you forgetting our deal? You live here now. You're mine for six months."

"*Tu sei pazzo,*" she spat at him. "I might have agreed to your crazy plan, but in no way, shape or form will your hands ever be on me again."

"*Tu sei pazzo?*" he murmured appreciatively. "I do believe your Italian's coming along. And, yes, I am crazy when it comes to you." He gently pushed against her shoulders and sent her back into the soft pillows. "Tomorrow we go over the ground rules. Tonight you rest."

"You are such a bully," she muttered wrathfully, too weak to defy him. "I have an early clinic tomorrow."

"I'll drive you there. You still have some clothes in the spare room you can wear."

He'd kept them? She'd left in such a hurry she'd taken only what would fit in a suitcase. Left all the beautiful gowns and jewelry behind.

"Yes, I kept them," he murmured, a bitter smile curving his lips. "Unlike you, I didn't give up on this marriage."

She closed her eyes. "You have no idea what you're talking about, Riccardo."

"Maybe you can enlighten me over the next six months, then. You never did grace me with an explanation."

Her gaze met his with blazing fury. "You never wanted to hear what I had to say."

The belligerent tilt of his chin matched hers. "Maybe now I do."

And maybe there was a blue-cheese moon out there tonight.

A jagged pain whizzed through her head. She winced and held a hand to her temple.

"*Hell*, Lilly," he bit out, waving a hand at her. "We're done arguing. Close your eyes and go to sleep."

She tried to fight it, but nature was having none of it. He tucked the covers up to her chin, then everything went black.

CHAPTER THREE

SEVEN HOURS OF sleep, one migraine-hangover-filled morning, three patients and one trip to the bank later, Lilly retreated to her office like a maimed fighter who'd escaped to her corner.

Coffee, she decided, setting her briefcase down. It was time to reintroduce the other banned substance in her life. Maybe it would help lift the paralysis that had gripped her since she'd woken up in her old bed this morning, dazed and confused at what had transpired.

She had agreed to become Mrs. Lilly De Campo again. The one thing she'd said she'd never do.

Worse, she'd let her husband see how deep her feelings ran. Distracted, she raised a hand to her hair and pushed it out of her face. The power Riccardo still held over her was disconcerting.

And *that* was the understatement of the year. She pressed her lips together, picked up her purse and let Katy, the receptionist at the small clinic she shared with another physiotherapist in SoHo, know she'd be in the café across the street. Scanning the menu board, she thought, *To hell with it,* and ordered the largest, creamiest latte they had, which would certainly knock her brain back into working order, and sat down to drink it in the window facing Broadway.

It helped. But with her escape hatch rapidly closing it was a case of avoiding the unavoidable. Her only alternative to accepting Riccardo's deal had been to secure the money at the bank. And she was pretty sure the bank manager would have laughed at her request if she hadn't officially reinstated her position as Mrs. Lilly De Campo by having it splashed across the morning papers.

She'd been getting to her feet when he'd given her a curious look and said, "Your husband is also a client, Mrs. De Campo. We'd be happy to draw up the papers with *him*."

She had given him a withering look. "No, thank you, Mr. Brooks. This is a personal matter."

He was an opportunist, she conceded, scraping the froth off the sides of her mug. Like almost everyone else in this city. Unfortunately Harry Taylor had also seen the news, if his multiple calls to her cell phone were any indication. A stomach-churning glance at her phone revealed she now had a message from him too. The latte seemed to curdle inside her. She'd been waiting, hoping there was some other solution that would allow her to call things off with Riccardo.

And who are you trying to fool? a voice inside her ridiculed. Their reconciliation was the subject of intense public speculation this morning. There was no getting out of it. And how could she when it was Lisbeth's only chance at survival?

She squirmed on the stool. What *was* she going to say to Harry? *I'm so sorry, Harry. I've gotten back together with the man who destroyed me?* Or, *I'm sorry for saying I wanted you when really I want my sexy, controlling somewhat ex-husband, who kissed me within an inch of my life last night and made me want more.*

Ugh. There was no good way to put it that wouldn't end up making her look like a horrible, horrible woman.

The café door chimed. She looked up to see the *other* person she was trying to avoid waltzing through the door.

"You really didn't think you could hide, did you?" Alex

asked grimly, tossing an order at the barista and plopping herself down on the stool beside her.

Lilly pushed her empty mug away. "I'm not avoiding you. I had a jam-packed morning."

Alex's eyebrows rose. "I'm your twin, remember? I can sense inner turmoil."

"I'm fine. Just a little groggy from the medication."

"Good." Her sister threw the words at her with a determined tilt of her chin. "So you can tell me what the hell's going on. Your autocratic husband ordered me out of the house before I could see if you'd actually lost your senses."

Lilly pulled in a breath. "It was like Riccardo said. It took a tough conversation for us to realize our feelings for each other."

Alex sat back in her chair and crossed her arms. "*Do not* try to spin me, Lilly. I know you too well. You walked in there last night intent on a divorce. What happened?"

"We talked...we came to some realizations..."

"Like what?" Alex waved her hand in the air. "Like the last hellish year of your marriage was just an apparition? Like he didn't almost annihilate you?"

"It takes two to tango," Lilly murmured. "Riccardo wasn't the only guilty party in our marriage."

"Only the majority holder." Her sister screwed up her face. "What about Harry? Last night you were telling me he's the one."

"I didn't say that. I said I wanted the opportunity to truly pursue things with him." She bit her lip, realizing how confused that sounded. *Dammit, she needed to make this believable. For Lisbeth's sake.*

"You know I've never really stopped loving Riccardo," she said quietly. And the fact that saying it didn't seem like too much of a stretch shook her to her core. "I want to give it another shot."

Alex's mouth tightened. "You left him to save yourself. And I for one don't relish being the one to pick up the pieces again when he reverts to being his domineering, controlling self."

"He's changed," Lilly lied.

"Men like him don't change. They come out of the womb like that."

Her mouth curved. "Probably true."

"What about his infidelity? Are you prepared to put up with that again?"

Everything around her faded, blurred into the series of carefully manufactured images she had created to keep herself in one piece. Control. Because to imagine Riccardo in bed with another woman—to imagine the man who'd promised to love her for life doing that to her—would damage her beyond repair.

"It won't happen again."

"How do you know?"

"Because he promised me."

In actual fact Riccardo had denied the whole thing. He'd put it down to the vicious money-making tactics of the tabloids. But Lilly had seen the photos. And photos didn't lie.

Her teeth clamped down on her bottom lip. The effort it took not to blurt out what was actually going on was immense. "You have to trust me," she forced out huskily. "I'm doing the right thing."

Her sister gave her a long, hard look. "You promise if things start to get bad you'll end it? You'll walk away?"

"I promise. And, Alex—this means we can get Lisbeth's treatment."

A light went on in her sister's cornflower-blue eyes. "Lilly Anderson, you promise me right now you are *not* doing this because of Lisbeth. I do *not* need two sisters in critical condition."

"I wouldn't do that," Lilly said firmly. "It's just a very wonderful outcome of this decision."

But she would. She would do anything it took to make Lisbeth well.

* * *

Riccardo came to pick her up at six. "You still don't look good," he said bluntly as she slid into his beast of a car.

She shrugged and pulled her seatbelt on. "You know what my migraines are like. It takes me a few days to get over one."

He put the car in gear and pulled out into traffic, the low-slung powerful machine reminding her of the man himself. Smooth, dangerous.

He flicked her a glance. "I'd forgotten just how bad they get."

She wondered if he'd done what she had. Used any method available to wipe her head clean of him—finding it impossible on so many levels.

Don't fool yourself, Lil. Riccardo wasn't the type to pine for anyone. Especially the woman who'd walked out on him.

Which begged the question: why hadn't he had other women over the past year? If she was to believe the highly sexed man she'd married was capable of celibacy, the question was why had he chosen it? Riccardo loved women. He lived for the contrast. Hard versus soft. Rational versus emotional. And with his superstar racing background they were like a feast that had been put on this earth for him to enjoy in endless supply.

She had fooled herself that she could be the only one for him.

She twisted her hands together in her lap and stared sightlessly out the window. They drove in a tense silence until he passed her street.

"What about my apartment? I need to get my stuff."

"I sent Mrs. Collins over to pick it up."

Her jaw dropped. He'd had Magda go through her stuff? Sift through the very fiber of her personal life?

"Stop the car."

He frowned over at her. "Lilly, it was—"

"Stop the car."

He swore under his breath and pulled to the curb. "It was the efficient way to get it done."

"Efficient?" she demanded, her voice shaking with anger. "You violated my privacy. My God, how did you even get in to my apartment?"

"I was the one who had the locks installed for you. You're overreacting, Lilly."

She clenched her hands in her lap for fear she might slap his handsome face. He'd pretended to be worried about the dismal state of the locks on her front door and had insisted on having them changed and a deadbolt added. She'd been grateful at the time, because in New York a solid set of locks was never a bad idea. But really it had just been another of his attempts to control her.

"You did that so you could spy on me," she hissed, pressing her head back against the seat. "How could I be so stu—"

"Stop." His eyes blazed into hers. His bronzed skin was pulled taut across his cheekbones. "You know I have security on you. You are still my wife and, like it or not, there are people out there who itch to get their hands on you. But I have never, *ever* spied on you."

"You knew about Harry."

"I *saw* you with Harry. You were eating at Nevaros the same night I was."

"You didn't introduce yourself."

"And say what? *How do you find my wife in bed? What would you rate her out of ten?*"

Her breath caught in her throat. "This is not going to work."

"You agreed to the bargain. You're my wife for the next six months. Deal with it."

She closed her eyes and pressed her palms against her thighs, forcing herself to take deep breaths. If she was to survive the next six months without having to go into emotional rehab she was going to have to learn to control her emotions.

She turned her gaze on him—defiant hazel on arrogant black. "Ground rule number one. You don't *ever* go into my apartment again without my permission and you do *not* enable someone to go through my personal possessions."

He nodded. *"Bene."*

Shocked at how easily he'd acquiesced, she kept going. "I want to go to my apartment now."

"Why?"

"Because I doubt Mrs. Collins packed my book. Or brought my two violets with her. And there's a few things I don't want hanging around."

"Like the sex toys you use with Harry?" he taunted.

"Why, yes. Harry knows how to keep things interesting."

He froze.

Her fingers curled around the door handle.

In a lightning-fast movement his hand slammed down on top of hers. "You know what a comment like that does to a guy like me, Lilly. Are you looking for me to up the ante? Because I can assure you Taylor doesn't make you scream like I do."

Lilly slunk back in her seat, her heart hammering in her chest.

He lifted his hand away from hers and returned it to the wheel. "Choose your fights carefully, *tesoro*. You know how many times you've won."

Never. She never won against Riccardo because he was too strong, too smart, and he knew her too well ever to let it happen.

They didn't speak during their brief stopover at her apartment, nor on the drive to the house.

Magda enveloped her in a warm hug when they walked through the door and told them dinner was ready when they were. Lilly went upstairs to change.

Riccardo was waiting for her in the small, private dining room when she came down. Magda had closed the doors to the terrace as the chill of the early May evening set in, and lit candles on the table in the warm dark-floored room with its elegant white wainscoting and glowing sconces. For a moment she stood standing in the entranceway, a sharp little pain tugging at her insides. She had been so desperate for her husband's attention in the latter days of their marriage that all she had dreamed about was coming home to a meal like this with him.

She took him in as he opened a bottle of wine, his muscular forearms flexing in the candlelight as he worked the cork out of the bottle. He hadn't bothered to change, but had taken off his suit jacket and tie and rolled his shirtsleeves up. In charcoal-gray trousers and white shirt he looked better than any man had a right to look. They molded his leanly muscular body into a work of art. She sank her teeth into her bottom lip. Women actually stopped in the street to stare at her husband. He was just *that* good-looking. In the beginning she hadn't minded, because she'd known she had him and they didn't.

In the end it had been crucifying.

Her gaze slid up to his face. He was watching her, the bottle in his hands, his dark eyes seeming to reach inside of her and read her every emotion. She shifted her weight to the other foot and stood her ground. Six-foot-four and broad-shouldered, he made the room seem stiflingly small.

He'd always been vastly intimidating. Except when he'd been naked beneath her. Those times *she* had been in control—her thighs straddling all that golden muscular flesh, his taut, powerful body beneath her tense, begging her for the release that had always bordered on the spiritual with them.

A glint entered his dark eyes. Her lashes swept down over hers. *What in God's name was she doing?*

"Rule number two, *cara*," he murmured. "No looking at me like that unless you intend to follow through with it."

Wildfire raced to her cheeks. *Dammit.* She walked jerkily across to him and took the glass of wine he'd poured.

Magda came in with their salads, her round face beaming. "How nice to see the two of you sitting down to a meal together."

"Yes, what a novelty," Lilly agreed. "I hardly remember how to converse."

Magda gave her a wary look, told them the casserole was in the oven and left.

"You will curb your tongue when others are around," Riccardo said curtly when the housekeeper was safely out of earshot. "Our deal depends on us being discreet."

"You liked it in the bedroom," she taunted.

"Right on the money, *tesoro*," he agreed, showing his teeth. "Knock yourself out."

She shrugged. "Since we won't be sharing a bedroom, I'll pass."

He took a sip of his wine, then lowered the glass with a slow, deliberate movement. "Here I am, speaking *your* native language, and still you don't get it."

"Get what?"

"We need to make this authentic, Lilly. We *will* be sharing a bedroom."

Her stomach dissolved into a ball of nerves. There was absolutely no way, with all the rooms in this house, that she was sharing *that* bedroom with *him*.

"Magda is completely trustworthy. There is no need to—"

"This isn't up for debate." He leaned back against the sideboard and crossed his arms over his chest. "Eyes are everywhere. People traipse through this house on a daily basis."

Lilly gave him a desperate look. "But I—"

"Rule number three." He kept going like a train, steamrollering right over her. "You will accompany me to all the social engagements I'm committed to over the next six months, and if I need to travel you'll do that too."

"I have patients who count on me, Riccardo. I can't just pick up and travel at will."

He shrugged. "Then you work around it. Our first engagement, by the way, is Saturday. It's a charitable thing for breast cancer."

She bit back the primal urge to scream that was surging against the back of her throat. She had a career, for God's sake. Responsibilities. And no wardrobe for a charity event. She was at least ten pounds heavier than she'd been when she'd been with Riccardo. None of her gowns upstairs would fit, and nothing she'd been wearing in her low-key life since then would be appropriate.

"Oh," he added, almost as an afterthought. "It's a fashion thing. They called today to ask if you'd model a gown when they heard our news."

She felt the blood drain from her face. "On a stage?"

"That's usually how they would do it, isn't it?"

The thought of modeling a gown in front of all those people with her new, curvier figure sent a sharp response tumbling out of her. "No."

He frowned. "What do you mean, no? It's for a good cause."

"Then *you* get up there and do it."

His gaze darkened. "Are you going to fight me on everything?"

"When you ask me to get up on a stage and parade myself around in front of a bunch of people when you know I hate that stuff, *yes*."

He tipped his head to one side. "You're a beautiful woman, Lilly. I never understood why you were so insecure."

And he never would. He had no clue how deep her insecurities ran. The demons she'd finally put to rest. And that was the way she preferred to keep it. Weakness left you vulnerable. Exposed. Open for people to pick at and slowly destroy you.

"I won't do it."

"You will," he returned grimly. "Ground rule number four. You will have no further contact with Harry Taylor."

The man she still hadn't had the guts to call back yet. "I have to talk to him. He's been trying to call me and he sounds—"

"Trying?" He lifted a brow. "I see your old patterns of avoidance haven't changed."

"Go to hell," she muttered. "You sandbagged me with this last night. I need a chance to explain it to him."

"One conversation, Lilly. And if I find out you've seen him after that—if I find out you've even chatted with him in the hallway—our agreement will be null and void."

It was fine for *him* to cheat in the public eye but when it came to her the same rules didn't apply!

He flicked a hand at her. "It's not like it should be a tough call, ending things. Or have you become such a tease you can kiss a man like you did me last night and still go back for more?"

She shook her head. "You're such a bastard sometimes."

A savage smile curled his lips. "You like it when I'm a son-of-a-bitch, *amore mio*. It excites you."

She turned her back on him before she said something she'd regret. She'd loved that about him in the beginning. That he'd called the shots and all she'd had to do was sit back and enjoy the ride. For a girl who'd been taking care of herself most of her life it had been a relief. An escape from the hand-to-mouth existence that had seen her work two jobs to put herself through college and graduate school to supplement the scholarship she'd won.

What she hadn't been prepared for was the flashy, no-end-to-the-riches lifestyle he'd dropped her into with no preparation, no defences for a girl from Iowa who'd never really grown into the hard-edged, sink-or-swim Manhattan way of life.

It had been her downfall. Her inability to cope.

"Ground rule number five," he continued softly. "You and I are going to be the old Riccardo and Lilly. The perfect couple. We're going to act madly in love, there will be no other men, and when you get weak and can't stand it anymore you'll come to me." He paused and flashed a superior smile. "I give you a week, max."

She spun around to face him, her gaze clashing with his. "I'm not the same person I was, Riccardo. You won't find me groveling at your feet for attention. And you won't walk all over me like you did before. You treat me as an equal or I'll leave and blow this deal to smithereens."

He lifted his elegant shoulders, as if he found her little outburst amusing. "But you want this house. Badly… I saw it in your eyes last night."

For a reason entirely other than what you think.

"Are you finished?" she asked quietly. "Because I suddenly seem to have lost my appetite. I'm going to go make sense of my stuff upstairs."

His gaze narrowed on her face. "Don't make yourself into a martyr. I've had enough of that to last a lifetime."

She lifted her chin. "Martyrs die for their cause. When this is over I'll be free of you. Eternally happy is more like it."

Lilly took her time unpacking her things, her arms curiously heavy as she hung her delicate pieces on hangers in the huge walk-in closet. Every item she unpacked was an effort, and her stomach was growing tighter with each piece she added with her usual military precision. Sweaters with sweaters, blouses with blouses, pants with pants. It was as if her old life was reappearing in front of her hanger by hanger, row by row.

And there was nothing she could do to stop it.

She'd said she'd never come back. What the hell was she doing?

She plunged on, doggedly working until everything was in its place. Then, when she was sure Riccardo was working in his study—which he undoubtedly would be until midnight—she slipped downstairs and made herself a snack. She wasn't remotely hungry, but skipping meals was a warning signal for her. She put some cheese and crackers on a plate, poured herself a glass of wine and took it to bed.

She had finished her snack and read about half a chapter of her supposedly scintillating book when her husband walked through the door. *It was only just past eleven. What was he doing?*

"You're coming to bed?"

A mocking smile twisted his mouth. "That's what it looks like, no?"

She shifted uncomfortably. "You usually work later than this."

"Maybe having my beautiful bride back in my bed is a draw."

Heat flared in her cheeks at the sarcasm in his voice. "As if," she muttered under her breath.

"What?"

"Nothing."

He flicked her a glance. "Mumbling is rude, Lilly. If you have something to say, say it."

She stuck her nose in her book. She didn't have to play this game. Except it was impossible not to sneak a glance at his bronzed, muscled chest as he whipped his shirt off. In keeping with his new harsher haircut, his body seemed even harder than before. As if someone had taken a chisel and worked away the remaining minute amounts of excess flesh until all that was left was smooth, hard, defined muscle, tapering down to that six pack she loved.

Hell. She buried her face back in her book. The rasp of his zipper and the sound of his pants hitting the floor had her desperately reading the same sentence over and over. His boxers flew across the room and landed in the hamper. Her breath seized in her throat. *She would not—would not—look.*

She took a deep breath as he sauntered into the bathroom and shut the door. Her passing out moment last night had meant she hadn't seen any of *that.* Her hectic pulse indicated she hadn't gotten any more immune to the show in the past twelve months.

This was just *so* not good it was laughable. No wonder she hadn't come near him in months. Because *this* happened.

She'd made it through a miraculous two pages when her husband emerged from the bathroom, the smell of his spicy aftershave filling her nostrils. A flash of skin in her peripheral vision revealed he hadn't lost his predisposition for sleeping in the nude.

She took another of those steadying breaths as he walked around the bed to his side, but all that did was overwhelm her with the cologne some manufacturer had for sure pumped full of every pheromone in the book. The bed dipped as the owner of the pheromones whipped the sheets back and got in. She made a grab for the material, feeling far too exposed in her short silk nightie, but not before her husband swept his eyes over her in a mocking perusal. She gritted her teeth and pulled the sheets up high over her chest.

Her husband's rich, deep laughter made her grit her teeth even harder. "I saw it all last night, Lil, and I have to say I like the changes. You look like a properly voluptuous Italian woman now. Your breasts are fabulous—and those hips..." He sat back against the headboard, a wicked smile pulling at the corner of his lips. "Without a doubt my favorite spot on a woman's body. That curve near the hipbone you can slide your hand over, and—"

"Stop." She flashed him a murderous look. "I may be

living with you for six months but these—these types of conversations are *not* happening."

He lifted his shoulders and pursed his lips. "This is the point where you'd usually freeze me out anyway."

She flinched. "It was always about sex. Sometimes I actually wanted to communicate."

"That's where men and women differ," he drawled. "When we're stressed we crave sex. It's the way *we* communicate."

"It was the *only* way you communicated. Too bad it wasn't conducive to working out our problems."

His face hardened. "You didn't want to work them out. You checked out, Lilly. You wanted us to fail."

"I wanted us to *work*." She blinked back the emotion stinging her eyes. "But we were light years apart. And we always have been. We were just too stupid to realize it."

He reached over and grabbed the book, tossing it on his bedside table. "You haven't read a thing since I walked into this room, *cara*. You're so busy trying to deny what's between us that you can't see a foot in front of you. That isn't light years apart—that's total avoidance."

"The easier way," she flashed. "Because we both know how it ends."

She took satisfaction in the frustrated flash of his eyes before she turned away from him and doused the light, curling up as far away from him as she could in the big king-sized bed. It was still impossible to ignore his presence. His warmth, his still, even breathing was everywhere around her.

She curled her fingers into the sheets and focused on keeping it together, shocked by the need, the almost physical ache for him to reach out and comfort her in the way he always had. When Riccardo had made love to her she had always known where his heart was. The problem had been when the cold light of day had dawned and their problems hadn't gone away.

She squeezed her eyes shut. Tomorrow she had to tell Harry it was over between them. It should have been a horrible thing to have to do. But with Riccardo back in her life, bearing down on her like a massive all-consuming storm, she knew her relationship with Harry was doomed.

There had only ever been one man who'd had her heart. Too bad he hadn't been worthy of it.

CHAPTER FOUR

RICCARDO WOKE UP Saturday morning with the need to hit something. To flatten something. Anything that got rid of the tension sitting low in his belly after he'd been jarred awake by some fool's motorcycle racing down the street.

Eternally happy. His wife's words echoed through his head, made worse by the paper-white state of her face when she'd returned home last night after ending things with Taylor.

He wanted to put a fist through the doctor's face.

He rolled over to glare at her, but there was only an imprint in the pillow where her head had been. Lilly? Out of bed before him? She liked to sleep more than any human being he knew.

He flicked a glance at the clock on the bedside table, his eyes widening as he read the neon green numbers. *Eight-thirty.* That couldn't be right. Sure, he was tired, because his wife was driving him crazy, but eight-thirty? A glance at his watch confirmed it was true.

Swinging his legs over the side of the bed, he struggled to clear the foreign-feeling fuzz in his head. He'd plowed through a mountain of work last night before coming to bed. To avoid the urge to come up here and make his wife eat her words. To pleasure her until she screamed and forgot Harry Taylor even existed.

A chainsaw would do it.

He picked up his mobile and called Gabe. There was a half-dead oak on their Westchester property that was a serious safety hazard. He'd been meaning to ask the landscapers to take it down, but suddenly the thought of a physical, mind-blanking task appealed to him greatly.

"Matteo got in last night," Gabe said. "I'll bring him and we can have some beer afterward."

"As long as you don't let him anywhere near the saw."

His youngest brother, who ran De Campo's European operations, and their father were in town for the annual board meetings. Which was probably another reason his gut was out of order. Whatever his father said in those meetings would make or break his chances of becoming CEO. And it had better go in his favor.

"We'll make him the look-out," Gabe said drily. "See you in forty-five."

Riccardo showered, put on an old pair of jeans and a T-shirt, and went to procure a travel cup of coffee in the kitchen. Lilly wasn't in there, or in the library she loved.

He was wondering if she'd made another run for it when she rushed into the front entryway just as his brothers arrived, a black look on her face, a curse on her breath.

"Matteo!" she exclaimed, her frown disappearing as his youngest brother stepped forward and scooped her up into a hug. "I had no idea you were in town."

Matteo gave her a squeeze and set her down. "If that means you two are busy making up for lost time, I'm good with that."

A flare of color speared Lilly's cheeks. She and Riccardo's youngest brother were close—or had been until their separation. Matteo was the more philosophical and expressive of the three brothers. Women naturally gravitated to him. Used his shoulder to cry on far too much, in Riccardo's opinion.

"It's so good you're here," Lilly said, pulling back and flashing his brother a warm smile. She gave Riccardo's boots and jeans a brief glance, her gaze staying well away from his glowering face, then looked back at Matteo. "Maybe I'll see you when you're back?"

Riccardo's shoulders shot to his ears. Where did she get off, giving his brother a smile like that when she hadn't offered him one in days?

He glanced at her purse and sunglasses. "You're going out?"

"I need to buy a dress for tonight."

"You have hundreds upstairs."

Her mouth tightened. "They don't fit."

He couldn't understand how at least *one* of those dresses didn't fit. Yes, she'd put on a few pounds since they'd been together, but they were undoubtedly in all the right places. *Women.* He lifted his shoulders. "You do still have the credit card?"

She flashed him a sweetly apologetic look. "Cut it into a million little pieces… But I have my own."

The urge to put her over his knee glowed like a red neon sign in front of him. Gritting his teeth, he dug in his pocket and fished the keys to his Jag out. He handed them to her. "Take the car. We'll go in Gabe's."

Her fingers curled around the keys, a hesitant look crossing her face. She loved driving that car. He knew it as surely as he knew where to kiss her to make her crazy. At the base of that beautiful long neck of hers, and most definitely between—

"Okay, thanks." She gave Gabe a kiss on the cheek and left, the car keys jangling from her fingers. Fury swept through him, raging through his veins. She might not think she had to put on a show for his brothers, but by God she was going to start acting the part—or she had a serious lesson coming her way.

Gabe gave him an amused look. "Glad to see you have everything under control."

"I can't believe you gave her the Jag," Matteo added,

leading the way outside. "She looked like she might drive it into a wall just for the fun of it."

Riccardo muttered something under his breath and took the front seat of the Maserati beside Gabe.

"She looks fantastic, though," Matteo said, sliding into the back. "Being away from you agrees with her."

"We all know you're in love with my wife," Riccardo shot back. "Why don't you spend your time finding one for yourself rather than drooling over mine?"

"Lilly needs someone in her corner with you as a *coniuge*," his brother returned, unperturbed. "You haven't exactly been husband of the year material."

Riccardo turned in his seat as Gabe backed out of the driveway. "What, exactly, does *that* mean?"

"You work fourteen-, sixteen-hour days and you treat Lilly as an afterthought," Matteo said belligerently. "I can't believe she put up with two years of it."

Riccardo was halfway into the backseat when Gabe threw up his hand. "*Sit the hell down. I'm* going to drive into a wall if you keep this up."

Riccardo sat back, pulling in a deep breath. "Keep your mouth shut until you know all the facts."

"You never talk so how would I know them?"

"Try living with the Ice Queen."

"She wasn't always like that," Matty murmured. "Maybe you should ask yourself what happened."

"Maybe you should mind your own business."

That set the tone for the forty-five-minute drive north of the city to Westchester. Riccardo kept his gaze on the scenery while Gabe and Matty caught up. Suburban New York blurred into a continuous stream of exclusive green bedroom communities. But if the scenery was tranquil, his mood was not.

What did they think? He was going to make the De Campo name a player in the North American restaurant business by being home for dinner at six every night?

That he was going to claim his birthright by being any less driven and focused than his father Antonio? He rubbed his hand across his unshaven jaw and shook his head.

"You never wanted to hear what I had to say," Lilly had lashed out at him the other night. "I'm through groveling at your feet, begging for your attention…"

Dio. Was he really that bad?

There'd been a time when he'd been much more laid-back. When he'd been driving a racecar for one of Italy's top teams and all he'd been focused on was winning. The shockingly alive feeling of driving a car at one-hundred-eighty miles an hour finally free of his father's iron grip. He had eaten up life with the appetite of a man determined to savor every minute.

And every beautiful woman who came along with it—like the froth on top of his espresso.

But Lilly had not been one of those easy-to-attain women who had chased him from track to track. Lilly had been the ultimate challenge. The one woman he could never have enough of. Her sharp wit, her loving nature—before she'd turned cold—and her bewitching sensuality had made her the hottest woman he'd ever touched. He had been consumed with the need to possess her, body and soul. And it had almost made him make the biggest mistake of his life.

He shifted in his seat. The sheer stupidity of what he'd almost done was something that would haunt him forever. He had kissed Chelsea Tate with the intent of taking her to bed at the absolute lowest point of his marriage. When Lilly wouldn't talk to him and he'd felt so alienated in his own home he hadn't been thinking straight. He'd wanted to prove he didn't need her, that he didn't love her so much that it was sending him straight to hell. But all it had done was backfire on him when he'd kissed Chelsea and realized Lilly was the only woman for him.

A bitter taste that had nothing to do with the espresso he

was consuming filled his mouth. Lilly, on the other hand, seemed to have moved on as easily as if she was shifting to the next course at dinner.

His fingers dug into the flimsy paper cup. If he had to sleep in that bed with her one more night with her freezing him out—warning him away from those sweet, soft curves that were his and his alone—he wasn't going to be responsible for his actions.

The tension in the car spilled out into the brisk morning as they parked in front of the Westchester house and stepped from the car. Riccardo took a big breath of the clean, woodsy air and felt the tension seep away as the soul-restoring properties of his home on the lake kicked in. He'd fallen in love with the beautiful rolling countryside on his first visit here, to a business associate's home on the Hudson River. When this estate had come up for sale he'd snapped it up as an escape for him and Lilly. But he'd been so busy they'd rarely ever made it out here.

Another promise to her he hadn't kept.

To hell with Matty.

Locating the chainsaw, he applied his frustration to the tree and they managed to take the huge old American white oak down without hitting the house—which was a good thing, since it had to be ninety feet tall and at least three feet in diameter.

Afterward they sat beside the huge old tree, now sprawled in front of them, drinking cold beer out of the can. As different as they all were—Gabe, the intense, serious one, obsessed with the craft of winemaking, who'd known what he'd wanted to do from the time he'd been a little boy; Riccardo, the rebel oldest son; Matty, the in-touch-with-his-feminine side youngest—they were as close as three brothers could be. Even scattered around the globe, with Gabe spending most of his time in Napa Valley, where their vineyards were located and Matty in Tuscany, where he oversaw the company's European operations.

Maybe it was because their mother Francesca, who had come from one of Europe's oldest families, hadn't been the nurturing type. Maybe that was what had bonded the three of them so tightly. Because they were all each other had alongside Antonio's domination. It was sink or swim in the De Campo family, and they had learned to survive—together.

Gabe set down his beer and looked at Riccardo. "Any idea where Antonio's head's at?"

He shook his head. They called their father Antonio because he was not only their father, he was the dominant, larger-than-life figure who had transformed the small, moderately successful De Campo vineyard his grandfather had passed along to him into a force to be reckoned with in the global wine industry.

Gabe shrugged. "Everybody knows it's going to be you. You've been the *de facto* head of the company since Antonio started scaling back."

Riccardo searched his brother's face for any sign that the logical heir to the De Campo empire harbored any bitterness toward him after his father's decision to put Riccardo in control of the company when he'd fallen ill—despite the fact that Gabe had been the obvious choice with Riccardo off racing. But his brother's face was matter-of-fact. As if he'd long ago given up fighting his father's predisposition for his eldest son.

Riccardo took a long swig of his beer. "It's impossible to predict what Antonio will do."

Particularly when teaching his eldest son a lesson seemed to be a greater priority than doing what was right. Antonio had never forgiven Riccardo for wasting his Harvard education on a racing career. No matter how good a driver he'd been—he'd been on track to win his first championship title when his father had fallen ill—Antonio had never forgiven him for his decision. He'd seen racing as a frivolous, ego-boosting activity that pandered to his son's

ego and was disrespectful to the family—to everything
Antonio had raised him to be. He hadn't talked to his eldest son for years, and had only relented when Riccardo
had returned to take the reins of De Campo.

Now Antonio was letting Riccardo sweat his guts out
in purgatory.

Rolling to his feet, he reached for the chainsaw. "Let's
get this done."

He worked his way from one end of the tree to the other,
with his brothers hauling and stacking the pieces. His muscles relaxed and his head cleared. He was nothing if not
a man who knew how to solve a problem. His wife might
think this was the way it was going to be, but she had it
all wrong. This icy détente was ending. And it was ending tonight.

Lilly adjusted the plunging bodice of the lavender gown
for the millionth time and asked herself why in the world
she'd allowed the owner of Sam's to convince her this gown
was *it*.

She felt conspicuous and exposed. Okay, sexy and de-
sirable too. But maybe it was *too much*. And the last thing
she wanted to do was attract any more attention than she
and Riccardo already would tonight. Their first appearance
as a reunited couple since their divorce party was going to
cause enough waves.

And as for when she came to model Antonia Abelli's
gown… All eyes would be on her, searching for and ex-
posing her flaws. And they were going to have a field-day
with her. With her less than perfect body, she could only
imagine what they'd say.

Her stomach rose to her throat. Her fitting with the designer had been humiliating. The eclectic woman, whose
romantic designs she'd always loved, had circled around
her, frowning at the tight fit of the chosen dress. "We'll

have to let some seams out," she'd muttered. "But it'll work."

Lilly had left, cheeks burning, wanting to tell her to make someone else wear the dress—someone it fit! The only problem with that was this was the *new* Lilly. The Lilly who wasn't going to care. The Lilly who was going to go out with Riccardo tonight, act like the perfect wife and not let anyone see how it got to her. She was older and wiser now—she'd gained perspective in the past year. She could handle this. And Lisbeth was all that mattered.

She heard Riccardo turn the water off in the shower. "Shoes," she murmured, ignoring the anticipatory surge of her pulse. And then she'd be ready.

She searched through a shelf full of shoes: slingbacks and stilettos in every shade of the rainbow. Her husband had walked in after his day with his brothers, taken one wary look at the pile of couture creations stacked on the floor for Magda to give away, and had said only, "Ready to leave in fifteen?"

"Aha!" She located her silver slingbacks on the top shelf. At least her shoes fit. They were her absolute weakness and, oh, did she love the strappy soft leather of these, which molded to her feet and felt like heaven...

She sat down on the bed and pulled them on. They made her legs seem a mile long, and if there was anything she needed tonight it was that. The fact she couldn't walk in them was of little consequence. Anything that increased her confidence level was worth it.

Her fingers clumsily refused to obey her as she struggled to thread the thin strap through the tiny loop. The fashion show was one thing. How she and Riccardo were going to fool all those people they knew and make them think they were still in love when they were in the middle of the War of the Roses was another matter entirely.

She managed to get one shoe done up, then started on the other, enduring the same frustrating process. Maybe what she needed were glasses, because the strap didn't seem to want to—

"Dammit."

"Need help?"

Riccardo's rich, sexy drawl sent the strap pinging out of her hand completely. "No, thanks," she murmured, snatching it up again and yanking it desperately through the loop. This time the pin slid right into the hole and stayed. Thank goodness. She didn't need a naked Riccardo any closer than he was right now because—

Hell. The blood had rushed to her head, bent over like that, but now, sitting up, her gaze moved over her husband leaning against the doorway of the bathroom and it seemed to congeal right there, pounding in her ears. *Not naked.* He'd wrapped a towel around his waist, but that was almost worse, because far, far too much mouthwatering muscled, bronzed flesh was still on display. Everything she hadn't let herself look at the other night.

She gulped in a desperate breath as that six-pack she'd loved to tell him turned her on stared her in the face. Her gaze moved lower, over the grooves in his abdomen only the most defined men had, skipped the next part, because really she couldn't go there, and ended up at his gorgeous thighs and calves. Riccardo had the best legs of any man she'd ever encountered. Muscled, strong and perfectly shaped. *Heavenly.*

No looking at me like that unless you intend to follow through with it.

She stood abruptly, teetering on the high shoes. "We should go. We're late already, and if we're going to get through traffic—" *He was so not listening to her.* His long-lashed dark gaze was conducting a thorough inspection of her physical assets that had begun with her face, swept down over the plunging neckline of her dress, over the flare of her hips in the clinging gown to her lavender-tipped feet.

Heat rushed to her face as his gaze lingered. Riccardo had always had a thing for feet.

Her feet in particular.

He turned, walked to the dresser and pulled something out of a drawer. Her heart-rate increased as he walked back toward her, a purposeful look on his face.

"We need to go," she repeated in a strangled voice. "We're already late."

He stopped in front of her, took her by the shoulders and turned her around.

"You need a necklace," he murmured, lifting her hair aside. "What are you worried about, Lilly? That I might tear this dress off you and end this détente?"

It wasn't as if he hadn't done it before... She shivered as he slid the necklace around her throat, the cold stones resting against her heated skin. "Riccardo..."

"Riccardo what?" Humor deepened his voice. "Tear the dress off?"

"Get the hell away from me."

"Because you don't trust yourself when I touch you?"

"Because this is a *charade,*" she hissed. "And when we aren't in public you *don't* touch me."

He fastened the clasp of the necklace. "Do you remember how we christened this?"

She stared down at the row of diamonds encircling her throat, sparkling against her skin like a ring of fire. As if she could ever forget. They had been out for dinner, wholly unable to keep their hands off each other, and he'd slapped his credit card on the table as soon as the entrées were removed and taken her home, where he'd ravished her with such urgent, sensual demand she had never been able to wear the necklace again without going back to that moment.

The fleeting sensation of his lips on her bare shoulder made her jump under his hands.

"You look stunningly beautiful in this dress, *tesoro.*

You could easily convince me to forget all about tonight and play hookey."

She would have replied, except his teeth nipped gently into her skin and a wave of heat swept through her. That would be one way of avoiding the fashion show...

Not worth the consequences.

She yanked herself out of his arms and fixed him with a glare. *Remember how he broke your heart. Remember this is only for six months...*

He watched her with a hooded gaze. "I take it that's a no?"

"Not ever," she agreed icily. "Shall we go?"

He inclined his head, stepped toward the closet and stripped off the towel. She averted her eyes and left to wait for him downstairs—but not before she got a full-on shot of his firm, beautiful behind.

CHAPTER FIVE

THE BALLROOM OF the historic hotel near Central Park glittered with light, muted laughter and a sense that time hadn't really moved on—it was just different souls passing through it.

Lilly stood at the entrance with Riccardo and took in the ambience with that same feeling. Massive chandeliers five feet in width still dominated the room, still exuded the elegance of decades past, the band was timelessly tasteful, filling the space with rich classical music, and the black-coated wait staff could have been from any time period. It was *her* that was different. Once she had walked in here with naive, trusting eyes that had seen only the sparkling beauty of so much loveliness in one place. Now she saw it for what it was—a backdrop for the rich and powerful, a symbol of how beauty could destroy and disfigure.

If you let it.

Her gaze shifted to the long runway that ran the center of the room. In an hour she would be up there, modeling Antonia Abelli's dress. If she didn't throw up first. It was a distinct possibility.

Heads turned. The open stares began. Her fingers dug into Riccardo's forearm as the room seemed to ignite with speculative conversation. The press had been all over them since the divorce party, coming up with a multitude of creative, vicious angles as to why they were back together.

Lilly was pregnant—thus her "added pounds," one tab-loid had said. Riccardo had had his fill of his mistress and wanted to start a family, said another. Worst of all had been the dirt they'd dug up on poor Harry Taylor—a former girl-friend citing his low libido as the reason Lilly had left him.

Riccardo looked down at her. "Just ignore them," he said quietly. "Ignore the rubbish they say and be true to yourself."

Lilly wished she had just an ounce of his self-confidence right now—or his supreme ability to focus on what was important and let everything else go.

"Let's get a drink," he murmured, sliding an arm around her waist. She leaned into him and allowed herself to absorb the innate strength that had once made her think nothing and no one could ever hurt her.

How wrong she'd been.

They procured martinis at the bar and were soon caught up in a rolling series of conversations with people eager to see if the rumors were true. Were the De Campos *really* back together?

Lilly tried to focus on the conversation, but the closer it got to nine o'clock and the fashion show the weaker her legs felt. She could feel the cold, assessing looks being thrown her way by the socialites who had claimed the limelight in her absence. And her stomach started to churn.

Riccardo shot her a look with those perceptive eyes of his, warning her to liven up. But Lilly was finished with the acting job she'd done for years. He wanted her as a wife? Then he was getting the real Lilly—not some plas-tic, manufactured replica of herself.

"Riccardo!"

The shrill voice of an outrageously beautiful blond just about took her ears off. About her own age, and so deli-cate a puff of wind might blow her away in her silver lamé dress, she threw herself into Riccardo's arms and landed a big kiss on either cheek before Lilly could blink.

Riccardo set the diminutive blond down, a smile pulling at the corners of his mouth. "Always a dramatic greeting, Victoria."

A rough-hewn, handsome man in a tux stepped up to shake his hand and clap him on the back. "She always did prefer you, De Campo."

Riccardo smiled—a guarded smile that didn't quite reach his eyes. "Alessandro Marino. This is the last place I'd expect to see you."

"My wife." Alessandro inclined his head with a rueful look. "We had a family wedding in the city. And of course my fashion-obsessed wife couldn't miss this."

Riccardo pulled Lilly forward, his hand firm at her back. "I don't believe you've met *my* wife. Lilly, this is Alessandro Marino, my former teammate, and his wife Victoria."

Lilly felt his fingers digging into her back. Surprised, she looked up at his face. He looked firmly in control, as always, but there was a tightness in his face that belied his easy smile. *Alessandro Marino.* It hit her. The man who had taken Riccardo's place as the star of TeamXT. She'd seen a cover story on him recently. He'd been described as "unbeatable."

Alessandro leaned forward and pressed a kiss to both her cheeks. His wife followed suit.

"So *you're* the woman stupid enough to walk out on Riccardo…" Victoria stood back, giving Lilly a once-over, her blue eyes assessing her as thoroughly as she might a prize filly. "Another few months and you might have been out of luck, with all those women lining up to catch him when he fell."

"Victoria." Alessandro bit out the word. "Not appropriate."

His wife shrugged. "It's the truth."

"How is the wine business?" Alessandro asked Riccardo. "De Campo's doing well."

"We had a good year. And you," he said, nodding at the other man. "You're at the top of the pack. Congratulations."

Alessandro shrugged. "You left big shoes to fill. No one is a daredevil like you, De Campo. I had to work on my style."

"Well, it's obviously working."

"He was the best, you know." Alessandro flicked a glance at Lilly. "He'd have a couple championship titles by now if he'd stayed."

Lilly nodded. "So I've heard."

Racing had always been a taboo subject with her and Riccardo. Anytime she'd brought it up her husband had shut down. As he looked like he was about to do right now, judging by the granite-hard expression on his face.

Their conversation with the Marinos deteriorated into an awkward, stilted back and forth that Lilly escaped as soon as she could with a trip to the ladies' room. When she returned to her husband's side he excused himself from the group of men he was speaking to and took her arm.

"Finished your little temper tantrum?"

"It wasn't a temper tantrum. I'm bored, and I'm tired about hearing how much women love you. I get it."

"Then why is smoke coming out of your ears?" He exerted pressure on her arm until she followed him through the crowd.

"Why didn't you defend me?" she burst out. "Why didn't you say something, like, *Good thing I'm madly in love with my wife,* or *anything* that would have made me feel less like an idiot?"

"What do you care? This is just an act for you, isn't it?"

She glared up at him. "I *don't* care. What bugs me is that all these people think we're back together and madly in love and *you're* letting *her* get away with *that.* You always do with women who fall all over you. You *eat* it up, Riccardo. You get that same look on your face like you had when you were standing on the podium splashing champagne over everyone after winning a race."

His jaw tightened. "All men like attention, Lilly. Especially when you get none from your wife."

Oh. She swung away from him before she hit him. "Is it unrealistic to expect you to stand up for me? You never reassure me. It's humiliating."

He led her onto the dance floor. "You know what's humiliating? Me having to tell everyone we know you've left and not knowing what to say because I didn't know why."

She absorbed that as he pulled her into his arms and wrapped his fingers around hers. "You brought it on yourself, Riccardo. Don't try and make me feel bad for you. One week with me out of the house and you were probably acting like 'Ravishing Riccardo' again."

His gaze sharpened at her use of the tabloid nickname for him. "You have a wicked mouth—you know that, *cara?*"

She stared mutinously at his chest as he pulled her closer. So he'd had to answer some questions about why she'd left? It couldn't possibly have matched the jealousy and humiliation *she'd* felt every time he'd left the house without her, wondering if he was with Chelsea. Wondering why she wasn't enough for him.

She studied his hard, proud profile. Maybe it hadn't been right for her to run as she had. She was sure it had been a knock to his pride for a man who was built around pride and honor, who had a public image to uphold, to admit his marriage had failed. But if she'd stayed in that house one more day she would have cracked in half.

Guilt lanced through her. "What did you tell them, then, when they asked where I was?"

He looked down at her, his expression cold and forbidding. "I told them we were taking some time off. And I let them talk. It was our business, not theirs."

"And you think I should do the same?"

"Let them think what they want. They can't hurt you if you don't let them."

"Have you ever read what they say about me?" she challenged. "Even once?"

"I don't have time to read those rags."

Her mouth tightened. "Today they called my figure 'less than fashionable' and insinuated I was pregnant."

"So what?"

So what? She clamped her mouth shut before she said something she'd regret.

"You need to recognize jealousy for what it is," he said impatiently. "They want to be you. That's why they try and tear you down."

She gave him a vicious look. "What would you know about it? You're Mr. Perfect. You have an affair and it only makes you sexier to them."

His eyes went so black she took a step backward. His fingers tightened around hers, drawing her forward in a slow, deliberate movement that wouldn't attract attention. His tone as he pinned her to the spot with his gaze was ice-cold. "Get over this obsession, Lilly. I did not cheat."

She swallowed back the nausea that circled her insides like a shark waiting to pounce. Eight time-lapse photographs didn't lie.

"I want to go."

"Well, we're staying. This is what you signed up for."

She hated him. At that moment she hated him as she'd never hated anyone in her life. "We should never have done this," she murmured huskily. "Look what we're doing to each other."

"We should have done this a long time ago," he disagreed roughly. "My big mistake was giving you time and space when what you really needed was for someone to shake some sense into you."

Her throat tightened. "What does it matter? We're past fixable."

A hard light glittered in his eyes. "That remains to be seen."

"No, it doesn't." She lifted her gaze to his. "This is a short-term solution, Riccardo. You become CEO and we're done."

It was as if her words bounced off his Teflon coating. His expression was inscrutable as he regarded her from beneath lowered lashes. "Matty told me I was a bad husband today."

Her mouth dropped open. "He did?"

"I expect I have been at times."

"At times?" Lilly was past being diplomatic. "That last year you couldn't have cared if I was on Mars as long as I showed up for whatever social function you dictated I appear at. So I could charm the Mayor or sweet-talk a difficult client."

He frowned. "That's an exaggeration. We supported each other. We were a team."

"A team?" She let out a bark of laughter that made a couple near them stare. "If by 'team' you mean I supported you while you ran roughshod over my career every time it was inconvenient for you, then you'd be right."

"Now you're being ridiculous."

"*Really?* You know why I was late that night we had dinner with the owner of Jacob's?" She waited while he paused, then shook his head. "Because I was consulting on the treatment for a little boy's legs. A little boy who'd just lost his mother in a car accident. I was crushed, devastated by what had happened, and all you did when I told you was nod and tell me to get to the table before the appetizers got cold."

"I did *not*. You did not tell me that story."

Her mouth tightened. "Oh, yes, I did. You just couldn't be bothered to listen. And you know what, Riccardo? I helped that little boy. I worked by his side for six months until he was walking again. I might not have been able to bring his mother back but I gave him the use of his legs back. And I'm damn proud of that."

"And so you should be. Lilly, I've always thought what you do is amazing."

"As long as it didn't interfere with the grand plan," she agreed bitterly. "With your obsession to win the CEO job."

A dark flush spread across his cheekbones. "It's my birthright to run De Campo. Why couldn't you ever understand that?"

"I understand it matters to you to the exclusion of everything else in your life. Please forgive me if I don't want to go along for the ride."

A muscle jumped in his jaw. "It won't last forever. Once I'm appointed CEO things will change."

"It'll never change. I think you left a piece of yourself on that racetrack, Riccardo. Nothing you do lives up to that, but you'll never stop looking, *needing* that adrenalin."

The color in his cheeks darkened to a deep, livid red. "Don't try and play psychologist, Lilly. You're not even close."

But she knew she was. She could see it in his face. And finally she felt she was starting to understand him. "Your need for a challenge will always be there. And everyone around you suffers. Our kids would have suffered if we'd been foolish enough to have had them."

"You know that would have changed things."

"No, I don't. We couldn't even keep a dog alive, Riccardo. How would a child have worked?"

The stormclouds in his eyes turned black and dangerous. "That's a ridiculous comparison. Brooklyn was a wild dog. There was nothing we could have done to prevent her death."

She knew he was right. From the day they'd found Brooklyn, a German Shepherd puppy, injured on their street and taken her in, she'd never lost her lust for adventure or for chasing cars.

"You promised you'd train her," she said roughly. "Just like you promised to be around more and you never were."

His mouth flattened into a grim line. "You just can't take your fair share for what happened, can you? You shut me out until I was tired of being verbally slapped in the face every time I walked through the door. And I'm the bad guy for not being around enough? You have a distorted view of the world, Lilly."

The couple beside them suddenly seemed awfully close, their curious gazes on the two of them. Lilly waited until Riccardo had steered them away. "We can talk until we're blue in the face but it isn't going to change the things that were wrong with us."

His fingers tightened around her waist. "Every marriage has its ups and downs. You work through them. You don't run away."

She swallowed hard. If only he knew how badly she'd tried to stick it out. To be what he needed.

His gaze burned into hers, radiating a warning that was impossible to ignore. "We are not over, Lilly."

"We will be in six months."

"And what a six months it's going to be…" He lifted his chin. "Buckle up, *tesoro,* it's going to be quite a ride."

A shiver ran through her. The flicker of the gorgeous two-carat canary-yellow diamond he'd bought to replace the one she'd told him she'd lost shimmered where her hand rested on his shoulder. If he seemed angry now, it would be nothing compared to how he'd react if he knew the truth about what had really happened to the ring.

The organizer of the fashion show waved at her. Her heart lifted to her throat. *She did not want to do this.* The guillotine seemed preferable. But she nodded back at her. The sooner she did this the sooner it was going to be over.

"I have to go."

The tremulous note in her voice drew her husband's eye.

He slid his fingers under her chin and drew her gaze up to his. "What's the matter?"

"Nothing."

"You're nervous."

"I'm not."

She waited for him to release her, but he pulled her closer instead, his eyes flashing as he anchored her against his hard, muscled length. "There was always one way to cure your nerves..."

Lilly started to protest, but he'd already brought his mouth down on hers. His palm cradled her jaw, holding her still while he explored the soft curves of her lips so thoroughly it felt as if he was memorizing them all over again. The heat that flashed between them was undeniable, as life-giving as it had been destructive. She told herself to stop, to end it, but it was impossible not to rise on tiptoes and kiss him back.

No one kissed like Riccardo. No one.

She stepped back, her gaze on his face, wanting him to feel as shaken, as flustered as she was. All she saw was a man still so firmly in control he looked as if he could have been carved out of stone. "Now you have color in your face," he murmured, releasing her and giving her a tap on the behind. "Off you go."

Confused, not sure which way was north and which was south, Lilly did as she was told, following the organizer, Kelly Rankin, to the temporary fitting rooms. Funnily enough, she *did* feel calmer.

Antonia Abelli stripped Lilly down to her underwear. "*Buon Dio,*" she breathed, casting a critical eye over the demure bra and panties Lilly had on. "Really?" She disappeared and came back with flimsy, lacy, non-existent underwear. She told Lilly to put it on. "They're yours. Riccardo will thank me later."

No, he wouldn't. Lilly tried to tell herself that as she closed the curtain on the tiny little changing space and exchanged her own "nothing" underwear for the exquisite lace. This was not a real marriage. And she was definitely not sleeping with Riccardo.

"You need to give me the dress," she told Antonia, peeking around the curtain. "I'm not going out there like this."

The designer whipped the curtain away and gave her a critical look. "You look hot in those."

"Yes, well—" She gasped as Antonia grabbed her arm and yanked her out. Shoulders slumping, cheeks on fire, she stood there, in the middle of all the pre-show chaos, a multitude of mirrors surrounding her, wanting to sink into the floor. Riccardo might have said he liked the changes, but there was too much flesh on her butt for comfort, and too much in her cleavage too, if the truth were told. And her thighs—well, they just looked big. She'd bet five of her extra pounds were *there,* as if she'd reached down and slapped a piece of chocolate cake on them.

"Turn," Antonia ordered, whipping her around with firm hands.

Lilly did her best to ignore all the rail-thin women being dressed around her. But it was hard to because that was her ideal. That was what she thought she *should* look like.

"You have an unrealistic view of your body that has nothing to do with reality." Her therapist's words echoed in her ears. *"You need to change the input you give your brain."*

She tried to look at herself objectively, but it was impossible to concentrate in the middle of a gazillion bodies racing around tucking people in, touching up hair and makeup and waving clipboards. She felt dizzy just watching them. Or was that because her chest felt so tight it was hard to breathe?

One pass down the runway, she told herself, pressing clammy palms together. That was all she had to do.

Antonia pulled the stunning white gown emblazoned with vibrant purple roses over her head and knelt to adjust the hem. Lilly's eyes connected with a hard-looking blond's in the mirror. "Hell," she muttered, her throat tightening. Lacey Craig. Gossip columnist and bitch extraordinaire. The woman who'd begun the end of her marriage.

Lacey sauntered up. "Nice to have you back on the scene."

Why? Because you missed having a punching bag? Lilly looked down at Antonia's updo for fear she might lose it. Lacey had been the worst of the worst when it had come to her and Riccardo's breakup. She'd splashed lurid details—some of them true, some of them not—across the pages of Manhattan's most widely read tabloid. And would have done worse if Lilly hadn't stopped her.

"You might want to watch the weight, though," Lacey commented, running her gaze over her. "Wouldn't want your sexy husband straying again."

Antonia rose to her full five-foot-two inches and nodded at a security guard. "Get her out of here."

Lacey shrugged. "Just a bit of friendly advice. You might have forgotten just how competitive the scene can be."

As if Lilly could ever forget her husband's infidelity. The room swayed around her, the floor tilting under her feet. Perspiration broke out on her forehead and she reached out an arm to steady herself against the wall. It must be a hundred degrees in here...

Antonia grimaced as the security guard ushered Lacey out. "Why can't she ever behave?"

Lilly closed her eyes and told herself to focus. To put the nasty words out of her head and concentrate on getting through this. But visions of those photos flashed through her head like a film strip that wouldn't stop. Riccardo in Chelsea Tate's apartment, standing face-to-face with her in intimate conversation, his dark head bent to hers as he kissed her. Remembering the rest of the blurry series made her stomach churn anew.

Bile rose up in her throat. The sense of betrayal had

been all-consuming. Had sucked her down into a cauldron of self-doubt so deep it had been impossible for her to climb out.

Antonia handed her some water. "Forget that horrible witch," she murmured as she slipped a different pair of shoes on Lilly, then decided she liked Lilly's own better with the dress. "You have a real woman's body that most would die for."

Lilly only barely registered the designer's words. Lost in the world that had destroyed her, she twisted her hands together and stared down at the blindingly beautiful ring on her finger.

The stage manager called for the models. "You need to go," Antonia said. "Keep your head up and don't slouch. I've left the hem a bit long."

She lined up behind the other women at the entrance to the stage, fourth in the queue, but she wasn't really there. All she could see was the brilliant smile on Chelsea Tate's face as she pulled Riccardo in for that kiss.

She ran the back of her hand across her damp forehead. The woman in front of her went out. The show director motioned that she was on.

"Go," he said, giving her a nudge.

She stepped onto the runway. The lights blinded her. The beat of the music pounded in her ears. She started walking, but her legs were shaking so much it was hard to make any progress. The hundreds of faces in rows around the stage were a blur. The long catwalk stretched like an endless sea of white in front of her.

She stumbled, looked down to gauge where she was. Her gaze collided with a handsome blond man sitting in the front row.

Harry.

He smiled at her. She couldn't move her lips out of their frozen curve. Of course he would be here. He worked for the hospital. Her gaze slid down the row to Riccardo, her stomach giving a sickening lurch. *Had they talked to each other?*

She forced herself to keep walking, but her trembling limbs made her misstep again. Her foot slid sideways in her shoe and she stumbled forward. *What the—?* she stuck a desperate hand out to steady herself, but the momentum of her body weight sent her careening off the side of the runway. A choked scream escaped her as the wooden floor rose up to meet her.

Bracing herself for impact, she felt the air hiss from her lungs as a pair of strong arms closed around her and hauled her in.

Winded and dazed, she stared up into the face of Harry Taylor.

"*Hell,* Lilly, are you okay?"

The pounding music made her head spin. The crowd gathering around her was claustrophobic.

She nodded. "I don't know what happened. I—"

"Lilly—" Antonia pushed through the crowd, a horrified look on her face. "I forgot to do up your shoe."

Lilly grimaced and put her hand on Harry's shoulder. "It's okay. I'm fine. You can put—"

"Her down." Riccardo stepped in, his gaze not leaving Harry's face.

No thanks for saving his wife from breaking a few bones. Not even a curt acknowledgement of what he'd done. Her husband stood glaring at Harry, his expression so dark Lilly was convinced most men would have dropped her and run.

But not Harry. He lowered her gently to the floor and held her steady as Antonia knelt and did up her shoe.

"You okay?" he asked again, keeping his hands on her arms until he was sure she had her balance.

Lilly nodded, humiliation washing over her until she wanted to shrivel up into a little droplet of water and disappear between the floorboards.

Kelly Rankin stepped forward. "I am *so* sorry, Lilly," she murmured. "Are you okay to get back up there and continue?"

Riccardo slipped an arm around her waist and pulled her to his side. "She's had enough. Go on without her."

Lilly's humiliation degenerated into a slow, explosive burn. He had been the one to make her do this. He had insisted on her doing something she clearly wasn't comfortable with. *How dared he act so concerned?*

If she didn't get back up there and hold her head high she would never get over it. Pressing her lips together, she turned to Kelly. "I'm fine. Let's do it."

The organizer gave her a relieved look and went backstage. Harry stepped back and went to his seat. Lilly went on tiptoe and put her mouth to Riccardo's ear. "Never, *ever* speak for me in public again."

Then she turned and followed Antonia, leaving her stunned husband staring after her.

"Good for you, getting back up there."

An attractive fifty-something brunette gave Lilly an encouraging smile as she touched up her lipstick in the ladies' room. "I'm not sure I would have."

Lilly flashed her a polite smile. "Not much else I could do."

The woman shrugged and tossed her perfume in her purse. "Well, you looked gorgeous. I hope you get to keep the dress."

She did, in fact. Riccardo had it outside, in a monogrammed Antonia Abelli bag that also held her own less-than-spectacular underwear. Although she doubted she'd ever wear the dress again. Not after tonight. Not after she'd crashed and burned so spectacularly in it.

She nodded at the woman and left. No less than a dozen people had come up to her since the show had ended. It would have been more if Riccardo hadn't acted as gate-keeper.

Her husband's mood had gone steeply downhill since she'd ended up in Harry's arms, and she'd been relieved at his suggestion they leave shortly after. Determined to avoid as many people as she could, she walked around the edge of the crowd toward the entrance.

"Lilly."

Harry Taylor stood in front of her, a determined look on his face.

"I wanted to make sure you're okay."

She smiled and gave him a kiss on the cheek. "More embarrassed than anything. Thank you for rescuing me."

His gaze sharpened on her face. "You sure? You looked like a ghost up there—not like yourself at all."

She nodded. "I'm fine, really. Just tired. We're leaving now."

He pulled at his tie and gave her a pained look. "You know I meant what I said the other day. I don't think Riccardo is the right guy for you. And I'm always here if you need me."

Lilly bit her lip. "Look, I shouldn't be talking to you, Harry—Riccardo will hit the roof."

"That's exactly what I mean," he pointed out, frowning. "Why should you have to worry about that? Dammit, Lilly, if that bastard starts treating you badly I swear I will—"

"What?"

She spun around to find her husband standing behind them, a barely restrained look of violence on his face.

"What will you do, Taylor? I'd like to know."

Harry stepped forward. He wasn't a short man, but Riccardo had three inches on him easily. That didn't seem to faze Harry as he stood toe to toe with him. "I will hold you accountable."

Riccardo gave him a silky look. "My wife and I and our

personal life are none of your business. Accept the fact that you never stood a chance, Taylor."

Harry's face turned bright red. Lilly stared as a man who never lost control balled his hand into a fist and sent it arcing toward her husband's face. Riccardo's reflexes, honed by years as a competitive athlete, were lightning-fast and he caught the other man's wrist in his hand before it connected.

Light exploded around them. Lilly looked up to see a half-dozen cameras pointed at them. *Oh, my God.* How could this be happening?

"Guys," she pleaded, pulling on Riccardo's arm. "Stop."

Her husband dropped his hand away but stayed toe to toe with Harry. "You come near my wife again and I will take you apart piece by piece."

Harry lifted his chin. "You don't scare me, De Campo. You—"

"Harry!" Lilly had the hysterical thought that if he'd acted more like *this*—more manly, more aggressive—he might have done it for her. She took a deep breath and gave both men a level look. "We are leaving. Goodnight, Harry."

Riccardo drove home like he was on a racecourse instead of in the middle of Manhattan, and was shocked when no police officer appeared to pull him over. Lilly was out of the car and flouncing up the walkway before he came to a complete stop in their driveway, but she'd forgotten he was the only one with keys and had to cool her heels while he parked and strolled leisurely up to the door. She stood back while he inserted his key and pushed it open, then swept by him, her head held high, fury in her hazel eyes. Her heels clicked on the hardwood floor as she charged upstairs without another word.

His own safety valve about to blow, he walked into his study and poured himself a Scotch. *"I don't think Riccardo is the right guy for you..."* Taylor's smug pronouncement:

"I'm always here if you need me." His blood burned in his veins, snaking through him like a river of fire. Taylor was there in the wings, waiting for her. Waiting for *him* to screw up. And what had he done to deserve it?

He took a swig of Scotch and stifled the urge to go back there and finish Taylor off. *He* was the only man Lilly was ever going to run to. He knew it and she knew it.

It was time he proved it to her.

He downed the Scotch in two gulps, slammed the glass down on the sideboard and took the stairs to their bedroom two at a time. When he arrived in the doorway Lilly was standing in front of the closet, her shoes in her hands. He sucked in a breath. She had taken her dress off and stood there in a very sexy, very skimpy lacy white panties and bra.

Desire slammed into him, hot and hard.

Lilly flicked her gaze over him, her cat eyes wary and defiant. "Get out."

He shook his head and leaned back against the door frame. "I don't think so."

Her eyes grew larger—big, bottomless pools of amber and green he could lose himself in. Her spine stiffened as she turned fully to face him. She was afraid of him, and with a savage inner growl he acknowledged that he didn't care.

He moved toward her, his steps slow and purposeful. "I warned you not to talk to him."

She planted her hands on her hips. "I fell off that runway because *you* insisted I model that dress. Harry just wanted to see if I was okay."

His mouth twisted. "He wanted to remind you he's still around."

"Good thing he was, or who would have caught me?"

She knew her mistake the minute he stepped in to trap her against the door. "You think I'm never there for you, Lilly? Well, here I am."

He could hear her agitated breathing, see the confusion and fire that swirled in her eyes. "Go to hell," she blazed, her shoulders pressing back into the door.

"I'd rather go down on you," he murmured, sliding the back of his hand over her rosy cheek. "I know how sweet you taste, *tesoro*. How much you love it when I— Ah—" He caught the hand she swung at him and twisted it behind her back. "Don't do that."

She bit out a curse and fought against his hold, but he held her firm. "Dammit, Riccardo, let me go."

He dropped her hand and stepped in closer, until his body was pushed up against hers. "Time to talk in the only way we know how."

She squirmed against him as he imprinted her with *his* brand of honesty—the hard, throbbing truth of his lust, which was quickly sending him over the edge. But she wasn't being very convincing and he could hear how her breathing had quickened.

"Give it up, Lilly," he murmured, lowering his mouth to hers. "We both know how this is going to end."

She said something against his lips and he replied with a hard, bruising kiss that was about control, not pleasure. She'd always liked it when he dominated, and he knew that hadn't changed.

She pressed her lips mutinously shut as he slid his tongue against the crease and demanded entry. Smiling at that, he trailed his hand down over the newly voluptuous curves of her breasts, over the nipple that jutted through the lacy material that covered her, and rolled the hard nub between his fingers. She made a sound low in her throat and twisted against him, but it wasn't the movement of a woman who wanted to go anywhere. Her eyes were closed and her lips had softened, and when he swept his thumb over the hard tip and made it come to full erectness she sagged against him.

Melted into him.

He buried his hands in the thick swath of hair at the nape of her neck. Then he kissed her again, and this time she opened for him and let him take the kiss deeper, into an achingly intimate caress that told her exactly what he wanted to do to her with his tongue and with his body.

The broken sound that came from her throat told him the battle had been won.

"*Basta*," he murmured. "Enough denying ourselves what we both want."

Lilly pressed her hands back against the door as he ran his palm down the trembling flatness of her stomach. "Ric—"

He slid his hand underneath the silk that covered her and his fingers delved into the hot cleft between her thighs. She gasped and arched against his hand. A primal surge of heat flashed through him. She was wet—oh, so wet for him—and he nearly lost it right there. But he savagely yanked back his control and stilled his fingers to growl, "Tell me you love it when I touch you, *tesoro*."

She nodded, but kept her eyes shut.

"Say it."

"Dammit, yes. Please—"

"And I'm the only man who's ever going to touch you like this?"

She moaned her assent. Satisfied, he slid his fingers against the warm silk of her and indulged his craving to touch her in every way possible.

Her sudden intake of breath and her hands against his chest took him off guard.

"Get your hands off me."

He drew back. "Lil—"

"That's what this is about, isn't it?" Her voice rose in furious accusation. "Control. *You* being the only one to ever have me. *Me* doing what you want."

He frowned. "You were as into that as I was."

"I was being stupid. *Stupid.* How could I forget what this

is all about? You—always you, Riccardo." She pushed her hair out of her face. "Claiming what's yours."

"You're being ridiculous."

Her eyes glittered. "No, I've finally got my head back. Lord forbid *I* forget to keep my eye on the prize. You certainly haven't."

He shook his head. "What are you talking about?"

"I am not something to be conquered," she said thickly. "I am your wife. You just can't understand that."

"Lilly—"

"Get out." Her face was a blotchy patchwork of red. "Get out or I will walk out of here and never come back, deal or no deal."

Deciding there was no reasoning with her while she was in this state, he turned on his heel and left, hearing the door slam behind him.

He took a cold shower in the guest bedroom, letting the freezing water pound down on his shoulders. *Was* he demented for even attempting this plan of his? To want to make Lilly pay for everything she'd done to him? The humiliation she'd caused him? Because he wasn't sure who was winning—her or him.

CHAPTER SIX

"*This is your* idea of convincing the board you're the man to lead De Campo?"

Gabe shoved a folded newspaper under Riccardo's nose.

He sat back in his office chair and glanced at the tabloid. It was the same one Lilly had waved in his face this morning on her way to work. Having the juiciest of all the coverage of the charity event, it sported the headline "Trouble in Paradise—Already?", which was set over a montage of three photos of him and Lilly laid out in timeline fashion.

The first was of him kissing her on the dance floor. He studied it critically. They *looked* very much in love, despite the fact they hadn't talked in days. The second was of Lilly falling off the runway into Taylor's arms. His mouth tightened. *That* he'd like to forget. The third was a shot of himself restraining the surgeon after he'd thrown that punch.

All in all, fairly damaging.

"What can I say?" He shrugged. "It's a slow news day."

Gabe lifted a brow at him. "What the hell happened? Fisticuffs aren't usually your style—although lately I have to say you're doing a pretty good job of it."

Riccardo spread his fingers in an expressive gesture. "He threw a punch."

Gabe sat on the edge of his desk. "Why?"

"He cornered Lilly and made it clear he was going to

be around to pick up the pieces when I broke her heart. I took offense at that."

His brother let out a low whistle. "I'm surprised you didn't slug him."

"That would have been giving the board far too much ammunition."

"And Lilly falling off the runway?"

"The designer forgot to do up her shoe."

"You're kidding?"

He crumpled up the paper and tossed it freethrow-style into the garbage can he kept across the room for exactly that purpose. "She was a trooper. She got right back up there and did it again."

"That's Lilly." His brother grinned. "She has *spirito*."

Until the end. When she'd become a shadow of her former self. When she'd had that same look on her face she'd had before going up on that stage *every* night before they'd gone out. As if she'd been dreading it.

A wave of remorse settled over him. He'd been the son-of-a-bitch who'd made her go up there. And, even though he had no idea what had set her off, it had been wrong to do it.

Dio. He picked up his coffee and glowered into it. Lilly had used to be comfortable in the center of it all. They'd been nicknamed the Golden Couple for their ability to work a room.

So what had changed?

She had accused him of never being there for her. The symbolic act of Taylor rescuing her and not him had been a brutal shot to his ego. Not just because he'd been five feet away and Taylor had sprung out of his seat like Sir Galahad on a white steed. But because it had once again reinforced the fact that she'd left him. That he wasn't the one she wanted. The fact that he had no clue *who* she really was.

His hand tightened around the coffee cup, red-hot anger slicing through him. It was time he and Lilly had a long conversation about a lot of things—not the least of which was what had really happened to her during those last few months of their marriage. Why she'd frozen him out. Become a ghost of who she'd been. It had to be about more than Chelsea. And he was sure that last night held the key to at least some of it.

Gabe glanced at his watch. "You ready?"

Riccardo nodded.

The cold war between him and Lilly couldn't go on forever. Not with this battle with the board and his father ahead of him. Not when he was intent on claiming what was rightfully his. Both at home and in the boardroom.

There was a knock on the door. He got to his feet as Paige, his PA, came in.

"The meeting's about to start."

He nodded and slipped on his jacket. It was possibly the most important meeting of his life, in which he was to lay out his plans for De Campo's future to the board, and here he was obsessing over his wife. His mouth twisted. Lilly would find that bitterly amusing, he was sure.

He picked up his laptop and followed Gabe out of the room.

"Ah…Riccardo?" Paige lifted a brow at him as he walked past her.

"Mmm?"

"Want the blueprints?"

The blueprints of their new restaurant in SoHo. The centerpiece of his presentation. He grimaced and took them from her. "What would I do without you?"

Antonio had the same salacious tabloid Riccardo had now seen twice this morning tucked in front of him when they walked into the room. Riccardo swept his gaze around the table. So did Phil Bedford and Chase Kenyon. *Hell.* Was his life a walking soap opera?

"Smoothing the way, I see," his father murmured as he

took his place beside him. "Did you know Phil Bedford plays golf with Harry Taylor?"

Riccardo deposited his laptop on the table with slightly more force than was necessary, picked up his father's paper and waved it in the air. "Looks like most of you have seen the paper this morning?"

Matty's mouth dropped open. Gabe looked fascinated. All the other extremely senior heads of their corporations sat there silently and stared at him. He shifted his gaze to Phil Bedford, the portly CEO of a consumer packaged goods company pushing fifty.

"Harry Taylor wants to date my wife. I don't consider that a valid proposition since she is *still* my wife. So I acted on it." He threw the paper down on the table like the trash it was and eyed the room. "If anyone would like to crucify me with this please do so now, so we can get on with business."

Phil Bedford stared down at his coffee. Chase Kenyon doodled on his notepad.

"Fine." Riccardo looked at Antonio. "All yours."

He could have sworn his father was holding back laughter as he got to his feet and opened the meeting. Antonio gave a holistic presentation on how the De Campo Group was performing worldwide, every bit the elegant global wine baron as he talked through the slides in his thick accent, then turned the meeting over to Riccardo for an update on the restaurant business.

Riccardo opened with an overview of the division's strong growth prospects, then ran through a presentation on the new jewel in the De Campo restaurant crown—Zambia, the SoHo restaurant set to open in six months. He saw the lights go on in the board members' eyes as he spoke of the twelve percent overall profit increase the restaurant division would bring in, and knew he'd driven home his message of where the future was for De Campo.

He sat down, his jaw clenched with satisfaction. He had nailed it.

Gabe stood to give an update on the California operations. Another board member gave a presentation on how lessons learned from the packaged goods industry could be applied to wine. Then they broke for lunch.

Antonio followed him into his office. *"Buon lavoro, figlio."*

Good job, son.

Caught off-guard by the compliment, he warily inclined his head. *"Grazie."*

"You keep this up and I might just throw my weight behind you."

He froze. *The son-of-a-bitch.* Even after the results he'd just presented Antonio was still stringing him along.

He dragged in a breath and let it out slowly. "I will be single-handedly responsible for that twelve percent profit you just gloated over. You start putting recognition where it's due or so, help me God, I will leave this company and not look back."

His father set his chin at that haughty angle he favored. "A De Campo would *never* utter those words."

"This one just did." Riccardo jammed his hands in his pockets and paced to the window. "Just out of curiosity, how long do you intend to make me pay?"

Antonio narrowed his gaze on him. "Is that what you think I'm doing?"

"I *know* that's what you're doing."

"Maybe I think Gabe would do a better job."

He stiffened, white-hot rage slicing through him. "We are not Cain and Abel, with you playing God, Antonio. I will *not* compete with my brother. Make a decision, but do not try and drive a wedge between us. Neither of us will tolerate it."

His father shrugged his broad shoulders. "Some think Gabe has the true love for this business. He's aggressive, with just the right amount of conservatism."

"Then why didn't you choose him to run the company while you were ill? You had the opportunity."

Antonio met his combative stare with one of his own. "Because, despite the fact that you dishonored this family by choosing a racing career over your heritage, you have the heart of a lion, Riccardo. You have the vision to take this company where it needs to go."

"So does Gabe."

His father shook his head. "Not like you. You have the ability to be brutal. To make the decisions no one else wants to make."

"Then do it," Riccardo gritted out. "Because I'm not waiting much longer. I've sacrificed too much."

Antonio pointed a beefy finger at him. "How long have I been waiting to hear you say that?"

Riccardo frowned. "What?"

"Sacrifice. You view De Campo as a sacrifice. As an impediment to your personal freedom. Not as the majestic birthright that's been handed to you."

"I love this company. I have killed myself for this company. I do *not* view it as a sacrifice. But I *have* sacrificed for it." He trained his gaze on his father. "As you did."

"Prove it." His father flicked his hand in the air in a dismissive motion. "I'm retiring in three months. The job is yours to lose."

"You might just kill me one of these days."

The big, burly football player wiped the sweat from his face and stepped off the treadmill. Lilly smiled and made a note of the time in her chart. What would normally have been a walk-in-the-park run for Trent Goodman had been a one-mile endurance test on a knee that had a whole lot of healing ahead before he stepped back on a football field.

"Admit it—you like coming to see me."

"Are you kidding?" He dropped the towel in his bag and slung it over his shoulder. "It's the highlight of my week.

The pain I can take, when I'm getting the inside scoop on all the gossip. You get more press than I do—and frankly," he admitted sheepishly, "that's not a good thing."

Lilly laughed. "Believe me—I'd happily pass it along if I could."

"I bet you would." He grinned. "That photo of your husband tangling with the doctor? Priceless."

Maybe somewhat less than priceless. She was now back as a fixture in all the gossip rags. She'd spent the weekend fuming at Riccardo's caveman tactics. Both with Harry and in the bedroom.

"He has his moments," she murmured, looking back at the clipboard. "Same time tomorrow?"

He nodded and blew her a kiss. She smiled and watched him leave. Muscular, gorgeous, charming and making millions…Trent would have had most women on their knees with his overt flirtatiousness. Lilly, however, was fixated on her own brutish male.

What in the world had gotten into her? She'd nearly toppled. Slept with him and done something she'd have sorely regretted. All because she still couldn't keep her hands to herself when it came to Riccardo.

She twirled a chunk of hair around her finger. They had exchanged a total of about a hundred words since that scene in the bedroom. If he was in the kitchen when she came down, she took her coffee onto the patio. If she came down first, he went and watched the news in his study.

It couldn't go on like this.

Unresolved issues lay between them like unexploded mines. Yet Saturday night had proved beyond a shadow of a doubt she never wanted to live the life of Riccardo's society wife ever again. That she'd been right to leave when she had.

That she wasn't *capable* of living it beyond the six months she'd committed to.

So why did everything feel so wrong? Why couldn't

she just do what she needed to in public and to hell with how things were at home? She tossed her clipboard on her desk and grabbed the notes on her afternoon patients so she could file them. She had pushed a set of notes into a folder and slid it back into the drawer before realizing she'd completely mixed the two patients up. *Damn.* She pulled the two folders out again.

A loud piano piece filled the air. She frowned. *Her new ringtone.* Note to self: change that. She pulled her phone out of her pocket and held it to her ear while she fixed the notes.

"Lilly Anderson."

"De Campo," Riccardo's rich drawl oozed across the line. "Really, Lilly, you have to get with the program."

"I don't use your name professionally. You know that."

"I don't like it. I'm calling to ask your permission to ask Katy to clear your schedule for Thursday and Friday."

Her husband's drily delivered request made Lilly frown and push the drawer of the filing cabinet shut with her foot. Riccardo asking for her permission to do something? Was he sick? On some type of mood-altering medication?

She cleared her throat and chose her words carefully. "I have clinics at the hospital on Thurdsay and Friday. Is it important?"

"I'd like to take you to Barbados for the weekend."

"The Caribbean island of Barbados?"

"The one and only," he confirmed, amusement lacing his tone. "A friend of mine offered up his place for the weekend."

She stuck a finger in her mouth and chewed on her nail. "So it's a business thing?"

"No." His voice deepened to that silky tone that made her toes squish in her shoes. "Definitely not business."

Heat filled her cheeks. "Riccardo—"

He sighed. "We need a truce. We need to talk, Lil. Somewhere by ourselves, with no photographers, no one interrupting us, neither of us rushing off to work… Just us."

She couldn't deny that. It was just that it sounded sort of...*terrifying*. She rested her hip on the corner of the desk and the guilty thought came to her that maybe, *maybe,* if she'd talked to him from the start instead of shutting down things *would* have been different.

A snapping sound filled the air. She pulled her finger out of her mouth and stared, horrified, at her broken nail. She hadn't bitten her nails in exactly twelve months.

"You still there?"

"Yes."

Another sigh. "I'm pretending I'm asking, but I'm not really, you know."

She smiled. At least she knew her husband hadn't been abducted by aliens. She stared down at her wreck of a nail and swallowed hard. "To be clear—this is a discussion? That's all?"

"A discussion," he agreed firmly. "That's all I'm asking for."

"Okay, then, yes." It would be closure for them both.

"Good. Will you tell Katy or will I?"

"I will."

"*Bene.* I'm off for dinner with the boys and Antonio." His voice took on a sardonic edge. "Wish me luck."

"Keep your cool. You'll be fine."

A meaningful silence came down the phone line. "Already lost it. *Ciao, bella.*"

"*Ciao.*"

Lilly pressed the end button, her skin tingling from the effects of those two softly spoken words. Would there ever come a day when *that* didn't make her want to throw caution to the wind and do exactly what she wasn't supposed to do?

She fought the sinking feeling she had just made a huge mistake and dialed her sister.

Alex answered with a distracted, "Hello."

"It's your sister. Got a sec?"

"Always. How are you holding up? Riccardo mix it up with anyone lately?"

"Very funny." Lilly pulled a pristine nail out of her mouth before she trashed that one too. "We have to re-schedule brunch. I'm going to be away this weekend."

"What lifestyle-of-the-rich-and-famous event is he tak-ing you to?"

"None. We're going to Barbados together."

"*Damn. I* would put up with him for a weekend like that."

Lilly smiled. "Gabe's still in town, you know."

"Mmm, yes—well, I'm afraid I'm not up for twenty-four-seven sparring. Dr. Overlea just called to say he's scheduled Lisbeth in for some pretreatments next week. I'm going to head home and keep her company so she doesn't stress."

Lilly's throat tightened. "I didn't think he was going to be able to get her in so soon."

"He needs to do this before he schedules treatment with the clinic in Switzerland."

"Right." She swallowed hard. "I—" *Hell.* The conver-sation with Riccardo was important, but her sister's health was more so.

"Lil—it's fine. I'll go." Her sister's voice softened. "You guys need time together."

She chewed on her lip. Alex probably thought she and Riccardo were having hot reunion sex every night… She so desperately wanted to tell her that, no, they weren't, that they were hardly talking to each other and she was hope-lessly confused, but she couldn't. Not if she was to keep her and Riccardo's deal.

"You'll call me if you need me? I'll come right back."

"I will. I promise."

Her shoulders sagged. "Okay."

"By the way—one of the girls here just showed me some

of the stuff the tabloids are saying about you. Please tell me you're not reading it?"

"I'm not reading it." Only a bit. One or two particularly horrid pieces...

"Yes, you are. I can tell. You have to stop it, Lil. It's awful, destructive stuff and not a bit true. I've never seen you looking so good."

Lilly sighed. "I'm fine, Alex. I promise." Only her sister knew how deep her body issues went and she called her on it when she needed to.

"You sure?"

"I gave my whole wardrobe to charity," she said drily. "Riccardo almost had a fit."

"The whole thing?" her sister squeaked.

"All of it."

"I can't tell you how glad I am to hear you say that."

"I know... Al?"

"Yeah?"

"Do you really think people never change?"

She sighed. "Are you talking about Riccardo?"

"Yes."

And why, exactly, was she?

Her sister cleared her throat. "When we were looking at those tabloids this morning, one of the girls here looked at that photo of you and Riccardo kissing—which is dreamy, by the way, and I don't *do* dreamy, as you know—and she got this stupid, expression on her face and said, 'I just want *that*. To be that much in love.'"

Lilly felt the stitches she'd triple-sewed around her heart rip, leaving it jagged and raw. *She* wanted to be that much in love again. But that wasn't her and Riccardo anymore, and telling herself that was possible was foolish.

"So," her sister continued, "while I think he might be the most arrogant son-of-a-bitch I've ever met, I know what you have is special, Lil, and that man is crazy about you in his own demented way. Which leads me to believe he's going to do whatever it takes to keep you."

Lilly stood there, wishing she'd never asked the question in the first place.

"Do me a favor?" Alex's voice lost its sarcasm and took on a serious note.

"Name it."

"Whatever you do, don't get pregnant."

Lilly stared at the phone, horrified. Then remembered her sister didn't know. Didn't know this was all a charade. "Of course I won't. That would complicate everything."

"Exactly."

Exactly. She glanced at her watch. "I'm done for the day, and Riccardo's out with the boys. You up to swimsuit-shopping? You're the only one I know who'll give me an honest opinion."

They made arrangements to meet and Lilly hung up, more worried with every passing moment that a "conversation" in Barbados with her sexier than hell husband was a disaster waiting to happen.

One thing she knew for sure. She could never, never tell him about why she'd entered into this deal. About Lisbeth. Because she didn't trust him not to use that against her. And Lisbeth was all that mattered.

CHAPTER SEVEN

LILLY STOOD ON the patio of Charles Greene's very beautiful, very exclusive Barbados estate overlooking Heron Bay. The sparkling, water-soaked playground of the world's rich and famous, the bay was dotted with luxury hotels and villas that sat on heavenly golden sand beaches and the most stunning clear turquoise water Lilly had ever seen.

If you were the world's most famous golfer you took over Heron Bay's five-thousand-dollar-a-night marquee hotel for a sunset marriage featuring heads of state, rock stars and movie icons. If you were Charles Greene, British billionaire and heir to a heavy machinery fortune, you bought this gorgeous six-bedroom villa on the ocean and kept it for yourself.

Charles and Riccardo had done business together on a few occasions, and had formed a close personal relationship in addition to their working one. With Charles away on business in the UK, the villa was theirs. A private oasis in paradise.

At any other time in her life Lilly would have been ecstatic to be here. But not tonight. Not when she was about to learn the truth about her marriage.

She kept her feet planted firmly on the concrete. Tonight was not about running. It was about facing her demons.

She drank in the sheet of shimmering perfect blue sea in front of her, its color morphing from light to dark turquoise, then to a marine blue the further out the eye traveled. Were relationships like that? she wondered. Were there gradations and depths she and Riccardo had yet to explore? Or would this be the end for them?

"I'm leaving now."

Mrs. Adams, the housekeeper who had greeted them and shown them to their rooms, appeared on the patio with a bottle of wine and a cooler in her hands. "Mr. De Campo thought you might enjoy a glass of wine while he showers."

Lilly forced a smile to her lips. "Thank you. He's off the phone, then?"

She nodded. "He said to tell you he'd be down in a few minutes." She set the cooler down on the table and took some glasses out of a cupboard. "Did you say you'd been here before?"

"Yes. A year ago."

Riccardo had come here on business and brought her with him. It had been right after news of his affair had surfaced and she'd spent the whole week trying to convince herself she shouldn't doubt him. Trying to save her marriage.

Until she'd seen the photos.

"It's a beautiful island," she murmured, realizing the woman was waiting for her response. "We stayed further up the coast."

Her brief response had the desired effect. The housekeeper nodded and stuck her hands on her hips. "I'll be back tomorrow to cook breakfast. Would you like me to pour you a glass of wine?"

"No, thank you. I can pour it."

"Okay, see you tomorrow, then."

"Goodnight."

Lilly kept the plastic smile on her face until the housekeeper had disappeared into the house. Her body vibrated with a tension that hadn't left her since they'd climbed aboard the De Campo jet and flown the five hours south to the island—a flight the entire duration of which Riccardo had worked. She pulled in a breath to steady herself, but the shallow pulls of air she managed to take in didn't help much.

She turned back to the sea and laced her hands together. *"Stay in the moment. Allow yourself to feel and move through the pain..."* Her therapist's words were a grounding force when all she wanted to do was run. It had been her coping mechanism since she was a teenager and her parents had been having their no-holds-barred fights to run when she was in pain. To refuse to feel it.

Making herself stand here was like being asked to walk over red-hot coals.

"You haven't had any wine."

Riccardo's low, smooth observation contrasted sharply with the imminent hysteria she felt building within her. This had always been the pattern with them. Him handling everything with reason—with well-thought-out premeditation. Lilly shooting from the hip—driven by emotion.

She turned around, a sharp condemnation on her lips. But he was so breathtakingly handsome in jeans and a navy polo shirt, his square-jawed, dark good looks only intensified by the casual attire, that the words fled her head.

He was beautiful beyond the meaning of the word. Charisma oozed out of him like oxygen for the female race. And she knew then that this had been a big, huge mistake.

Just as it had been to think she could claim ownership over a man every woman wanted.

She turned back to look at the ocean. "You can pour me some now."

The knot in her stomach grew to an almost incapacitating level as she heard him walk across the patio and pour the wine. The sound of bubbling liquid hitting glass was deafeningly loud on the night air.

He came to stand beside her, the smoky, spicy scent of him wrapping itself around her.

"What's wrong?"

She swiveled to face him. "You've been talking on that phone non-stop since we left. I thought we had a no work rule."

His mouth tightened. "It's off now. I just had a few last things to go through with Gabe. By the way," he added, raising a brow, "he asked Alex out for dinner and she turned him down flat. Said she was going back to Mason Hill for the weekend." His gaze narrowed on her face. "You two *never* go home. Is everything okay with your family?"

She blanched. "Everything's fine. Can we just get this over with?"

He kept that watchful dark gaze on her. Then handed her the glass of wine.

She wrapped her fingers around the stem. The glass shook in her hand.

"Lil—" His eyes moved from her shaking fingers to her face.

"I'm fine," she murmured. "You—you start."

He exhaled harshly, the nostrils of his perfectly straight Roman nose flaring.

"What happened the night of the fashion show? Why were you so afraid to do it?"

She blinked. She had not expected that to be his first question. "You know I've never been comfortable in that type of setting. I told you that when we first started dating."

"But you got over it. You thrived on it."

"I hated every minute of it. I trained myself to do it so I wouldn't let you down."

Confusion flickered in his eyes. "Why? Why would a woman like you have confidence issues? You had the position, the wealth, the looks to back you. Why would you feel inferior?"

She gave a twisted smile. "I come from a town of two thousand, five hundred people, Riccardo. I will always feel small-town, no matter how you dress me up or how many places you take me or how many etiquette rules you teach me." She shook her head. "You swept me up into this glamorous life I had no coping skills for, tossed me into the deep end and expected me to swim."

He frowned. "But you never said anything. To me— you were just fine."

Her shoulders stiffened. "I was doing what I had to do. That was my *job*. My role as Lilly De Campo."

He exhaled heavily. "No one would ever have known you felt that way."

Her lips twisted in a bitter smile. "I became extraordinarily good at faking it. And why not? I faked my way through our entire marriage."

His gaze sharpened on her face, a dangerous glint firing in its dark depths. "I think you'd better explain that."

"I never wanted that life, Riccardo. I told you that when you knocked me off my feet in that bar in SoHo. But you wouldn't listen…you kept pushing until I said yes."

"We were in love with each other," he growled.

"We were infatuated with each other," she corrected. "There was still time to recognize how wrong it was for me. How self-destructive all the attention and criticism was."

"How so?"

She set her wine down on the railing and pushed her hair behind her ears. "I've never been secure in the way I look. It's always been a tough one for me. But as your wife I couldn't put on five pounds without the tabloids noticing and pouncing on me."

"I told you. Stop reading them."

"That's overly simplistic. They were everywhere. I couldn't avoid them all."

His brows drew together. "But where does it come from, then, this insecurity about your looks? Beyond what the tabloids say?"

She turned away from his penetrating barrage of questions. But her therapist's words haunted her, refused to let her back away. *"Above all be honest, Lilly. Be honest with yourself and those around you."*

She took a deep breath. "I was very unhappy as a teenager. My parents' marriage was a mess for a long time. The farm wasn't doing well and the stress of having no money was getting to them. The kids—we had no life. We spent all our time helping out on the farm. We barely had time for schoolwork, let alone social lives."

"I knew you weren't happy at home and that's why you left," he said quietly. "But I didn't know it was that bad."

She nodded. "My parents' fights would dissolve into screaming matches. Plates would fly and my mother would threaten to leave. My dad had an affair with the farmer's wife down the road." She hugged her arms around herself and looked up at him. "It was a disaster. A huge mess."

There was a pregnant silence. His face paled. *Yes,* she thought viciously. *That's why what you did hurt so much.*

She kept going, afraid that if she stopped she'd never tell him the truth. "David seemed immune to it all. Lisbeth was too young to know what was happening. Alex dealt with it by getting into trouble—running with the wrong crowd. I internalized it. I thought if I could control everything about my life beyond them, beyond what was happening at home, I'd be okay."

Her mouth felt wooden, her lips thick, and the desire to stop talking was so strong it was hard to make herself form the words. "My big thing was food. I hated the way I looked so I controlled everything I put in my mouth." She swallowed hard. "To the point where I was hardly eating."

His eyes darkened with an emotion she couldn't read. "But you can't ever have been fat. Why in the world would you hate yourself so much?"

"I was a 'chunky, healthy, solid-boned farmgirl,' as my mother would say," she said with a derisive smile. "And I hated it. No one wanted to date me. No one wanted to be with me."

"I find that hard to believe."

"It wasn't until I was in my twenties that I bloomed. Came into myself. You met me not long after that."

He frowned. "So why is it still so bad? I've seen men lust after you, Lilly. You know they do. That must give you some confidence."

"Yes." She turned back to look at the brilliant sunset staining the sky now, the giant ball of orange and red sinking into the horizon. She swallowed past the hard, round mass in her throat that felt as if it was choking her, as if revealing her shameful secret might bring her to her knees. "But not before I developed anorexia."

There was a long silence. He scraped his hand over his jaw and stared at her. "I had no idea."

She made a face. "It's not something you drop into casual conversation, like the fact I had a dog named Honey when I was little."

"*Dio,* Lilly." He stepped forward and took her by the shoulders. "That's not what I'm talking about. This is key to who you are. Essential information I need to know about you. I would never have put you through any of this if I'd known that."

She lifted her chin. "I didn't want you to know."

"Why?" He threw up his hands. "Because for once I might see who the real Lilly De Campo is?"

"No, I—"

"Lilly, we've been as intimate as two people can be. We've spent hours devouring each other. Yet you still can't tell me these profound truths about yourself? No wonder we're messed up."

She shook her head and took a step back. "Sex and intimacy are two different things."

"They most certainly are," he agreed tightly. "And the minute you turned into the Ice Queen and froze me out any intimacy we had was blown to bits."

She winced. "I wasn't trying to hurt you. I was trying

to protect myself. My anorexia was my deep, dark secret. It was the thing no one knew about me in my new life. The thing I never wanted anyone to know about me. Most of all you."

A muscle jumped in his jaw. "Why?"

She pressed her lips together. "You're a perfect human being, Riccardo. Everything about you is so damn perfect that everyone wants you, everyone admires you. I've never felt I could live up to it. *Be* that woman who's worthy of you."

"That's ridiculous."

She stamped her foot. "*It's how I feel, dammit*. Everything—*everything* about my life with you was about keeping up appearances. Making sure we were that Golden Couple. And the balance I'd tried so hard to inject into my life in order to stay healthy went out the window. How could it not when I was constantly in the spotlight? Constantly being judged?"

He raked his hand through his hair. "I wish you'd told me so I could have helped you."

Her heart throbbed in her chest. "I didn't want to add myself to your list of issues. You had enough going on with De Campo business."

He shook his head. "Did *I* ever put any pressure on you about your weight?"

"You never reassured me."

"I *always* told you how gorgeous you looked."

"Yes, but when I said things like, 'I feel fat,' to get some reassurance from you, you told me to go to the gym."

"That's because that's what *I* do when I feel like that. I work out, get the tension out, and I feel better about myself. *Hell,* Lilly…" He was staring at her as if she was a creature from another planet. "Has there ever been any doubt about how much I love your body?"

Her gaze skipped away from his. "I've put on weight since we were together."

"And that scene the other night wasn't enough to convince you I like the changes?"

"Why wasn't I enough, then?" She yelled the words at him, her control snapping. "If you think I'm beautiful, if I'm *enough* for you, then why did you have to have an affair with Chelsea Tate?"

All the color drained out of his face. "It didn't happen. You're the only woman I want, Lilly. Chelsea never came close to meaning anything like that to me."

"Then tell me the truth," she raged, pointing a finger at him. "This is my life, Riccardo. Not a tabloid page. When I left you I was in the fetal position for three days. *Three days.* And if Alex hadn't come along to dig me out I might still be there. So do *not* tell me any more lies. I can't take it."

He stared at her with the glazed look of a man who didn't know where to go. What to do. She watched him take a deep breath and steady himself and felt her heart sink into the depths of hell.

"You need to give me a chance to explain…"

She bit back the bile that rose in her throat. "Believe me—you have my full attention."

He raked a hand through his hair and set his jaw. "Chelsea and I were once close—you know that. But once I met you that all ended and you were the only woman in my life. The *only* one, Lilly." He frowned when she gave no reaction. "When things got so bad between us I was completely at a loss as to what to do. It was impossible to believe a marriage could go from one-fifty to zero in a matter of months—but somehow ours did, and I couldn't figure out why or what to do about it. You refused to be with me, my pride was stinging, and I think we were both questioning our marriage."

She forgot to breathe. Forgot she *had* to.

"I was hurt at what had become of us. Angry at what you were doing to me." His mouth flattened into a grim line and his eyes half closed, as if he couldn't believe what he was saying. "So I called Chelsea and invited her to dinner."

Lilly felt as if a train was headed for her, but she couldn't move. Couldn't do anything to avoid it.

"I wanted to prove I didn't need you—I didn't love you," he continued hoarsely. "And maybe I wanted to hurt you too. Make you hurt as much as I was hurting."

Lilly pressed her hands to her ears, but he stalked forward and dragged them away.

"I drove her home, I went up to her apartment with every intention of taking her to bed. And then I kissed her and everything felt wrong."

Lilly felt the ground sway beneath her and, cursing, Riccardo scooped her up in his arms. He carried her over to the bench and sat down with her cradled against him. A tortured expression filled his eyes as he stared down at her. "You haunted me. No matter how much you pushed me away you were the only one I wanted."

She sat there in his arms like a strange, disembodied presence that could hear what he was saying but couldn't actually register it. When she managed to speak, her voice was low and thready. "You kissed her but you didn't sleep with her?"

He nodded. "I came home to you and never saw her again."

Something reached inside her and tore her heart out. "What kind of a kiss was it?"

He cursed low under his breath. "You can't torture yourself like that."

"*Yes, I can!*" she shrieked, stumbling off his lap and facing him on shaking legs. "You betrayed me, Riccardo. I saw those photographs. You didn't just kiss her. You had sex with her!"

He frowned. "There were no photographs taken of us. We were in Chelsea's apartment."

"There were *eight*. Eight photos of you in various states of undress. Dammit, stop lying."

He stood up and took her by the shoulders. "You will watch your tongue and tell me what you're talking about."

"Lacey Craig," she threw at him, knowing this might well put the final nail in their marriage, but past caring. "After we got back from Barbados I called her up and asked what proof she had to support her story. She showed me photos of you and Chelsea. *Intimate* photos of you. And she let me buy them to spare me the humiliation of having them splashed across every gossip magazine in the country."

He blinked at her, a look of complete incomprehension on his face. "Let me get this straight," he said slowly. "You called a gossip columnist, demanded information about my infidelity and paid her for fake photos?"

"They weren't fake," she cried. "Everybody in New York knew you were having an affair! Too bad I was the last to know."

His fingers tightened around her shoulders. "They *are* fake photos because I did not sleep with Chelsea Tate— ever—after our relationship began."

His rage and the icy, menacing look on his face vibrated through her like a sledgehammer. Riccardo had never lied to her. Not once in their marriage. Until Chelsea. Truth was like a badge of honor to him—it was the De Campo creed, the way he conducted his life. Better to be brutal and get it over with.

What if she was wrong?

"Lilly?"

She yanked herself out of his grasp and turned away. Her brain moved wildly through the possibilities. Photos could be doctored. They were doctored all the time. Maybe those *hadn't* been shots of him and Chelsea. It had been hard to see their faces after that initial shot of them kissing…

A cold, buzzing feeling descended over her. Would Lacey Craig have dared to sell her fakes? Wouldn't she have been worried Lilly would take them straight to Riccardo, who would have pronounced them as such and sued the hell out of her?

Or maybe Lacey hadn't known they were fake...

Oh, God.

Riccardo took a step toward her, his face hard and determined. "How much did you pay for those photos?"

She shook her head.

"How much?"

"One hundred thousand dollars."

"A hundred thousand?" His brow furrowed. "They wouldn't give you a full-page ad for a hundred grand..."

Lilly felt her world fall apart.

His gaze sharpened on her face as understanding dawned in his eyes. "That was the money you said you sent your parents?"

"Yes."

He sucked in a breath, his fists clenching at his sides. "You trusted me so little you would do that without talking to me?"

"You kissed her, Riccardo! You went home with her, intending to sleep with her. Where in that is there anything that says I should have trusted you?"

His jaw clamped shut. He was silent for several long moments, each one driving the stake that was impaling her heart deeper and deeper.

Finally he raised his gaze to hers and asked quietly, "Was there ever any point in our marriage you were happy?"

She fought the fire burning the back of her eyes. "That first year after we married was the most amazing year of my life. I loved you, Riccardo. I worshipped the ground you walked on. You were my knight in shining armor who'd swooped into my life and made it whole again. But somewhere along the way I lost my glitter when it came to you. You didn't want me the same way you did before. And it was torturous for me to be with you like that." She looked down at the sparkling ring on her finger. "So I left."

"You left because you thought I didn't love you anymore?"

"I left because we were destroying each other. You became obsessed with that job—obsessed with having your birthright. And you left me alone to deal with the fallout of being Lilly De Campo. Something I couldn't do on my own."

He was silent, a granite mask stretching across his face. She hugged her arms around herself and listened as a chorus of tree frogs filled the air with their haunting, rhythmical song.

"You never once thought I might be struggling too? That I might need my wife?" He said the words quietly, deliberately, his face devoid of emotion.

"How would I have known? You're like Mount Vesuvius. You keep everything inside until you explode. And when you do there's nothing for me to respond to but the anger."

His dark gaze rested on her. "I could say the same about you."

"Yes, you could." She nodded. "I have a ton of baggage, I know. But at least I acknowledge mine."

His mouth pulled tight as her arrow hit home. He swung away and walked to the edge of the terrace, rested his elbows on the railing as he looked out at the sea. "I always thought if you wanted something bad enough you made it happen. That we could resolve our differences because we loved each other that much."

The lump in her throat grew so large it felt as if she was aching all over. "Sometimes," she choked, "love isn't enough."

He turned around, his broad shoulders silhouetted against the setting sun. The dull look on his face made the rest of her shrivel away.

"A marriage needs trust to survive. And between the two of us I think we've proved we have none."

And there it was, she thought miserably. Their marriage summed up in one glaring truth.

"It was never going to work."

Her words sat flat and lifeless on the night air between them. Riccardo's head snapped back, a flare of angry color slashing across his cheekbones. His steps as he closed the distance between them were jerky, full of a barely leashed rage that made her suck in a breath. When he stopped in front of her, his furious glare leveled on her face, her heart seemed to stop.

"We may have spoken a lot of truths tonight, Lilly, but do not, *do not* absolve yourself of the responsibility you carry for this marriage. You checked out. You left me. You *chose* to give up. And you *will* own that."

She pulled in another breath, but it wasn't enough, and desperately she dragged in another. There never seemed to be enough oxygen on the planet when she was with Riccardo because he sucked it out of her. Stripped her bare.

He stared at her for a long moment, waiting for her to respond, waiting for her to give him what he demanded of her, but she couldn't force the words out of her mouth.

He spun away and stalked toward the French doors.

"Ric—"

"I need some space."

He disappeared inside. Lilly watched him go, too numb to react. *Where was he going?* The sound of the front door slamming made her heart drop. *He was leaving?*

She ran to the front door and threw it open, but only the glaring darkness of the Caribbean night stared back at her. She would have heard the car if he'd taken it. He must have gone on foot.

She closed the door and fumbled with the deadbolt to lock it. Unsure of what to do next, she turned and leaned against it, pulling in deep, long breaths. Then she slid down to the floor and did the thing she hadn't let herself do since the week she'd left Riccardo.

She sobbed her heart out.

Tears streamed down her face in a barrage that it seemed would never end. Her worst fear about her marriage had been both proven and unproven in one explosive conversation that had left her so raw and exposed she wasn't sure she would ever be able to close herself back up again.

Riccardo had kissed Chelsea Tate with the intent of sleeping with her. And even though he hadn't been able to do it, the fact that he'd kissed Chelsea—the *thought* of him kissing her—splintered Lilly's heart into a million pieces.

How could he? The man who'd promised to love and protect her that day in the cathedral when they'd been married, whom she'd let down all her barriers for, had betrayed her in the worst way possible. Because, she thought numbly, wasn't kissing the most intimate act of all?

Somewhere, someplace deep down inside her, she'd been hoping she was wrong. That Riccardo had been telling her the truth when he'd said nothing had happened between him and Chelsea and that her early naive belief that nothing could touch them was true.

But it wasn't something she could hang onto anymore. She and Riccardo *were* fallible and his message had been clear. *She* had driven him into Chelsea's arms. He had wanted to hurt her as she'd been hurting him. And that, she realized, swiping the tears from her face, was something she'd never thought of. That cool, hard-as-rock Riccardo could be hurt in any way. That *she* had the power to hurt him like that.

But in the end it had been as she'd always known it would be. She hadn't been capable of being what he needed. She hadn't been enough for him. Otherwise he never would have gone to Chelsea.

Her severed heart throbbed with a misery that said there was still some life in it. She closed her eyes and breathed.

To leave had been her survival mechanism. To stop trying to be something she could never be.

But Riccardo's relentless assault continued to unpeel her layers, as if once started it would never stop. Emotions that had been bottled up far too long bubbled over and tumbled into her consciousness. She remembered that perfect day before everything had unraveled, when they'd rescued their dog, Brooklyn, from the street, taken her to the house in Westchester and spent the weekend there. Her gorgeous husband had scooped up Brooklyn in one hand and Lilly in the other and tucked them all into bed. Throwing out the heart-stopping comment as the puppy lay snoring at their feet that maybe they should make theirs a family of four.

She'd been so excited, her mind whirring like the hamster's wheel from her childhood, that she hadn't slept that night. Like the luckiest of little girls on Christmas morning, she'd felt as if she'd been given everything she'd ever dreamed of. She had Riccardo, a great career and a home. A *real* home, where love reigned—not dramatic tension that would take her who knew where next. And for the first time since she'd left Iowa as a teenager, scared and unsure of her future, she'd known everything was going to be okay.

She would have a family of her own—one that wasn't living a hand-to-mouth existence. A family that wasn't a dysfunctional, sordid mess.

Dreams could come true, she'd told herself, falling asleep in Riccardo's arms at dawn.

The impossibly perfect memory made her suck in a breath.

She was still in love with her husband.

No matter how hard she tried to deny it, no matter how much she told herself they shouldn't be together, it was never going to go away. That deep, gnawing pain that had started when she'd left him and never stopped.

She pried her eyes open and stared dully up at the grandfather clock in the hallway. Its rhythmical tick-tock was

deafeningly loud in the still villa. She was mad about a
man who'd spoken of their love in the past tense tonight.
As if he was as sure as she was they'd done too much harm
to each other ever to be able to recover from it.

And he was right. About all of it. She *had* shut down
on him. She should have told him about her anorexia. She
should have told him about the photos. Instead she'd run,
like she always did.

But he had kissed Chelsea. And that wasn't something
she was sure she could forgive.

She bit her lip, vaguely registering the metallic taste of
blood. The clock droned on...tick-tock, tick-tock. She had
made huge mistakes in her marriage. But at least tonight
she'd taken her first step forward. She'd told the truth. And
that was something.

She bit her lip, refusing to give in to the fresh set of tears
burning the back of her eyes. If it was clear they were over,
then that was for the best. They had closure. In six months
she was going to have to walk away from Riccardo, this
time for good.

She was going to have to move on.

At least now she could.

She got to her feet, splashed cold water on her face and
went back out to the terrace to wait for Riccardo. Two, three
hours passed—she wasn't sure. A million stars blanketed
the dark Caribbean sky as she drank wine and listened to
the rhythmic pull of the ocean.

Her eyes started to drift shut.

The clocks chiming midnight woke her. Disoriented and
half asleep, she padded inside to a dark, empty villa. And
realized her husband wasn't coming back.

CHAPTER EIGHT

RICCARDO ENDED UP nursing a glass of ten-year-old rum on the front steps of a local rum shack in Holetown. Neat, as the grizzly old proprietor had suggested.

He'd needed a place he could think, away from the glitzy west coast hotels and restaurants. A place where he could digest his mind-blowing conversation with his wife. Because if he'd suspected before that he didn't know all of her it was now brutally apparent he hadn't even scratched the surface of who Lilly De Campo was.

Mind reeling, he'd wandered down the road from the villa until he'd come to the local hotspot—a red-and-cream-painted clapboard house emblazoned with the logo of a local beer company, one of dozens of such dwellings scattered around the island. There had been a handful of Bajans sitting on the front steps, chatting about last night's cricket game, and zero expectations of socializing.

Perfetto.

He took a sip of the rum and was glad the proprietor had talked him into drinking it neat. It brought out the oaky molasses flavor of the blend and right now he needed its smooth burn. Needed to quell the tumult raging through his brain.

His wife had trusted him so little she'd paid a gossip columnist one hundred thousand dollars for pictures that weren't even of him. Then she'd lied to him about where the money had gone.

Che diavolo.

He pulled in a deep breath. What state of mind must she have been in to do something like that? To air their dirty laundry to a tabloid journalist and expose their private lives rather than come to him? He wanted to shake her. To chastise her for being so stupid. Except it had also been his fault. *He* had given her reason to be jealous. *He* had violated the trust in their marriage.

He had almost smeared the past in her face without knowing it by being unfaithful to her like her father had her mother.

He uttered a smothered oath. The bombshells had just kept coming. His wife had been suffering from an eating disorder he hadn't known about. She had been struggling with a disease only made worse by the limelight she'd been thrust into and *he hadn't noticed*. How had he not noticed? It was inconceivable to him. He wasn't an expert on eating disorders, but didn't women usually make themselves throw up when they had one? He knew for sure he hadn't missed that. Lilly hated throwing up, and when she did so because of her migraines she was miserable.

So where had been the signs he'd been supposed to see?

She'd always been tall and thin, and he'd thought that was her natural predisposition, but now that he thought about it she *had* been curvier when they'd met. She'd consistently lost weight throughout their marriage until she'd been ultra-thin at the end, but he'd thought that was because she'd wanted to fit into the designer dresses she'd worn. In hindsight, he admitted, shifting uncomfortably on the steps, her penchant for skipping meals near the end should have raised alarm bells. It was just that he hadn't been home enough to monitor it.

A memory of Lilly, exhausted and seemingly emotionally spent, begging him to let her stay home the night of the financial district's Christmas ball filled his head. He'd thought she was just being difficult and had insisted on her attending because it was a De Campo-sponsored event.

She'd obviously been struggling.

His hands tightened around the glass. He could have destroyed her by not knowing. By continuing to push her. Had he really been that oblivious? Was he so set on perfection in those around him she'd felt she couldn't come to him? Couldn't talk to him?

Had he been, as Lilly had accused, so caught up with his obsession of becoming CEO he hadn't seen anything but the end goal?

An intense feeling of shame washed over him. There had been one month in that last year when he'd only been home one night because he'd been traveling so much, opening restaurants. *One night.*

And maybe there had been more months like that…

"You left me alone to deal with the fallout of being Lilly De Campo."

Was that what he'd done?

He took a swig of the rum and stared out at the cars whizzing by on the snakelike coastal road. Their ability to hurt each other was monumental. The breakdown in communication between them breathtaking. How had something so good gone so wrong?

He watched as a new arrival joined the other grizzled old men on the steps. They clapped him on the back and kept on talking about last night's game, which apparently had been a barn-burner. He was struck by how absolutely insane his life had become. He was a machine, not a man. He no longer remembered what it was like to live because he was too busy planning for tomorrow.

He nursed the glass between his hands and stared down at the brilliant amber liquid. It was time he simplified his life. Step one had been this weekend with Lilly, to discover the truth. Step two would be in three months, when

Antonio ceded control to him. Step three was going to be about honesty.

"I faked my way through our entire marriage."

The statement had made his blood boil. He might have done things all wrong but Lilly had owed him honesty. She had owed that to their marriage. And nothing, *nothing* made up for the fact that she'd walked out on him. And left *him* to deal with the fallout of their marriage.

"It was never going to work."

Her words danced in front of him like a red cape, egging on an enraged bull. If his wife thought she was going to check out again now, when the honesty had just started between them, she was sadly mistaken. Lilly was about to find out what it was like to follow through on a promise. What it was like to pay as he'd been paying for the past year. Because De Campos didn't divorce. They stuck it out—even if they were in a loveless partnership like his parents.

He drained his glass and set it down with a thud that drew the eyes of the faction of grizzled old men. Standing up, he went back inside and slapped his glass on the counter. "Another," he said hoarsely. "Make it a double."

This time he *had left* her.

Lilly stood on the balcony of their villa, staring at the ocean as it sparkled in the moonlight. It was pushing one o'clock and still her husband hadn't come home. He had decided the muddled, mass of confusion his wife undoubtedly was wasn't CEO wife material. Wasn't worth the effort.

Hot, silent tears ran down her cheeks. She'd kept her secrets because she'd known if she'd told the truth about who she was she'd lose him. But in the end it hadn't mattered. She'd lost him anyway.

Had he been repulsed by her secret—by the anorexia that had been her Achilles' Heel? Or had it been the dishonesty? The lies she'd told to save herself?

She didn't blame him for not wanting her. She'd only just started to learn how to appreciate herself.

"I thought you'd be asleep."

Her husband's deep voice came from behind her. She spun around, her heart in her mouth as her gaze moved over his strained, somber features.

"You came back."

"Of course I did." He closed the distance between them. "I told you this is not over between us."

That had been before tonight. Before they had annihilated each other.

His gaze moved over her face. "I've never seen you cry."

She raised a hand to swipe the tears from her face. Telling him she still loved him, that she'd thought she'd lost him forever, wasn't going to happen. Not when she was sure he hated her for what she'd done to him. But she couldn't stop the emotion that was suffocating her, threatening to spill over into something she couldn't control.

His eyes darkened and the strain on his face deepened, looking even harsher in the moonlight. "This is not over," he repeated. "Get that through your head, Lilly. We are only getting started."

How could that be? This reconciliation of theirs was only for six months. And it wasn't real. But tell that to her brain. He did away with the last few inches between them, a look of intent on his face so deliberate her heart stopped in her chest.

"Ric—"

The hand she held out to ward him off was captured and folded against his chest as he pulled her into him. "No more talking," he murmured, moving his lips to the upper curve of her cheek, where the tears were still falling. "We've done enough talking for a lifetime tonight."

She knew she should protest, but then he was kissing away her tears one by one, following the hot, salty path down over the curve of her jaw. As if with every one he dispensed with he was wiping the past away. A sigh was torn from deep inside her as she arched her neck back. If this was supposed to be comfort she couldn't quite envision it, because he was setting her blood on fire.

His big hands swept the straps of her négligée aside so his lips could continue their exploration down the sensitive skin of her neck and over the roundness of her shoulder.

The honesty of this—the honesty of them together like this—had never been in question. And tonight she needed for him to heal them.

To hell with the consequences.

She moved willingly against him as he pulled her up on tiptoes and kissed her—a slow, drugging caress she felt down to her toes. It was like an anesthetic to her soul, his touch, as if the only thing she'd been put on this planet to do was kiss him in these deep, never-ending caresses that devoured the essence of each other.

A shiver ran through her—anticipatory, all-consuming. She buried her fingers in the thick muscles of his shoulders, rediscovering the feel of him under her hands, the way the sharp tug of her teeth on his bottom lip made him groan low in the back of his throat.

"You are killing me," he murmured, sliding his hands down over her silk-covered bottom and yanking her closer.

The feel of his big, warm hands on her, shaping her against the muscular hard length of him made her whimper. His thick erection made her gasp.

"*Esattamente,*" he muttered, scooping her up into his arms. She breathed in the familiar, heady male scent of him as he carried her into the bedroom. It was like coming home.

Light from the big, fat, almost-full moon flooded the beautiful blue-and-white-striped bedroom that looked as if it had come straight out of a magazine. But all Lilly had eyes for was her husband as he let her slide down his body to the floor, the silk catching between them. He was the most smoking hot man she'd ever encountered on so many levels.

Intense, like the night. Exciting, like a summer storm that made everything electric. Earthy, like a man who knew how to savor every moment like the fine wines his family created.

Her heart thumped at the foot of her throat as he slid his fingers under the straps of her négligée and dropped it to the floor. She closed her eyes as his gaze moved over her naked flesh. She had never been perfect but she was definitely less than that now.

"Dio, Lilly. *Come sei bella."*

His raspily intoned observation made her eyes fly open. The look of pure lust on his face made her knees go weak. "I don't look like I used to," she whispered.

He slid his hands down her back to her bottom and tugged her forward, until her naked flesh was flush against his still clothed body. "I told you," he murmured. "I love the curves... If anything, I want you more than I did before."

Oh. Liquid fire raced through her veins as his fingers tangled in the hair at the nape of her neck and he tipped her head back to receive his kiss. Open-mouthed, and hotter than Hades, it immersed her in a pool of want that threatened to eat her alive.

Her control snapped. The depth of her emotion for this man was frightening, endless, but to have him again like this made her frantic, desperate.

"Ric," she muttered against his mouth. "Please."

He abandoned her lips in favor of a fingertips to bare skin exploration of the weight of her breasts. "Do you know how hard it's been for me to keep my hands off you?" he breathed, brushing his thumbs over the tips of her nipples. "I took down a ninety-foot tree in Westchester, I was so crazed."

Lilly squeezed her eyes shut as her nipples hardened beneath his touch. "I can't believe you didn't kill yourself."

"Gabe helped. Matteo got in the way."

She smiled and wriggled against him, trying to get closer, but he closed his hands down hard over her shoulders and held her away.

"Not so fast, *tesoro*. It's been a long time since I've had you like this."

She eased back reluctantly. "Did you really go a year without sex?"

"I'm a man, Lilly. I found ways to ease the tension."

"Oh."

His soft laughter filled the night air. "Don't worry—you were still the star attraction."

The erotic image of him pleasuring himself—stroking that beautiful muscular body of his and thinking about her—sent another hot flash through her body that made her feel vaguely feverish. But then he was kissing his way down her throat toward the sensitive spot at the base of her neck—the spot he knew drove her crazy.

Hot. So hot.

She moved desperately against him.

He slid a hand down over her trembling stomach, over her navel to the juncture of her thighs. "Spread your legs for me, sweetheart."

Lilly swallowed hard and relaxed her grip, letting him push her legs apart.

"Did you ever touch yourself, thinking about me?" he questioned, sliding his fingers against the most private part of her.

"Ric—"

"The truth," he insisted.

"Yes," she murmured. God help her, yes, she had.

He rotated his thumb against the hard, aching center of her. "But it wasn't as good as the real thing, was it? Because I know it wasn't for me."

"No," she groaned. "It wasn't."

He lowered his head and kissed her, made her remember exactly how good he could make her feel. She grabbed a hold of his shirt to steady herself as he slid a finger inside her, his touch so unbearly good she thought she would scream.

"More," she murmured against his lips.

He withdrew and slid two fingers inside her, filling her deeper, harder. She arched against his hand as the ache inside her became unbearable.

"Please," she moaned.

He dropped to his knees in front of her. Lilly made a sound of protest, reaching down and grabbing his arms to pull him back up to her. She felt too exposed, too raw to have him do this to her right now.

But he shook her hands off and looked up at her, eyes glittering. "Immersion therapy, Lilly. Relax and enjoy it."

She squeezed her eyes shut, too hot, too aroused to do anything but obey. And then he was parting her with gentle fingers, his raspy, *"Bella..."* filling the air before he bent and feasted on her. She held the back of his head as he slid his tongue against her aroused flesh. The rush of pleasure that swirled through her was so incredibly good she felt as if every nerve in her body was concentrated right *there*.

"Ric—I need—"

"I know," he murmured against her skin. "Let go, Lilly."

Her legs started to tremble wildly. He slid his fingers inside her again and shot her into another stratosphere. *God.* She just needed him to curve his fingers like—*that.*

"Oh."

He kept his fingers there and flicked his tongue over the hard bud at the center of her. Her insides contracted as she came in a rush of such sweet, hot pleasure he had to hold her upright. It was white-hot, blinding. All-consuming.

She was floating on a sea of pleasure when he got to his feet, scooped her up into his arms and carried her to the bed. "You are so sexy," he murmured, leaning down to kiss her. "Your reactions…everything about you turns me on."

The taste of herself on his lips was unbearably intimate. And she felt her last barrier come tumbling down.

He left her to pull his shirt over his head, his impatient, jerky movements so unlike him she smiled. "Need some help with your pants?"

He stepped closer and brought her hands to his belt.

She took in the hard muscles of his torso, the perfectly defined six-pack, the undeniably hot vee that disappeared beneath his jeans. She had undressed him hundreds of times, but this time her hands were shaking and her throat was dry.

She worked his belt buckle open and fumbled with the button of his jeans.

"Lilly," he murmured, covering her hand with his. "Are you okay?"

She nodded and bit her lip. With a smothered curse he stepped back and shoved his jeans and boxers off. The masculine beauty of his body made her want like a woman who'd been stranded in the desert far too long. When he sank down on the bed and reached for her she straddled his muscular thighs, wanting to give him as much pleasure as he'd given her.

He was hard, aroused, barely leashed male power beneath her, and she wanted him inside her more than she wanted her next breath.

He buried his lips in her shoulder, a tremor running through his big body. "I can't play around like this much longer..."

"Who's playing?" She sat back on her haunches, her eyes riveted to his beautiful toned body. "I'm not," she assured him, sliding her fingers to the insides of his thighs.

His gaze moved to her hands. *"Lilly..."*

She curved her fingers around him and reveled in his sharp intake of breath. He was smooth and hard like steel, pulsing underneath her fingers. With a muffled curse he sank his hands into her waist and lifted her over him, the movement bringing her swollen flesh into contact with his engorged length.

Ruddy color dusted his cheekbones. "*Maledizione,* Lilly…"

She slid the thick head of him inside her, her body so aroused, so wet, she accommodated him easily. He cursed under his breath, the muscles of his arms bulging as he braced them on either side of himself. She took more of him, and more, until she felt as if she couldn't go further. She'd forgotten how big he was, how the length of him caressed every last centimeter of her. Closing her eyes, she focused on taking him, adjusting her hips until he slid in to the hilt.

Her gasp split the air.

He stayed completely still beneath her while her body adjusted to his, his jaw clenched, his face a picture of grim self-control. "Are you okay?"

"Fine," she breathed, relaxing into him. "You're just so damned big."

He closed his eyes. "That's not usually a complaint."

"It's not, it's j— *Oh, God,* you feel so good."

"*I'd* feel better if I could move," he rasped.

She leaned down and kissed him. "Let me."

She rode him slowly, deliberately at first, every movement designed to drive him wild. He twisted his hips and tried to control the rhythm but she shook her head. "Like this."

He clamped his jaw shut and let her take the lead. Lilly shut her eyes and just *felt.* Felt the size and girth of him stroke her, reach every nerve-ending. Her body clamped around him as she remembered the pleasure he could give her, cried out desperately for it.

No man had ever been able to turn her on this much. Only Riccardo.

She threw her head back and let herself go. Every powerful stroke of his body up into hers was filling her from the inside out—filling the lonely place inside her that had never gotten over the loss of him. And when she looked down at him the dark glitter in his eyes told her he felt it too.

"Are you with me?" he demanded hoarsely. "Please tell me you're with me."

"Always," she whispered.

Something tilted in his face. A look of such raw, uncensored emotion that she felt it in a place she'd never felt it before. He might not love her anymore, but he wasn't devoid of emotion.

She committed it to memory, held onto it as he surged up inside her and demanded she ride him harder, faster. Something told her she was going to need it as he made her drown in the sensations he was creating. As he branded her with his touch and found that sweet spot he knew would take her over the edge. Her fingernails dug into his shoulders as he stroked her deliberately, repeatedly, until she felt the white-hot beginning of her release. Once, twice, three times he drove into her, and she screamed, her body contracting around his in an orgasm stronger and more shattering than the first.

He cursed under his breath and fell back onto his elbows, his body surging up inside her. She felt him throb even bigger, watched his face as he lost control. His hands clamped down on her hips and his body shook in a release that rocked them both.

Winded, shaken to her core, she collapsed forward onto his chest, listening to his heart thunder beneath her ear. This was the time when he'd used to whisper that he loved her in Italian. When he'd tuck her into his side and cradle her until she slept. When she had been sure beyond a shadow of a doubt of his feelings for her.

The hot, humid Caribbean air throbbed around them—heavy and full. A loaded silence stretched between them. They stayed like that for several long minutes. Then Riccardo lifted her off his chest and tucked her beneath the sheets.

"You need to sleep."

She wanted to beg him to hold her. To prolong what they'd shared for just a few more minutes. She heard him snap off the lights and come back to the bed, felt the mattress dipping beneath his weight. Then he reached for her and pulled her into his arms, curving her back against the warm length of him. She exhaled in a long, slow breath. This was enough. Being back in the place where everything felt right. Even for one night.

She fell asleep almost immediately.

Her pounding head woke her at two a.m. She stumbled into the bathroom and grabbed her painkillers out of her bag. She had unscrewed the bottle and downed two tablets with a glass of water when the unthinkable occurred to her.

In the hustle of traveling this morning she'd forgotten to take her birth control pill.

It had been almost twenty-four hours since she had.

"Do me a favor." Alex's words rang in her ear. *"Whatever you do, don't get pregnant."*

She pulled the birth control pills out of her bag and desperately shoved one in her mouth. It hadn't even been twenty-four hours… It would be fine.

But even as she reassured herself she knew it had been stupid, *stupid*. How could she have complicated a relationship in which the only thing that *was* clear was that it didn't need complicating?

CHAPTER NINE

LILLY WOKE UP with such a supreme feeling of well-being she thought she might have been accidentally transported to a land of paradise, where everything was silk sheets, hard male and a bone-meltingly familiar sense of satisfaction she never wanted to end.

Turning her head from its face-down planting in the pillow, she slid her palm across the sheet in search of more warm, hard male. Nothing but silk. Her eyes flickered open. She was alone in the huge king-sized bed.

She flipped over, settled back against the mountain of pillows and stared out at the brilliant blue sky. She might almost think it had been a dream, the ridiculously hot sex she'd had with her husband. But the ache between her legs begged to differ. And in the blinding light of morning everything seemed magnified by ten.

She'd let the man she was still madly in love with, who didn't love her anymore, strip her of the defenses she'd spent a decade building. Then she'd slept with him in a moment of madness without using protection, which demonstrated exactly what a moment of madness it had been.

Damn.

She squeezed her eyes shut. It had been a monumentally stupid thing to do. The one thing she'd never been able to deny was the connection they'd had in bed. And once that took over all bets were off.

It was the reason she'd refused to see him for so long. Because she didn't trust herself around Riccardo.

Her stomach churned. Both she and Riccardo had extremely fertile families. But hadn't it taken her girlfriend, Darya, forever to conceive? Surely it wouldn't happen in one night?

Finding the whole thing entirely too disconcerting, she threw back the covers and swung her legs out of bed. Riccardo would have been up hours ago. He'd probably swum fifty lengths of that Olympic-sized pool and gone through every set of weights in the exercise room by now.

She padded restlessly over to the patio doors and threw open the curtains. The humid heat hit her immediately, and the perfume-soaked, salty, heavy air was filled with the scent of dozens of exotic flowers. It begged complete lethargy—a sunchair, a book and a drink, followed by a cool swim.

She blinked and shaded her eyes against the brilliant sunlight. And found her guess had been right. But rather than laps her husband was slicing through the ocean with a powerful front crawl that ate up the distance between the raft that bobbed about a mile out and the beach.

She watched as he hit the shore and walked up the beach, water sluicing down over his washboard abs. The drool that formed in her mouth was swift and uncontrollable. As if having him so completely last night had done nothing to stem the urge she had for him.

He lifted a hand to swipe the water from his face. And saw her standing there.

A heart-meltingly sexy smile curved his mouth. He walked up the beach and came to stand below the balcony, a fully relaxed, content-looking Riccardo who turned her insides to mush.

"You coming down?"

A smile twisted her lips. "If you'll come swimming with me. I'm sweating already."

"We have fifteen minutes before breakfast is ready. Get your suit on and get down here."

She slipped off her négligée and pulled on the fuchsia bikini she'd bought with Alex. She might have made the huge mistake of sleeping with Riccardo last night, but that didn't mean she had to continue her foolish behavior today. She needed to focus on keeping her head. She bit her lip as she pulled on a short cotton dress over her bathing suit. So what was she doing, running down to swim with him? And what had he meant when he'd said, *"This is not over. We are only getting started"*?

It didn't matter what he'd said! She swiped some sunscreen across her cheeks and nose. Riccardo *was* a lethal banned substance for her. Best to accept that last night had been inevitable between them, like a storm reaching its conclusion, and find a way to make it through the next six months without killing each other.

Hot sex wasn't going to accomplish that.

A rational brain would.

Tell that to her hormones, she thought as she joined Riccardo on the tiny private beach in front of the villa, the sand as smooth as silk between her toes. Because the intensity of her husband's dark gaze on her was making her overheating problem a virtual crisis.

"You'd better lose the dress," he advised. "Nowhere down here to leave it."

She darted a self-conscious glance around her. The bikini wasn't French Riviera material but it was revealing enough. She would rather have just gotten in the water, but since there really wasn't anywhere to leave her cover-up on the beach she walked up to the terrace, draped it over a chair and headed back down to him, self-conscious in her halter top bikini.

The smell of bacon wafted through the air. "Mrs. Adams is cooking?"

He nodded. "We thought we'd let you sleep in. You needed it."

She walked toward him, ultra self-conscious in her halter top bikini.

Her husband took her in from beneath veiled lashes. "And here I thought we had declared a truce."

She frowned. Looked down at herself. *Pink*. Her swimsuit was pink.

Heat filled her cheeks. "It was the only suit that didn't make me look like an adult movie star."

He reached for her, his fingers closing over her forearm. "Why go for modest when you look that good, *cara?*"

She sucked in a breath as he pulled her against his hard, dripping wet body. "Did you listen to a word I said last night?"

"*Si*. I am intent on desensitizing you."

She pressed a hand against his chest to balance herself. "You can't just wave your fairy wand and cure me, Riccardo. Anorexia is something I'll carry with me for the rest of my life, even if I have it under control."

"I know," he said, bringing his lips down on hers as he swung her up in his arms. "But I'm going to do it anyway."

She smiled at his arrogance. His lips were warm from the heat of the sun, his kiss as leisurely as the mood he seemed to be in, and she found she just didn't have the willpower to fight him.

He walked into the sea, and the water was so warm it barely registered on her heated skin. Then he wrapped her legs around him so they floated on the buoyant sea.

"Riccardo…"

"What?"

"I—I don't think this is appropriate."

He gave her an amused look. "We're married. What's inappropriate about it?"

She focused her gaze on his Adam's apple. "Last night

was…amazing…but I think anymore of that is just going to complicate things between us."

He lifted her chin with his fingers. "If you mean sex, Lilly, then I'm going to have to disagree. Sex breaks down the barriers between us, and if you think, now that we're finally talking, I'm going to let you put them up again, you're mistaken. By the end of this weekend there isn't going to be anything I don't know about you."

She went rigid. "There isn't anymore to say."

He pressed his lips together. "How did you keep it from me? I never saw the signs."

"My anorexia?"

He nodded.

She pressed her hands against his chest to put some distance between them, but he kept his arms firmly banded around her. "I was better when I met you. I'd gotten control over it. I'd spent my career practicing physiotherapy, learning how incredible the human body is—how strong it is—and how much more important it was to honor your body than do what I'd been doing to it."

She swallowed hard. His gaze on her face was making her feel as if she was under a microscope.

"It started to get bad for me again after that first year, when our honeymoon with the media wore off and they made a game out of criticizing how I looked or what I wore."

"Which they do with anyone who's in the limelight like that," he interjected.

"Yes. But for me it was harder. Anorexia isn't something with a lot of outward signs. It's insidious. I withdraw. I stop eating. It becomes impossible for me to look at my body objectively. Everything gets distorted."

He frowned. "I thought it was a vanity thing. The need to look perfect."

A rueful smile curved her mouth. "The need to not hate myself would be more accurate."

His jaw hardened. "Was I really that impossible to talk to? Did I really demand that much perfection from you?"

"It comes with your life, Riccardo. It's *expected* from those around you."

His jaw hardened. "We could have made adjustments to our life to make things easier for you."

She shook her head. "You're going to be the head of a ten-billion-dollar conglomerate when you take over from your father. You couldn't make those changes even if you wanted to."

His dark eyes glittered. "We could have. We could have done what was necessary and let the rest go."

"You're a dreamer," she bit out. "You needed a new wife. And you refused to admit it."

His lip curled. "I did not need a new wife. I needed a wife with the guts to tell me what was wrong. I needed a wife who was there for me at one of the lowest points of my life and instead you were *gone*."

She recoiled. "I had lost myself, Riccardo. I had lost the ability to keep myself in balance. If I hadn't left I would have reverted back to my old bad habits and destroyed myself."

A muscle jumped in his jaw. "You couldn't have waited until I'd gotten back? Been there for me?"

She pushed hard against his chest and this time he let her go. Finding the sandy bottom with her feet, she stood facing him. "What happened in Italy? All I knew was that you'd been summoned there on Antonio's orders."

He scraped his wet hair out of his face. "It doesn't matter now. We're talking about why you left."

"Goddammit, Riccardo." She took a step closer and jabbed her finger in his face. "We *are* talking about why I left. You never talk. You never tell me how you're feeling. What the hell happened in Tuscany?"

His face tightened into a stony stillness. "I knew the restaurant business was the future for De Campo. Knew we needed to diversify. Antonio didn't agree. He forbade me to proceed with the plans I had for Orvietto." He paused. "I signed the lease anyway."

She let out a slow breath. "He lost his mind...?"

"He threatened to strip me of my title and kick me out of the company."

"What?" Her mouth dropped open. "He wouldn't have done that."

"He would have!"

She took a step back as he practically yelled the words at her.

"The only reason he didn't was because my decision was right. I *proved* him wrong. Orvietto proved him wrong. But when I came back to New York that night I thought I'd lost everything. I'd given up the sport I loved for an old man who didn't give a damn, I was about to lose my job at De Campo, and then I walked into our house—into our *empty* house—to find the only person who could make me feel better and a teary Magda informed me you'd gone. *Gone.*" His gaze, dark and tormented, swept over her. "I hadn't slept in forty-eight hours. I just looked at her and said, 'Gone? What do you mean, gone?'"

Lilly felt a wave of nausea sweep over her. She'd been so lost in her own private hell she'd been numbed against the bizarre, disjointed tone of his voice when he'd called that night from overseas.

"I'm sorry," she whispered, tears stinging the back of her eyes. "I'm so sorry."

He looked away, the sun reflecting off the hard line of his jaw. "It isn't always about you, Lilly."

She wrapped her arms around herself. "I never thought it was."

The waves lapped gently around them, the only sound in this private slice of paradise.

"How did things ever get so bad between you two?"

He looked back at her. "Between Antonio and I?"

She nodded.

"The day of my graduation from Harvard I told him I'd signed with TeamXT. It was a once-in-a-lifetime opportunity I couldn't say no to. I'd been driving every summer, whenever I could, but this—this was my chance. I told Antonio I needed a couple of years to get it out of my system—that I'd join De Campo after that." He shrugged. "I knew he wasn't going to be happy, but I thought, given the opportunity, he might understand." A bitter note filled his tone as he continued. "I should have known better. He gave me an ultimatum instead. Join De Campo or forget ever being a part of it."

"You walked away?"

"We didn't speak after that until he became ill and asked me to take over."

"He expected you to come back after all that?"

He exhaled roughly. "You have to understand Antonio's background. His father was a tyrant. He browbeat Antonio into running the business when all my father ever wanted to do was work with animals. He wanted to raise prize-winning racehorses, not prize-winning vines, but his father had built a thriving business and Antonio was expected to take over."

"So by following your dream with racing you became everything he'd ever wanted to be?"

"*Sì.* I was the ultimate insult."

"So why not choose Gabe to head the company? He has such a love for it."

He grimaced. "Antonio is old-fashioned. He could never get past the fact that his eldest son should carry on as CEO. And, despite the animosity between us, we have always been the same. Tough sons-of-bitches who know how to get what we want."

How true *that* was. She blinked, trying to absorb it all. "And what about your mother? She didn't interject through all of this?"

"You've met her," he said roughly. "My mother toes the party line. Their marriage is based on mutual ambition. Emotion doesn't have anything to do with it. Not with her boys, either. She would have carted us off to boarding school in true aristocratic fashion if my father hadn't insisted we learn the wine business."

Emotions swirled inside her. Suddenly she wasn't certain of anything anymore. Whether she'd been right to leave him. Whether she should have worked harder at her marriage. It was all riddled with intricacies she had no way of assimilating.

"So what now?" she asked huskily. "You wait while Antonio strings you along?"

He shook his head. "He's retiring in three months. He's promised to hand De Campo over to me then. *If*," he murmured bitterly, "I continue to prove to him I deserve it."

She flinched. "You could walk away. Go back to racing…"

His expression turned black as night. "I can't go back."

"You can do anything you want. You're a winner, Riccardo. You move mountains when you need to."

"You think I don't want to?" The words exploded out of him. "Every morning when I was driving I woke up feeling lucky to be on this planet. I was free. I was *alive*. Everytime I stepped on that racetrack I challenged the very core of myself. I was the *best*. The adrenalin, that charge that came at the starting line from driving a vehicle more powerful than any other on the planet—it *defined* me."

"So do it," she urged. "You don't owe Antonio anything. This is your life, not his."

His broad shoulders stiffened. "This is about honor. Not about doing what I want. Something I'm not sure *you* know much about. You walked away from your family and you walked away from me. But sometimes you have to hang in there, Lilly. Sometimes you have to fulfill the promises you've made. Even if it interferes with the grand plan."

His anger rippled through her, the depth and fury of it rocking her back on her heels. It was too much. Too much had passed between them. There was no going back.

"I think we should get some breakfast," she murmured, needing to break the intensity. "Mrs. Adams must have it ready by now."

"By all means." He nodded savagely. "Wouldn't want the eggs to cool while you do a little soul-searching."

She turned her back on him and started walking. Five and a half months. She could do this.

If it was possible to spend the day in heaven and feel as if you were in hell, then Lilly had managed to capture perfectly that peculiar and miserable experience. She'd spent the day on the private beach with an introspective version of her husband, surrounded by a shimmering sexual tension that was impossible to ignore despite the fact it seemed they were a million miles apart.

Somehow guilt had taken center stage. She should have been there for Riccardo when he'd been struggling. His account of coming home to find her gone had torn her heart out. No matter what she'd been going through, she should have been there for him.

She'd been incredibly selfish. Not only with her marriage. With her life. She'd had a dream for herself. To leave Mason Hill and never look back. But in pursuing that dream she'd hurt a lot of people. Her parents, Lisbeth—who'd been left alone and defenseless, even if she *had* been too young to come with them—and her brother, who'd been left with her and Alex's work on the farm. And, although she would do the same thing over, she'd had to leave to be who she was now, she was starting to realize that by being so wrapped up in herself she'd neglected the people she loved.

Her heart gave a painful squeeze. Even now she was

here and not with Lisbeth, helping her through her treatment.

When she got better, Lilly was going to bring her to New York to stay with her. She was going to make up for leaving her alone in Iowa.

"What are you thinking about?"

Riccardo's idly delivered question was one of the few he'd uttered over their evening meal at the beachfront restaurant on Barbados's south coast. It pulled her out of her thoughts and focused her attention on the man sitting across from her. Not that she'd been able to avoid acknowledging how good he looked. Dressed in jeans and a gray T-shirt, he had a relaxed and dangerously attractive air about him that every woman in the restaurant had already noticed. Including the Hollywood A-lister and the Mediterranean Princess sitting at right angles to them.

He hadn't looked at one of them.

"So?" He lifted his hand and waved it at her.

She took a sip of her wine—just because Riccardo had refused alcohol tonight it didn't mean she had to. "Is this going to be your new occupation? Analyzing me at every moment?"

His gaze narrowed. "Until I'm sure you're telling the truth—*si,* it is."

She waggled her fingers at him. "No secrets left here. I'm an open book."

Except I still love you desperately.

"You're thinking about something."

About how she'd like to skip dessert, rush home and enjoy that incredible body of his as the final course... Which was absolutely, positively not going to happen.

His mouth tilted up at the corners. "You know the rules. You look at me like that—we leave." He reached into his jeans pocket and threw his wallet on the table.

She stared at the wallet, her heart pounding. "I wasn't

looking at you like that. And we should at least look at the dessert menu."

"Why? You never eat dessert." He handed his credit card to the waiter. "Tell me what happened to your wedding rings."

She set her glass down with a jerky movement. "I told you I'm not sure where they are."

He lifted a brow. "I may be a lot of things, *tesoro,* but I'm not a fool. You're far too careful with things to lose them. So where are they?"

Her gaze slid away from his. "I'm not sure you want to know."

He lifted his brow higher.

"They might be in the East River."

"Scusi?"

She swallowed hard. "I threw them off the Brooklyn Bridge."

His jaw dropped. "You threw your fifty-thousand-dollar engagement ring off the Brooklyn Bridge?"

"I was angry."

"You were *angry?*" For the first time in their married life her husband looked speechless.

She lifted her chin. "The day I left I was so mad, so hurt. I had a clinic in Brooklyn and on my way back I lost it. I felt so betrayed—about Chelsea, about what you'd done to us—that I asked my cab driver to stop and I just…"

"Threw them in," he finished grimly.

"Sure I can't get you anything else?" Their waiter popped a leather folder on their table.

"I wanted to have a liqueur." Lilly searched desperately for anything that wouldn't involve them being alone together.

"We can have one at the villa."

"I'd prefer to have it here." She looked desperately at the little bar that sat beside this restaurant on the beach. There was loud Calypso music playing and lots of locals hanging out on the front patio. "Why don't we have one *there?* It looks like fun."

He followed her gaze. "Trying to avoid the inevitable, Lil?"

"I'm trying to have a good time. You might try that every once in a while."

The antagonism that flared in his gaze made her stomach do a little flip. He threw some money on the table and stood up.

"One drink."

Breathing deeply at her momentary reprieve, Lilly settled herself on a stool at the beachside bar and smiled at the tall, dreadlocked Bajan bartender.

He eyed them up. "On your honeymoon?"

Lilly choked.

"I wish we were," Riccardo interjected drily. "The *signora* would like a drink."

Mr. Dreadlocks, whose hair reached further down his back than her own, shifted his oh-so-cool gaze to her. "What can I get you?"

"How about the house specialty?"

He blinked. "The house specialty?"

"Sure. Sounds good."

"Lewis," he introduced himself, sticking a hand out. She took it, then he did the same to Riccardo. "The same?"

"Wouldn't miss it. But make mine a half—I'm driving."

Lewis pulled about five different bottles off the shelf and started mixing. Lilly could tell she'd made a big mistake by the time he got to bottle number three, which had no label on it and looked as if it was a home brew.

Riccardo held his glass up to hers, a challenging glitter in his ebony eyes. "Bottoms up."

It was so strong it was all Lilly could do not to plug her nose and drink it that way. Those who liked straight alcohol might have found it passable, and Riccardo wasn't having any trouble with it, but for Lilly, who wasn't used to drinking liquor neat, every sip felt like a fire in her mouth and throat.

Every sip was also making her feel looser and much less inhibited. She permitted herself a good look at her drool-worthy husband. Imagined stripping off that T-shirt and exploring every inch of his hard pecs and chest. *Would allowing herself one more night be such a huge mistake?* After all, it wasn't as if this was easy, being here in such a romantic place. Maybe after this weekend, back in New York, she'd be able to keep a much firmer grip on her head.

Determinedly she rattled on to Lewis about how much she loved the island and asked him a million questions about himself.

Riccardo drained his glass and set it on the bar. "Time to go."

She scrunched her face up and downed the rest of her drink. She was going to need it. She was definitely going to need it. Lewis waved goodnight and made them promise to come back.

Their walk to the car was filled with a weighty silence that played on Lilly's nerve-endings like a bow. Her whole body felt as if it was on fire.

"What the hell was in that drink?" she muttered, leaning against the car while Riccardo opened her door.

He whipped the door open, then pushed her back against the Lamborghini. "I'm not sure I want to know."

Her fingers curled into his shirt as he leaned down and took her mouth in a hard, punishing kiss that told her he was still furious about the rings. But it was the heat behind it that made her feel light-headed.

This was going to be off the scale.

Riccardo considered himself a skilled driver, but there was no finesse in the way he handled Charles Browne's sleek sports car as they drove the windy coastal road home. Lilly was all over him. It was all he could do to keep the car on the road with her unbuttoning his shirt and sliding her hands over his chest.

"Lilly," he groaned. "What are you doing?"

"What's the matter, Mr. Racecar Driver?" she taunted, sliding her hands to his belt. "A little distraction and you can't cope?"

He sucked in a breath as she tugged hard on the leather. "I never should have let you have that drink."

"So true," she murmured. The rasp of his zipper was agonizingly loud in the quiet confines of the car. "Too late now."

Her fingers brushed over him. He jerked so hard the car went sliding across the road. He shoved her away from him and yanked hard on the wheel to avoid a ditch. "If you want to live, keep your hands off me."

She slunk back against the seat. He glanced at her impatient expression. *Dio.* What had gotten into his wife? He hadn't seen this Lilly since—when? He couldn't remember.

His body throbbing with an urgency that was near combustible, he started inwardly reciting the specs of the engine under the Lamborghini's hood. One after another he went through the parts, until he'd exhausted every single screw and cap and they were on the side road to the villa.

He brought the car to a growling halt in the garage, walked around to Lilly's side and pulled her out. "You're paying for that," he promised, pushing her in front of him and out of the garage. "That was seriously stupid, Lilly."

His wife appeared not to care. In fact she stood there, her cat's eyes challenging him, focused on him, as he unlocked the door to the villa. He urged her inside and locked it. The want in her gaze undid him.

He threw her over his shoulder and headed upstairs.

"You know I like this," she teased.

"Your payment hasn't even begun."

He set her down on the floor of their bedroom, then shrugged out of his shirt, ripped off his belt and ditched his pants. Lilly's eyes were big as saucers as he pushed her against the wall and ran his hand over the soft flesh of her breasts, temptingly full under her cotton dress, then down over her trembling stomach.

"Ric—"

He moved his hands over her hips and under the flirty dress that had been driving him crazy all night. Her flesh was warm, and toned, and control was in short supply.

"Feel free to tell me when the punishment is over."

He pushed her thighs apart and slid the heel of his hand up over the heat of her. "You will know."

She was trembling under his hands. He reached up, snagged his fingers in the sides of her barely-there thong and pulled it down over her long legs. She was beautiful and intoxicating, his Lilly, and she whispered something unintelligible as he stood and buried his fingers in her hair, kissing her senseless. She had the most perfect lips he'd ever encountered in a woman—full, perfectly shaped, and without a collagen injection in sight. And if he hadn't been so intent on teaching her a lesson he would have suggested she wrap them around another part of his anatomy.

But payback was paramount. He slid a hand between her thighs, seeking and finding her hot wetness. She moaned and pressed closer, inviting him in as he slid a finger inside her.

"Ric—"she said brokenly, shaking like a leaf.

"Not over," he said harshly, adding another finger and working her in a rhythm he knew would send her close to the edge.

Her breathing was quick and tortured against his mouth. Her hips writhed against his hand. And he knew the point at which she would beg...

"Please—I—"

He removed his fingers from her and pushed her toward the bed. "I never make a promise I don't keep, *amore mio*."

The front of her knees butted up against the edge of the

mattress. He placed a palm in the small of her back and pushed her forward until her hands were braced on the bed.

"Almost over," he murmured. "Because I know you like it like this too."

She bit back a gasp as he pushed her dress up and nudged her legs apart.

"Ric—"

"Shh." He leaned over and pressed a kiss against her back. "Keep your hands there and don't move."

She stayed where she was. He felt his composure waver as he brushed himself against the wet heat of her, hard steel against soft velvet. Lilly groaned and grasped the bedcovers. She was as hot for him as he was for her, but he kept a torturous hold on himself as he slid into her slowly, inch by inch. She was incredibly vulnerable in this position and he needed her trust.

"Good?" he asked hoarsely, giving her body a chance to adjust to the size and girth of him.

She let out a strangled, urgent moan. He closed his eyes and let himself go. Let the desperate urgency of a man who was haunted by a woman take over as he drove into the tight, wet heat that embraced him like a glove.

Too long he had wanted her. Too much he had missed her.

His hands tightened on her hips as he took her close to the edge, then pulled back, wanting this to last, wanting to torture her as she'd tortured him. Wanting to give them both maximum pleasure. But his body tensed and swelled; his mind fixed on the torturously perfect fit of being inside of her again. Then the world splintered apart.

He wanted, *needed* her to be there with him, and he almost cried out with relief when he felt her body contract around his, drawing out his own release until his harsh moan split the night air. The tightening of her body rolled over him like a shockwave, sending surge after surge of explosive pleasure through him.

Dio. He scooped her trembling body off the bed and sat down with her limbs wrapped around him. She buried her head in his shoulder as if she couldn't bear to break the connection. And the force of his emotion hit him like a tidal wave, stealing his breath.

He was not over her. He was not even close to being over her.

She had walked out on him without a backward glance. He had spent every night after that for at least a month thinking she would change her mind and come home.

She hadn't.

He stood up with an abrupt movement and deposited Lilly on the bed. She stared up at him, a dazed look on her face, all tangled long limbs and physical satiation.

Great sex, he told himself. *That's all it is.* But it was enough to severely mess a man's head up.

"I'm going to go make sure everything's locked up," he said roughly.

She was curled in a ball on her side of the bed when he came back. A tightness seized his belly so strong he almost reached down to gather her in his arms. But he kept his hands clenched tightly by his sides.

She deserved to suffer.

He'd suffered every night for a year. Let her feel his pain.

CHAPTER TEN

LILLY PEEKED HER head around her sister Lisbeth's hospital room door, checking to see if she was awake. Their brother David, who'd driven Lisbeth down to New York last night for a series of tests before her treatment abroad, was sitting in a chair by the window.

"Lilly!" Lisbeth practically screamed the word across the room at her, her blue eyes shining brightly. "You're here!"

Lilly crossed the room, gave her older brother a hug, then pressed a kiss to her sister's cheek. Lisbeth had an IV tube sticking out of her arm and looked so pale and small that a lump formed in her throat. This had to work. There was no alternative.

"Where is Riccardo? Did you bring him?"

Lilly shook her head and sat back. She needed to tell Riccardo about Lisbeth, and soon, because she and Alex intended on going to Switzerland with her. But it never seemed like the right time—not with the rollercoaster of emotion going on between them. "I will soon, sweetie. How are you feeling?"

Her sister made a face. "Crappy, but the doctor's hoping after all this I'm going to feel a whole lot better."

Lilly's heart contracted, feeling too big for her chest. "Six weeks, Lizzie. You can do it."

"Does you and Riccardo being back together mean I can

come stay with you guys when I'm better?" Lisbeth looked at her with eager eyes.

Lilly kept her face straight, because to do anything else would be to reveal far too much to her sister and brother about her and Riccardo's relationship. "You can come stay with us anytime."

You can come stay with me *anytime.*

A satisfied smile curved her sister's lips. "I think I need a life."

Lilly squeezed her hand. "Conserve your energy so we can fight this battle together. Then we'll talk about it."

They stayed until Lisbeth got tired and David had to leave for home. Kissing their sister goodbye, they walked out into the hallway.

"She's going to be okay, right?" Lilly asked, looking up at her older brother.

David pulled her into a hug. "Of course she is."

She hugged him tight, her head feeling far, far too full. She loved her serious, hardworking sibling, even with his strict sense of right and wrong—which had clearly labeled her and Alex's defection nine years ago *wrong*. Seeing him again after so long—what had it been? A year and a half? Two years—reminded her how much she missed him.

Her brother pulled back. "You okay? You look like hell, sis."

No. She most definitely was not okay. But she couldn't talk to David about it.

"I'm fine. Just worried."

"Pretty damn amazing we can get her this treatment. She'll be fine, Lil. We didn't raise her to be a strong, sturdy farmgirl for nothing."

She nodded. "You sure you want to head back tonight? You could stay and start out early tomorrow. A few hours isn't going to make a difference."

"It will the way things are now." Her brother rubbed a hand against his face. "Even with the extra money you've been sending and the extra help we've hired we've all been working from sun-up till sun-down."

Guilt mixed with the maelstrom of emotion swirling through her. She felt as if she was hanging on by a thread. "I'm sorry," she whispered. "You know we had to go."

The lines of fatigue softened around the corners of his mouth. "I know. In some ways I think Mom and Dad even understand too. But staying away isn't going to change the past. It's only driving the wedge deeper and deeper between you guys."

"I know." And she knew she had to do something about it. "Are things any better between them?"

"Not unless you count the fact they've given up fighting with each other." He lifted his shoulders. "I think they're just numb to it all now."

She wasn't sure if that was a good or bad thing. "I was thinking of coming home for Mom's birthday."

"She would love that. She misses you, Lilly. She doesn't say anything—you know Mom—but she does."

A lump formed in her throat. "About Lisbeth..."

He shook his head. "She needs to get out. We can't keep her where she doesn't want to be."

"But the farm..."

"We'll manage. The extra money is helping a lot."

At least something good was coming out of a reconciliation that only seemed to get more complicated with every day that passed.

Speaking of which... She glanced at her watch. "I need to go. I'm late for dinner with Riccardo."

She hugged her brother, watched as he headed in the direction of the parking garage and then pushed through the front doors of Memorial Sloan Kettering. Flagging a cab, she slid in and gave the driver directions to the restaurant where she was to meet Riccardo.

She rested her head against the seat and closed her eyes. It had been seven weeks since her and Riccardo's weekend in Barbados. Seven weeks during which she'd been telling herself she could walk out when their deal was done. Then she'd walked into her doctor's office this morning to confirm what she'd been desperate to deny.

She was pregnant. Exactly seven weeks pregnant. With her soon-to-be ex-husband's baby.

If she'd consciously set out to create a bigger disaster, she couldn't have done so.

How was a baby going to fit into all this?

She stared numbly out at the rush-hour Manhattan traffic, bumper to bumper, horns blaring. She'd spent the past seven weeks trying to blend her and Riccardo's lives in a way that eased confrontation. She'd done the things she had to do for her practice, refused to give up the friends and essential things that had made her life her own over the past year—*and* fulfilled her commitments as Riccardo's wife. Surprisingly, it had worked rather well.

Riccardo seemed bent on reducing the stress placed on her, and had instructed Paige to accept only the social invitations that were essential to De Campo's interests. He was like a guard dog, monitoring her with annoying persistence. And it made her wonder if there would have been a different outcome for them if it had been like this all along.

Pain stabbed at her insides. The ache inside her was deep and all-consuming. She'd been trying so hard to ignore her feelings for him—to keep herself intact. But every time she tried to put distance between them Riccardo would knock the walls down. He came home early, insisted they eat together, and this time around they actually talked. About which way the board was leaning toward a CEO. How delayed tiles meant Zambia would open a week late. About Antonio being a piece of work.

And then there were the nights… He had followed through on his promise that there would be sexual intimacy. And it was the one thing she couldn't deny him. Or herself.

It was becoming harder and harder to remind herself that

this was a business arrangement when in so many ways this was the marriage she'd never had.

The cab swung to a halt in front of Toujours, a new, eclectic French bistro in the financial district which Riccardo was courting to stock De Campo's new Napa Valley vintages. She had met the owner, Henri Thibout, formerly a chef in Paris, at a party a few weeks before, and knew Toujours was at the top of her husband's expansion list.

Henri stood as the maître d' ushered her to the table. Lilly's eyes widened when she saw the tall man standing behind him. *Antonio.* What was he doing here? Riccardo hadn't mentioned anything about him being in town.

"Lilly." Henri, a short, balding man in his mid-fifties, who made up for it with bucketloads of charm, brushed twin kisses to her cheeks and introduced her to his head sommelier, Georges, and his wife Joanna.

Riccardo stood and brushed a similar kiss to both her cheeks. She felt the tension radiating from him. *Great,* she thought, turning to Antonio. Exactly what she needed tonight. The battle of the De Campos.

The big, burly, aristocratic man, with his hook nose and formidable features, failed to intimidate her tonight.

Maybe because she was *pregnant.* If she said it ten more times maybe she'd believe it.

Henri reached for the sparkling wine chilling on the table and pulled Lilly's glass toward him. "This will do the trick after a long day," he said jovially. "Riccardo says you work long days."

"None for me, thank you," Lilly said quickly. "It *has* been a long day. I might actually fall flat on my face if I do."

Riccardo shot her a quizzical look. If there was anything Lilly loved it was a good sparkling wine. She averted her gaze and answered Joanna's question about what she did for a living.

The five-course tasting menu was superb, but the smell

of seafood was making her nauseous. She did her best, but by the time she'd forced herself to eat half of her third course chicken dish she thought she was going to choke. She set her fork and knife down in an abrupt movement that sent the clang of fine china echoing throughout the restaurant.

Conversation stopped. "Is it not to your liking?" Henri enquired, frowning. "I can get you some—"

"It's delicious," Lilly assured him. She reached for her water. "Apologies—my appetite is a bit off."

Riccardo kept that watchdog look on her, his gaze darkening. She stumbled through the sorbet and cheese course, so desperate to be home alone with her thoughts that she almost jumped out of her seat at the end of the meal.

"Thank you," she murmured to Henri after he'd promised Riccardo feedback on the wine list by next week. "It was lovely to see you again."

Antonio stayed behind to enjoy an aperitif with Henri. She watched her husband's mouth tighten at the interaction. Antonio was in town without Francesca, as usual, who preferred not to travel to North America. He and Henri had obviously hit it off.

Riccardo led her through the restaurant, his firm grip on her elbow keeping her by his side. When they'd stepped out of the busy restaurant onto the sidewalk he spun her around.

"What is up with you? *Dio*. It's like you've had a gallon of coffee in one go."

She pulled her arm out of his. There was *no way* she was telling him her news on a busy Manhattan sidewalk.

"Like I said. It's been a long day. What was Antonio doing here?"

"Sticking his nose where it doesn't belong, as usual," he growled. "Don't deflect, Lilly. You were a disaster in there. You hardly ate a thing. In fact you've hardly eaten a thing for weeks. This is ending *now*."

She focused her gaze a centimeter to the right of his. "I'm feeling a bit nauseous, that's all."

"Then we're going to see your doctor," he said grimly. "I will not have you go through this again."

"I did see my doctor. I'm fine."

"Then what's wrong?" He stalked closer and captured her wrist in his. "We are not moving until you tell me."

"I think we should—"

"Lilly!" The valet who had been headed toward them stopped in mid-stride as Riccardo bellowed the word at her. "Spit it out."

His anger, her terror, and the complete loss of control she was feeling all hit her at once. "I'm pregnant!" she yelled at him. "I'm pregnant, goddammit, Riccardo. There—are you happy?"

He went chalk-white under his olive skin. The valet swiftly changed direction. The two of them faced off like prize fighters on the busy sidewalk. Then Riccardo grabbed her arm and pulled her under the awning of the restaurant, away from the flow of people.

"Is it mine?"

Her jaw dropped open. "I can't believe you're asking me that."

"It could be Taylor's."

She put a hand on her stomach. "I'm seven weeks pregnant. *Exactly* seven weeks pregnant. It's yours."

He went even paler, raking a hand through his hair. "We're not having this conversation here."

"I was trying to avoid it," she muttered. "And I sincerely hope that valet doesn't realize what a scoop he has on his hands."

Riccardo walked over to the valet stand and said something to the young guy, who practically ran to the lot across the street. He came back minutes later with the Jag.

Riccardo opened the door. "Get in."

They didn't talk for the entire drive home. Her husband's

knuckles were white on the steering wheel, his attention focused on the road. When they got to the house he opened the door, slammed it behind her and directed her inside.

She flicked on the lights in the front sitting room and sat down on the sofa. Riccardo poured himself a Scotch and paced the room like a restless, lethal animal that had no idea what its next move would be.

Finally he stopped by the fireplace and rested an elbow on the mantel, his gaze sinking into her. "It happened in Barbados if that's the timing."

She nodded. "I forgot my pill that morning we flew down. I didn't realize it until after we'd had sex."

His gaze narrowed. "You didn't see fit to tell me?"

She pressed her lips together. "The chances of anything coming from it were minuscule."

"Well, it happened," he growled. "You should have told me."

She got to her feet, feeling too vulnerable while he towered over her. "What difference would it have made? It happened. Now we're going to have to decide how we're going to deal with it."

He was in front of her so fast her head spun, his fingers biting into her arms. "We are *having* this baby."

"Of course we are." She stared at him, aghast. "Well, technically *I* am having this baby, and *we* are going to have to figure out how it'll work after we separate."

"Separate?"

She watched him digest the word as if it were a particularly tough piece of steak.

"We are not carting this baby back and forth between the two of us, Lilly."

"What are you suggesting, then?" she demanded flippantly. "That we stay together and live happily ever after?"

His lips curved in a smile that showed his teeth. "That's exactly what I'm suggesting, *tesoro*. Glad you're keeping up with me."

A feeling akin to shock settled over her. She studied his face, searching for some sign he was joking, but other than his twisted smile there was nothing but grim determination. Her chin lifted. "There is no way in hell I'm staying in an unhappy marriage. I know what it's like to grow up like that, and I won't do it to a child."

"You think it's better to subject them to a tug of war between two adults?"

"I think it's better to create an amicable separation where we both have this baby's best interests at heart."

"*Buona prova,* Lilly," he drawled. "But I'm not about to let your baggage destroy the future of our child. You contest this and I'll make it a court battle of epic porportions."

She shrugged out of his hold. "You are crazy. *This* is crazy." She looked at him desperately. "It will never work."

"It will work because we'll make it work." He crossed his arms over his chest and stood looking down at her like the impenetrable force he was. "Haven't we proved the last few weeks we can compromise?"

"About our social schedule," she said dully. How would a child fare in a marriage based solely on sex? In a marriage so far gone there was no pulling it back?

He lifted her chin with his fingers. "We have been good together lately, Lil. And we once had a fantastic marriage. We can make this work."

Or the bitterness between them would consume both them *and* their child, just as it had her.

She went for the jugular. "Don't you remember what it was like to live as part of a business partnership? Do you want that for yourself? For your child?"

"If what we've been doing in bed is a business partnership, then I'm all for it," he returned with a mocking smile. "Sign me up."

"You are—" She spun away, frustration burning a path of fire through her.

"A man who wants the family that was promised to

him," he rasped. "You are having my child, Lilly. De Campos don't divorce. So this is it. And I want more than one. My brothers are the most precious thing I have. I want that for our child."

Once she would have been sure he would say *she* was the most precious thing he had. Wrapping her arms around herself, she stared up at him. "So you were never going to let me walk away?"

"You would have been free to walk when our deal was up. But I would never have remarried."

Why? She wanted to scream it at him, but her throat felt as if it was closing over as the inevitability of what had happened hit her. How could she have been so stupid as to allow this to happen? To do the one thing that would bind her to the man she loved forever when she would never have his love back?

"I'm tired," she said abruptly, sure that if she attempted one more word she was going to sob. "I need some rest."

He let her go.

Overwhelmed and exhausted, she climbed the stairs to the bedroom, unzipped her dress and left it on the floor. She washed her face and brushed her teeth and slipped beneath the silk sheets of their bed. The dark, silent room finally allowed a refuge for her tears. They ran hot, silent, down her face.

What once would have been the news that completed her and Riccardo's dream had only driven them further apart.

She cried for that dream. She cried for her childhood. She cried for Riccardo's. She cried for the damage they had done to each other. And when he came after her and reached for her with strong, comforting hands she curled into him and let him hold her until her tears soaked his shirt.

"Don't be sad, *amore mio*," he murmured. "The past is the past. *We* are in control of our future and I promise you we can make this work."

My love. He'd said it not in the taunting tone he'd adopted of late, but the way he'd used to say it to her. Her sobs gradually subsided into big, hiccuping breaths that shook her body. When she was silent against him he undressed her and moved over her, kissing every inch of her skin. His passionate tenderness revealed more to her than he ever could have said with words.

They had a chance. He might not have meant the words literally—maybe they had just been to comfort her—but as her head rested on his chest and the solid warmth of him put her to sleep her heart told her differently. She had seen that look on his face before.

He cared more than he was saying.

Could she hope his feelings would eventually turn into love again, for the sake of their unborn child? Or was she just fooling herself in a very dangerous game?

CHAPTER ELEVEN

WHEN LILLY WAS a little girl she'd dreamed of attending a Hollywood movie premiere on the arm of a handsome man, with paparazzi flashbulbs exploding in her face as they made their way down the red carpet. She would blink, steady herself on his arm, and continue on, a big smile on her face as she showed off her very fabulous dress.

Never once, outside of those dreams, had she allowed herself to believe she would actually live that life. Not Lilly the awkward, shy farmgirl. Not even Lilly the graduate physiotherapist with a budding career in front of her, living in one of the most exciting cities in the world where red carpets were a star-studded fixture.

Then she'd met Riccardo. And her life had *become* that dream. Only for her to realize how lonely and empty a life it was.

She walked into her office and shut the door, feeling as if her life had come full circle. Tonight she was to walk the red carpet for the premiere of this summer's hottest blockbuster with her very own dark and dangerous male. The man she was falling more in love with every day she was with him.

She didn't want the dream. She wanted what was real. She wanted *him*.

She sank down in her office chair and dropped her head into her hands. She had married Riccardo for the man he'd been early in their marriage. And ever since they'd returned from Barbados she'd seen glimpses of him again.

He'd been by her side through all the doctor's appointments and tests, asking the pertinent questions her scrambled brain didn't think to. He'd made her sit down to a proper meal every night, and sent her to bed early. And when he did he would stay for a few minutes before he started working again. He would cradle her against him and talk to her, even confide in her if his mood was right. She was realizing how complex a man her husband was— that she'd never really *known* him in their two years of marriage.

Or one, if you counted the year they'd stopped talking.

He'd sacrificed so much for De Campo. And she was starting to see what becoming CEO would do for his soul. It was the final piece in the puzzle that was Riccardo De Campo.

She wondered how she'd never seen it before.

Weariness swept over her and she closed her eyes just for a moment. The weight of the decision she had to make was killing her. Was she going to follow her heart, agree to stay with Riccardo and hope she was right about his feelings for him? Or was she going to run and fight him all the way to the bitter end for custody of a child who would become a pawn in their tug of war?

She'd promised herself she would stop running. Which also meant running from herself.

She blinked to keep herself awake, so exhausted she wanted to crawl onto her desk and sleep there. She had nothing to wear tonight that fit, and hadn't had time to shop since she'd really started showing.

She wanted to walk the red carpet like she wanted a hole in her head.

But it was important to De Campo, this sponsorship, and she didn't really have a choice.

A knock sounded on the door. She pulled herself up off

her desk, expecting to see Katy. Instead Riccardo strolled through the door, looking as if he'd just slayed ten dragons and was ready to move on to the next. The smile on his face faded into a frown when he saw her wipe a trail of drool from the corner of her mouth.

"*Dio,* Lilly, you're sleeping at your *desk?*"

"Resting," she corrected, sitting up straight and smoothing her hair. "Wasn't I meeting you at home?"

"My meetings were canceled this afternoon." He walked over to her desk and leaned against the edge of it, his gaze resting on hers. "This is ridiculous. You're asleep on your feet."

"I'm fine," she murmured, standing up. "Just give me a minute to gather my stuff."

He waved her on. She shoved a file she was working on in her briefcase, along with the antacids that had become a new food group for her, and went to retrieve her sweater off the coat rack near the door.

"Jim—Riccardo here."

She turned to see her husband on his phone.

"Lilly and I can't make it to the premiere tonight. Can you and your wife attend in our place?"

Her eyes widened. She waved at him to say she was fine, but he held up a hand.

"Great. We'll drop off the tickets on our way home."

She stared at him as he disconnected the call. "I can't believe you just did that."

He lifted his shoulders. "Jim's the head of North American sales… It'll be a great networking opportunity for him."

"I would have been fine."

He crossed over to her. "I know you would have. You've been a trooper, *tesoro.* But enough's enough. I'm worried about you."

She pushed her hair out of her face. "It just hit me how tired I am."

"You're not getting enough rest." He ran his fingers down her cheek. "You have big black bags under your eyes."

"Heartburn," she lied. "But I am glad you canceled."

"Because you have nothing to wear?" His dark gaze slashed over her in a reprimand. "You refuse to go buy new clothes, because that would be admitting you're gaining weight, and you don't like the way you look. So I went out and bought some for you."

Her jaw dropped. "You mean you had Paige get me a dress for tonight?"

"No, *I* bought you a dress for tonight—plus the rest of the wardrobe you need." He shrugged. "I'm sure I forgot something, but it's a start."

"You went shopping?"

His teeth flashed white. "I run one of the world's top ten beverage companies, *cara*. A trip to a recommended fashion house isn't beyond my means."

She couldn't believe what she was hearing. "How did you know my size?"

He lifted his hands. "I told them you were this tall and like this." He arced his hands in the shape of an hourglass. "You did?"

"I did. It's all in the car." He looked supremely satisfied with himself as he took her sweater and pushed her out the door in front of him. "I think I have pretty good taste."

He had exquisite taste. In everything. Lilly stared at the cream silk sweater draped over her arm. It was exactly the right size and style she would have chosen. As were the T-shirts, blouses, jeans and gowns he'd picked out.

He had forgotten nothing.

A lump the size of Mount Everest formed in her throat. The little pieces of her heart she'd thought shattered forever started to put themselves back together again.

His attention to detail wasn't surprising. What got her

was how in tune a big, macho man like him could be with what she loved. Who she was.

She pulled the last couple of items out of the bag—a sexy lilac-colored silk nightie she was sure Riccardo had chosen with himself in mind, and a pair of yoga pants. Fuchsia yoga pants. Her mouth twisted in her first real smile of the day.

She slipped her too-tight pants off and pulled on the pink pair. And sighed. To be in something that fit, that didn't make her feel like an overstuffed sausage, was heavenly. She added a T-shirt, pulled her hair into a ponytail, and went downstairs to find Riccardo.

She found him in the den—a cozy, comfortable room that housed their big screen TV and library.

"I ordered us Chinese," he told her. "Should be here in a few minutes."

"I've decided you are always to shop for me," she murmured, moving toward him. Lifting on tiptoe, she brushed a kiss across the light stubble that dusted his cheek. "Since you do such a good job."

He slid his arms around her waist. "I closed my eyes when I handed the woman the yoga pants."

"You get bonus points for those," she murmured, lifting her chin and inviting his kiss. She was rewarded with a hard, possessive one that left her breathless.

"You need to cut down on your schedule."

"I'm not taking any new patients. It'll gradually lessen."

He pressed his lips together, consciously controlling his automatic response, which she was sure would have been, *Cut it down now.*

"You also have to accept the changes in your body. They're natural and healthy."

"I'm getting there," she murmured. "It's just hard when it feels like my body is out of control. The control part is the hardest for me."

He spread his hands wide. "Just hand it over to me, *cara,* and I'll take care of it for you."

She made a face at him. "You would love that, wouldn't you?"

He caught her hand in his much larger one, the teasing light in his eyes darkening into seriousness. "No more keeping things inside, Lil. If you're struggling you need to tell me."

"I will. I promise."

He put some classical music on—a haunting piece of Mozart she knew was his favorite—then pulled her into his arms on the sofa while they waited for the food. She closed her eyes and rested her head against his chest. *This* was what she'd always wanted. The way they were when they were together like this.

At that moment she knew with certainty that everything he'd been holding back, everything he hadn't said to her these past few weeks, had been because she'd hurt him so badly. Because she'd deserted him when he'd needed her the most.

Because she had failed him.

"Ric?"

He pressed his lips to her hair. "Mmm?"

"I'm sorry for walking out on you. I'm sorry I gave up on us."

He stiffened. Then his arms tightened around her. For a long moment silence bound them together, her husky admission sitting on the air between them. Then he bent and pressed a kiss to her shoulder. "I've made so many mistakes too," he said thickly. "It wasn't just you."

Her eyes burned. Her throat was clogged with so much pent-up emotion she wasn't sure she could articulate it all. "I hurt you."

He turned her around so their gazes met. "We hurt each other."

"I want to make this work." Her voice came out husky, edged with the fear she felt.

His eyes were razor-sharp. "What do you mean?"

She sucked in a shuddering breath. "I was so angry with you at first—threatening to turn this into a custody battle, not giving me any choice in the matter. But then I realized you were right. It's time for me—for *us*—to move on. To let go of the past. To give this marriage the shot it deserves. To give our *baby* the home it deserves."

An emotion she wished desperately she could identify flashed in his eyes. He lifted his hands to frame her face.

"But I want *you,* Riccardo," she said shakily. "I don't want the Golden Man from the Golden Couple. I want the Riccardo De Campo who charmed me out of my phone number in that bar. The man who just wanted to be with me."

His gaze darkened to midnight. "You will have him," he promised huskily. "You have always been the only woman for me."

"You won't want me in a few months," she murmured. "I'll be so far from the woman you married you'll be repelled by me."

A smile curved his lips. "Don't you know there's nothing you could ever do to make me want you less? You're like a fire in my blood, *cara.* I want you all the time."

The heat in his eyes stole her breath. The reverence of his hands as he slipped her T-shirt over her head and cupped her breasts in his palms made it catch in her throat. And when he stripped the bra from her and set his mouth to her flesh she moaned her appreciation.

The pink yoga pants went next, landing on the floor in a heap. "This part you hate so much," he whispered, sliding his hands up over her hips, "allows you to carry my baby. And *that* is a miracle."

Her heart turned over and emotion so sharp it was almost painful sliced through her. When he was touching her, when he was holding her like this, his reverence eclipsed her insecurities and made her feel like the most beautiful woman on the planet.

She got the buttons undone on his shirt, divested him of his jeans and boxers, and then there was only his magnificent body, free for her to touch at will. She dropped to her knees and worshipped him, moved her lips over his perfect chest, his powerful abs, then down over the hard, throbbing length of him that telegraphed his desire for her. Reveling in his sharp intake of breath, she teased him until he begged—begged for her to take him into the heat of her mouth—and then, when he'd had all he could take of that, he begged for her to end the torture.

She crawled up his body and hooked her legs around his waist. Slowly, torturously, she took him inside her, prolonging it until sweat beaded on his forehead and he cursed out loud.

Her gaze locked with his. She wanted to look away, *needed* to look away, because surely her love for him was written across her face. But she'd promised honesty. To herself and to him. She kept her eyes on his as he allowed her to drive him crazy with shallow, then deeper twists of her hips. His eyes were closed. His big body was shaking with need. She had control. But she knew it was an illusion. She was about to take the biggest risk of her life. Bigger even than that day when she and Alex had driven out of Iowa, a dust cloud rising up behind the beat-up old car they'd paid a hundred dollars for, which had barely been moving, with nothing but hope and determination in their hearts.

He could cheat on her again. He could actually cheat this time. And there was nothing she could do but believe he would never do it. And she did. Because he was the only man who could turn her world from dark to light.

She could only hope that this didn't turn out to be her biggest mistake. That once he saw the messy, frightened truth of her he didn't run in the opposite direction.

Pleasure coursed through her, wave after wave, as his body swelled inside her, making it impossible to think. To worry. She closed her eyes and rocked her hips and took him over the edge. And let go of everything except her love for him.

CHAPTER TWELVE

THE DEEP TIMBRE of male voices greeted Lilly as she let herself into the townhouse. Her husband's smooth, rich baritone slid down her spine in a delicious reminder of how he'd woken her up this morning. A husky prompt to get out of bed, her own teasing reply, then a spark that burst into a flame that put both of them fifteen minutes behind schedule.

She kicked off her shoes. She was happy—so happy she felt as if she was floating on air. As if she'd figured out the secret of life.

Gabe's voice floated in from the terrace. A male with a deeper, more heavily accented tone responded. *Antonio?*

A twinge of disappointment sliced through her. She'd been hoping for another quiet night at home with Riccardo. Tonight she'd intended on telling him about Lisbeth. She couldn't hold off any longer because she was to fly to Switzerland in a couple of weeks. Finally she felt sure enough of what she and Riccardo had to tell him.

She was making peace with the past. She'd gone home for her mother's birthday a week ago. It hadn't been perfect. But it was progress. And now she would wipe any remaining secrets from her and Riccardo's relationship.

She waved at Magda in the kitchen before joining the men on the terrace.

"*Cara.*" Riccardo's dark eyes lit with pleasure. "You're just in time to celebrate with us."

She crossed to his side and smiled up at him. "Celebrate what?"

Antonio strolled over and pressed a kiss to her cheeks. "I've just told Riccardo I am backing him as the next CEO of De Campo."

Her gaze lifted to her husband's. A quiet gleam of satisfaction burned in his eyes.

"Congratulations," she murmured, reaching up to brush a kiss across his cheek.

His lifted brow told her she would do better than that later. She smiled and tamped down her anxiety at the confirmation of what she'd known was coming but had secretly been dreading.

They had just gotten themselves back on track. Now the craziness would begin.

"Content to tend your vines?" she teased Gabe, walking over to greet him.

He smiled that serious Gabe smile she loved and kissed her. "The most crucial job in the company—*si.*"

She laughed and drew back. "But of course."

"I intend to endorse Riccardo tomorrow at the board meeting," Antonio said, nodding at his son.

Her throat tightened. *It was all happening so quickly.*

She moved back to Riccardo's side and slipped an arm around his waist. He would make a far better leader for De Campo than Antonio had. He would inspire the best in those who worked for him without using fear or intimidation as a threat. And she—she would shine for him. Riccardo needed her by his side, needed her to be the softness when everything else was a million-dollar decision. And this time she would not let the pressure get to her. She had the tools in place to manage her stress.

The De Campo men stayed for dinner. Tonight there was no need for Gabe to be his usual buffer between Antonio and Riccardo. There was rare harmony at the table. And she wondered, moving her gaze over her handsome, quietly confident brother-in-law, what it must have been like always to be the peacekeeper—always to be second best. In any other company Gabe would have made a brilliant CEO. Instead he made brilliant wine.

And maybe that was all he wanted.

After dinner Antonio excused himself to make a call. Lilly checked with Magda about dessert, then slipped out onto the terrace to get a breath of fresh air. The summer night was on the chilly side and she wrapped her arms around herself and stared up at the sky. It was so rare to see stars in Manhattan that the smattering overhead held her attention.

"My son's about to become one of the most powerful men on the planet." Antonio stepped out of the shadows and slid his mobile phone into his pocket. "Are you ready for this, Lilly?"

She wrapped her arms tighter around herself. What was it about these De Campo men, always trying to intimidate her?

"You must think I can or you wouldn't have mandated our reconciliation."

"Scusi?"

She gave him a level look. "Your condition, Antonio, for throwing your weight behind Riccardo. I take it our reconciliation has cemented your choice?"

He lifted a brow. "The performance of the company dictated my choice."

"But you wanted us to reconcile?"

He shrugged. "You're good for my son. I've always thought you had an excellent grounding effect on him. But it had nothing to do with my decision."

Her brain spun in a confused circle. "But you made our reconciliation a condition for your support."

An amused look spread across his face. "If Riccardo

said that he was using it as a way to get you back. You must know my son by now... He is solely focused on getting what he wants and damn the consequences."

She felt the blood drain from her face. Either Antonio or Riccardo was lying.

She prayed it was her father-in-law.

An icy numbness spread through her limbs. She lifted trembling hands to her face. "I—I think I'm going to go back inside. It's getting chilly out here."

She was halfway across the patio when Antonio's voice stopped her. "You look upset—but why? Riccardo may be ruthless in going after what he wants, *mia cara,* but is it so bad if he loves you that much?"

It *was* bad if he had lied to her without compunction. If he had preyed upon her in a moment of weakness, dangling a divorce in front of her she now wasn't sure he'd ever intended to give her.

"De Campos don't divorce."

He had never intended to let her go.

She excused herself from dessert, uncaring of her husband's concerned glance, sweeping upstairs before he had a chance to press her. She immersed her three and a half months pregnant body in a hot bath, desperate for something to soothe her. Desperate not to believe the man she had fallen in love with all over again could have lied to her like that when he had demanded honesty from *her*.

Damn him. She struggled to come up with a reason, an alternative explanation for why he'd done what he'd done. But there weren't any. There was nothing that excused what he'd done.

She closed her eyes and let the steaming water attack the numbness that had consumed her. Riccardo hadn't technically lied when he had talked about what had happened with Chelsea Tate. But it had been a lie by omission. And now he had lied again.

It was crazy. She'd *wanted* him to want her that much.

She'd *wanted* him to do exactly as she'd fantasized in the limo the night of their divorce party. To ride down her street on a white horse, climb through her window and carry her home.

But now she was afraid he was still the same old Riccardo, just cloaked in a new suit. The Riccardo who would use any weapon at his disposal to get what he wanted.

No. She slapped her hand against the water, sending bubbles flying. He had stood there on that terrace in Barbados and sworn to her they were going to create a marriage based on honesty and trust. And she had eaten it up like the naive Iowa farm girl she obviously still was.

Her insides crumbled. She'd made herself completely vulnerable to him. She had trusted him with her darkest secrets, trusted him to take care of her and their baby. And he had violated that trust.

Just like with everything else in her past—every time her parents' relationship had gone through a good patch and they'd actually been happy together, every time the farm had gone into the black and she'd been able to buy a new dress, or that bittersweet moment in Westchester when she'd thought she had everything she'd ever wanted—this brief moment of happiness had been taken from her. Just as she'd feared it would be.

She didn't know what was real anymore.

The moment he entered the room she sensed him. The air thickened around her. His grim appraisal as she opened her eyes made her sink further under the water.

"What's going on, Lilly?"

She swallowed past the lump in her throat. "You promised me honesty. You promised we could trust each other."

He nodded, his dark gaze fixed intently on her. "*Si.* Have I given you any reason to doubt me?"

She sat up and reached for the sides of the tub with shaking hands. "You *lied* to me, Riccardo. You lied to me about this whole crazy deal."

He paled. "What did Antonio say to you?"

"That you're a selfish bastard who'll do whatever it takes to get what you want." She stood up and jabbed a finger at him. "I trusted you. You told me we were starting over without any lies between us."

He took a step toward her. "I might have taken some artistic liberty with my wording, but Antonio *did* want us back together."

"You told me Antonio's support *depended* on us getting back together." She was shaking so hard she could hardly get the words out. "It was a bold-faced lie."

"What was I supposed to do?" he shot back tightly. "You wouldn't see me, you wouldn't talk to me, but you knew I wasn't going to give up."

Heat blazed through her. "You were supposed to *woo* me. You were supposed to come sit on my doorstep every night for a week, like you did when we first started dating. You were not supposed to *coerce* me into a reconciliation."

She stood there shivering violently. He grasped her wrists and pulled her out of the tub, wrapped a towel around her.

"Wooing wasn't working."

"The deal was a lie," she said dully. "And the only reason I accepted it was because of Lisbeth."

"Lisbeth?"

"Her leukemia is back. She needed treatment and I needed the money. So I agreed to your deal."

His expression darkened. "You agreed to reconcile with me because Lisbeth needed treatment? *Hell,* Lilly, what kind of a monster do you think I am that I wouldn't have given you that money if you'd told me?"

"I didn't want to be beholden to you. I didn't trust you. And look—" she threw her hands up in the air "—guess I was right."

His mouth flattened into a thin line, the nostrils of his Roman nose flaring. "You accuse *me* of not being completely honest when you are withholding things like that from me?"

"It has nothing to do with us."

"It has *everything* to do with us. We are a family, Lilly. We support each other."

"Well, now you've got your family," she bit out, feeling her world fall apart. "Wife, baby—you've got everything you ever wanted, just like you always do."

He closed his eyes, his long dark lashes sweeping down over his cheeks. "It was never about that," he denied huskily. "I swear to you—it was never about that. I was—I was desperately in love with you, Lilly, and I needed you back."

Her heart stopped. She took a deep breath, forcing herself to breathe, forcing her heart to start again—because surely he would not use that tactic on her now. Not after she'd spent weeks desperate to hear him say it.

She pulled the towel tight around her, fingers clenching the material. "How many other things have you lied to me about?"

"Nothing." His voice vibrated with emotion. "Lilly—"

She held up a hand. "No more."

He ignored her and pulled her into his arms. The strength and breadth of him dwarfed her, so achingly familiar she wanted to howl at the want in her.

His gaze bored into hers. "You are not a possession. You and this baby we are going to have are the most precious things in my life. How could I have let myself lose you? I couldn't let that happen."

Hot tears escaped her eyes, running down her cheeks like a river of fire. She beat her hands against his chest, desperate for him to hurt as much as she was hurting. "I needed this to be real. I needed *us* to be real this time."

"We are. Lilly—"

"No." She wrenched herself out of his arms, the towel falling into a heap on the floor. "You know what Alex said to me before we left for Barbados? 'Whatever you do, don't get pregnant...' Because that was the one thing that would complicate a relationship that didn't need complicating." She closed her eyes. "And what do I do? I let exactly that happen. And *now* look at us."

He eyed her wild, naked stance apprehensively, as if she were a keg of dynamite poised to go off. "Let's get some clothes on you," he suggested quietly, "and then we'll talk."

She stalked past him into the bedroom and reached for the first piece of clothing she could lay her hands on. He followed, watching as she pulled on a T-shirt and jeans.

"Listen, I know you're emotional, *cara,* but—"

"I am not emotional." She wrenched her hair from underneath her T-shirt and whipped to face him. "I am crushed and I am saddened and I am *disappointed* in you. But I am *not* hormonal."

If she sounded insane she was past caring. "I need some time to myself," she muttered, turning back to search for a sweater. "Away from here. Away from you."

"You are not running away again."

"You're right." She swiped a sweater off a chair and shoved her arm in a sleeve. "I'm walking. Maybe to the Brooklyn Bridge. Who knows?"

He moved forward, took her by the shoulders and spun her around. His eyes were black, stormy. "You can throw away a million rings and I will still come after you."

She squared her shoulders. "I need time. Do not follow me. Don't have anyone follow me, for that matter. Or I swear to God you'll push me over the edge."

She turned and walked out the door. The stars were still shining brightly when she climbed into Riccardo's Jag and reversed it down the driveway. But this time she didn't look up.

CHAPTER THIRTEEN

RICCARDO KNOTTED HIS tie with fingers that weren't quite steady. This should have been the most important day of his life—the day his father anointed him the new head of De Campo. It should have been the crowning glory of three years spent proving to Antonio that he had what it took—that this was *his* company and his vision was the future. That the passion in his veins ran as deep as it did through his father's.

But his wife was gone. His *pregnant* wife was gone. And he had no idea where she was, what her state of mind was, or what he was supposed to do with the unfamiliar feeling of helplessness pulsing through him. Giving a speech to the board that painted a vision of De Campo's future seemed inconceivable.

His hands dropped away from his tie. Lilly had made it clear she needed space. If he had denied it to her, gone after her, he would have lost her.

If he hadn't already.

He shrugged on his jacket, lifted his collar clear of the dark gray Armani that was his good luck suit—the suit he'd been wearing the night he'd met Lilly in that bar—and refused even to contemplate the possibility. Instead he thought about the twists and turns life could take. Antonio had wanted to raise racehorses. He'd ended up with vines and a company that had brought him success beyond his wildest dreams. Motor racing had been *his* passion, but he'd grown to love the business that was bigger than him, bigger than his brothers and his father now. De Campo had come to signify luxury and refinement on a global scale. It was bigger than all of them. He would be the man who took it to new heights. Who exploited its raw potential.

Sometimes things happened that were beyond your control.

Sometimes you made them happen with your own arrogance and stupidity.

He stared at his reflection in the mirror, searching for some sign of life in his perfectly tailored appearance. A machine stared back at him. None of this meant anything without Lilly. He could handle the dull throb he woke with every day he wasn't racing as long as she was by his side. But he could not fathom the future without her.

His chest ached with the need to have his wife back.

Shaking it off—shaking it off because he had to—he straightened his shoulders and went downstairs to where Tony was waiting with the car. His longtime driver said hello, gave him a quick look, and eliminated his usual witty banter.

Riccardo slid into the backseat and pressed his head against the leather. He'd felt justified in coercing Lilly into the deal because it had been the only weapon he'd had against her refusal to see him. Because he loved her. He was so used to having to fight tooth and nail to get what he wanted from Antonio he'd carried that same demeanor into his personal life. Strategize and conquer. But with all of his and Lilly's trust issues he should have known better. He should have at least come clean when he'd had the chance to in Barbados.

Muddled thinking from a man who had seen the destructive effects of secrets harbored.

He clasped his hands together in his lap and looked down at the gleaming gold wedding band Lilly had placed on his finger. He'd been forgiven once. Would he be forgiven again? Or had he made one mistake too many?

The urge to put his fist through the bulletproof window overwhelmingly strong, he switched his attention to the traffic on Fifth Avenue instead, curling his fist on his lap. Lilly had called in to her clinic to say she wouldn't be in. After she hadn't picked up her cell he'd called Alex, to see if she was with her. Which had, in turn, opened him up to her sister's sarcastic demand to know what he'd done *now*.

He ran a hand over his chin, his uneven shaving job making him frown. Where in *Dio's* name was she? And why wouldn't she at least pick up the phone and let him know she was okay?

Paige handed him a stack of messages when he walked in. He crumpled them up and threw them on his desk.

"Everyone's here," she murmured, moving her gaze from the wad of paper back to him. "You okay?"

Did he *look* okay? He gave her a curt nod, dropped his briefcase by his desk and took his laptop out.

His father gave him a nod as he walked into the boardroom. *"Siete pronti?"*

"Pronto." Ready.

Gabe took the chair beside him. "You look like hell, *fratello*. Too much champagne last night?"

"I can't find Lilly."

His brother blinked. *"Scusi?"*

He powered up his laptop. "We had a fight last night and she needed some space."

"You have no idea where she went?"

"None." His jammed his palm against the table. She was pregnant. Driving his far too powerful car. And emotional.

Antonio opened the meeting and ran through the agenda. Riccardo looked down at the notes for his speech. There were only five words on the cue card. *Vision. Courage. Expertise. Timing. Domination.* They would define De Campo's future.

His father began his pitch to endorse his son as CEO. Riccardo checked his messages on his phone. *Nothing*.

"As you have seen over the past three years, my son Riccardo has transformed De Campo into the multifaceted global brand that it is today..."

Antonio's voice droned on, blurred into nothingness. It was only when his father turned to him and put his hands together, and the board followed suit, that he realized it was time.

"I am throwing my full support behind Riccardo De Campo for the position of CEO of this company."

The board members stood and clapped.

It was happening.

This time as he made his way to the podium and shook Antonio's hand there was no mistaking the pride gleaming in his father's eyes. He felt strong and weak at the same time—as if he was both that boy who'd trailed after his father into the vineyard asking a million questions and the man he'd become.

He cleared his throat and stepped to the microphone.

"For the last three years I have watched the De Campo Group grow from a fledgling global brand to a force to be reckoned with in the industry. We gambled. Our vision was big. Our vision was ambitious. But our vision was right." He paused and cast his gaze around the room. "And now we sit poised on a precipice. We can either move with the future or we can lose our way, as so many other brands have done. I say we move—that we have the guts and the vision to—"

Paige stepped into the back of the room. It was highly unusual for her to interrupt a meeting of this importance, and the look on her face stopped him cold.

Lilly. He knew it as instinctively as he knew the sun rose in the east.

"Excuse me." He stepped down from the podium and walked toward the back of the room. Antonio frowned and stood up as he passed. The buzzing in his ears got louder the closer he got to Paige. Her eyes were glued to his face and she stood wringing her hands together—something his PA never did.

Antonio announced they would take a quick break.

"I have Lilly on the line," Paige whispered to him. "Riccardo, she doesn't sound good."

He sprinted to Paige's desk and picked up the line. *"Lilly?"*

"Riccardo?"

"Yes," he barked. Her voice was faint. Not right. "Lilly, where are you?"

"I—I'm not feeling well. Ric, I—"

"Lilly?"

The line went dead. He slammed the receiver down and stood staring at it.

Paige's hand flew to her mouth. "She said her phone was dying."

He was already halfway into his office. "Call the security company and have her phone traced. *Now.* I need to know where she is."

Antonio and Gabe joined him in his office.

"What the hell are you doing?" his father demanded. "They're waiting to hear from you."

"There's something wrong with Lilly," he said grimly. "I've got to find her."

Antonio gave him an incredulous look. "Surely it can wait fifteen minutes?"

"No, it can't!" Riccardo roared. "Gabe, I need your keys."

His brother dug them out of his pocket. "I'll come with you."

"You should stay here and hold down the fort."

"I'm not sure you should—"

He ripped the keys out of his brother's hand. "I'll call when I know something."

Mid-morning traffic was still thick. He crawled forward, trying not to think about how weak and scared Lilly had sounded. Why had he let her go last night?

Paige called. Lilly had last been tracked in Westchester. *She was at the house.* He changed lanes and headed for the interstate, relieved, and then his heart started to pound as all sorts of disturbing images crammed his head. What if something was wrong with her pregnancy? The house was on the water. What if she'd taken one of the boats out and started to feel ill? Or gotten weak while swimming?

What if she was lying somewhere helpless?

He put his foot down on the accelerator and gunned the Maserati, weaving in and out of traffic as if he was in the Monaco Grand Prix. When he hit the interstate he put the pedal to the floor. The powerful car ate up the miles, but it wasn't fast enough. Not for the torturous images running through his head.

The guy in front of him was driving like his grandmother in the left lane. He jammed his foot on the accelerator and sent the car to twice the legal speed limit, passing him on the inside.

The sirens started ten minutes out of Westchester. Red flashing lights blazed in his rearview mirror. For a split second he contemplated ignoring them. He could outdrive them in this car, he knew. But the whir of a helicopter overhead convinced him the cop on the ground wasn't the only one after him.

He slowed down and pulled onto the side of the road. The cop pulled in behind him and got out of his car. He'd just explain what was going on and then he'd be on his way...

A tall, beefy cop stopped by his window. "License and registration."

Riccardo handed it to him. "Officer—I—"

"Do you have any idea how fast you were going, sir?"

"About a hundred. But, Officer, I—"

The cop jabbed a finger at him. "You, sir, are a danger-ous driver. You aren't walking away with this car today. I can tell you that."

"Look, I—"

The officer looked at his license and started to laugh. "You're kidding me? Riccardo De Campo the racecar driver?"

"Former racecar driver," Riccardo corrected. "I can ex-plain why I was driving so fast. My—"

"Save it. You're not the first superstar to think you can flaunt the rules."

"*Officer!*" Riccardo yelled. "My wife is sick. She's preg-nant. I was racing to get to her."

The cop blinked. "Where?"

"Our Westchester house. It's ten minutes from here."

"Did you call an ambulance?"

He closed his eyes. "No. *Why hadn't he?*"

The cop gave him a considering look. "You better be telling the truth."

"I am," Riccardo rasped desperately. "Can I go?"

"You will follow me," the cop said sternly. "You so much as step one inch out of line and I will impound both you *and* your car."

Riccardo nodded and gave him directions. The cop put on his siren and thankfully was no slouch in the speed de-partment either, getting them to the house in just under fifteen minutes.

He found Lilly in the living room, lying on the sofa.

"Cara." He dropped down on his knees beside her. She was curled in the fetal position, her face about five shades paler than it normally was.

"I didn't mean to scare you," she murmured. "The phones here aren't working and my cell phone died."

"They've been working on the lines out here. Lil—" He took her hands in his. "Can you tell me what doesn't feel right?"

She bit her lip. "I don't know. I—I'm nauseous and I'm having bad pains."

Riccardo looked up at the cop, who'd come in behind him, but the officer was already on his radio, calling for an ambulance.

A tear rolled down her cheek. "I didn't want to bother you. You had that meeting..."

He gripped her hands tighter. "I don't care if I'm having lunch with the Pope. You need me—you call me."

A river of tears ran down her cheeks.

"Are the pains getting worse or better?"

"Worse. There's more of them now."

His insides went cold. "When did they start?"

"A couple hours ago." She closed her eyes as a tremor ran through her slim body. "Ric—something's wrong. I don't feel right."

He sat down and pulled her into his arms. "It's going to be all right, *tesoro,* I promise you. The ambulance is on its way."

She burrowed into him. The tension in her body made his own stiffen with fear.

"I'm so sorry. You should be in that meeting, and if I screw up your ch—"

"Ssh." He pressed a kiss against her hair. "You're the most important thing in the world to me, Lilly."

"Yes, but the job is—"

He pressed his fingers to her mouth. "The job is nothing without you. *I* am nothing without you. Haven't you realized that yet? I do these stupid things because I love you. Because I can't bear the thought of losing you."

Her lashes fluttered down over those beautiful hazel eyes. "I spent the morning walking along the river, thinking."

His heart jammed in his chest.

The tears streamed harder down her face now, running

over the edge of her chin. "I love you, Riccardo. I've never stopped loving you. Not even for a minute."

He felt as if the sun had come out on this dreary, overcast summer day. The flash of joy that swept through him was powerful. Followed by sick, overwhelming relief that he hadn't lost her.

"Please forgive me," he whispered. "That was my last big mistake. Ever."

She shook her head. "It was my running too. I can see that now. I was so scared that once you saw the truth of me—how messed up I am still—you wouldn't want me anymore."

He brought her hand to his mouth and pressed his lips to her knuckles. "We all have our baggage, *cara*. Look what you've done with your life. You help little boys walk again. Nothing I've ever done comes close to that."

Her eyes glittered with an emotion that stole his breath.

"We have to be honest with each other. No more lies. No matter how little or how painful the truth."

"Agreed." He held her tightly as another shudder racked her body and glanced up at the cop. The officer held up two fingers.

"I mean it." Lilly bumped her hand against his chest. "Three strikes and you're out, Riccardo De Campo."

"Then it's a good thing I don't need anymore," he murmured. "*You* are all I need."

"Ambulance is here." The cop abandoned his post at the window. "Let's go."

Riccardo picked up Lilly and strode outside. She was going to be fine. She *had* to be fine. There was no other way to think.

CHAPTER FOURTEEN

THE GRAY-HAIRED emergency room physician walked into the waiting room where Riccardo, Gabe, Alex and—surprisingly—Antonio, who'd shown up a couple of hours ago sat, just over three hours after they'd taken Lilly in. He wore the unsmiling, grim look of a man who'd been working too many hours straight.

Riccardo's heart dropped to the floor.

The elderly physician stopped in front of him, a tired smile curving his mouth. "They're both fine. Lilly's suffering from pre-eclampsia—a high blood pressure condition associated with pregnancy. Very common, but she'll need to see her doctor often."

His shoulders sagged with relief. "And the pain?"

"Under control. You can take her home as soon as we can do the paperwork, but you'll need to schedule an appointment with her obstetrician as soon as possible. Get some more detailed tests done."

He released the breath he'd been holding in a long, heavy exhale. *Lilly was fine. Their baby was fine.*

Thank God.

The doctor smiled. "Glad I could give out some good news today. There hasn't been a surplus of it."

"*Grazie,*" he murmured huskily. "I can't say it enough."

The doctor waved him off and headed back into the chaos. Alex went in and spent a few minutes with her sis-

ter before Riccardo took her home. Gabe went to get him
a cup of coffee for the ride.

He rested his elbows on his thighs and dropped his head
into his hands. Moisture stung the backs of his eyes, mixing with a relief so profound it was all-consuming.

A hand gripped his shoulder. "Your mother suffered
from pre-eclampsia. Lilly will be fine."

He looked up at Antonio through glazed eyes. He'd been
shocked when his father had arrived and waited with them
without a word. The emotion darkening his father's silver
eyes shocked him even more.

Antonio straightened, as if the show of affection had
thrown him off balance. "You don't need to worry about
the board," he said roughly. "I made sure you have a hundred and ten percent of their support."

Riccardo held his gaze for a long moment. *"Grazie."*

He had Lilly. Now he could think about the future.

Lilly prided herself on the toughness at her core. It had
carried her out of Iowa and into a life she could only have
dreamed of. It had helped her give that same strength to
her patients when they were intent on giving up. But the
vulnerability she felt walking toward the front door of the
hospital was so soul-searing it was hard to keep walking
in a straight line.

A nurse pushed the door open for her and she walked out
into the light drizzle to Riccardo, waiting with the car at
the curb. Her legs trembled as her husband walked toward
her—tall, imposing, with a determined set to his mouth
that made her want to fling herself into his arms.

What if he hadn't come after her? What if she'd lost him?

Her knees wobbled as he took the last couple of steps and
pulled her into his arms. She closed her eyes and absorbed his strength, that determination. It was enough for
both of them.

"Let's go home," he said quietly.

They made the drive back to Manhattan in silence, an acknowledgement of what they'd almost lost heavy in the air. Riccardo held her hand in his lap the entire way, as if he couldn't bear to let her go.

Their stately old limestone townhouse awaited them— the scene of her rollercoaster marriage which had run from perfect to miserable to all she'd ever wanted. Majestic, it glimmered in the late-afternoon sunlight, so solid with its heavy brick façade it would stand forever.

She stepped out of the car, her mind traveling back to that night four and a half months before, when limos had lined up in this driveway to witness the destruction of her and Riccardo.

Tonight it was unusually quiet. There were no limos. No drivers chatting. No false illusions of perfection on either part. There was only the here and now and what they chose to do with it.

Riccardo came around the car and slid his arm around her waist. "What are you thinking?"

"We have a blank slate," she said huskily. "The story is ours to write."

He tugged her closer and lifted her chin with his fingers. "I predict a very happy ending."

She drank him in—the hard, strong lines of his face that could soften into devastating humor, the sensuous pull of his lips that could make her crazy for him. He loved her. He was crazy about her. That much she was sure of. And that was enough.

Her lips curved. "You think so, Signor De Campo?"

"I know so, Signora De Campo."

He swung her into his arms and carried her up the front walk.

For her and Riccardo this past year had been simply a twist in the road of a lifetime together.

And tomorrow was another day.

EPILOGUE

Westchester, New York

"I DON'T KNOW about you, but I think he needs a strong, manly name to match his personality."

"Papà."

One-and-a-half-year-old Marco ducked under Lilly's arm and ran as fast as his short, stumpy legs would carry him across the terrace to where her husband stood, indecently attractive in a navy pinstriped suit. Her heart contracted as her son flung himself around Riccardo's legs. The two males had a love affair going on that was a joy to watch.

She would normally have let herself drool a little longer over the suit that set off her husband's swarthy good looks to perfection, but the squirming bundle of fluff in his arms demanded her attention.

It looked suspiciously like a chocolate-brown Labrador Retriever puppy.

"*Cucciolo!*" Marco squealed, tugging on his father's pant leg. "*Giù,*" he ordered, in an imperious tone that was already so close to his father's Lilly was afraid he was going to skip the baby stage entirely and move straight to domination.

Riccardo bent and set the puppy on the ground. Marco

grabbed onto its fur so hard the puppy backed up and cowered against Riccardo's leg.

"*Dolcemente,*" her husband instructed, scooping the puppy up in one arm and Marco in the other. "You are a brute, Marco De Campo."

"Just like his daddy." Lilly sighed. "Well, most of the time anyway," she teased, standing up on tiptoe to kiss him. But between the squirming, licking puppy and the delighted Marco it was a pretty fruitless effort.

"Hold that thought," Riccardo murmured. "I have a surprise for you too, but you'll get it later."

Heat rose to her face.

He laughed—a low, sexy rumble that did jittery things to her insides. "*That* is a given, *tesoro*. But I also stumbled upon something else I thought you'd like."

Mortified that her thoughts always seemed to involve her husband and some sort of naked activity, she took the puppy from him and felt her heart melt at the tiny bundle of fur, the big brown eyes and giant paws. "I thought this was happening in the spring?"

He lifted his shoulders. "The breeder had someone cancel at the last minute. I made the mistake of going to see him, and well…"

She smiled as the puppy licked her face with boundless enthusiasm. "I wouldn't have been able to resist him either."

"His name's Dutch. But we can rename him."

She lifted a brow.

"Dutch chocolate?"

She hated it. "We'll rename."

"Thought so. You were about to swim?"

She nodded. "We didn't expect you for hours."

Her husband's gaze rested on her face with that singular intensity he devoted to everything he focused on. "I ducked out early. I missed you."

A lump formed in her throat. Her life was as close to perfect as a life could be. So perfect, in fact, that some days when it seemed *too* perfect, as if it could never last, she re-treated to the back porch of the house here in Westchester, where they'd move for the summer, and stayed there until her heart stopped racing and the feeling went away. It was where Riccardo inevitably found her. And instinctively he'd always know what to say, because this beautiful, au-tocratic man who'd suffered plenty of his own heartaches knew her better than anyone.

He'd been there every step of the way.

She ran her fingers down the hard lines of his face. They still had their blow-outs—and, boy, were they blow-outs when they happened. That had never changed. But they were few and far between, and beneficial from the point of view that they both got their feelings out and moved on.

Marco scrunched up his face and shoved a beefy little hand against Riccardo's chest. "Swim. *Cucciolo.*"

Lilly laughed. "Maybe no swimming for the puppy today. But we can."

They splashed in the shallow end of the pool and Ric-cardo changed, then joined them. Lilly sat on the edge of the pool, dangling her legs in the water while her husband tossed Marco high. Her son's delighted yelps filled the air.

Her husband lifted a brow. "Enjoying your part-time life?"

"Oh, yes." She'd opted to cut back to part-time hours after Marco had been born, sharing her workload with another physiotherapist who also had a family. It allowed her to focus on work *and* her family, and she was loving every minute of it.

Marco slapped his hand on the water and sprayed water in Riccardo's face. Her lips curved. He was not only a solid little dark-haired mirror image of his father he was just as much of a daredevil. Fearless. Willing to try everything. Nothing like his mother had been like as a child. And she was glad for that.

Marco Alfonso De Campo. Named after Riccardo's racing hero and former teammate Marco Agostino, who'd died in a crash just weeks before their Marco had been born. His second name was after Riccardo's grandfather, who had built the first De Campo vineyard in Tuscany.

She blinked, her eyes stinging with the bittersweet emotion that seemed to define her life now. With the naming of Marco her husband seemed to have moved on, to have made amends with the past. He no longer shut down if racing came up. He acknowledged the subject, then moved on.

She had moved on too. It would never be a perfect relationship, but she was making strides with her parents. They were in love with Marco, and she visited a few times a year to give them a chance to spend time together. And somehow that was enough.

Riccardo caught her eye across the water. "Lisbeth's met an investment banker. She had stars in her eyes when he dropped her off the other night."

Oh, no. Of all the men in New York, investment bankers had to be the most arrogant. "Did you *do* something about it?"

A smile tugged at the corners of his mouth. "What was I supposed to do? Put the fear of God in him?"

"Yes. You should have." Her sister had been in remission for six months now. She'd come to live with them in New York after her treatment and was set to start college in the fall. She was so much like her former vibrant self it felt almost as if a miracle had happened, but Lilly was still fiercely protective of her. She was so vulnerable in so many ways.

But then again, she reminded herself, she'd been the same way when she'd moved to New York, and it had done her a world of good to stand on her own two feet in a city as tough as Manhattan.

"On second thought," she murmured, "maybe this is a good thing. She *should* have her heart broken a few times. It'll teach her how to deal with you alpha males."

His dark eyes glittered. "Maybe so. You've figured out how to have *this* one hopelessly within your power."

She glanced at him from beneath lowered lashes. "You think so?"

"Undoubtedly."

She put the heat in his gaze on hold while they enjoyed the afternoon, took care of the puppy, then fed and put their son to bed. Riccardo read to Marco while she changed. Her soft, cream-colored jersey dress that showed an ample amount of cleavage was meant to put his theory to the test. Her husband's deep velvet stare as she walked out onto the terrace gave her the answer she was looking for.

Just tamable enough.

He finished mixing their drinks. "New dress?"

"Yes."

"Come here."

Her heart went pitter-patter in her chest as she closed the distance between them. "What is *that?*" she questioned, staring at the murky dark liquid in the glass he handed her.

A satisfied smile touched his lips. "It so happens Lewis, our Bajan bartender friend, has become an international celebrity. The recipe for his house specialty has made it into one of the top food and beverage magazines."

"You're kidding?"

"Would I lie to you about something like that? He calls it his 'love potion'. The 'ultimate aphrodisiac.'"

An all-over body flush consumed her. *A love potion?* She could only think of three words. Hottest. Sex. Ever.

Riccardo read her expression. "Exactly," he drawled. "Drink up."

She took a sip. "Doesn't taste any better than I remember."

"It gets better the more you drink. Remember that?"

She sipped on the potent drink, wincing as the alcohol hit her empty stomach.

"What's that?" she asked, pointing at the tabloid he'd set on the bar. "I thought we weren't reading that stuff."

"You should read Jay Kaiken's column."

Ugh. "Really?"

"Yes. Read it."

She took another sip of her drink, thinking she might need it. Jay Kaiken's column was an account of the posh benefit she and Riccardo had attended for former supermodel Gillian King's Manhattan clinic for eating disorders. A friend of Gillian's, Lilly had instantly seen the value of a place where women could go to be surrounded by those who were going through the same thing they were. And when Gillian had asked her to speak at the event she'd decided it was time for her to tell her story publicly. Even if it only helped one person, that was enough.

"Perhaps the most poignant moment of the evening was Lilly De Campo's account of her struggle with anorexia," Kaiken had written. *"Courageous and truthful, its honesty no doubt made an impression on everyone in attendance. I'm pretty sure there wasn't a dry eye in the crowd."* And, in true Kaiken tongue-in-cheek fashion, he'd added, *"PS— can I say how good it is to have the De Campos back together? I always did want to believe in fairytales..."*

She looked up at Riccardo, her vision blurring.

"It *was* very courageous of you," he said quietly. "But then again you're the most courageous woman I know, Lilly De Campo."

She stepped in to kiss him as she'd wanted to this afternoon. Heat swept through her veins, licked at her nerve-endings as he claimed her mouth in a thorough, possessive kiss that seemed to promise a million forevers.

"I love you," she whispered. *"Io ti amo per sempre."*

I will love you forever.

He pulled back, his gaze so dark it was almost black. "Finish that drink," he muttered roughly. "Dinner can wait."

She downed the last gulp and gasped when he swung her up in his arms and headed for the stairs. Up he climbed, to the bedroom that overlooked the river, the room where her dream of their family had begun. It occurred to her as Riccardo slid his hands to the back of her dress and unzipped it, letting the silky material slip to the floor, that her dream had finally come true. The puppy sleeping downstairs in a basket in the kitchen had been the final piece.

She smiled and wrapped her arms around her husband's neck, pulling his mouth down to hers.

From a divorce party to forever. Who would have known?

* * * * *

A sneaky peek at next month...

MODERN™

INTERNATIONAL AFFAIRS, SEDUCTION & PASSION GUARANTEED

My wish list for next month's titles...

In stores from 18th October 2013:

❑ Million Dollar Christmas Proposal — Lucy Monroe

❑ The Consequences of That Night — Jennie Lucas

❑ Visconti's Forgotten Heir — Elizabeth Power

❑ A Touch of Temptation — Tara Pammi

In stores from 1st November 2013:

❑ A Dangerous Solace — Lucy Ellis

❑ Secrets of a Powerful Man — Chantelle Shaw

❑ Never Gamble with a Caffarelli — Melanie Milburne

❑ The Rogue's Fortune — Cat Schield

Available at WHSmith, Tesco, Asda, Eason, Amazon and Apple

Just can't wait?

Come home this Christmas to Fiona Harper

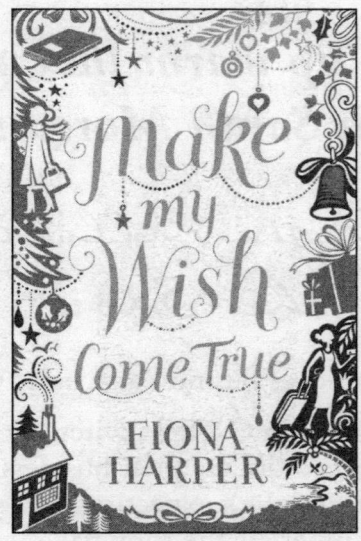

From the author of *Kiss Me Under the Mistletoe* comes a
Christmas tale of family and fun. Two sisters are ready
to swap their Christmases—the busy super-mum, Juliet,
getting the chance to escape it all on an exotic Christmas
getaway, whilst her glamorous work-obsessed sister,
Gemma, is plunged headfirst into the family Christmas
she always thought she'd hate.

www.millsandboon.co.uk

Wrap up warm this winter with Sarah Morgan…

Sleigh Bells in the Snow

Kayla Green loves business and hates Christmas.

So when Jackson O'Neil invites her to Snow Crystal Resort to discuss their business proposal… the last thing she's expecting is to stay for Christmas dinner. As the snowflakes continue to fall, will the woman who doesn't believe in the magic of Christmas finally fall under its spell…?

4th October

www.millsandboon.co.uk/sarahmorgan

1013/MB435

Join the Mills & Boon Book Club

Want to read more **Modern**™ books?
We're offering you **2 more** absolutely **FREE!**

We'll also treat you to these fabulous extras:

- 🌹 **Exclusive offers and much more!**

- 🌹 **FREE home delivery**

- 🌹 **FREE books and gifts with our special rewards scheme**

Get your free books now!

visit www.millsandboon.co.uk/bookclub
or call Customer Relations on 020 8288 2888

The World of
Mills & Boon®

There's a Mills & Boon® series that's perfect
for you. We publish ten series and, with new
titles every month, you never have to wait
long for your favourite to come along.

Blaze.
Scorching hot, sexy reads
4 new stories every month

By Request
*Relive the romance with
the best of the best*
9 new stories every month

Cherish
*Romance to melt the
heart every time*
12 new stories every month

Desire
*Passionate and dramatic
love stories*
8 new stories every month